Grouped around the far perimeter of the pool, half buried in the sand, were such things as nightmares are made of! Their dingy yellowish-green skins were scaled with the stigmata of the reptile. Dard estimated that they were from seven to ten feet long.

The head of the larger thing snapped up, swaying back and forth, a snake preparing to strike! Then it was on its feet, towering far over Dard and Santee. From the fanged jaws came a hiss which gathered volume until it rivaled the piercing whistle of a steam-powered engine.

Santee shot. The nerve-paralyzing projectile of the stun rifle struck fair between those murderous yellow, unblinking eyes. The skull shattered with a spatter of green ooze. But the thing waded the pool to rush them, tearing claws outstretched. It should have been dead. But with a broken, empty skull, blinded, it came on!

"No brain in the head!" Dard shouted. "Jump!"

Baen Books
By
Andre Norton

Time Traders
Time Traders II
Star Soldiers
Warlock
Janus
Darkness & Dawn
Gods & Androids
Dark Companion
Masks of the Outcasts
Moonsinger
Crosstime
From the Sea to the Stars
Star Flight
Search for the Star Stones

STAR FLIGHT

Andre Norton

STAR FLIGHT

This is a work of fiction. All the characters and events portrayed in this book are fictional, and any resemblance to real people or incidents is purely coincidental.

The *Stars are Ours* copyright © 1954 by The Estate of Andre Norton; *Star Born* copyright © 1957 by The Estate of Andre Norton.

A Baen Book

Baen Publishing Enterprises
P.O. Box 1403
Riverdale, NY 10471
www.baen.com

ISBN: 978-1-4391-3272-2

Cover art by Stephen Hickman

First Baen paperback printing, June 2009

Distributed by Simon & Schuster
1230 Avenue of the Americas
New York, NY 10020

Library of Congress Cataloging-in-Publication Data:
2007023560

Printed in the United States of America

10 9 8 7 6 5 4 3 2 1

CONTENTS

THE
STARS ARE
OURS

For **HARLAN ELLISON**
Who is a veteran of galactic voyages and an ever
prepared guide to the realms of outer Space

BOOK ONE

TERRA

PROLOGUE

(Except from the Encyclopedia Galactica)

THE FIRST GALACTIC exploratory and colonization flight came as a direct outgrowth of a peculiar sociological-political situation on the planet Terra. As a result of a series of wars between nationalistic divisions atomic power was discovered. Afraid of the demon they had so loosed the nations then engaged in so-called "cold wars" during which all countries raced to outbuild each other in the stock piling of new and more drastic weapons and the mobilization of manpower into the ancient "armies."

Scientific training became valued only for the aid it could render in helping to arm and fit a nation for war. For some time scientists and techneers of all classes were kept in a form of peonage by "security" regulations. But a unification of scientists fostered in a secret underground movement resulted in the formation of "Free Scientist" teams, groups of experts and specialists who sold their services to both private industry and governments as research workers. Since they gave no attention to the racial, political, or religious antecedents of their members, they became truly international and planet-, instead of nation-, minded—a situation both hated and feared by their employers.

Under the stimulus of Free Scientist encouragement man achieved interplanetary flight. Terra was the third in a series of nine planets revolving about the sun, Sol I. It possessed one satellite, Luna.

Exploration ships made landings on Luna, and the two neighboring planets, Mars and Venus. None of these worlds were suitable for human colonization without vast expenditure, and they offered little or no return for such effort. Consequently, after the first flurry of interest, space flight died down, and there were few visitors to the other worlds, except for the purpose of research.

Three "space stations" had been constructed to serve Terra as artificial satellites. These were used for refueling interplanetary ships and astronomical and meteorological observation. One of these provided the weapon the nationalists had been searching for in their war against the "Free Scientists."

The station was invaded and occupied by a party of unidentified armed men (later studies suggest that these men were mercenaries in the pay of nationalist forces). And this group, either by ignorant chance or with deliberate purpose, turned certain installations in the station into weapons for an attack upon Terra. There are indications that they themselves had no idea of the power they unleashed, and that it was at once beyond their control.

As a result the major portion of the thickly populated sections of the planet were completely devastated and no one was ever able to reckon the loss of life.

Among those who were the sole survivors of an entire family group was Arturo Renzi. Renzi, a man of unusual magnetic personality, was a believer in narrow and fanatical nationalist doctrines. Because of his personal loss he began to preach the evil of science (with propaganda that the Free Scientists themselves had turned the station against the earth that had apparently been carefully prepared even before the act) and the necessity for man to return to the simple life on the soil to save himself and Terra.

To a people already in psychic shock from the enormity of the disaster, Renzi appeared the great leader they needed and his party came into power around the world. But, fanatic and narrow as he was, his voiced policies were still too liberal for some of his supporters.

Renzi's assassination, an act committed by a man arbitrarily identified as an outlawed Free Scientist, touched off the terrible purge which lasted three days. At the end of which time the few scientists and techneers still alive had been driven into hiding, to be hunted down one by one through the following years as chance or man betrayed them.

Saxon Bort, a lieutenant of Renzi's, assumed command of the leader's forces and organized the tight dictatorship of the Company of Pax.

Learning, unless one was a privileged "Peaceman," became suspect. Society was formed into three classes, the nobility as represented by the Peacemen of various grades, the peasantry on the land, and the work-slaves—descendants of suspected scientists or techneers.

With the stranglehold of Pax firmly established on

Terra, old prejudices against different racial and religious origins again developed. All research, invention, and study was proscribed and the planet was fast slipping into an age of total darkness and retreat. Yet it was at this moment in her history that the first galactic flight was made.

SEE ALSO:
Astra: First Colony
Free Scientists
Renzi, Arturo
Terra: Space Flight

— 1 —
THE ROUNDUP

DARD NORDIS PAUSED beneath the low-hanging branches of a pine, sheltered for the moment from the worst of the cutting wind. The western sky was striped with color, dusky purple, gold, red almost as sultry as if this were August instead of late November. But for all their splendor the colors were as bleakly chill as the wind whipping his too-thin body through the sleazy rags of clothing.

He shrugged his shoulders, trying to settle more evenly the bundle of firewood which bowed him into an old man. There came a tug at the hide thong serving him as a belt.

"Dard—there's an animal watching—over there—"

He stiffened. To Dessie, with her odd kinship for all furred creatures, every animal was a friend. She might now be speaking of a squirrel or—a wolf. He looked down to the smaller, ragged figure beside him and moistened suddenly dry lips.

"Is it a big one?" he asked.

Hands, which wrappings of sackcloth made into shapeless paws, projected to measure off slightly more than a foot of air.

"So big. I think it's a fox—it must be cold. Could we—could we take it home?" Those eyes, which seemed to fill about a quarter of the grimy little face turned up to his, were wistful as well as filled with a too-old patience.

He shook his head. "Foxes have thick fur skins—they're warmer than we are, honey. He probably has a home and is going there now. Think you can pull the wood all the way down to the path?"

Her mouth twisted in an indignant pout "'Course. I'm not a baby any more. It's awfully cold, though, isn't it, Dardie? Wish it were summer again."

She gave a quick jerk on a piece of hide and brought into grudging motion the flat piece of battered wood winch served as a sled. It was piled high with branches and a few pieces of shredded bark. Not much of a haul today, even combining Dessie's bits and patches with his own load. But since their axe had vanished it was the best they could do.

He followed the little girl down the slope, retracing the tracks they had made two hours before. There was a frown drawing deep lines between his black brows. That axe—it hadn't just been mislaid—it had been stolen. By whom? By someone who knew just what its loss would mean, who wanted to cripple them. And that would be Hew Folley. But Hew had not been near the farm for weeks—or had he—secretly?

If he could only get Lars to see that Folley was a danger.

Folley was a landsman which made him a fanatic servant of Pax. The once independent farmers had always believed in peace—true peace, not the iron stagnation imposed by Pax—and they had early been won over as firm followers of Renzi. When their sturdy independence had been entirely swallowed up by the strangle controls of those who had assumed command after the death of the Prophet, some had rebelled—too late. Landsmen were now as proud of their lack of education as they were retentive of the few favors allowed them. And it was from their ranks the hated Peacemen were recruited.

Folley was a fervid follower of Pax and for a long time he had wanted to add the few poor Nordis acres to his own holding. If he ever came to suspect their descent—that they were of Free Scientist blood! If he ever guessed what Lars was doing even now!

"Dardie, why must we run?"

Dard caught his breath in a hall sob and slowed. That prick of frantic panic which had sent him plunging down to the main trail still goaded him. It was always this way when he was away from the farm even for an hour or two. Each time he feared to return to . . . Resolutely he closed his mind to the picture his imagination was only too ready to supply him. He forced his lips into a set half-smile for Dessie's sake.

"Going to be dark early tonight, Dessie. See those big clouds?"

"Snow, Dardie?"

"Probably. We'll be glad to have this wood."

"I hope that the fox gets home to his den before the snow comes. He will, won't he?"

"Of course he will. We'd better, too. Let's try to run, Dessie—here along the trail—"

She regarded doubtfully the almost shapeless blobs of wrappings which concealed her feet "My feet don't run very well, Dardie. Too many coverings on them, maybe. And they're cold now—"

Not frostbite—not frostbite! he prayed. They had been lucky so far. Of course they were always cold, and very often, hungry. But they had had no accidents, nor serious illnesses.

"Run!" he commanded sharply, and Dessie's short-legged shuffle became a trot.

But, when they reached the screen of second-growth brush at the end of the north field, she halted in obedience to old orders. Dard shrugged off the bundle of firewood and dropped to his hands and knees, crawling forward under cover until he could look down across the broken field-stone wall to the house.

Carefully he examined the sweep of snow about the half-ruined dwelling. There were the tracks he and Dessie had made about the yard. But the smooth expanse of white between house and main road was unbroken. There had been no invaders since they had left Thankfully, though without any lessening of his habitual apprehension, he went back to gather up the wood.

"All right?" Dessie shifted impatiently from one cold foot to the other.

"All right."

She jerked the sled into motion and plodded on along the wall where the snow had not drifted. There was a fatal gleam of light in one of the windows below. Lars must be in the kitchen. Minutes later they stamped off snow and went in.

Lars Nordis raised his head as his daughter and then his brother entered. His smile of welcome was hardly more than a stretch of parchment skin over thrusting bones and Dard's secret fear deepened as he studied Lars anxiously. They were always hungry, but tonight Lars had the appearance of a man in the last stages of starvation.

"Good haul?" he asked Dard as the boy began to shed his first layer of the sacking which served him as a coat.

"Good as we could do without the axe. Dessie got a lot of pine cones."

Lars swung around to his daughter who had squatted down before the small fire on the hearth where she began to methodically unwind the strips of burlap which were her mittens.

"Now that was lucky! Did you see anything interesting, Dessie?" He spoke to her as he might have addressed an adult.

"Just a fox," she reported gravely. "It was watching us—from under a tree. It looked cold—but Dardie said it had a home—"

"So it did, honey," Lars assured her, "A little cave or a hollow tree."

"I wish I could have brought it home. It would be nice to have a fox or a squirrel—or something—to live with us." She stretched her small, grime-encrusted, chapped hands out to the fire.

"Maybe someday . . ." Lars' voice trailed off. He stared across Dessie's head at the scanty flames.

Dard hung up the cobbled mass of tatters which was

his outdoor coat and went to the cupboard. He lifted down an unwholesome block of salted meat as his brother spoke again.

"How are supplies?"

Dard tensed. There was more to that question than was merely routine. He surveyed the pitiful array on the shelves jealously.

"How much?" he asked, unable to keep out of his voice the almost despairing resentment he felt.

"Maybe enough for two days—if you can put up such a packet."

Swiftly Dard's eyes measured and portioned. "If it is really necessary—" he couldn't stop that half-protest. This systematic robbing of their own, too scanty hoard—for what? If Lars would only explain! But he knew Lars' answer to that, too: The less one knew, the better, these days. Even in a family that could be so. All right, he'd make up that packet of food and leave it here on the table and in the morning it would be gone—given to someone he didn't know and would never see. And within a week, or maybe a month it would happen again. . . .

"Tonight?" He asked only that as he sawed away at the wood-like meat.

"I don't know."

And at the tone of his brother's answer Dard dropped the dull knife to turn and watch Lars' face. There was a new light in the man's eyes, a brightness about him that his younger brother had never seen since Dessie's mother had died two years before.

"You've finished," Dard said slowly, hardly daring to believe what might be true, that they might be free!

"I've finished. They'll pass the word and then we'll be sent for."

"Honey," Dard called to Dessie, "bring in the pine cones. We'll have a big fire tonight."

As she scampered toward the shed Dard spoke over her head.

"There's a heavy snow on the way, Lars."

"So?" the man at the table did not appear worried. "Well, snow's never stopped them from coming before." He was relaxed, at peace.

Dard was silent but his eyes flickered beyond Lars' shoulder to the objects leaning against the wall. They were never mentioned, those crutches. But in deep snow! Lars never went outside in winter, he couldn't! How could they get away unless the mysterious others had a horse or horses. But perhaps they did. That was always his greatest fault—worrying over the future—borrowing trouble ahead, as if they didn't have enough already to go around!

Dessie was back: to feed the fire slowly one come at a time. Dard scraped the meat slivers into the iron pot and added a shriveled potato carefully diced. Then he grew reckless and wrenched off the lid of a can to pour its treasured contents to thicken the water. If they were going away they'd need feeding up to make the trip and there would be little sense in hoarding supplies they could not carry with them.

"Birthday?" Dessie watched this move in wide-eyed surprise. "But my birthday's in the summer, and Daddy's was last month, and yours," she counted on her fingers, "is not for a long time yet, Dardie."

"Not a birthday. Just a celebration. Get the spoon, Dessie, and stir this carefully."

"Celebration," she considered the new word thoughtfully. "I like celebrations. You going to make tea, too, Dardie? Why, this is just like a birthday!"

Dard shook the dried leaves out on the palm of his hand. Their aromatic fragrance reached him faintly. Mint, green and cool under the sun. He sensed that he was different from Lars—colors, scents, certain sounds meant more to him. Just as Dessie was different in her way—in her ability to make friends with birds and animals. He had seen her last summer, sitting perfectly still on the wall, two birds on her shoulders and a squirrel nuzzling her hand.

But Lars had gifts, too. Only he had been taught to use them. Dard shook the last crumbling leaf from his hand into the pot and wondered for the thousandth time what it would have been like to live in the old days when the Free Scientists had the right to teach and learn and experiment. It probably had been another kind of world altogether—the one which existed before the Big Burning, before Renzi had preached the Great Peace.

All he could remember of his early childhood in those days was a vague happiness. The purge had come when he was eight and Lars twenty-five, and after that things simply got worse and worse. Of course, they'd been lucky to survive the purge at all—belonging to a Scientific family. But their escape had left Lars a twisted cripple. He and Lars and Kathia had come here. But Kathia was different— she forgot everything, mercifully. And after Dessie had been born five months later it had been like caring for two babies at once. Kathia had been sweet and obedient and lovely, but she lived in her own dream world and neither of them had ever tried to bring her out of it. Seven, almost eight years now, they had been here. But in all that time Dard had never quite dared to believe they were safe. He lived always on the ragged edge of fear. Maybe Kathia had been the luckiest one of all.

He took over the stirring of the stew and Dessie set the table, putting out the three wooden spoons, the battered crockery bowl, the tin basin and the single clapped soup dish, the two tin cups and the graceful fluted china one, which had been Dessie's last birthday gift after he had found it hidden on a rafter out in the barn.

"Smells grand, Dard. You're a good cook, son." Lars offered praise.

Dessie bobbed her head in agreement until her two pencil-thick braids flopped up and down on shoulders where the blades, as she moved, took on the angular outlines of wings. "I like celebrations!" She announced. "Tonight may we play the word game?"

"We certainly shall!" Lars returned with emphatic promptness.

Dard did not pause in his stirring though he was alert to every inflection in Lars' voice. Did he read a special significance into that last answer? Why did Lars want to play the word game? And why did he himself feel this aroused wariness—as if they were secure in a den while out in the dark danger prowled!

"I have a new one," Dessie went on, "It sings—"

She put her hands down on the table on either side of

her soup plate and tapped her little broken nails in time to the words she receited:

"Eesee, Osee, Icksee, Ann,
Fullson, Follson, Orson, Cann."

Dard made an effort and pushed the rhythm out of his mind—no time now to "see" the pattern in that. Why did he always "see" words mentally arranged in the up and down patterns of lines? That was as much a part of him as, his delight in color, texture, sight and sound. And for the past three years Lars had encouraged him to work upon it, setting him problems of stray lines of old poetry.

"Yes, that sings, Dessie," Lars was agreeing now. "I heard you humming it this morning. And there is a reason why Dard must make us a pattern—" he broke off abruptly and Dard did not try to question him.

They ate silently, ladling the hot stuff into them, lifting the dishes to drink the last drops. But they lingered over the spicy mint drink, feeling its warmth sink into their starved, chilled bodies. The light given out by the fire was meager; only now and again did it reach Lars' face, and shadows were thick in the corners of the room. Dard made no move to light the greased fagot supported by the iron loop above the table. He was too tired and listless. But Dessie rounded the table and leaned against Lars' crooked shoulder.

"You promised—the word game," she reminded him.

"Yes—the game—"

With a sigh Dard stooped to pick up a charred stick

from the hearth. But he was sure now about the suppressed excitement in his brother's voice. With the blackened wood for a pencil and the table top for his writing pad he waited.

"Suppose we try your verse now, Dessie," Lars suggested. "Repeat it slowly so Dard can work out the pattern."

Dard's stick moved in a series of lines up, down, up again. It made a pattern right enough and a clear one. Dessie came to look and then she laughed.

"Legs kicking, Daddy. My rhyme make a picture of legs kicking!"

Dard studied what he had just done. Dessie was right, legs kicked, one a little more exuberantly than the other. He smiled and then glanced up with a start, for Lars had struggled to his feet and was edging around the table without the aid of his crutches. He looked at the straggling lines, his brows drawn together in a frown of concentration. From the breast pocket of his patched shirt he look out a scrap of peeled bark they used for paper—keeping it half-concealed in the palm of his hand so that what was noted on it remained a secret. Taking the writing stick from Dard he began to make notations, but the scratchings were all numbers not words.

Erasing with the side of his hand now and again he worked feverishly until at last he gave a quick nod as if in self-reassurance, and let his last combinations stand among the line pattern Dard had seen in Dessie's nonsense rhyme.

"This is important—both of you—" his voice was almost a whip lash of impatient command. "The pattern

you see for Dessie's lines, Dard—but—these words."
Slowly he recited, accenting heavily each word he spoke.

"Seven, nine, four and ten.

Twenty, sixty, and seven again."

Dard studied the smudged diagram on the table top until he was sure that it was engraved on his memory for all time.

When he nodded, Lars turned and tossed the note chip into the fire. Then his eyes met his brother's in a straight measuring look over the little girl's bent head.

"It's all yours, Dard, just remember—"

But the younger Nordis had only said, "I'll do it," when Dessie, uncomprehendingly, broke in.

"Seven, nine, four and ten," she repeated solemnly. "Twenty, sixty, and seven again. Why, it sings just as mine does—you're right, Daddy!"

"Yes. Now how about bed." Lars lurched back to hits chair. "It's dark. You'd better go, too, Dard."

That was an order. Lars was expecting someone tonight, then. Dard raked two bricks away from the fire and wrapped them up in charred pieces of blanket. Then he opened the door to the crooked stairs which led to the room overhead. There it was dark and the cold was bitter. But moonlight made a short path from the uncurtained window—enough to show them the pile of straw and ragged bed covers huddled close to the chimney where some heat came up from the fire below. Dard made a nest with the bricks laid in to warm it and pushed Dessie back as far as he could without smothering her. Then he stood for a moment looking out across the moonlit snow.

They were a safe mile from the road and he had taken

certain precautions of his own to insure that no sneaking patrol of Peacemen could enter the lane without warning. Across the fields was only Folley's place—though that was a lurking danger. Behind loomed the mountains, which, wild as they were, promised safety of a kind. If only Lars were not crippled they could have gone into the hills long ago.

When they first reached the farm it had seemed a haven of safety after two years of hiding and being hunted. There was so much confusion after Renzi's assassination and the following purge, with the Peacemen busily consolidating their power, that small fry among the remaining techneers and scientists had managed to stay free of the first nets. But now patrols were combing everywhere and some day, sooner or later, one would come here—especially if Folley revealed his suspicions to the right people. Foley wanted the farm, and be hated Lars and Dard because they were different. To be different nowadays was to sign your own death warrant. How much longer would they escape the notice of a roundup gang?

Dard was aroused from the blackest of forebodings to discover that he was biting savagely on the knuckles of a balled fist. With two quick steps·he crossed the small zoom and felt along the shelf. His heart leaped as his groping fingers closed about the haft of a knife. Not much good against a stun rifle maybe. But when he held it so, he did not feel completely defenseless.

On impulse he put it inside his clothing, against skin which shrunk from the icy metal. And then he crawled into the nest of straw.

"Hmm—?" came a sleepy murmur from Dessie.

"It's Dardie," he whispered reassuringly. "Go to sleep."

It might have been hours later, or minutes, when Dard came suddenly awake. He lay rigid, listening. There was no sound in the old house, not even the creak of a board. But he pulled out into the cold and crawled to the window. Something had awakened him, and the fear he lived with put him on guard.

He strained to see all the details of the bright white and black landscape. A shadow moved between moon and snow. There was a 'copter coming down, making a silent landing just before the house. Figures leaped out of it and flitted to right and left, encircling the dwelling.

Dard ran back to scoop Dessie out of the warmth of the bed, clapping his hand over her mouth. Her eyes opened, wide with fear, as he put his lips close to her ear.

"Go down to Daddy," he ordered. "Wake him!"

"Peacemen?" She was shaking with more than cold as she started down the stairs.

"Say that I think so. They came in a 'copter." That was the one thing he had not been able to guard against— surprise from above. But they had so few of the 'copters left, now that it was forbidden to manufacture any of the prepurge machines. And why should they use one to raid an insignificant farmhouse sheltering a child, a cripple and a boy? Unless Lars' work was important—so important that they dared not allow him to pass along his findings to the underground.

Dard watched the dark shapes take cover. They were probably all around the house by this time, moving in. They wanted to take the inhabitants alive. Too many cornered scientists in the past had cheated them. So they would move slowly now—slow enough to—Dard's smile was no more than a drawn grimace. He still had one secret, one which might save the Nordis family yet.

Having watched the last of the raiders take cover, Dard ran down into the kitchen. The fire was still burning, and before it crouched Lars.

"They came by air. And they have the house surrounded," Dard reported in a matter-of-fact voice. Now that the worst had at last happened he was surprisingly calm. "But they don't have their trap completely closed—as they are going to discover!"

He brushed past Lars and jerked open the cupboard doors. Dessie stood beside her father, and now Dard threw her a bag.

"Food—everything you can pack in," he ordered. "Lars, here!"

From the pegs he pulled down all the extra clothing they had. "Get dressed to go out."

But his brother shook his head. "You know I can't make it, Dard."

Dessie went on stuffing provisions into the bag. "I'll help you, Daddy," she promised, "Just as soon as I can."

Dard paid no attention to his brother. Instead he ran to the far end of the room and raised the trap door of the cellar.

"Last summer," he explained as he came back to gather up the clothing, "I found a passage down there, behind the wall. It leads out to the foundations of the barn. We can hide there—"

"They know we are here. They'll be looking for a move such as that," objected Lars.

"Not after I cover our trail."

He saw that Lars was pulling on the remnants of a coat Dessie was almost ready to go and now she helped her father not only to dress but to crawl across the floor to the hole. Dard gave her a pine knot torch before he went to work.

The doors and all the downstairs shutters were barred. Those ought to hold just long enough—

He took a small can from the cupboard and poured its long-saved contents liberally about the room. Then he withdrew to the head of the cellar ladder before hurling a second blazing torch into the nearest patch of liquid. A billow of fire sent him hurtling down with just enough time to pull the trap door shut behind him.

As he shoved aside the rotting bins which concealed the opening to the passage, he could hear the crackling above, and smoke drifted down through the flooring cracks.

A moment later Dessie scuttled into the passage ahead as Dard hauled Lars along with him. Over their heads the house burned. These outside might well believe that their prey burned with it. At the very least the blaze would cover their escape for the precious minutes which meant the difference between life and death.

⇥2⇤
HIDING OUT

BEFORE THEY REACHED the outlet below the barn, Dard brought them to a halt. There was no use emerging into the arms of some snooping Peaceman. It was better to stay in hiding until they could see whether or not the enemy had been fooled by the burning house.

The passage in which the three crouched was walled with rough stone and so narrow that the shoulders of the two adults brushed both sides. It was cold, icy with a chill which crept up from the bare earth underneath through their ill-covered feet to their knees and then into their shivering bodies. How long they could stay there without succumbing to that cold Dard did not know. He bit his lip anxiously as he strained to hear the sound from above.

He was answered by an explosion, the sound and shock of which came to them down the passage from the house. And then there was a slightly hysterical chuckle from Lars.

"What happened?" began Dard, and then answered his own question, "The laboratory!"

"Yes, the laboratory," Lars said, leaning against the wall. These was relaxation in both his pose and voice. "They'll have a mess to comb through now."

"All the better!" snapped Dard. "Will it feed the fire?"

"Feed the fire! It might blow up the whole building. There won't be enough pieces left for them to discover what was inside before the blast."

"Or who might have been there!" For the first time Dard saw a ray of real hope. The Peacemen could not have known of this passage, they probably believed that the dwellers in the farmhouse had been blown up in that explosion. The escape of the Nordis family was covered— they now had a better than even chance.

But still he waited, or rather made Lars and Dessie wait in hiding while he crept on into the barn hole and climbed up the ladder he had placed there for such a use as this. Then, making a worm's progress crawling, he crossed the rotting floor to peer out through the doorless entrance.

The outline of the farmhouse walls was gone, and tongues of blue-white flame ate up the dark to make the scene daybright. Two men in the black and white Peace uniforms were dragging a third away from the holocaust. And there was a lot of confused shouting. Dard listened and gathered that the raiders were convinced that their prey had gone up with the house, taking with them two officers who had just beaten in the back door before the explosion. And there had been three others injured. The round up gang was hurrying away, apprehensive of other explosions. Peacemen, who prided themselves on their lack of scientific knowledge, were apt to harbor such suspicions.

Dard got to his feet. The last man, trailing a stun rifle, was going around the fire now, keeping a careful distance from the chemically fed flames, such a distance that he plunged waist deep through snow drifts. And a few moments later Dard saw the 'copter rise, circle the farm once, and head west. He sighed with relief and went back to get the others.

"All clear," he reported to Lars as he supported the crippled man up the ladder. "They think we went up in the explosion and they were afraid there might be another so they left fast—"

Again Lars chuckled. "They won't be back in a hurry then."

"Dard," Dessie was a small shadow moving through the gloom, "if our house is gone where are we going to live now?"

"My practical daughter," Lars said. "We will find some other place. . . ."

Dard remembered. "The messenger you were expecting! He might see the blaze from the hills and not come at all!"

"And that's why you're going to leave him a sign that we're still in the land of the living, Dard. As Dessie points out we haven't a roof over us now, and the sooner we're on our way the better. Since our late callers believe us to be dead there's no danger in Dessie and I staying right where we are now, while you do what's necessary to bring help. Follow the wall in the top pasture to the corner where the old woods road begins. About a quarter of a mile beyond is a big tree with a hollow in it. Put this inside." Lars pulled a piece of rag out of his wrappings. "Then come back here. That'll bring our man on down even if he sees an eruption going on. It tells him that we've escaped and are hiding out waiting to make contact. If he doesn't come by morning—we'll try moving up closer to the tree."

Dard understood. His brother daren't attempt the journey through the snow and brush at night. But tomorrow they could rig some kind of a board sled from the debris and drag Lars into the safety of the woods. In the meantime it was very necessary to leave the sign. With a word of caution to them both, Dard left the barn.

By instinct he kept to the shadows cast by the trees and brush which encroached on the once fertile fields. Near the farm buildings was a maze of tracks left by the Peacemen, and he used them to hide the pattern of his own steps. Just why he took such precautions he could not tell, but the wariness which had guided every move of his life for years had now become an ingrown part of him. On the other hand, now that the raid he had feared for so long had come, and he and his were still alive and free, he felt eased of some of the almost intolerable burden.

As he tramped away from the dying fire the night was very still and cold. Once a snowy owl slipped across the sky, and deep in the forest a wolf, or one of the predatory wild dogs, howled. Dard did not find it difficult to locate Lars' tree and made sure that the rag was safe in the black hollow of its trunk.

The cold ate into him and he hurried on his back trail. Maybe they might dare light a small fire in the cellar pit, just enough to keep them from freezing until morning. How close was the dawn, he wondered, as he stumbled and clutched at a snow-crowned wall to steady himself. Bed—sleep—warmth. He was so tired—so very tired—

Then a sound ripped through the night air. A shot! His face twisted and his hand went to the haft of the knife. A shot! Lars had no gun! The Peacemen—but they had gone!

Clumsily, slipping, fighting to keep his footing in the treacherous snow drifts, Dard began to run. Within a matter of minutes he came to his senses and dodged into cover, making his way to the barn in such a manner as to provide no target for any marksman lurking there. Dessie, Lars—there alone without any means of defense!

Dard was close to he braiding when Dessie's scream came. And that scream tore all the caution from him. Balancing the knife in his hand, he threw himself across the churned snow of the yard for the door. And his sacking covered feet made no sound as he ran.

"Got ya—imp of Satan!"

Dard's arm came up, the knife was poised. And, as if for once Fortune was on his side, there was a sharp tinkle of breaking glass from the embers of the house and a following sweep of flame to light the scene within the barn.

Dessie was fighting, silently now, with all the frenzy of a small cornered animal, in the hands of Hew Folley. One of the man's hard fists was aimed straight for her face as Dard threw the knife.

The months he had practiced with that single weapon were now rewarded. Dessie flew free as the man hurled her away. On hands and feet she scuttled into the dark. Hew turned and bent over as if to grope for the rifle which lay by his feet. Then he coughed, and coughing, went down. Dard grabbed the rifle. Only when it was in his hands did he come up to the still-coughing man. He pulled at Folley's shoulder and rolled him over. Bitter hatred stared up at Dard from the small dark eyes of the other.

"Got—dirty—stinkman—" Folley mouthed and then coughed. Blood bubbled from his slack lips. "Thought— he—was—hiding—right— Kill—kill—" The rest was lost in a gush of blood. He tried to raise himself but the effort was beyond him. Dard watched grimly until it was over and then, fighting down a rising nausea, undertook the dirty business of retrieving his knife.

The sun did not show when he came out of the barn with Dessie after some hours which he did not want to remember. From a gray sky whirled flakes of white. Dard regarded them blankly at first and then with a dull relief. A snow storm would hide a lot. Not that anyone would ever find Lars' poor twisted body, now safely walled up in the passage. But Folley's people might be detained, by a heavy storm if they started a search. The landsman had been a tyrant and the district bully—not beloved enough to arouse interest for a sizable searching party.

"Where are we going, Dardie?" Dessie's voice was a monotone. She had not cried, but she had shivered continually, and now she looked at the outer world with a shadow of dread in her eyes. He drew her closer as he shouldered their bag of supplies.

"Into the woods, Dessie. We'll have to live as the animals do—for a while. Are you hungry?"

She did not meet his eyes as she shook her head. And she made no effort to move until his hand on her shoulder drew her along. The snow thickened in a wild dance, driven by gusts of wind to hide the still smoldering cellar of the farmhouse. Pushing Dessie before him Dard began the hike back along his path of the night before—toward the hollow tree and the meeting place. To contact Lars' messenger might now be their only chance.

Under the trees the fury of the storm was less, but the snow packed against their bodies, clinging to their eyelashes and a wisp of hair which hung across Dessie's forehead so that she brushed at it mechanically. Food, heat, shelter, their needs made a pattern in Dard's mind and he clung to it, shutting out memories of the past night Dessie could not stand this tramping for long. And he was almost to the end of his own strength. He used the rifle as a staff.

The rifle—and three shells—He had those. But he dared not use the weapon except as a last resort. The sound of a shot carried too far. There were only a few guns left and they were in the hands of those whom the Peacemen had reason to trust. Anyone hunting for Folley would be attracted by a shot. If their escape became suspected. . . . He shivered with something other than cold.

Herding Dessie at a steady pace he fought his way to the hollow tree. There was no need to worry about the trail they had left, the snow filled it in a matter of minutes. But they must stay near here—for Lars' messenger to find them.

Dard set Dessie to treading back and forth in a space he marked out for her. That not only kept her moving and so fighting the insidious cold numbness, but it packed down a flooring for the shelter he built. A fallen tree gave it backing and pine branches, heaped up and covered with snow; provided a roof.

He could see the hollow in the tree from this lair and he impressed upon Dessie the necessity of watching for anyone coming along the path.

They ate handfuls of snow together with wooden bits of salted meat. But the little girl complained of sleepiness and at last Dard huddled in the shelter with Dessie in his arms, the rifle at hand, fighting drowsiness to keep his grim vigil.

At length he had to put the rifle between his feet, the end of the barrel just under his jaw, so that when he nodded, the touch of the cold metal nudged him into wakefulness. How long they dared stay there was a question which continued to trouble him. What if the messenger did not come today or tomorrow? There was a cave back in the hills which he had discovered during the past summer but—

The jab of the rifle barrel made his eyes water with pain. The snow had stopped falling. Branches, heavily burdened, were bent to the ground, but the air was free. He pulled back his top covering and studied Dessie's pinched face. She was sleeping, but now and again she twisted uneasily and once she whimpered. He changed position to aid his cramped legs and she half roused.

But right on her inquiring "Dardie?" came another sound and his hand clamped right across her lips. Someone was coming along the woods trail, singing tunelessly.

The messenger?

Before Dard's hope was fully aroused it was dashed. He saw a flash of red around a bush and then the wearer of that bright cap came into full view. Dard's lips drew back in a half-snarl—

Lotta Folley!

Dessie struggled in his arms and he let her crawl to one side of the tiny shelter. But, though he brought up the rifle, he found he could not aim it. Hew Folley—betrayer and murderer—yes. His daughter—though she might be of the same brutal breed—though he might be throwing away freedom and life—he could not kill!

The girl, a sturdy stout figure in her warm homespuns and knitted cap, halted panting beneath the very tree he must watch. If she glanced up now—if her woodsight was as keen as his—and he had no reason to doubt that it was.

Lotta Folley's head raised and across the open expanse of snow her eyes found Dard's strained face. He made no move in a last desperate attempt to escape notice. After all he was in the half-shadow of the shelter, she might not see him—the protective "playing dead" of an animal.

But her eyes widened, her full mouth shaped a soundless expression of astonishment. With a kind of pain he waited for her to cry out.

Only she made no sound at all. After that first moment of surprise her face assumed its usual stupid, slightly sullen solidity. She brushed some snow from the front of her jacket without looking at it, and when she spoke in her hoarse common voice, she might have been addressing the tree at her side.

"The Peacemen are huntin'."

Dard made no answer. She pouted her lips and added, "They're huntin' you."

He still kept silent. She stopped brushing her jacket and her eyes wavered around the trees and brush walling in the old road.

"They say as how your brother's a stinkman—"

"Stinkman," the opprobious term for a scientist. Dard continued to hold his tongue. But her next question surprised him.

"Dessie—Dessie all right?"

He was too slow to catch the little girl who slipped by him to face the Folley girl gravely.

Lotta fumbled in the breast of her packet and brought out a packet folded in a piece of grease-blotted cloth. She did not move up to offer it to Dessie but set it down carefully on the end of a tree stump.

"For you," she said to the little girl. Then she turned to Dard. "You better not stick around. Pa tol' the Peacemen about you." She hesitated. "Pa didn't come back las' night—"

Dard sucked in his breath. That glance she had shot at him, had there been knowledge in it? But if she knew what lay in the barn—why wasn't she heading the hue and cry to their refuge? Lotta Folley, he had never regarded her with any pleasure. In the early days, when they had first come to the farm, she had often visited them, watching Kathia, Dessie, with a kind of lumpish interest. She had talked little and what she said suggested that she was hardly more than a moron. He had been contemptuous of her, though he had never showed it.

"Pa didn't come back las' night," she repeated, and now he was sure she knew—or suspected. What would she do? He couldn't use the rifle—he couldn't—

Then he realized that she must have seen that weapon, seen and recognized it. He could offer no reasonable explanation for having it with him. Folley's rifle was a treasure, it wouldn't be in the hands of another—and surely not in the hands of Folley's enemy—as long as Folley was alive.

Dard caught the past tense. So she did know! Now—what was she going to do?

"Pa hated lotsa things," her eyes clipped away from his to Dessie. "Pa liked t' hurt things."

The words were spoken without emotion, in her usual dull tone.

"He wanted t' hurt Dessie. He wanted t' send her t' a work camp. He said he was gonna. You better give me that there gun, Dard. If they find it with Pa they ain't gonna look around for anybody that ran away."

"But why?" he was shocked almost out of his suspicion.

"Nobody's gonna send Dessie t' no work camp," she stated flatly. "Dessie—she's special! Her ma was special, too. Once she made me a play baby. Pa—he found it an' burned it up. You—you can take care of Dessie—you gotta take care of Dessie!" Her eyes met his again compellingly. "You gotta git away from here an' take Dessie where none of them Peacemen are gonna find her. Give me Pa's rifle an' I'll cover up."

Driven to the last rags of his endurance Dard met that with the real truth.

"We can't leave here yet—"

She cut him off. "Some one comin' for you? Then Pa was right—your brother was a stinkman?"

Dard found himself nodding.

"All right," she shrugged. "I can let you know if they come again. But you see to Dessie—mind that!"

"I'll see to Dessie." He held out the rifle and she took it from him before she pointed again to the packet.

"Give her that. I'll try to git you some more—maybe tonight. If they think you got away they'll bring dogs out from town. If they do—" She shuffled her feet in the snow. Then she stood the rifle against the hollow tree and unbuttoned the front of her packet. Her hands, clumsy in mittens, unwound a heavy knitted scarf and tossed it to the child.

"You put that on you," she ordered with some of the authority of a mother, or at least of an elder sister. "I'd leave you my coat, only they'd notice." She picked up the rifle again. "Now I'll put this here where it belongs an' maybe they won't go on huntin'."

Speechless Dard watched her turn down trail, still at a loss to understand her actions. Was she really going to return that rifle to the barn—how could she, knowing the truth? And why?

He knelt to wind the scarf around Dessie's head and shoulders. For some reason Folley's daughter wanted to help them and he was beginning to realize that he needed all the aid he could get.

The packet Lotta had left contained such food as he had not seen in years—real bread, thick buttered slices of it, and a great hunk of fat pork. Dessie would not eat unless he shared it with her, and he took enough to flavor his own meal of the wretched fare they had brought with them. When they had finished he asked one of the questions which had been in his mind ever since Lotta's amazing actions.

"Do you know Lotta well, Dessie?"

She ran her tongue around her greasy lips, collecting stray crumbs.

"Lotta came over often."

"But I haven't seen her since—" he stopped before mentioning Kathia's death.

"She comes and talks to me when I am in the fields. I think she is afraid of you and—Daddy. She always brings me nice things to eat. She said that some day she wanted to give me a dress—a pink dress. I would very much like a pink dress, Dardie. I like Lotta—she is always good— inside she is good."

Dessie smoothed down the ends of her new scarf.

"She is afraid of her Daddy. He is mean to her. Once he came when she was with me and he was very, very mad. He cut a stick with his knife and he hit her with it. She told me to run away quick and I did. He was a very bad man, Dardie. I was afraid of him, too. He won't come after us?"

"No!"

He persuaded Dessie to sleep again and when she awoke he knew that he must have rest himself and soon. Impressing upon her how much their lives depended on it, he told her to watch the tree and awaken him if anyone came.

It was sunset when he aroused from an uneasy, night-mare-haunted sleep. Dessie squatted quietly beside him, her small grave face turned to the trail. As he shifted his weight she glanced up.

"There was just a bunny," she pointed to small betraying tracks. "But no people, Dard, Is—is there any bread left? I'm hungry."

"Sure you are!" He crawled out of the shelter and stretched cramped limbs before unwrapping the remains of Lotta's bounty.

In spite of her vaunted hunger Dessie ate slowly, as if savoring each crumb. The light was fading fast, although there were still red streaks in the sky. Tonight they must remain here—but tomorrow? If Lotta's return of the rifle to the barn did not stop the search—then tomorrow the fugitives would have to take to the trail again.

"Is it going to snow again, Dardie?"

He studied the sky. "I don't think so. I wish it would."

"Why? When the snow is deep, it's hard to walk."

He tried to explain. "Because when it snows, it is really warmer. Too cold at night . . ." he didn't finish that sentence, but encircled Dessie with a long arm and drew her back under the shelter with him. She wriggled about, settling herself more comfortably, then she jerked upright again.

"Someone's coming!" her whisper was warm on his cheek.

He had heard that too, the faint creak of a foot on the icy coated snow. And his hand closed about the haft of his knife.

⊰3⊱

THE CLEFT DWELLERS

HE WAS A SMALL MAN, the newcomer, and Dard overtopped him by four inches or more. And that gave the boy confidence enough to pull out of the shelter. He watched the stranger come confidently on, as though he knew just how many steps lay between himself and some goal. His clothing, what could be seen of it in the fast deepening dusk, was as ragged and patched as Dard's own. This was no landsman or Peaceman scout. Only one who did not hold all the important "confidence cards" would go about so unkempt. Which meant that he was an "unreliable," almost as much an outlaw as a techneer or a scientist.

The newcomer stopped abruptly in front of the tree. But he did not raise his hand to the hollow, instead he studied the tracks left by Lotta. But finally he shrugged and reached into the hole.

Dard moved and the other whirled in a half-crouch.

There was the gleam of teeth in his bearded face, and another glint—of bare metal—in his hand.

But he made no sound and it was Dard who broke the quiet.

"I am Dard Nordis—"

"So? . . ." The single word was lengthened to approximate a reptile's hiss.

And Dard sensed that he was facing a dangerous man, a menace far worse than Hew Folley or any of his brutal kind.

"Suppose you tell me what has happened?" the man added.

"Roundup raid—last night," Dard returned laconically, his initial relief at the other's coming considerably dampened. "We thought we had escaped. I came up to leave that message for Lars." He motioned to the rag. "When I got back Lars was dead—killed by the neighbor who probably set them on us. So Dessie and I came here to wait for you."

"Peacemen!" the man spat. "And Lars Nordis dead! That's a bad piece of luck—bad." He made no move to put away the gun he held. It resembled a hand stun gun, but certain peculiarities of the stub barrel suggested that it was more deadly a weapon than that.

"And now," the man moved a step or two in Dard's direction, "what do you expect me to do with you?"

Dard moistened dry lips with a nervous tongue. He had not considered that, without Lars and what Lars had to offer, the mysterious underground might not wish to burden themselves with an untrained boy and a small child. Grim necessity was the law among all the present outlaws, and useless hands coupled with another mouth to feed were not wanted. He had a single hope. . . .

Lars had been so insistent about that word pattern that Dard dared now to believe that he must carry his brother's discovery in that memorized design of lines and numbers. He had to believe that and impress the importance of his information upon this messenger. It would be their passport to the underground.

"Lars had finished his work," Dard schooled his voice to conversational evenness. "I think you need the results—"

The man's head jerked. And now he did put away that oddly shaped gun.

"You have the formula?"

Dard took a chance and touched his own forehead. "I have it here. I'll deliver it when and if I reach the proper persons."

The messenger kicked moodily at a lump of snow. "It's a long trip—back into the hills. You have supplies?"

"Some. I'll talk when we're safe—when Dessie is safe—"

"I don't know—a child—the going's pretty tough."

"You'll find we can keep up," Dard made a promise he had no surety of keeping. "But we had better start now—there's just a chance that they may be after us."

The man shrugged. "All right. Come ahead—the two of you."

Dard handed the bag of supplies to the other and took Dessie's hand. Without another word the man turned to retrace the way he had come and the other two followed, keeping as well as they could to the trail he had broken.

They traveled on all that night. Dard first led and then

carried Dessie, until, after one halt, the guide waved him on and raised the little girl to his shoulder, leaving Dard to stumble along unburdened. They rested at intervals but never long enough to relax, and Dard despaired of being able to keep up the pace. This messenger was a tireless machine, striding as might a robot along some hidden trail of which he alone knew the landmarks.

At dawn they were close to the top of a rise. Dard pulled himself up the last of a steep slope, panting, to discover the other waiting for him. With a jerk of his thumb, the man indicated the crest of the divide.

"Cave—camp—" he got out the two words stiffly and put Dessie down. "Can you make it by yourself?" he asked her.

"Yes," her hand sought his confidently. "I'm a good climber."

There was a hint of smile, an awkward smile, pulling long forgotten muscles about his tight mouth. "You sure are, sister!"

The cave was fairly deep, the narrow entrance giving little hint of the wide room one found after squeezing through. It was a revelation to Dard as the guide snapped on a hand beam from a tiny carrying case he took from a ledge by the entrance. This was, the boy gathered, a regular camping place used by the underground travelers. He sank down on a bed of leaves and watched their companion pull out a black box, adjusting a dial on its side. Within seconds they began to feel the heat radiating from it. Free Scientist—equipment all of this—all top contraband. Dard had dim pre-purge memories of such aids to comfort.

Dessie gave a sigh of pure content and curled up as

close to that wonder as she could get. She watched with sleepy eyes the owner of this marvel break open a can of soup and pour its half-frozen contents into a pan which he set on top of the heating unit. He rummaged through the bag of supplies Dard brought grunting at the scantiness of the pitiful collection.

"We didn't have much time to pack," said Dard, finally irritated by the other's unspoken contempt.

"What brought them down on you?" the man asked, squatting back on his heels. He had the strange gun out checking the clip which carried its charge, squinting down its few inches of barrel.

"Who knows? There was a landsman—he wanted the farm. He was the one who shot Lars."

"Hmm—" The man peered into the now bubbling soup. "Then it may have been only a routine raid after all—sparked by just general malice?"

That, Dard gathered from his tone, was the answer more desired by this stranger. And his own thoughts went back to the last evening in the farm house when Lars had made his announcement of success. The raid had followed too aptly—almost as if Lars' discovery at all costs had to be prevented from reaching those who might make use of it. What had Lars been working on, and why was it so important? And did he, Dard Nordis, actually know anything about it?

"What's your name?" Dessie eyed their companion over the cup of soup he had poured for her. "I never saw you before—"

For the second time that shadow smile appeared on the guide's lips.

"No, you never saw me, Dessie. But I've seen you—several times. And you may call me Sach."

"Sach," she repeated. "That is a funny name. But this is very good soup, Sach. Is this a celebration?"

He looked startled. "Don't know about its being a celebration, Dessie. But it is going to be a day of sleep for all of us. We still have a long way to go. Suppose you bed down over there and close your eyes."

Dard was nodding over his own supply of food and a very short time later followed the same orders.

He awoke with a start. Sach was stooping over him, his grimed hand over Dard's mouth as he shook him by the shoulder. As soon as he saw the awareness in the boy's eyes, he dropped down on one knee to whisper:

"There's a 'copter circling—been up and around overhead for a half hour. Either we've been trailed or they've found out about this cave and put a watch on it. Now you listen and get this straight. What Lars Nordis was doing means more than life to the Cleft Dwellers. They've been waiting for the results of his last tests." He paused and in quite a different voice as if repeating some talisman added two words Dard had once heard from Lars, "Ad astra." Then in a harsh command he continued, "They've got to have it and have it quick. We're some five miles from the valley. Set a line straight to the peak you can see from this cave entrance and keep to it. Give me a good start and watch. If the 'copter follows me, then it's okay for you to make a break to reach the peak. Keep undercover all you can. There's only one long stretch where you cross the river that you have to be in the open."

"But you—" Dard was trying to pull his sleep scattered thoughts together.

"I'll go down slope the opposite way. If they are suspicious of this hiding hole and are watching it, they may take out after me. And I've played this type of hide and seek before, I know the game. You watch from the entrance while I go—now!"

Dard followed him to the narrow opening where Sach lingered just within the shadow listening. Now Dard could hear it too, the faint whine of a 'copter beating through the cold afternoon air. It grew to a steady drone, passed overhead, and faded. Sach still waited. Then he gave a curt nod to Dard and melted away.

The boy crawled to the very edge of the concealing overhang. Sach by some trick had won a good ten feet down slope. It would be difficult for anyone sighting him now to guess just where he had appeared from. He slid down, in only enough hurry to suggest that he was bolting from a position he considered dangerous.

Now the 'copter was on its way back—either on a routine sweep or because the dark figure of Sach had been sighted. He leaped into the shelter of a pine grown thicket, but not soon enough to escape detection. The 'copter circled down. There was a loud crack awaking echoes from the surrounding rocks. Somebody had shot at the fugitive.

"Dardie!"

"It's all right," the boy called reassuringly over his shoulder into the cave. "I'll be back in a minute."

Sach had probably wormed his way down to the edge of the deep woods. The 'copter made another smaller and tighter circle and came closer to the ground, to allow three men to leap into the snow. Before they could gain their feet and their balance a pencil of green light beamed a tight ray at one. He screamed and threshed the snow into a high shower of drift. The others threw themselves flat but continued to snake toward the wood from which that attack had come, and the 'copter swooped to spray death into the silent trees. Sach had not only drawn the attention of the trackers, he was using every means of keeping it on him. The 'copter soared above the trees, westward, away from the cave. When the two men broke into the brush undercover Dard watched them out of sight.

It would be evening soon. And the eastern slope was well provided with cover. There were sections of bare rock on the slope where no snow clung. Dard's eyes narrowed—footprints were easy to see from the air. But there was another way of getting down to the valley, one which would leave no such tell-tale traces. He went inside and clicked on the light Sach had left.

"Time to go, Dardie?" Dessie asked.

"First we eat." He made himself move deliberately. If Sach's information was right they still had a long trip before them. And they must not start it with empty stomachs. He used supplies recklessly before tying up enough of the remains to provide them with food for at least one more day.

"Where is Sach?" Dessie wanted to know.

"He had to go away. We will travel alone now. Eat all that, Dessie."

"I am," she answered almost peevishly. "I wish we could stay here. That box makes it so nice and warm."

For a moment Dard was tempted to do just that. To venture out on an unknown trail through the snow and cold when they could lay snug here seemed not only foolish but almost criminal, especially when it involved taking Dessie into the wilderness. But the urgency which had sent Sach out into the very mouth of danger to draw off pursuit could not be denied. If Sach believed that the information they carried was as important as that—Well, they would uphold their part of the bargain. And there was always the fear in his mind since the coming of the 'copter, that the cave had been marked down and was known to the Peacemen.

It was dusk when they came out into the snap of the cruel night air. Dard pointed to the nearest ledge of bare rock sloping downward.

"We must walk along that ledge so as not to leave tracks in the snow."

Dessie nodded. "But where the rock ends, Dardie, what do we do then?"

"Wait and see!"

They edged along the ledge and it seemed to Dard that the chill struck up from the stone with double intensity. But Dessie flitted ahead and was teetering back and forth on the very edge as he caught up.

"Now," he told her, "we are going to jump. Into the big drift down there."

He had meant to make that leap first, and was tensing his muscles for the spring, when Dessie went over. Whether she had voluntarily thrown herself over or whether she had lost her balance he could not tell. But before he could move she had disappeared, and a plume of snow puffed to mark her landing place. Dard crouched there uncertainly until he saw the wave of an arm. Then he plunged, calculating his fall to land him apart from Dessie. He was a moment in the frosty air and then deep in snow which choked his mouth and blinded his eyes.

When they had fought their way out of the drift Dard glanced back up the slope. They had won into the shadow of the woods where their trail would be concealed from 'copter spies. His ruse had succeeded!

Now, he swung to the east, five miles Sach had said. Their progress would depend upon drifts and footing. It wouldn't be too hard going in the shelter of the trees. Luckily this was no dense forest. And by steering with the peak and the river they could reach their ultimate goal.

In the beginning the journey appeared simple and Dard was lighthearted. But before morning dawned they were caught in a nightmare. They had reached the river's bank, only to find the ice crust there too thin to use as a bridge. Time and time again, as they hunted along its bank, they sank knee deep into the powdery snow. Dard carried Dessie again and had to abandon the bag of supplies. He knew with a sinking heart that the periods of struggle between the rests were growing shorter and shorter. But he dared not give up and try to camp—being sure that if he once relaxed he would never rise again.

Morning found them at the one place where the river might be crossed. An arch of ice, snow crowned, made a perilous bridge over which they crept fearfully. The peak stood needle-pointing into the sky—probably, the boy thought bitterly, looking closer than it was.

He tried to keep to the cover afforded by brush and

trees, but the rays of the rising sun reflected from the snow confused him and at last he plodded on, setting each foot down with exaggerated care, grimly determined only upon keeping his feet, with or without protection from a 'copter.

Dessie rested across his shoulder, her eyes half-closed. He believed that she was unconscious now, or very close to it. She gave no protest when he laid her body down on a fallen tree and leaned against another forest giant to draw panting gasps that cut his lungs with knives of ice. Some instinct or good fortune had kept him on the right course—the peak was still ahead. And now he could see that it guarded the entrance to a narrow cleft through which a small pathway led. But what lay beyond that cleft and how far he would still be from help if he could reach it he had no idea.

Dard allowed himself to rest until he had counted slowly to one hundred, and then he lifted Dessie again and lurched on, trying to avoid the clutching briars on neighboring bushes. In that moment, as he straightened up with the girl in his arms, he thought that he had sighted a strange glint of light from near the crown of the peak. Sun striking on ice, he reasoned dully as he plodded on.

He was never to know if he could have made the last lap of that journey under his own power. For, before he had gone a hundred yards, his fatigue-dulled ears caught the ominous sound of a 'copter engine. And, without trying to locate the source, he threw himself and his burden into the bushes, rolling through the snow and enduring the lash of branches.

The whine of the machine's supporting blades sounded

doubly clear through the morning air. And a second later he saw splinters fly from a tree trunk not a foot away. Dragging Dessie he pulled back into thicker cover. But he knew that he was only prolonging the end. They knew that he was alone except for the child, they would conclude that he was unarmed. They had only to land men and take him at their leisure.

But, though the 'copter swept back and forth over the tangle of brush into which he had burrowed his way, it made no move to land anyone. So, thinking that he now was screened from their sight, Dard squatted down holding Dessie tightly, trying to think.

Sach—Sach and the green ray which had brought down the Peacemen back on the heights by the cave; that was it. They knew that he carried no rifle. But they were afraid that he might be armed with one of those more potent weapons such as Sach had used. Dessie whimpered and clung closer to him as the 'copter made another dive above their hiding place—one which leveled off only inches above the branches which might have tangled in the undercarriage.

The crack of rifle fire punctuated the whine of the engine. Again he watched splinters fly—one close enough to score his cheek. By will alone he held himself immovable and kept Dessie captive, though her little body flinched at the sound of each shot. Those above could not see their quarry or they would not be spraying bullets so indiscriminantly. This raking of the brush was to force him out.

And the worst of it was that they could do just that! Dard knew that the searching stream of death quartering the thicket would either kill them or force them to move.

He blinked at the bushes and made his first constructive move, stripping Lotta's scarf off Dessie's head and shoulders. Quickly he tangled the thick wool in some thorned branches. Then he put Dessie on her knees in the snow and pushed her away from that thorn bush. She obediently wormed her way off as Dard followed, moving by inches. Luckily the 'copter was now making the rounds of the perimeter of the thicket and for a minute or two there had been no shooting. Dard traveled on until the scarf end pulled taut in his hand, until he could keep his grip on the loose end only with thumb and forefinger at the full extent of an outstretched arm. Then he lay waiting.

The 'copter was moving in again while more than one marksman added to a crisscross fire. Dard bit deep on the soft inner side of his lip. Now! By the sound the 'copter was just in the right position. As a rifle cracked, Dard gave two quick jerks of the scarf, and was answered by a loud burst of fire. Then he screamed wildly, and Dessie, shocked out of her bewilderment, echoed him thinly. Another tug at the scarf for good measure and then he was racing on hands and knees, bumping Dessie before him. If they would only believe that he, or Dessie, or both had been hit! That should bring them down, set them fighting their way to the spot where he had fastened the scarf. And then there would be a slim chance, a terribly slim chance, to get away.

Dard cringed at the sound of the vicious attack the 'copter riders were still centering behind him—an attack delivered without any call to surrender. All that blind hatred which had boiled over during the purge was still smoldering in those who were now hunting them. He had always known that anyone of proven scientist blood would have little chance if the Peacemen tracked him down, but now the last faint hope of mercy for the helpless was gone.

Pulling Dessie he reached the end of the thicket in which they had taken refuge. By some blind chance they had come out on the side which faced the peak. But before them lay a wide open sweep of ground, impossible to cross undetected. Dard faced it bleakly. The brightness of the sunlight somehow made that last blow harder.

But, even as his misery and despair weakened him, he suddenly noted again flashes of light on the peak—coming in too regular a pattern to be sun fostered. While he was still gaping up at that, a shadow swept over. The 'copter landed directly on that virgin expanse of snow before him. He sagged and his arms tightened about Dessie who gave a muffled cry as his grip hurt her. This was the end—they could not run any more.

The Peacemen were taking their time about leaving the 'copter. It looked as if they were still reluctant to approach that thicket. What had Sach done that made them so wary?

Two of them crept around the tail of the machine, and, Dard saw the gun mounted on the 'copter's roof swing about to cover them. The men crawled slowly through the snow. But before they had reached beyond the length of the 'copter, that blink of light on the peak stepped up into a steady glow. Dard's eyes dropped from it to the Peacemen and so he did not see deliverance arrive.

There was a swish of sound followed by a tinkle as if

glass had splintered. Green fog bellowed out about the machine—the same fatal green of the ray Sach had used on the cave slope.

Without knowing why, he threw himself face down, carrying Dessie with him, as traces of the fog wafted slowly toward the thicket. It must be gas, and those men were now floundering in it. Then the world went black and Dard fell into deep space, a place where Dessie, too, was swept away from him.

—4—
AD ASTRA

DARD LAY ON HIS back staring up into unfamiliar gray reaches. Then a pinkish globe swam into position over him and he concentrated upon it. Eyes, nose, a mouth that was opening and shutting, took proper place.

"How is it, fella?"

Dard considered the question. He had been face down in the snow, there had been Peacemen creeping after him and—Dessie! Dessie! He struggled to sit up and the face of that figure above him moved.

"The little girl, she's all right. You're both all right now. You are the Nordis kids?"

Dard nodded. "Where is here?" he formed the inquiry slowly. The face crinkled into laughter.

"Well, at least that's a variation on the old 'where am I?' You're in the Cleft, kid. We saw you trying to make it across the river valley with that 'copter after you. You managed to delay them long enough for us to lay down the fog. Then we gathered you in. Also we're a 'copter and some assorted supplies to the good, so you've more than paid your admittance fee—even if you weren't Lars Nordis' kin."

"How did you discover who we are?" Dard asked.

Dark brown eyes twinkled. "We have our little ways of learning what is necessary for us to know. And it is a painless process—done while you're asleep."

"I talked in my sleep? But I don't!"

"Maybe not under ordinary circumstances. But let our medico get the digester on you and you do. You've had a pretty hard pull, kid, haven't you?"

Dard levered himself up on his elbows and the other slipped extra support behind him. Now he could see that he was stretched out on a narrow cot in a room which seemed to be part cave, for three of its walls were bare rock, the fourth a smooth gray substance cut by a door. There were no windows, and a soft light issued from two tubes in the rock ceiling. His visitor perched on a folding stool and there was no other furniture in the cell-like chamber.

But there were coverings over him such as he had not seen for years, and he was wearing a clean, one piece coverall over a bathed body. He smoothed the top blanket lovingly. "Where is here—and what is here?" he expanded his first question.

"This is the Cleft, the last stronghold, as far as we know, of the Free Men." The other got to his feet and stretched. He was a tall, lean-waisted man, with dark brown skin, against which his strong teeth and the china-white of his eyeballs made startling contrast. Curly black hair was cropped very close to his round skull, and he had only a slight trace of beard. "This is the gateway to Ad Astra—" he paused, eyeing Dard as if to assess the effect those last two words had on the boy.

"Ad Astra," Dard repeated. "Lars spoke of that once."

"Ad Astra means 'to the stars.' And this is the jumping off place."

Dard frowned. To the stars! Not interplanetary—but galactic flight! But that was impossible!"

"I thought that Mars and Venus—" he began doubtfully.

"Who said anything about Mars or Venus, kid? Sure, they're impossible. It would take most of the resources of a willing Terra to plant a colony on either of them—as who should know better than I? No, not interplanetary flight—stellar. Go out to take our pick of waiting worlds such as earth creepers never dreamed of, that's what we're going to do! Ad Astra!"

Galactic flight—his first wild guess had been right.

"A star ship here!" In spite of himself Dard knew a small thrill far inside his starved body. Men had landed on Mars and Venus back in the days before the Burn and the Purge, discovering conditions on both planets which made them almost impossible for human life without a vast expenditure which Terra was not willing to make. And, of course, Pax had forbidden all space flight as part of the program for stamping out scientific experimentation. But a star ship—to break the bounds of Sol's system and go out to find another sun, other planets. It sounded like a very wild dream but he could not doubt the sincerity of the man who had just voiced it.

"But what did Lars have to do with this?" he wondered aloud. Lars' field had been chemistry, not astronomy or the mechanics of space flight. Dard doubted whether his brother could have told one constellation from another.

"He had a very important part. We've just been waiting around for you to wake up to get the report of his findings."

"But I thought you got the full story out of me while I was unconscious."

"What you personally did in the past few days, yes. But you do carry a message from Lars, don't you?" For the first time some of the dark man's lightheadedness vanished.

Dard smoothed the blanket and then plucked at it with nervous fingers. "I don't know—I hope so—"

His companion ran his hands across his tight cap of hair.

"Suppose we have Tas in. He's only been waiting for you to come around." He crossed the room and pushed a wall button.

"By the way," he said over his shoulder, I'm forgetting introductions. "I'm Simba Kimber, Pilot-astrogator Simba Kimber," he repeated that title as if it meant a great deal to him. "And Tas is First Scientist Tas Kordov, biological division. Our organization here is made up of survivors from half a dozen Free Scientist teams as well as quite a few just plain outlaws who are not Pax-minded. Oh, come in, Tas."

The man who entered was short and almost as broad as he was tall. But sturdy muscle, not fat, thickened his shoulders and pillared his arms and legs. He wore the faded uniform of a Free Scientist with the flaming sword of First Rank still to be picked out on the breast. His eyes and broad cheek bones had Tartar contour and Dard believed that he was not a native of the land in which he now lived.

"Well, and now you are awake, eh?" he smiled at Dard. "We have been waiting for you to open those eyes—and that mouth of yours—young man. What word do you bring from Lars Nordis?"

Dard could hesitate about telling the full truth no longer. "I don't know whether I have anything or not. The night the roundup gang came Lars said he had finished his job—"

"Good!" Tas Kordov actually clapped his hands.

"But when we had to clear out he didn't try to bring any papers with him—"

Kordov's face was avid as if he would drag what he wanted out of Dard by force. "But he gave to you some message—surely he gave some message!"

"Only one thing. And I don't know how important that may be. I'll have to have something to write on to explain properly."

"Is that all?" Kordov pulled a notebook out of his breeches' pocket and flipped it open to a blank page, handing it to him with an inkless stylus. Dard, equipped with the tools, began the explanation which neither of these men might believe.

"It goes way back. Lars knew that I imagine words as designs. That is, if I hear a poem, it makes a pattern for me—" he paused trying to guess from their expressions whether they understood. Somehow it didn't sound very sensible now.

Kordov pulled his lower lip away from his yellowish teeth and allowed it to snap back. "Hmm—semantics are not my field. But I believe that I can follow what you mean. Demonstrate!"

Feeling foolish, Dard recited Dessie's jingle, marking out the pattern on the page.

"Eesee, Osee, Icksie, Ann; Fullson, Follson, Orson, Cann."

He underlined, accented, and overlined, as he had that evening on the farm and Dessie's kicking legs came into being again.

"Lars saw me do this. He was quite excited about it. And then he gave me another two lines, which for me do not make the same pattern. But he insisted that this pattern be fitted over his lines."

"And those other lines?" demanded Tas.

Dard repeated the words aloud as he jotted them down.

"Seven, nine, four and ten; twenty, sixty and seven again."

Carefully he fitted the lines through and about the numbers and handed the result to Kordov. To him it made no possible sense, and if it didn't to the First Scientist, then he would not have had Lars' precious secret at all. When Tas continued to frown down at the page, Dard lost the small flicker of confidence he had had.

"Ingenious," muttered Kimber looking over the First Scientist's shoulder. "Could be a code."

"Yes," Tas was going to the door. "I must study it. And look upon the other notes again. I must—"

With that he was gone. Dard sighed.

"It probably doesn't mean a thing," he said wearily. "But what should it be?"

"The formula for the 'cold sleep,'" Kimber told him.

"Cold sleep?"

"We go to sleep, hibernate, during that trip—or else the ship comes to its port manned by dust! Even with all the improvements they have given her—the new drive—everything—our baby isn't going to make the big jump in one man's lifetime, or in a number of lifetimes!" Kimber paced back and forth as he talked, turning square corners at either end of the room. "In fact, we didn't have a chance—we'd begun thinking of trying to make a stand on Mars—before one of our men accidentally discovered Lars Nordis was alive. Before the purge he'd published one paper concerning his research on the circulatory system of bats—studying the drop in their body temperature during their winter sleep. Don't ask me about it, I'm only a pilot-astrogator, not a Big Brain! But he was on the track of something Kordov believed might be done—the freezing of a human being so that he can remain alive but in sleep indefinitely. And since we contacted him, Lars has continued to feed us data bit by bit."

"But why?" Why, if Lars had been working with this group so closely, hadn't he wanted to join them? Why had they had to live in a farmhouse on a starvation level, under constant fear of a roundup?

"Why didn't he come here?" It was as if Kimber had picked that out of Dard's mind. "He said he wasn't sure he could make the trip—crippled as he was. He didn't want to try it until the last possible moment when it wouldn't matter if he were sighted trying—or traced here. He believed that he was under constant surveillance by some enemy and that the minute he, or any of you, made a move out of the ordinary, that enemy would bring in the Peacemen, perhaps before he had the answer to our problem. So you had to live on a very narrow edge of safety."

"Very narrow," Dard agreed. There was logic in what Kimber said. If Folley had been spying on them, and he must have or else he would not have appeared in the barn, he would have suspected something if any of them had not shown around the house as usual. Lars could never have made the journey they had just taken. Yes, he could see why his brother had waited until it was too late for him.

"But there's something else." Kimber sat down on the stool again, his elbows resting on his knees, his chin supported by his cupped hands.

"What do you know about the Temple of the Voice?"

Dard, still intent upon the problem of the cold sleep, was startled. Why did Kimber want to know about the innermost heart of the neighboring Pax establishment?

The "Voice" was that giant computer to which representatives of Pax fed data—to have it digested and to receive back the logical directives which enabled them to control the thousands under their rule. He knew what the "Voice" was, had had it hazily described to him by hearsay. But he doubted whether any Free Scientist or any associate of such proscribed outlaws had ever dared to approach the "Temple" which housed it.

"It's the center of the Pax—" he began, only to have the pilot interrupt him.

"I mean—give me your own description of the place."

Dard froze. He hoped that his panic at that moment

was not open enough to be marked. How did they know he had been to the Temple—through that mysterious digester which had picked over his memories while he was unconscious?

"You were there—two years ago," the other bored in relentlessly.

"Yes, I was there. Kathia was sick—there was just a chance of getting some medico to attend her if I could show a 'confidence card.' I made a Seventh Day visit but when I presented my attendance slip to the Circle they asked too many questions. I never got the card."

Kimber nodded. "It's okay, kid. I'm not accusing you of being a Pax plant. If you had been that the digester would have warned us. But I have a very good reason for wanting to know about the Temple of the Voice. Now tell me everything you can remember—every detail."

Dard began. And discovered that his memory was a vivid one. He could recall the number of steps leading into the inner court and quote closely enough every word that the "Laurel Crowned" speaker of that particular Seventh Day had spouted in his talk to the faithful. When he finished he saw that Kimber was regarding him with an expression of mingled amazement and admiration.

"Good Lord, kid, how do you remember everything— just from one short visit?"

Dard laughed shakily. "What's worse, I can't forget anything. I can tell you every detail of every day I've lived since the purge. Before then," his hand went to his head, "before then for some reason it's not so clear."

"Lots of us would rather not remember what happened since then. You get a pack of fanatics in control—the way

Renzi's forces have taken over this ant hill of a world—and tilings crack wide open. We've organized our collective sanity to save our own lives. And there's nothing we can do about the rest of mankind now—when we're only a handful of outlaws hiding out in the wilderness. There's a good big price on the head of everyone here in the Cleft. The whole company of Pax would like nothing better than to round us up. Only we're planning to get away. That's why we have to have the help of the Voice."

"The Voice?"

Kimber swept over the half interruption. "You know what the Voice is, don't you? A computer—mechanical brain they used to call them. Feed it data, it digests the figures and then spews out an answer to any problem which would require months or years for a human mind to solve. The astrogation course, the one which is going to take us to a sun enough like Sol to provide us with a proper world, is beyond the power of our setting up. We have the data and all our puny calculations—but the Voice has to melt them down for us!"

Dard stared at this madman. No one but a Peaceman who had reached the rarified status of "Laurel Wearer" dared approach the inner sanctuary which held the Voice. And just how Kimber proposed to get there and set the machine to work on outlawed formula, he could not possibly guess.

Kimber volunteered no more information and Dard did not ask. In fact he half forgot it during the next few hours as he was shown that strange honeycomb fortress, blasted out of the living rock, which served the last of the Free Scientists as a base. Kimber was his guide and escort along the narrow passages, giving him short glimpses of Hydrogardens, of strange laboratories, and once, from a vantage point, the star ship itself.

"Not too large, is she?" the pilot had commented, eyeing the long silvery dart with a full-sized frown. "But she's the best we could do. Her core is an experimental model designed for a try at the outer planets just before the purge. In the first days of the disturbance they got her here—or the most important parts of her—and we have been building ever since."

No, the ship wasn't large. Dard frankly could not see where all the toiling inhabitants of the Cleft were going to find berths on her, whether in the suspended animation of hibernation or not. But he didn't mention that aloud. Instead he said:

"I don't see how you've been able to hide out without detection this long."

Kimber grinned wickedly. "We have more ways than one. What do you think of this?" He drew his hand from his breeches' pocket. On his dark palm lay a flat piece of shining metal.

"That, my boy, is gold! There's been precious little of it about for the past hundred years or so—governments buried their supplies of it and sat tight on them brooding. But it hasn't lost its magic. We have found many metals in these mountains and, while this is useless for our purposes, it still carries a lot of weight out there." He pointed to the peak which guarded the entrance to the Cleft. "We have our trading messengers and we fill hands in proper places. Then this is all camouflaged. If you were to fly across this valley in a 'copter, you'd see only what our techneers want you to. Don't ask me how they do it—some warping of the light rays—too deep for me." He shrugged. "I'm only a pilot waiting for a job."

"But if you are able to keep hidden, why 'Ad Astra'?"

Kimber rubbed the curve of his jaw with his thumb. "For several reasons. Pax has all the power pretty well in its hands now, so the Peacemen are stretching to wipe out the last holes of resistance. We've been receiving a steady stream of warnings through our messengers and the outside men we've bought. The roundup gangs are consolidating— planning on a big raid. What we have here is the precarious safety of a rabbit crouching at the bottom of a burrow while the hound sniffs outside. We have no time for anything except the ship, preparing to take advantage of the thin promise for another future that it offers us. Lui Skort—he's a medico with a taste for history—gives Pax another fifty to a hundred years of life. And the Cleft can't last that long. So we'll try the chance in a million of going out—and it is a chance in a million. We may not find another earth-type planet, we may not ever survive the voyage. And, well, you can fill in a few of the other ifs, ands, and buts for yourself."

Dard still watched the star ship. Yes, a thousand chances of failure against one or two of success. But what an adventure! And to be free—out of this dark morass which stunted minds and fed man's fears to the point of madness—to be free among the stars!

He heard Kimber laugh softly. "You're caught by it, too, aren't you, kid? Well, keep your fingers crossed. If your brother's stuff works, if the Voice gives us the right course, if the new fuel Tang concocted will really take her through—why—we're off!"

Kimber seemed so confident that Dard dared now to ask that other question.

"She isn't very big. How are you going to stow away all the people?"

For the first time the space pilot did not meet his eyes. With the toe of his shabby boot Kimber kicked at an inoffensive table savagely.

"We can stow away more than you would believe just looking at her, if we are able to use the hibernation process."

"But not all," Dard persisted, driven by some inner need to know.

"But not all," Kimber agreed with manifest reluctance.

Dard blinked, but now there was a veil between his eyes and the sleek, silver swell of the star ship. He was not going to question farther. There was no need to, and he had no desire for a straight answer. Instead he changed the subject abruptly.

"When are you going to try to reach the Voice?"

"As soon as I hear from Tas—"

"And what do you wish to hear from Tas?" came a voice from behind Dard. "That he has succeeded in making sense of gibberish and 'kicking legs' and all the rest of the fantastic puzzle this young man has dumped into his head? Because if that is what you wait for, wait no longer, Sim! The sense has been made and thanks to Lars Nordis and our messengers," Kordov's big paw of a hand reached up to give Dard's shoulder a reassuring squeeze, "we can now take off into the heavens at our will. We wait only for your part of the operation."

"Good enough." Kimber started to turn when Dard caught his arm.

"Look here. You've never been to the Temple of the Voice."

"Of course not," Tas cut in. "Is he completely crazy? Does one thrust one's hand into raw atomic radiation?"

"But I have! Maybe I can't work your computations but I can guide you in and out And I know enough about the official forms to—"

Kimber opened his mouth, plainly to refuse, but again the First Scientist was too quick for him.

"Now that makes very good sense, Sim. If young Nordis has already been there—why, that is more than any of the rest of us have done. And in the disguise you have planned the risk is less."

The pilot frowned and Dard prepared for an outright refusal. But at last Kimber gave a half-nod. Tas pushed Dard after him.

"Go along with you. And mind you bring him back in one piece. We can do many things among us, but he remains our only space pilot, our only experienced astrogator."

Dard followed Kimber along rock passages, back through the maze of the Cleft dwelling to a flight of stairs crudely hacked from the stone. The stairs ended in a large room holding a 'copter which bore all the markings of a Pax machine.

"Recognize it? This is the one which you played tag with out in the valley. Now—get into this and hurry!"

From the 'copter he took a bundle of clothing which he pitched over to Dard. The boy put on the Peaceman's black and white, buckling around him as a finishing touch a belt supporting a hand stun gun. Although the clothes were large the fit was good enough to pass in the half-light of evening. And they had to visit the Voice at night to have any chance at all.

He took his place gingerly beside the pilot inside the 'copter. Overhead a cover had rolled back so that the sky was open to them. As Dard secretly gripped the edge of his seat Kimber took the controls. And Dard continued to hold on as the machine started the slow spiral up into the air.

—5—
NIGHT AND THE VOICE

DARD SURVEYED the country over which the 'copter flew. It required only a few minutes to cover the same rugged miles across which he and Dessie had fought their way. And he was sure that he saw traces of that trip left on the snow below.

The machine skimmed over the heights which concealed the cave. And then, for the first time in crowded hours, Dard remembered Sach. It was down this very slope that the messenger had led the chase.

"You've heard from Sach?" He was anxious to be reassured concerning that small, wary man.

But Kimber didn't reply at once. And when he did, Dard was aware of the reservations in his tone.

"No news yet. He hasn't reported at any of our contacts. Which reminds me—"

Under the pilot's control the 'copter swung to the right and headed away from the path Dard had followed into the hills. He was unreasonably glad that they were not going to wing over the charred ruins of the farmhouse.

Instead, within a short space, they were circling another farm, one in much better condition than the farm which had sheltered the Nordis family. In fact, the buildings gave such an air of Pax-blessed landsman prosperity that Dard wondered at Kimber's visiting the place. Only a man with the brightest of prospects under the new rule would dare to keep his buildings in such good repair. And the volume of smoke curling fatly from the chimney spoke of unlimited warmth and food, better conditions than anyone but a staunch supporter of the Company of Pax could attain.

Yet Kimber set the 'copter down without hesitation on a stretch of packed snow not too far from the house. Once down however the pilot made no move to leave the machine.

The house door opened and a man wearing the good farm homespun of an "approved" landsman—another Folley by all outward signs—crossed the yard. For one wild moment Dard was inclined to doubt the man beside him, being still more uneasy when the round plump face of the landsman was thrust close to the window of the 'copter.

Pale blue eyes in a weather-beaten face flicked over them both, and Dard did not miss the fact that they widened a fraction as they passed from Kimber's impassive face to his flashy uniform. The landsman turned and spat at a hound that approached, showing white teeth and growling.

"Time?" he asked.

"Time," Kimber returned. "Get moving on tonight if you can, Harmon."

"Sure we've been packin' some stuff already, Th' boy's got th' road cleared—"

Then those blue eyes slid back to Dard. "Who's th' youngster?"

"Nordis' brother. He got in with the Nordis girl. Lars is dead—raid."

"Yeah. Heard a rumor they all were—that th' roundup got 'em. Glad to know that ain't th' truth. Well—be seein' you—"

With a wave of the hand he headed back to the house. And Kimber took them aloft.

"I didn't think—" Dard began. Kimber chuckled.

"You didn't think a man such as Harmon would be one of us? We have some mighty odd contacts here and there. We have men who drove ground trucks and men who were first rank scientists—before the purge. There's Santee—he was a non-com of the old army—he can read and write his name—and he's an expert with weapons—to us he's as important a part of the Cleft as Tas Kordov, who is one of the world's greatest biologists. We ask only one thing of a man—that he believes in true freedom. And Harmon is going to be more important in the future. We may know how to grow hydro-style—you had a meal or two with us and know that—but an honest dirt farmer will be able to teach us all better tricks. Added to that, Harmon's been our biggest ace in the hole all along. He and his wife, their son, and their twin girls—they've been playing a mighty hard role for more than five years— doing it splendidly, too. But I can well believe that he welcomed my news that it is over. Double lives are tough going. Now, back to work."

The 'copter wheeled and flew due west into a sky now painted with sunset colors. It was warm inside the cabin, and the clothing about his thin body was the finest he had worn in years. Dard relaxed against the padded cushion, but far inside him was a warming spark of excitement, an excitement no longer completely darkened by fear—Kimber's confidence in himself, in the eventual success of their mission was comforting.

Below ran a ribbon of road, and by the churned snow, it was a well-traveled one. Dard tried to identify landmarks. But, never having seen the country from above, he could only guess that they were now being guided to town by that same artery which had tied Folley's holding and the tumbledown Nordis place to the overgrown village which was the nearest approach to a pre-Burn city.

Another farm road, rutted and used, cut into the main road and its curve was familiar. It was Folley's! And it had seen considerable travel since the storm. He thought briefly of Lotta—wondered if she had gone back to the message tree with some food for Dessie as she had promised. Dessie!

Dessie!

Hoping he could keep from revealing to Kimber his own secret problem, the one which had gnawed at him ever since he had seen the star ship, he asked a question:

"I didn't see any children in the Cleft."

Kimber was intent upon flying; when he answered it was with a faint touch of absent-mindedness.

"There're only two. Carlee Skort's daughter is three and the Winson boy—he's almost four. The Harmon twins are—ten, I think—but they don't live in the Cleft."

"Dessie is six—almost seven."

Kimber grinned. "Bright little trick, too, isn't she? Took to Carlee right away—after we had persuaded her you were going to recover. Last I heard she'd taken command in the nursery quarters, Carlee was surprised at how sensible she was."

"Dessie's a pretty big person," Dard said slowly. "She's old for her years. And she has a gift, too. She makes friends with animals—not just tame ones—but the wild things. I've seen them come right up to her. She insists that they talk."

Had he said too much? Had he labeled Dessie as one so far outside the pattern that she would not "fit" into a ship's company where a farmer was considered important? But surely, a child's future was worth more than an adult's! Dessie must be considered—she must be!

"Carlee thinks she is quite a person, too." That was certainly noncommittal enough. But, although he did not know Carlee, her approbation was comforting to Dard. A woman, a woman with a little girl of her own, would see that another little girl would get a fair break. As for himself—resolutely he refused to think ahead for himself. Instead he began to watch the twilight-cloaked road and think of the problem immediately before them.

"The 'copter park is at the back of the Temple. And you can't fly over the building—nothing crosses the sacred roof."

"Then we circle. No use taking chances. Park well guarded?"

"I don't know. Only Peacemen get inside. But I'd think that in the dark, and with this machine—"

"We could brazen it out? Let us hope they don't ask for any recognition signals. I'm going to try to land as close to the edge as I can and in the darkest part—unless they have floodlights—"

"Town lights!" Dard interrupted, intent on the sparks of yellow. "The Temple is on that rise to the south. See!"

It was easy enough to see. The lights of the town houses were small and sickly yellow. But above and beyond them were concentrated bars of vivid blue and startling white, somehow garish and out of place against the purple-blue of the sky. Kimber circled.

The Temple occupied about a third of the rise which had been leveled off to form a wide platform. Behind the building itself was a floodlit space in which they could see a row of 'copters.

"Ten down there," Kimber counted, the lighting of the instrument panel showing the planes and hollows of his face. "You'd think they would have more. This is a center for their control and they don't do much raiding by night. Or at least they haven't in the past."

"They may now. They struck our place at night."

"Anyway, the fewer the better. Look, that's a nice long shadow—one of their floods must have burnt out. I'm going to see if I can bring us down in it!"

They lost speed, it was something like coasting, much like floating, Dard decided. Then the lights arose about them and a second later the undercarriage made contact. They didn't bounce. Kimber shook hands with himself vigorously, in congratulation.

"Now listen, kid," the pilot's voice was a faint murmur. "That's a stun gun you have in your belt. Ever use one?"

"No."

"It doesn't require training to point it and push the button. But you're not to do that unless I give the word, understand? You have only two charges and I have the same in mine—we can't afford to waste them. Nothing—absolutely nothing must happen to prevent our interview with the Voice!" There was a passionate determination in that. It was an order, delivered not only to Dard, but to Destiny or Fortune herself. "Afterward we may have to fight our way out—though I hope not. Then the stun guns will be our hope. But we've got to use bluff to get us in!"

The Peacemen hoarded the remains of pre-purge invention, Dard noted as he matched his steps to Kimber's across the park at an unhurried pace, but their maintenance of such appliances was not promising. Several of the floodlights were out and there were cracks in the concrete under his boots. There couldn't be too many techneers left in the slave-labor camps of the Temple gangs. Some day no 'copter would rise from this park, no light would burn. Had the leaders of Pax thought of that, or didn't they care? The old cities built by the techneers were rubble fit only for bats and birds. Now there were only grubby villages slipping back and back, with the wilderness edging down across the field to nibble at man's building.

So far they had not met anyone, but now they approached the western gate of the Temple and there was a guard. Dard straightened his shoulders, lifted his chin, summoned that arrogance of bearing which cloaked a Peaceman as rightly as the gaudy uniform. Kimber had the right presence. He strode along with a damn-devil air suitable to a Laurel Wearer. Dard did his best to copy that But the boy couldn't quite suppress a half-sigh of relief when the guard did not attempt to stop them and they crossed the threshold unchallenged.

Of course, they were still far from the sanctuary of the Voice. And Dard's knowledge of the place would not take them farther than the second court.

Kimber stopped and touched his companion's sleeve. Together they slipped out of the direct path of the light up to the shadowed obscurity behind one of the massive pillars.

Before them lay the inner court where the commoners might gather—in fact were expected to gather—to hear words of wisdom as mouthed from the August Sayings of Renzi by one of the Laurel Wearers. It was now deserted. After dark none of those not "Wedded to the Inner Peace" dared enter the Temple. Which would make the venture more precarious since they would be alone among the Peacemen and might betray themselves by ignorance of custom. Dard's hand twitched, but he kept it off the stun gun.

"The Voice?"

Dard pointed to the archway at the other end of the inner court. What they sought lay beyond that, but where—he wasn't sure. Kimber went on, flitting from pillar to pillar, and Dard followed on a woodman's sure, silent feet. Twice they stiffened into inanimateness as others tramped into the open. Peacemen, two Laurel Wearers and, just as they had almost reached the archway, a third party—two shuffling labor slaves carrying a box under the malicious eye of a single lounging guard.

Kimber leaned back behind a pillar and drew Dard in beside him.

"Lots of traffic." The whispered comment was tinged with laughter and Dard saw that the pilot was smiling, an eager fire in his eyes.

They waited until slaves and guard were gone and then stepped boldly into the open and through the archway. They were now in a wide corridor, not too well lighted, broken at regular intervals with open doorways through which came solid blocks of illumination to trap the passerby. But Kimber went on with the assurance of one who had a perfect right to be where he was. He did not attempt to steal a look at any of the rooms—it was as if he had seen their contents a thousand times.

Dard marveled at his complete confidence. The Voice— where was it housed in this maze? He never suspected all this to lie beyond the inner court They had neared the end of the corridor before Kimber slackened pace and began glancing from right to left With infinite caution he tried the latch of a closed door. It gave, swinging silently open to disclose a flight of stairs leading down. Kimber's grin was wide.

"Down here! It has to be down—" his lips shaped the words.

Together they crept close to the edge of the stairway and peered over into a cavern where the best lighting arrangements of the Temple made little headway against a general gloom. The hollow went deep, it was the heart of the eminence upon which the Temple stood. And on the floor far below was the Voice—a bank of metal, faceless, tongueless, but potent.

Two guards stood at the bottom of the stairs, but their attitudes suggested that they had no fear of being called upon to carry out any duties. And on a curved bench before a board of dials and levers lounged a third man wearing the crimson and gold tunic of a second circle Laurel Wearer.

"The night shift," mouthed Kimber at Dard's ear, and then he sat down on the platform and proceeded to remove his boots. After a moment of hesitation Dard followed the pilot's example.

Kimber, boots swinging in one hand, started noiselessly down the staircase, hugging the wall. But he did not draw the gun at his belt· and Dard obediently kept his own weapon sheathed.

It was not entirely quiet in the chamber. A drowsy hum from the internals of the Voice was echoed and magnified by the height and width of the place.

Kimber took a long time—or what seemed to Dard a very long time—to descend. When they were still on the last flight of steps above the guard the pilot reached out a long arm and pulled Dard tight against him, his lips to the boy's ear.

"I'll risk using my gun on that fellow on the bench. Then we jump the other two with these—"

He gestured with the boots. Four steps—five—side by side they crept down. Kimber drew his stun gun and fired. The, noiseless charge of the ray hit its mark. The man on the bench twisted, turning a horribly contorted face to them before he fell to the floor.

In that same instant Kimber hurled himself out and down. There was one startled shout as Dard went out into space too. Then the boy struck another body and they went to the floor together in a kicking clawing fury. Dodging a blow Dard brought his boots down club fashion in the other's face. He struck heavily three times before hands clutched his shoulders and wrenched him off the now limp man. Kimber, a raw and bleeding scrape over one eye, shook him out of the battle madness.

Dard's eyes focused on the pilot as the terrible anger drained out of him. They tied the limp bodies with the men's own belts and lacings before Kimber took his place on the bench before the Voice.

He pulled a much-creased sheaf of papers from the breast of his blouse and spread them out on the sloping board beneath the first rank of push buttons. Dard fidgeted, thinking the pilot was taking entirely too long over that business.

But the boy had sense enough to keep quiet as Kimber rubbed his hands slowly together as if to clear them of moisture before raising his eyes to study the row upon row of buttons, each marked with a different symbol. Slowly, with a finicky touch and care, the pilot pressed one, another, a third. There was a change in the hum of the Voice, a faster rhythm, the great machine was coming to life.

Kimber picked up speed, stopping only now and again to consult his scrawled notes. His fingers were racing now. The hum deepened to a throb which, Dard feared, must certainly be noticeable in the Temple overhead.

The boy withdrew to the stairway, his attention as much on the door at the top as on Kimber. He drew his gun. As Kimber had said, the mechanism of the arm was childishly simple—one pointed it, pushed the button on

the grip—easy. And he had two charges to use. Caressing
the metal he looked back at the Voice.

Under the light Kimber's face displayed damp drops,
and now and again he rubbed his hand across his eyes. He
was waiting—his part of the job finished—waiting for the
Voice to assimilate the data fed it and move in its ponderous
way to solve the problem. But every minute they were
forced to linger added to the danger of their position.

One of the captives rolled over on his side, and, over
the gag they had forced into his jaws, his eyes blared red
hate at Dard. The hum of the Voice faded to a lulling
murmur. There was no other sound in the cavern. Dard
crossed to touch Kimber's shoulder.

"How long?" he began.

Kimber shrugged without taking his eyes from the
screen above the keyboard. That square of light remained
obstinately empty. Dard could not stand still. He had no
timekeeper, and he believed that they had been there too
long—it might be close to morning. What if another shift
of watcher and guards was due to come on presently?

A sharp demanding chime interrupted his thoughts.
The screen was no longer blank. Across it slowly crawled
formula, figures, equations. And Kimber scrambled to
write them down in frantic haste, checking and rechecking
each he scribbled. As the last set of figures faded from the
screen the pilot hesitated and then pushed a single button
far to the right on the board. A moment of waiting and five
figures flashed into being on the screen.

Kimber read them with a sigh. He thrust the sheets of
calculations back into safety, before, with a grin playing
about his generous mouth, he leaned forward and pushed

as many buttons as he could reach at random. Without pausing for the reply, though the Voice had gone into labor again, he joined Dard.

"That will give them something to puzzle out if they try to discover what we were after," he explained. "No reading that back. Not that I believe any of these poor brains would have the imagination to guess what brought us here. Now—speed's the thing! Up with you, kid."

Kimber took the steps at a gait Dard had a hard time matching. It was not until they stood directly before the corridor door that the pilot stopped to listen.

"Let us hope that they've all gone to bed and are good sound sleepers," he whispered. "We've, had a lot of luck tonight and this is no time for it to run out"

The corridor was as empty as it had been on their first trip. Some of the blocks of light from the rooms were gone. They had only three such danger spots to cross now. Two they negotiated without trouble, but as they stepped into the third, it was broken by a moving shadow, a man was coming out of the room. He wore a scarlet and gold tunic, with more gold on it than Dard had ever seen before—plainly one of the hierarchy. And he stared straight at them with annoyance and the faint stirrings of suspicion.

"Pax!" the word was hardly the conventional and courteous greeting, it carried too much authority. "What do you here, brothers? These are the night watches—"

Kimber drew back into the shadows and the man unconsciously followed him, coming out into the corridor.

"What—" he began again when the pilot moved. Both his dark hands closed about the other's throat, cutting off voice and breath.

Dard caught the hands clawing at Kimber's hold and together they dragged the struggling captive through the archway into the dimly lighted inner court.

"Either you come quietly," Kimber fussed, "or you don't come at all Make your choice quick."

The struggles ceased as Kimber pulled him on.

"Why try to take him?" Dard wanted to know.

Kimber's grin was no longer pleasant, it was closer to a wolfish snarl. "Insurance," he returned concisely. "We aren't out of this place yet. Now move!" He gave the captive a vicious shove, keeping one hand clamped on the nape of the other's neck, as the three moved on toward the outer door and freedom.

—6—
FIVE DAYS—FORTY-FIVE MINUTES

A GRILLE of bars and metal wire was down across the entrance of the outer court. When they reached it their captive snickered. He had snapped out of his first panic-surprise, and though he was quite helpless in Kimber's hands, the voice with which he asked a question now was entirely self-possessed.

"How do you propose to get past this?"

The pilot met that demand almost jauntily. "I suppose that this is equipped with a time lock?"

The Laurel Wearer did not reply to that, he had a second demand: "Who are you?"

"What if I should say—a rebel?"

But that was the wrong answer. The man's lips thinned to a single cruel line.

"So—" his half-whisper was soft but it promised deadly reprisals, "Lossler dares this, does he? Lossler!"

But Kimber had no time for that. He shoved the captive into Dard's ready hands before he applied a black disc to the grille's lock. There was a crackle, a shower of spitting sparks. Then Kimber struck the barrier with his shoulder and it yielded. Taking the prisoner with them, they went out into the freedom of the night.

The town was in darkness, a dark broken only by a scattering of street lights. The full moon picked out light and shadow in vivid black and white across the snow on roofs and yards.

"March!" Kimber pushed the captive before him in the direction of the 'copter park. Dard trotted behind, nervously alert, not yet daring to believe that they had been successful.

Before they came onto the crumbling concrete of the take-off Kimber had instructions for the Laurel Wearer.

"We're going to take a 'copter," he explained—bored—as if he were discussing a dull report, "and, once we do that, we shall have no more use for you, understand? It remains entirely up to you in what condition you shall be left behind—"

"And you can tell Lossler from me," the words came slowly, ground out one by one between teeth set close together, "that he is not going to get away with this!"

"Only we are getting away with it, aren't we? Now step right ahead—we are all friends—in case there is a guard on duty. You shall see us off and we will trouble you no more."

"But why?" protested the other. "What did you want here?"

"What did we want? That is a minor problem and you

shall have all the rest of the night to solve it—if you can. Now, where's the guard?"

When the man made no answer Kimber's hand moved and brought a gasp of pain from the captive.

"Where—is—the—guard?" repeated the pilot, his patience iced by frigid promise of worse things to come.

"Three guards—gate and patrol—" came the gritted return.

"Excellent. Try to answer more promptly next time. You shall escort us through the gate. We are being sent by you on a special mission."

Just as Dard saw the black and white coat at the entance the command snapped out:

"Halt!"

Kimber obediently brought their procession of three to a stop.

"Speak your piece," he whispered.

"Pax, brother."

Dard was alert—waiting for some warning to that sentry. But Kimber must have taken precautions, for the voice of the Laurel Wearer sounded natural.

"Laurel Wearer Dawson on special business on the Company—"

The guard saluted. "Pass, Noble Dawson!"

Dard closed in on the heels of Kimber and Dawson with all the military bearing he could muster. He held the pose until they were passing along the row of idle 'copters. Then Kimber spoke to his fellow conspirator.

"There's the little matter of fuel. Climb into that baby and check the reading on the top dial in the row directly before the control stick. If it registers between forty and sixty—sing out. If it doesn't, we'll have to try the next"

Dard crawled into the seat and found the light button. Between—between forty and sixty! White figures danced crazily until he forced his nerves under control "Fifty-three," he called out softly.

What Kimber intended to do with Dawson Dard never learned. For, at the moment, the Laurel Wearer gave a sudden heave, throwing himself down and trying to drag the pilot with him. At the same time he shouted, and that cry must have carried not only across the field, but into the Temple as well.

Dard hurled himself at the door of the 'copter. But before he could get out he saw an arm rise and fall in a deadly blow. A second scream for help was cut off in the middle and the pilot jumped for the machine. Dard found himself face down while the pilot scrambled over him to the controls. The 'copter lurched, the open door banging until Kimber was able to pull it to. They were air borne, and not a moment too soon as the whip crack of a shot testified.

The boy pulled up on the seat, trying to see behind them. Was that another 'copter rising? Or would they have more of a start before pursuit would be on their tail?

"Couldn't expect our luck to last forever," Kimber murmured. "How about it, kid? Do they have anything up yet? Evasive action right now would be tough."

There was an ominous wink of red light now in the sky.

"Someone's coming up—wing lights showing."

"Wing lights, eh? Well, well, well, aren't we both the forgetful boys though." Kimber's hand went out to snap down a small lever.

From the corner of his eye Dard saw their own tell-tale wing-tip gleams disappear. But the pursuer made no move to shut his off—or else he did not care if he betrayed his position.

"I have now only one question," the pilot continued, half to himself. "Who is Lossler and why did our dear friend back there expect trouble from him? A split within the ranks of Pax—it smells like that. Too bad we didn't know about this Lossler complication sooner."

"Would such a split make any difference in your plans?"

"No, but we could have had a lot more fun these past few months. And playing one group against the other might have paid off. Like tonight—this Lossler may take the blame for us, and no one will come nosing around the Cleft for the crucial time we have left here. What the—!"

Kimber's body strained forward, he was suddenly intent upon the dials before him. Then he reached out to rap smartly on the very indicator he had told Dard to check before they had taken the 'copter. The needle behind the cracked glass remained as stationary as if it were painted across the numbers it half obscured. A line drew Kimber's brows together. Again he struck the glass, trying to jar loose the needle. Then he settled back in the seat.

"Dear me," he might have been remarking on the brightness of the night, "now we do have a problem. How much fuel? Is the tank full, part full, or deuced near empty? I thought this was all a little too smooth. Now we may have to—"

The smooth purr of the motor caught in a cough, and

then picked up beat again. But Kimber shrugged resignedly.

"It is now not a question of 'may have to,' that cough was a promise that we are going to walk. How about our friend behind?"

"Coming strong," Dard was forced to admit.

"Which makes the situation very jolly indeed. We could do with less of this blasted moonlight! A few clouds hanging about would help."

The engine chose that moment to cough again and this time the pickup was delayed longer than before. "Three or four drops more, maybe. Better set her down before we have to pancake. Now where're a lot of nice dark shadows? Ha—trees! And there's only one 'copter behind us—sure?"

"Sure." Dard verified that point before he answered.

"So, we have to do it the hard way. Here we go, m'lad."

The 'copter came down a field away from the road they had followed, landing heavily in a sizable drift. On the other side of a low wall was a clump of trees. And— Dard was pretty sure—he had sighted the outline of a house beyond.

They scrambled out and jumped the wall, struggling out of the soft snow into the grove. From behind came the sound of the other 'copter. Those in it must have sighted the machine on the ground at once, they were heading unerringly toward it.

"There's a house that way," Dard panted as Kimber plowed ahead with the determination of breaking beyond the thin screen of trees.

"Any chance of finding some transportation there?"

"None of the landsmen have surface cars any more. Folley had a double A rating, and Lotta said his application for one was turned down twice. Horses—maybe . . ."

Kimber expelled a snort. "Horses, yet!" he addressed the night. "And me not knowing which end of the animal is which!"

"We'd get away faster mounted," Dard sputtered as he slipped on a piece of iced crust and fell into the spiky embrace of a bush. "They'll probably put hounds on us—we're so near to town.

Kimber's pace slowed. "I'd forgotten those pleasures of civilization," he observed. "Do they use dogs a lot in tracking?"

"Depends on how important the tracked are."

"And we're probably number one on their list of public enemies now. Yes, nothing like being worthy of dogs—and no meat to throw behind us! All right, let's descend upon this house and see how many horses or reasonable facsimile or same we can find."

But when they reached the end of the grove they stopped. Lights showed in three house windows and they reached far enough across the snow-crusted road to reveal a 'copter there. Kimber laughed without any amusement at all.

"That bird by the machine is waving a rifle."

"Wait!" Dard caught at the pilot as Kimber started out of the brush.

Yes, he had been right—there was another 'copter coming! He felt Kimber tense in his hold.

"If they have any brains at all," the pilot whispered, "they'll box us up! We've got to get out."

But Dard held him fast.

"You're trying for the road," the boy objected.

"Of course! We daren't get lost now—and that is our only guide back. Or do you know this country well enough to go skating off into the midst of nowhere?"

Dard kept his hold on the other. "I know something— that this is the only road leading to the mountains, yes. But we can't take it unless . . ."

He took his hands from Kimber and pulled up the edge of the Jacket he wore—the black jacket trimmed in white. With numb fingers he pulled buttons roughly out of holes and stripped off the too large garment. He had been right! The black fabric was completely lined with the same white which made the deep cuffs and the throat-fretting stand-up collar. And the breeches were white, too. With frantic haste he thrust sleeves wrongside out. Kimber watched him until he caught on and a minute later the pilot was reverting his own coat White against white—if they kept in the ditches—if dogs were not brought—they still had a thin chance of escaping notice.

They half fell, half plunged into the ditch beside the road just as a second 'copter came to earth. Dard counted at least six men fanning out in a circle from it, beginning a stealthy prowl into the grove they had left.

Neither of the fugitives waited longer, but, half crouched, scurried along between the dry brush which partly filled the ditch and the ragged hedges walling the fields. The skin between Dard's shoulder blades crawled as he expected momentarily to feel the deadly impact of a bullet. Tonight death was a closer companion than the pilot whose boots kicked snow into his sweating face.

Some time later they reached the curve of a farm lane and dared to venture out in the open to skim across it The cold pinched at them now. As warm as the uniform had seemed when they rode in the heated 'copter cabin, it was little defense against the chill cut of the wind which powdered them with scooped-up puffs of snow. Dard watched the moon anxiously. No clouds to dim that. But clouds meant storm—and they dared not be caught in the open by a storm.

Kimber settled down to a lope which Dard found easy to match. How far they now were from the Cleft he had no way of knowing. And how long was it going to take them to get back? Did Kimber know the trail after they had to turn off the road? He himself might be able to find the path which led from the farm. But where was the farm?

"How far was your farm from that town?"

"About ten miles. But with all this snow—" Dard's breath made a white cloud about his head.

"Yes—the snow. And maybe more of it later. Look here, kid, this is the important part. We haven't too much time—"

"They may wait until morning to trail us. And if they bring dogs—"

"I don't mean that!" It appeared to Dard that Kimber waved away the idea of pursuit as if that did not matter. "This is what counts. The course the Voice set for us—I asked before we left how long it was good for. The answer was five days and two hours. Now I figure we have about five days and forty-five minutes. We have a blast off within that time or try a second visit to the Voice, Frankly, I think that would be hopeless."

"Five days and forty-five minutes," Dard echoed. "But, even if we have luck all the way it might take two—three days to reach the Cleft. And we haven't supplies—"

"Let us hope Kordov has kept things moving there," was Kimber's only comment. "And waiting here now isn't adding to our time. Come on."

Twice through the hours which followed they took to cover as 'copters went over. The machines ranged with an angry intentness in a circle and it hardly seemed possible that the fugitives could escape notice. But maybe it was their white clothing which kept them invisible.

The sun was up when Dard caught at the end of a time-eaten post projecting from the snow, swinging around to face the track it marked.

"Our farm lane," he bit off the words with economy, as he rocked on his feet To have made it this far—so soon. The 'copter must have taken them a good distance from town before it failed.

"Sure it is your place?"

Dard nodded, wasting no breath.

"Hmm." Kimber studied the unbroken white. "Prints on that are going to show up as well as ink. But no help for it."

"I wonder. The place was burnt—no supplies to be found there."

"Got a better suggestion?" Kimber's face was drawn and gaunt now."

"Folley's."

"But I thought—"

"Folley's dead. He ran the place with three work slaves. His son was tapped as a Peaceman recruit a month ago. Suppose we were to smarten up and fast tramp in. Say that our 'copter broke down in the hills and we walked in to get help—"

Kimber's eyes snapped alive. "And that does happen to these lame brains often enough. How many might be at the farm?"

"Folley's second wife, his daughter, the work slaves, I don't think he got an overseer after his son left"

"And they'd be only too willing to help Peacemen in distress! But they'll know you—"

"I've never seen Folley's wife—we didn't visit And Lotta—well, she let me go before. But it's a better chance than trying to get into the mountains from here."

They tramped on, in the open now. And, at the end of Folley's lane, they reversed their jackets, shaking off what they could of the snow. They were still disheveled but a 'copter failure should account for that.

"After all," Kimber pointed out as they climbed the slight rise to the ugly farmhouse, "Peacemen don't explain to landsmen. If we ask questions and don't volunteer much we'll only be acting in character. It all depends on whether they've heard about the chase—"

Smoke arose from the chimney and Dard did not miss the betraying twitch at one of the curtains in a window facing the lane. The arrival was known. Lotta—everything depended now upon Lotta. He shot a glance at Kimber. All the good humor and amusement were wiped from that dark face. This was a tough—very tough muscle-boy, a typical Peaceman who would have no nonsense from a landsman.

The door on the porch which ran the side length of the

house opened before they had taken two steps along the cleaned boards. A woman waited for them, her hands tugging smooth a food-spattered apron, an uneasy half-smirk spreading her lips to display a missing front tooth.

"Pax, noble sirs—Pax." Her voice was as fat and oily as her body and sounded more assured than her expression.

Kimber sketched a version of the official salute and rapped out an answering "Pax—" in an authority-heavy tone. "This is—?"

Grotesquely she bobbed in an attempt at a curtsey. "The farm of Hew Folley, noble sir."

"And where is this Folley?" Kimber asked as if he expected the missing landsman to spring up before him.

"He is dead, sir. Murdered by outlaws. I thought that was why—But come in, noble sirs, come in—" She waddled back a step leaving the entrance to the kitchen open.

The rich smell of food caught at Dard's throat, until, for a second, he was almost nauseated. There were thick dishes on the stained table, and congealed grease, a fragment of bread, a half cup of herb tea, marked the remains of a late breakfast.

Without answering the woman's half-question Kimber seated himself on the nearest chair and with an outstretched arm swept the used dishes from before him. Dard dropped down opposite to the pilot, thankful for the support the hard wooden seat gave his trembling body.

"You have food, woman?" Kimber demanded. "Get it. We have been walking over this forsaken country for hours. Is there a messenger here we can send into town? Our 'copter is down and we must have the repair crew."

She was busy at the stove, breaking eggs, real eggs into a greasy skillet.

"Food, yes, noble sirs. But a messenger—since my man is dead I have only the slaves, and they are under lock and key. There is no one to send."

"You have no son?" Kimber helped himself to a piece of bread.

Her nervous smirk stretched to a smile. "Yes, noble sir, I have a son. But only this month he was chosen by the House of the Olive Branch. He is now in training for your own service, noble sir."

If she expected this information to unbend her visitors and soften their manners she was disappointed for Kimber merely raised his eyebrows before he continued:

"We can't walk to town ourselves, woman. Have you no one at all you can send?"

"There is Lotta." She went to the door and called the girl's name harshly. "With Hew gone she must see to the cows. But it is a long walk to town, noble sir."

"Then ride—or how do you get there when you go, woman?" Kimber slid three eggs onto his plate and pushed the still laden platter over to Dard, who, a little dazed by the sight of such a wealth of food, made haste to help himself before it vanished.

"There is the colt. She might ride," the woman agreed reluctantly.

"Then let her get to it. I don't intend to sit out the whole of this day waiting for help. The sooner she goes, the better!"

"You want me?"

Dard knew that voice. For a long moment he dared

not look up. But that inner compulsion which made him always face danger squarely raised his eyes to meet those of the girl standing in the half-open door. His fingers curled around the handle of the fork and bent it a trifle. But Lotta's stolid expression did not change and he could only hope that his own face was as blank.

"You want me?" she repeated.

The woman nodded at the two Peacemen. "These gentlemen—their 'copter broke down. They want you should take a message to town for them. Git the colt out and ride."

"All right." The girl tramped out and slammed the door behind her.

—≈7≈—
BATTLE AT THE BARRIER

DARD CHEWED mechanically on food which now had no savor. As Kimber forked a thick slice of ham he spoke to the pilot:

"Shall I give the girl instructions, sir?"

Kimber swallowed. "Very well. Be sure she gets it straight. I don't propose to sit around here waiting for a couple of days. Let her tell the repair master they may find us at the 'copter. We'll go back there after we thaw out But get her started right away—the sooner she leaves the sooner they will come for us."

Dard went out into the farmyard. Lotta was saddling a horse. As his boots squeaked on the snow she looked up.

"Where's Dessie? Wotta you done with her?"

"She's safe."

Lotta studied his face before she nodded. "That's the truth, ain't it? You really want I should go to town? Why? You ain't no Peaceman—"

"No. And the more you can delay your trip in, the

better. But Lotta—" he had to give her some protection. If later she were suspected of aiding their escape her fate would not be pleasant. "When you get in and report at the Temple, tell them you are suspicious of us. We'll be gone from here by then."

With her chin she pointed to the house. "Don't you trust her none. She ain't my ma—Folley wasn't really my pa, neither. My pa was kin and Folley, he wanted the land pa left so they took me in. Don't you trust her none at all—she's worse'n Folley was. I'll ride slow goin' in, and I'll do like you say when I git there. Lissen here, Dard, you sure Dessie's gonna be all right?"

"She is if we can get back to her. Shell have a chance to live the way she ought to—"

The small eyes in the girl's pasty face were shrewd, "And that's a promise! You git outta here and take her too. I'll make up a good story for 'em. I ain't," she suddenly smiled at him, "I ain't near as dumb as I look, Dard Nordis, even if I ain't one of your kind!"

She scrambled awkwardly into the saddle and slapped the ends of the reins so that the horse broke into a trot.

Dard went back to the house and sat down at the table with a better appetite. Kimber broke off man-sized bites of apple tart, and between them he addressed his junior.

"Now that it's day, I've been thinking that we may be able to check the bus over ourselves. You, woman," he said to their unwilling hostess, "can you direct them on to join us if we don't return?"

Dard pressured Kimber's foot with the toe of his boot in warning. And received a return midge of acknowledgement.

"Which way you goin'?" she asked. Dard thought that

some of her deference was gone. Was she beginning to suspect that she was not really entertaining two of the new lords of the land?

"North. We'll leave a trail, have to back track on your own. Suppose you put us up some grub so we'll have something at noon. And just send the repair crew along."

"Yes, noble sirs."

But that acknowledgement was almost grudging and she was spending a long time putting aside some pieces of cold meat and bread. Or did his jumpy nerves make him imagine that, wondered Dard.

A half hour later they left the house. They kept to the lane and then to the road leading north until a grove cut off their path from any watcher. It was then that Kimber faced west.

"Where now?"

"There's a trail farther on that doubles back up into the hills," Dard informed him. "It cuts across the old woods road near that tree where I met Sach."

"Good, I leave the guide duty up to you. But let's move! That girl may make a quick trip in—"

"She'll delay all she can. She knows—"

Kimber's lips shaped a soundless whistle. "That will help—if she is working for us."

"I told her that it meant saving Dessie. Dessie's the only one she cares about."

The warmth, good food, and short rest they had had at Folley's gave them heat and strength for the trail ahead. After two false tries Dard found the woods road. Along it there was an earlier trail breaking the snow, made by Lotta, he guessed.

Kimber set an easy pace, knowing the grueling miles which still lay ahead. They took a lengthy rest at the rude lean-to by the message tree. The woods were unnaturally still and the sun reflected from patches of snow, making them squint against the glare.

From the message tree on, it was a matter of following the traces he himself had helped to make. Luckily, Dard congratulated himself, there had been no more snow and the broken path was easy to follow. But both were tired and slowed against their will as they slogged their way toward the heights which held the cave. There they could rest, Dard promised his aching body. They paused to eat, to breathe, and then on and on and on. Dard lost all track of time, it was a business of following in a robot fashion those other marks in the snow.

They had reached the lower slopes of the rise which would take them to the cave when he leaned against a tree. Kimber's face, stark and drawn, all the easy good humor pounded out of it by fatigue, was in outline against a snowbank.

It was in that moment of silence that Dard caught the distant sound—very faint, borne to them by some freak of air current—the bay of a hunting dog running a fresh and uncomplicated trail Kimber's head jerked up. Dard ran his tongue around a dry mouth. That cave up there with its narrow entrance! He wasted no breath on explanation, instead he began doggedly to climb.

But—there was something wrong about the stone before them. Maybe his eyes—snow blindness—Dard shook his head, trying to clear them. But that different look remained. So that he was partly expecting what he found when he reached the crest. Sick, shaken to the point of nausea, he stared at the closed door of the cave—closed with rocks and something else—and then he reeled retching to the other side of the hill top.

He was scrubbing out his mouth with a handful of snow when Kimber joined him.

"So, now we know about Sach—"

Dard raised sick eyes. The pilot's mouth was stone-hard. "Left him there like that as a threat," muttered Kimber, "and a warning. They must have discovered that this was one of out regular posts."

"How could any one do that?"

"Listen, son, somebody starts out with an idea—maybe in the beginning a good one. Renzi wasn't a crook, he was basically a decent man. I heard his early speeches and I'm willing to agree that much he said was true. But he had no—well, 'charity' is the best word for it He wanted to force his pattern for living on everyone else, for their own good, of course. Because he was great and sincere in his own way he gained a following of honest people. They were sick of war and they were terribly shocked by the Big Burn, they could readily believe that science had led to evil. The Free Scientists were too independent—they made closed guilds of their teams. There was a separation between thinking and feeling. And feeling is easier to us than thinking. So Renzi appealed to feeling, and against the aloofness of science he won. He was joined by other fanatics, and by those who want power no matter how it comes into their bands. Then there have always been some human beings who enjoy that sort of thing—what we just saw over there. They're lower than animals because animals don't torture their own kind for pleasure. Fanatics, power lovers, sadists—let them get a tight hold on the government and there is no room for decency. The best this world can hope for now is a break in their ranks, an inner struggle for control.

"This type of fight against freedom of thought and tolerance has happened before. Centuries ago there was the Inquisition in the name of religion. And daring the twentieth century the dictators did the same under political systems of one kind or another. Fanatic belief in an idea— a conviction that an idea or a nation is greater than the individual man—it has scrourged us again and again. Utter power over his fellow men changes a man, rots him through and through. When we are able to breed men who want no influence over each other—who are content to strive equally for a common goal—then we'll pull ourselves above that—" He gestured to that pitiful thing now hidden from their eyes. "The Free Scientists came close to reaching that, point. Which is why Renzi and his kind both hated and feared them. But they were only a handful—drops lost in a sea. And they went under as have others before them who have followed the same vision. Nothing worse can be done to man than what he has done to himself. But listen to this—"

Kimber's head was high, he was watching that peak which guarded the distant Cleft. Now he repeated slowly:

"'Frontiers of any type, physical or mental, are but a challenge to our breed. Nothing can stop the questing of men, not even Man. If we will it, not only the wonders of space, but the very stars are ours!'"

"The stars are ours!" echoed Dard. "Who said that?"

"Techneer Vidor Chang, one of our martyrs. He helped to bring the star ship here, ventured out on the first fuel research and— But his words remain ours.

"That's what we've geared our lives to, we outlaws. It doesn't matter what a man was in the past—Free Scientist, techneer, laborer, farmer, soldier—we're all one because we believe in freedom for the individual, in the rights of man to grow and develop as far as he can. And we are daring to search for a place where we can put those beliefs, into practice. The earth denied us—we must seek the stars."

Kimber started down slope. Dard caught up to point out the ruse which he had used with Dessie and which might now baffle the hounds. They found a higher ledge and made a more perilous dive, so that Dard landed on pine boughs and spilled to the earth with a jolt which drove the breath out of his lungs until Kimber pounded air back into him.

To his surprise the pilot did not keep to cover now. The night was falling fast and they could not hold their present pace without rest But Kimber plunged on until they came to the open space flanking the river. There the pilot brought out the same flat disc with which he had cut their way out of the temple barrier, and hurled it out into the open.

A column of green fire shot from it up into the night, standing steady for at least five minutes. In the dusk it made a good show, turning the surrounding snow and the faces of the fugitives verdant as it burned.

"Now we wait," Kimber's voice held a faint shadow of the old humor. "The boys will be down to pick us up before Pax can connect."

But waiting was not so simple when each minute meant the difference between life and death. They swallowed the last of the food and bedded down between two fallen trees at the edge of the clearing. The flame died down, but a core of green glow would continue to shine for several hours, Kimber said.

A wind was rising. And its wails through the trees did not drown out the distant yapping of the hounds. Dard fingered his stun gun—two charges for him, one in Kimber's weapon. Little enough with which to meet what panted on their trail. The trailers would be armed with rifles.

Kimber stirred and then scuttled on hands and feet out from their shelter. From the night sky a dark shape came down—a 'copter. But the pilot summoned Dard to meet with it. A door opened and he was shoved into the machine by his companion. Then as they were air borne Dard rested his head against a cushion, only half hearing the excited questions and answers of the others.

When he awoke the whole wild adventure of the past forty-eight hours might only have been a dream, for he was back on the same cot where he had rested before. Only now Kimber was not with him. Dard lay there, trying to separate dream from reality. Then a clang which could only have been an alarm brought him up. With clumsy hands he pulled on the clothes lying in a heap on the floor and opened the door to peer out into the corridor.

Two men, pushing before them a small cart, crossed its lower end. The cart wheel caught on the edge of a doorway and both men cursed as they worked swiftly to pry it loose. Dard padded in that direction, but before he could join them they were gone. He followed as they broke into a trot and started down a ramp leading into the heart of the mountain.

This brought them to a large cave which was a scene of complete confusion. Dard hesitated, trying to pick out of the busy throng some familiar face. There were two parties at work. One was carrying and wheeling boxes and containers out into the narrow valley where the star ship was berthed. And in this group women toiled with the men. The second party, which had been joined by the men with the cart, was wholly masculine and all armed.

"Hey, you!"

Dard realized that he was being hailed by a black-bearded man using a rifle as a baton to direct the movements of the armed force. He went over there, only to have a rifle thrust into his hands and to be urged into line with the men taking a tunnel to the right. They were bound for a defense point, he decided, but no one explained.

The answer came soon enough with a crackle of rifle fire. What had once been the narrow throat-valley leading into the Cleft proper had been choked up by a fall of tumbled rock and earth cemented by snow, broken in places by the protruding crown or roots of a small tree. Up this dam men were crawling, dragging after them an assortment of weapons, from ordinary rifles and stun guns to a tube and box arrangement totally strange to Dard.

He counted at least ten defenders who were now ensconced in hollows along the rim of the barrier. Now and again one of these fired, the sound being echoed by the rock walls to twice its normal volume. Dard clambered over the slide, cautiously testing his footing, until he reached the nearest of the snipers' hollows. The man glanced up as a rolling clod announced his arrival.

"Get your fool head down, kid!" he snapped. "They're still trying the 'copter game. You'd think that they'd have learned by now!"

Dard wormed his way along—until he rubbed shoulders with the defender and could look down into the weird battlefield. He tried to piece out from the wreckage there what had been happening in the hours since he and Kimber had returned.

Two burnt-out skeletons of 'copters were crumpled among rocks. From one of them thin wisps of vapor still spiraled. And there were four bodies wearing black and white Pax Every. But as far as Dard could see there was nothing alive down there now.

"Yeah. They've all taken t' cover. Trying to think up some trick that'll get us away from here. It'll take time for 'em to get any big guns back in these hills. And they don't have time. Before they can shake us loose the ship's going to blast off!"

"The ship's going to blast off!" So that was it! He was now one of an expendable rear guard, left to hold the fort while the star ship won free. Dard studied the rifle he held, with eyes which did not see either the metal of barrel or wood of stock.

Well, he told himself savagely, wasn't this just what he knew was going to happen—ever since that moment when Kimber had admitted with his silence that all those in the Cleft would not go out into space?

"Hey!" a hand joggling his elbow snapped his attention back to the job at hand. "See—down there—"

He followed the line set by that dirty finger.
Something moved around the wreckage of the 'copter
farthest from the barrier—a black tube. Dard frowned as
he studied its outline. The tube was being slued around to
face the barrier. That was no rifle—too large. It was no
form of gun he had seen before.

"Santee! Hey, Santee!" his companion shouted.
"They're bringing up a burper!"

A man scrambled up and Dard was shoved painfully
against a tree branch as the black beard took his place.

"You're right—damn it! I didn't think they had any of
those left! Well, we've got to stay as long as we can. I'll
pass the word to the boys. In the meantime try a little
ricochet work. Might pick off one or two of that beauty's
crew. If we're lucky. Which I'm beginning to think now we
certainly ain't!"

He crawled out of the hollow and Dard got thankfully
back into station. His companion patted down a ridge of
dirt on which to rest the barrel of his rifle. Dard saw that
he was aiming, not at the ugly black muzzle of the harper,
but at the rock wall behind the gun. So—that was what
Santee meant by ricochet work. Fire at the rock wall and
hope that the bullets would be deflected back against the
men serving the burper. Neat—if it could be done. Dard
lined the sights of his own weapon to cover what he hoped
was the proper point. Others had the same idea. The shots
came in a ragged volley. And the trick worked, for with a
scream a man reeled out and fell.

"Why don't they use that green gas?" asked Dard,
remembering his own introduction to the fighting methods
of the Cleft dwellers.

"How do you think we crashed those 'copters, kid? And the boys got a couple more machines the same way out by the river. Only something went wrong when they triggered the blast to seal off the valley this way. And the gas gun—with a couple of very good guys—came down with this—underneath!"

For a space the burper did not move. Perhaps the defenders had wiped out its crew with the ricochet volley. Just as they were beginning to hope that this was so, the black muzzle, moving with the ponderous slowness of some big animal, eased back into concealment. Dard's partner watched this maneuver sourly.

"Cookin' up something else now. They must have had a guy with brains come in to run things. And if that's so, we're not going to have it so good. Yahh!" His voice arose sharply.

But Dard needed no warning. He, too, had seen that black sphere rising in a lazy course, straight at the barrier.

"Head down, kid! Head—"

Dard burrowed into the side of the hollow, his face scratching across the frozen dirt, his hunched shoulders and arms protecting his head. The explosion rocked the ground and was followed by a scream and several moans. Dazed, the boy shook himself free of loose earth and snow.

To the left there was a sizeable gap in the barrier. With a white patch halfway down—not snow but a hand buried to the wrist in the slide the explosion had ripped down.

"Dan—and Red—and Loften got it. Nice bag for Pax," his fellow sniper muttered. "Now was that Just a lucky shot—or do they have our range?"

The forces of Pax had the range. A second ragged tear was sliced across the rock and earth dam. Before the stones stopped rattling down, Dard was shaken out of his crouch roughly.

"If you ain't dead, kid, come on! Santee's passed the word to fall back, to the next turn of the canyon. On the double, because we're going to blow again, and if you get caught on this side—it's your skin!"

Dard tumbled down the barrier behind his guide, falling once and scraping both sleeve and skin from his forearm in the process. Seconds later eight defenders, their sides heaving, their dirty faces haunted and drawn, gathered around Santee and were waved on down the canyon. Santee himself stood counting off seconds aloud. At "ten" he plunged his hand down on the black box beside him.

There was a dull rumble, less noise than the burper shots had made. Dard watched in a sort of fascinated horror as the whole opposite cliff moved majestically outward into space before it crashed down to make a second and taller wall. The stones and earth had not ceased to roll before Santee was leading his force up it to dig in and face the enemy. Once more Dard lay in wait with a rifle, this time alone.

The burper sounded regularly, systematically pounding down the first barrier. But, save for that, there was no sign of Pax activity. And how long would it be before they brought the burper up to this assault? Then would the few left retreat again and blow down another section of the mountain?

There was a flicker of movement down at the first

barrier, and it was answered by a shot from the defense. A second later more shots, all down by the battered dam. Dard guessed what had happened, wounded and left behind, one of the Cleft dwellers was firing his last round to delay the victors. The flurry of fire was only a prelude to what they were waiting to see—the black snub nose of the burper rising above the rubble.

—8—
COLD SLEEP

UNABLE TO SEE the burper's crew the defenders had only the narrowest and most impossible mark to shot at—the gun's muzzle. Perhaps that action was only to occupy their minds, by concentrating on that menace, by seeing or thinking of nothing else, they could, each and everyone, forget for a space that the ship they fought for could only take a numbered few—that when it blasted off, some of the Cleft would still be here.

Dessie! Dard twisted in the hole he had hollowed with his body. Surely Dessie would be aboard. There were so few children—so few women—Dessie would be an asset!

He tried to think only of a shadow he thought he saw move then. Or a shadow he wanted to believe had moved as he snapped a shot at it. When this battle had begun, or rather when he had come on the scene—it had been mid-morning. Once during the day he had choked down some dry food which had been passed along, taking sips from a shared canteen. Now the dusk of evening lengthened the patches of gloom. Under the cover of the dark the burper would rumble up to them, to gnaw away at this second barrier. And the defenders would withdraw—to delay and delay.

But maybe the end of that battle would not wait upon nightfall after all. The familiar sound of blades beating the air was a warning which reached them before they saw the 'copter skimming up, its undercarriage scraping the top of their first wall.

Dard watched it resignedly, too apathetic to duck when its occupants hurled grenades. He crouched unmoving as the machine climbed for altitude. The explosion caught him in his hollow a second later. There was the sense of being torn out of hiding, of being flung free. Then he was on his hands and knees, creeping through a strangely silent world of rolling stones and sliding earth.

Some feet away a man struggled to free his legs from a mound of earth. He clawed at his covering with a single hand, the other, welling red, lay at a queer twisted angle. Dard crept over and the man stared at him wildly, mouthing words Dard could not hear through the buzzing which filled his head. He dug with torn fingers into the mass which held the other prisoner.

Another figure loomed over them and Dard was shoved aside. The huge Santee knelt, scooping away soil and rock, until together they were able to pull the injured man free. Dard, his shaking head still ringing with noise of its own, helped to lift the limp body and carry it back into the inner valley of the star ship. Santee stumbled and brought all three of them down. Dard got to his knees and turned his head carefully to blink at what be saw behind him.

Those in the 'copter had not ripped apart the barrier as they had planned. The grenades had jarred some hidden fault bringing down more tons of soil and rocks. Anyone viewing that spot now would never believe that there had once been an opening there.

Of the defenders who had held that barricade only the three of them remained,—he, Santee, and the wounded man they had dragged with them.

Dard wondered if he had been deafened by the explosion. The roaring in his head, which affected his balance when he tried to walk, had no connection with normal sound and he could hear nothing Santee was saying. He ran his hands aimlessly across his bruised and aching ribs, content to remain where he was.

But the enemy was not satisfied to leave them alone Spurts of dust stung up from the rock wall. Dard stared at them a second or two before Santee's heavy fist sent him sprawling, and he realized that the three of them were cut off in a pocket while snipers in the 'copter tried to pick them off. This was the end—but to think that brought him no sensation of fear. It was enough to just lie still and wait.

He brought his hands up to support his buzzing head. Then someone tugged roughly at his belt, rolling him over. Dard opened his eyes to see Santee taking the stun gun from him. Out of that thick that of black hair which masked most of the man's face his teeth showed in a white snarl of rage.

But there were only two charges in the stun gun. Maybe he was able to say that aloud, for Santee glanced at him and then examined the clip. Two shots from a stun gun wasn't going to bring down a 'copter. The humor of that pricked him and he laughed quietly to himself. A stun gun against a 'copter!

Santee was up on his knees behind the rock he had chosen for protection, his head straining back on his thick neck as he watched the movements of the copter.

What happened next might have astonished Dard earlier, but now he was past all amazement. The 'copter, making a wide turn, smashed into some invisible barrier in the air. Through the twilight they saw it literally bounce back, as if some giant hand had slapped at an annoying insect. Then, broken as the insect would have been, it came tumbling down. Two of its passengers jumped and floated through the air, supported by some means Dard could not identify. Santee scrambled to his feet and took careful aim with the stun gun.

He picked off the nearer. But a second shot missed the other. And the big man ducked only just in time to escape the return fire of the enemy. Making contact with the ground the Peaceman dodged behind the crumpled fuselage of the 'copter. Why didn't he just walk across and finish them off, Dard speculated fretfully. Why draw out the process? It was getting darker—darker. He pawed at his eyes, was his sight as well as his hearing going to fail him?

But, no, he could still see Santee who had gone down on his belly and was now wriggling around the rocks, proceeding worm-fashion along a finger of the slide toward the 'copter. Though how he expected to attack the man hidden there—with his bare hands and an empty stun gun—against a rifle!

Dard's detachment persisted. He watched the action

in which he was not involved critically. Wanting to see how it would end he pulled himself up to follow Santee's slow progress. When the crawler disappeared from his range of vision Dard was irritated. Suppose the man waiting over there was to believe that they were trying to escape down valley—wouldn't all his attention be for that direction—not at Santee?

Dard felt about him in the gloom, hunting stones of a suitable size, weighing and discarding until he held one larger than both his fists. Two more he lined up before him. With all the strength he could muster he sent the first and largest hurling down the valley. A flash of fire answered its landing.

The second and third rock followed at intervals. Each time he saw the mark of answering shots. His hearing was coming back—he caught the faint echo of the last one. New stones were found and sent after the others—to keep up the illusion of escape. But now there was no shot to reply. Had Santee reached that sniper?

The boy sprawled back against the wall of the cleft and waited, for what he did not altogether know. Santee's return? Or the star ship's blast off? Had they bought time enough for the frenzied workers back there? Was tonight going to see Kimber setting that course they had won from the Voice, piloting the ship out into space before he, too, went under the influence of Lars' drug and began the sleep from which there might be no awakening? But if the voyagers did awaken! Dard drew a deep breath and for a moment he forgot everything—his own aching, punished body, the rocky trap which enclosed him, the lack of future—he forgot all these in a dream of what might lie beyond the sky which he now searched for the first wink of star-light. Another world—another sun—a fresh start!

He started as a shape loomed out of the dark to cut off the sight of that star he had just discovered. Fingers clawed painfully into his shoulders bringing him up to his feet. Then, mainly by Santee's brute force of body and will, they picked up the rescued man and started in a drunken stagger back into the valley. Dard forgot his dream, he needed all his strength to keep his feet, to go as Santee drove him.

They made a half-turn to avoid a boulder and came to a stop as lights blinded them. The ship was surrounded by a circle of blazing flares. The fury of industry which had boiled about it during the loading had stemmed to a mere trickle. Dard could see no women at all and most of the men were gone also. The few who remained in sight were passing boxes up a ramp. Soon that would be done, and then those down there would enter that silvery shape. The hatch would close, the ship would rise on fire.

Muted by the pain in his head he heard the booming shout of a deep voice. Below, the loaders stopped work. Grouped together they faced the survivors of the barrier battle. Santee called again, and that group broke apart as the men ran up to them.

Dard sat down beside the injured man, his legs giving way under him. With detachment he watched the coming of that other party. One man had his shirt badly torn across the shoulder—would he land on another world across the void of space with that tatter still fluttering? The problem had some interest.

Now a circle of legs walled the boy in, boots spurted

snow in his face. He was brought to his feet, arms about his shoulders, led along to the ship. But that wasn't right, he thought mistily. Kimber had said not room enough— he was one of the expendables—

But he could find no words to argue with those who helped him along, not even when he was pushed up that ramp into the ship. Kordov stood in the hatch door waving them ahead with an imperious arm. Then Dard found himself in a tiny room and a cup of milky liquid was thrust against his lips and held there until he docilely swallowed its contents to the last tasteless drop. When that was in him he was lowered onto a folding seat pulled down from the starkly bare metal wall and left to hold his spinning head in his hands.

"Yeah—the force field's still holdin'—"

"Won't be able to plow through that last slide, eh?"

"Not with anything they've got now."

Words, a lot of words, passing pack and forth across him. Sometimes for a second or two they made good sense, then meaning faded again.

"Can pretty well take your own time now—" Was that rumble from Santee?

And that quick, crisp voice cutting in, "What about the kid?"

"Him? He's some scrapper. Got a head on him, too. Just shaken up a lot when that last blowup hit us, but he's still in one piece."

Kimber! That had been Kimber asking about him. But Dard hadn't strength left to raise his head and look for the pilot.

"We'll patch up Tremont first and send him under. You

two will have to wait a while. Give them the soup and that first powder, Lui—"

Again Dard was given a drink—this time of hot steamy stuff which carried the flavor of rich meat. After it there was a capsule to be swallowed.

Bruises and aches—when he moved his body he was just one huge ache. But he straightened up and tried to take an interest in his surroundings. Santee, his shirt a few rags about his thick hairy shoulders and arms, squatted on another pull-down seat directly across from Dard. Along the passage outside there was a constant coming and going. Scraps of conversation reached them, most of which he did not understand.

"Feelin' better, kid?" the big man asked.

Dard answered that muffled question with a nod and then wished that he hadn't moved his head.

"Are we going along?" he shaped the words with difficulty.

Santee's beard wagged as he roared with laughter, "Like to see 'em throw us off ship now! What made you think we weren't, kid?"

"No room—Kimber said."

Laughter faded from the eyes of the man opposite him.

"Might not have been, kid. Only a lot of good men died back there puttin' such a plug in the valley that these buggers aren't going to git in 'til too late. Since the warp's still workin', flyin' won't bring 'em neither. So we ain't needed out there no more. An' maybe some good fightin' men will be needed where this old girl's headed. So in we come, an' they're gonna pack us away with the rest of the cargo. Ain't that so, Doc?" he ended by demanding of the tall young man who had just entered.

The newcomer's parrot crest of blond hair stood up from his scalp in a twist like the stem of a pear and his wide eyes glowed with enthusiasm.

"You're young Nordis, aren't you?" he demanded of Dard, ignoring Santee. "I wish I could have known your brother! He—what he did—! I wouldn't have believed such results possible if I hadn't seen the formula! Hibernation and freezing—his formula combined with Tas's biological experiments! Why, we've even put three of Hammond's calves under—what grass they'll graze on before they die! And it's all due to Lars Nordis!"

Dard was too tired to show much interest in that. He wanted to go to sleep—to forget everything and everybody. "To sleep, perchance to dream"—the old words shaped patterns for him. Only—not to dream would be better now. Did one dream in space—and what queer dreams haunted men lying in slumber between worlds? Dard mentally shook himself—there was something important—something he had to ask before he dared let sleep come.

"Where's Dessie?"

"Nordis' little girl? She's with my daughter—and my wife—they're already under."

"Under what?"

"In cold sleep. Most of the gang are now. Just a few of us still loading. Then Kimber, Kordov and I. We'll ride out until Kimber is sure of the course before we stow away. All the rest of you—"

"Will be packed away before the take-off. Saves wear

and tear on bodies and nerves under acceleration," cut in Kimber from the doorway. He nodded over the medico's shoulder at Dard. "Glad to have you aboard, kid. Promise you—no forced landings on this voyage. You're to be sealed up in crew's quarters—so you'll wake early to see the new world!" And with that he was gone again.

Maybe it was the capsule acting now, maybe it was just that last reassurance from a man he had come to trust wholeheartedly, but Dard was warm and relaxed. To wake and see a new world!

Santee went away with Lui Skort, and Dard was alone. The noise in the corridor died away. At last he heard a warning bell. And a moment later the pound of heavy feet in a hurry roused him. The haste of that spoke of trouble, and with the support of the wall he got up to look out Kimber was coming down a spiral stairway, the center core of the ship. In his hand was one of the snubnosed ray guns Sach had had. He passed Dard without a word.

Bracing his hands against the wall of the corridor, Dard shuffled along in his wake. Then he was peering out of an airlock to see the pilot squatting on the ramp. It was black night out—most of the flares had gone out.

Dard listened. He could hear at intervals the blast of the burper. The Peacemen were still doggedly attacking the cleft barrier. But what had Kimber come to guard and why? Have some important possessions been left in the caverns? Dard slumped against the lock and watched lights spark to life in the mouth of the tunnel. A man came out running, covering the ground to the foot of the ship's ramp in ground-eating leaps. He dashed by Kimber, and Dard had just time enough to get back as Santee burst in.

"Get going!" The big man bore him along to the corridor and Kimber joined them. He touched some control and the hatch-lock was sealed.

Santee, panting, grinned, "Nice neat job, if I do say so myself," he reported. "The space warp's off an' the final charge is set for forty minutes from now. We'll blast before that?"

"Yes. Better get along both of you. Lui's waiting and we don't want to scrape a couple of acceleration cases off the floor later," returned Kimber.

With the aid of the other two Dard pulled his tired body up the stair, part various landing stages where sealed doors fronted them. Kordov's broad face appeared at last, surveying them anxiously, and it was he who lifted Dard up the last three steps. Kimber left them—climbing on through an opening above into the control chamber. He did not glance back or say any goodbyes.

"In here—" Kordov thrust them ahead of him.

Dard, brought face to face with what that cabin contained, knew a sudden repulsion. Those boxes, shelved in a metal rack—they too closely resembled coffins! And the rack was full except for the bottommost box which awaited open on the floor.

Kordov pointed to it. "That's for you, Santee—built for a big boy. You're lighter, Dard. We'll fit you in on top over on the other side."

A second rack stood against the farther wall with four more of the coffins ready and waiting. Dard shivered, but it was not imagination—disturbed nerves which roughened his skin, there was a chill in the air—coming from the open boxes.

Kordov explained. "You go to sleep and then you freeze."

Santee chuckled. "Just so you thaw us out again, Tas. I ain't aimin' to spend the rest of my life an icicle, so you brainy boys can prove somethin' or other. Now what do we do—climb in?"

"Strip first," ordered the First Scientist "And then you get a couple of shots."

He pulled along a small rolling tray-table on which were laid a series of hypodermics. Carefully he selected two, one filled with a red brown liquid, the other with a colorless substance.

As Dard fumbled at the fastenings of the torn uniform he still wore, Santee asked a question for them both.

"An' how do we wake up when the right time comes? Got any alarms set in these contraptions?"

"Those three—" Kordov indicated the three lower coffins on the far rack, "are especially fitted. Arranged to waken those inside, Kimber, Lui, and me, when the ship signals that it has reached the end of the course set, which will be when the instruments raise a sun enough like Sol to nourish earth-type planets. We feed that into her robot controls once we are free in space. During the voyage she may vary the pattern—to make evasion of meteors or for other reasons. But she will always come back on the set course. If we are close to a solar system when we are awakened, and Kimber has done everything possible to assure that, then we shall arouse you others needed to bring the ship down. Most of you won't be awakened until after we land—there isn't enough room."

Kordov shrugged, "Who knows? No man has yet

pioneered into the galaxy. It may be for generations."

Santee rolled his discarded clothing into a ball and waited stoically for Kordov to give him the shots. Then with a wave of one big fist he climbed into the coffin and lay down. Kordov made adjustments at either end. Icy air welled up in a freezing puff. Santee's eyes closed as the First Scientist moved the lid into place before setting the three dials on the side. Their pointers swung until the needles came to rest at the far end. Kordov pushed the box back onto the rack.

"Now for you," he turned to Dard.

The top box lowered itself on two long arms from the top of the other rack. Dard discarded his last piece of clothing with a vast reluctance. Sure, he could understand the theory of this—what his brother had worked out for them. But the reality—to be frozen within a box—to go sightlessly, helplessly into the void—perhaps never to awake! With his teeth set hard he fought back the panic those thoughts churned up in him. And he was fighting so hard that the prick of the first injection came as a shock. He started, only to have Kordov's hand close as a vise upon his upper arm and hold him steady for a second.

"That's all—in with you now, son. See you in another world."

Kordov was laughing, but Dard's weak answering smile as he settled himself in the coffin had no humor in it. Because Kordov could be so very right. The cover was going on, he had an insane desire to scream out that he wasn't going to be shut in this way—that he wanted out, not only of the box, but of the whole crazy venture. But the lid was on now. It was cold—so cold—dark—cold. This was space as man had always believed it would be—cold and dark—eternal cold and dark—without end.

BOOK TWO

ASTRA

—★ 1 ★—
AWAKENING

IT WAS WARM and there was a light, striking redly through Dard's closed eyelids. The warmth was good, but he wanted to twist his head away from the demands of that light. To move—but movement required effort he had not yet the strength to make. It would be better to slip back into the pleasant darkness—to sleep. . . .

A sharp stab of pain shook him out of that floating ease. Dard made a great effort and forced his eyelids up. Cloudy masses of color moved above him, sometimes changing position in quick jerks which removed them entirely from his area of vision. The cloudiness slowly disappeared and lines tightened, drew together. A face— vaguely familiar—hands which descended to his level of sight.

He became aware of the hands moving across his body and another prick of pain followed. There was sound— staccato bursts. Talking—talking—Dard willed his mouth to open, his tongue to move. But obedience came with agonizing slowness, as if those particular motions had not been made for a long, long time. How long? Long—? He began to remember, and his hands turned to feel for the confines of the coffin. But they met no barrier—he was no longer imprisoned in that box!

"Drink up, kid—"

The words sorted themselves into coherent speech as he sucked on the tube which had been placed in his mouth. The drink was hot, warmth tingling inside him as well as without, driving the chill which had immobilized his muscles. Strangely he was drowsy again and this time the hands did not work to keep him conscious.

"That's right. Take it easy—we'll be seeing you . . ."

That reassurance carried into sleep with him. It held through to his second awakening. This time he raised himself up and looked around. He had been stretched on a soft thick pad on the floor of the oddest room he had ever seen. Half lying in a cushioned chair swung on webbing was a dark-haired man, intent upon a wide screen set in the wall before him.

There were two more such seats, each before a board of controls. And Dard saw three more such floor mats as the one he rested upon, each equipped with a set of straps and buckles. He drew his feet up under him to sit cross-legged, while he studied the cabin and put together bits of recollection.

This could not be anything but the control cabin of the star ship. He was awake—had been aroused—which meant—! His hand went to his mouth in an involuntary gesture. Now he wanted to see what was on that screen his cabin companion watched. He must see!

But his body moved so slowly. Rusty joints—slack muscles. Why—he creaked! Hands and eyes told him that he was clothed. Though the cloth of the breeches and blouse was sleek and smooth, like no other fabric he had ever seen, colored in a mixture of brown and green. He put out the feet in their queer soft boots and inched forward to grab at the nearest swinging chair.

The watcher turned his head and smiled. It was Kimber—the same Kimber he had last seen on his way to this cabin on the night the voyage had begun. How long ago had that been?

"Greetings!" The pilot pointed to the chair beside his own. "Sit down—you haven't got your ship's legs yet. Did you have good dreams?"

Dard moved his tongue experimentally, "Can't remember any," the words came out easily now—at least his voice hadn't rusted away. "Where are we?"

Kimber chuckled. "Space only knows. But we're near enough to a reasonable goal for the old girl to awake Kordov and me. Then we added you to the company—and will probably bring around a couple more before we land. See?"

On the screen three specks of light dotted the dark glass.

"That's it, a new solar system, m'boy! Luck—Lord, Luck's ridden on our rockets most of the way. That?"— Kimber pointed to the largest of the dots—"that is a yellow sun, approximate temperature 11,000 degrees, approximate size—same as Sol. In fact, it could be Sol's twin brother. And being Sol's twin we can hope that one of its three planets is enough like Terra to make us welcome."

"Three planets—I only see two."

"Other's behind Sol II now. We've seen her—in fact Tas and I have had a week to chart this system since the ship controls roused us. Give us another day and we shall pick out the world we want and land the ship—"

Three worlds—and a yellow sun. Dard wished that he knew more, that his education was better than a collection of scraps and patches. Back on earth under Pax it was a feat to be able to read and write—he had entertained some pride in his learning. But now—he felt that to be nothing at all!

"Why did you waken me?" he asked. "I can't help with the ship. You said that Kordov and you—" He was trying to remember. There had been a third man to be aroused early—

Kimber's attention was again given to the screen. Now he answered quickly:

"You were available and you can help Kordov. Lui didn't make it."

Lui Skort—that young medico who had been so enthusiastic about Lars' drug! He had been that third man.

"What—what happened?"

"We can't tell now. All of this—the ship, her course, the freeze boxes were constructed on hope alone. We had no way of testing anything properly. The ship awakened Kordov and me. But Lui—"

"How long have we been cruising in deep space?"

"At least three hundred years—maybe more. Time in space may be different from planet time. That is one of the points scientists have argued about. We have no accurate way of telling."

"Was it only Lui's box that failed?"

Kimber's face was grim now as it had been on that night they fought their way back to the Cleft.

"Until we land and start to rouse the whole company we can not tell. The freeze boxes must not be opened until their occupants are ready for revival. And the ship is too small to do that before landing—"

Coffins! Coffins were what they resembled, and coffins they might be for the whole inert cargo the star ship carried! Perhaps the three of them were the only survivors.

"We can hope for a high percentage of survivals," Kimber continued. "Lui's box had the special controls— that may have been the trouble. But out of four, three of us are all right. Kordov—".

"Yes—and what does Kordov do?" asked the hearty voice behind them.

The stocky First Scientist elbowed his way between the two swinging seats and handed the occupant of each a round plastic bulb from which a tube projected. He cradled a third in his own hand as he settled in the other chair.

"Kordov," he answered his own question, "continues to see after your puny bodies, my friends. And you should be glad of his personal interest in them. You will now consume what you hold in your paws and be thankful!" He inserted the bulb tube in his mouth and took a smacking suck.

Dard discovered that he had to drink the same warm salty stuff that had been given to him on his first awakening. And it satisfied him completely. But he only took one experimental drag before he demanded:

"I heard about Lui. How many others?"

Tas Kordov wiped his mouth with the back of his square hand.

"That we can not tell. We dare not investigate the boxes too closely until a landing has been made. Yes, all of us want an answer to that question, young man. How many—? We can hope that most came through. I propose to open two more from the crews' quarters—there are men in them whose skills we need. But—for the rest— their slumbers must continue until we have the new world to offer them. And that too," he waved at the visa-screen, "presents problems. We have found the proper sort of sun. But remember Sol had nine planets, on only one of which mankind could live at ease. Here are three planets— perhaps a Mars, a Venus, a Mercury, and no Terra. Which one do you think we should try, Sim?"

The pilot drank before he replied. "Judging by the charted orbits, I'll settle for the middle one. It's closer to Sol II than Terra was to Sol I, but it has the nearest approach to a Terran orbit."

"I don't know anything about astronomy," Dard ventured. "You expect this sun to produce an earth-type planet because it is a 'yellow' one, but if one of those three worlds is another Terra—what about intelligent life on it? Couldn't the same general conditions have produced the same type of dominant life form?"

Kordov leaned forward, disturbing the precarious balance of his swinging seat.

"Intelligent life—maybe. Humanoid or Man—only perhaps. If on one planet the primate is the ruling form, on another it may be the insect or the carnivora."

"Don't forget this!" Kimber held up one hand and flexed its fingers in front of the screen. "Man's hand helped to make him the ruling form. Suppose you had only—say, a cat's paw. Even if intelligence went with it, and I defy anyone to tell me that a cat is not an intelligent creature; its brains may work in a different pattern, perhaps, but no one who has lived with one can deny that it can alter its environment to suit its convenience, in spite of the general stupidity of the human beings that it must deal with and through. But if we had been born with paws instead of hands—no matter what super brains we had, could we have produced tools, or other artifacts? Primates on Terra had hands. And they used them to pull themselves up to a material civilization, just as they used monkey chatter and worse than monkey manners to break up what they themselves had created. No, if we had not possessed hands we would have achieved nothing."

"Very well," Kordov returned, "I grant you the advantage of hands. But I still say that some ruling species, other than primates might well have developed under slightly different conditions. All history, both man-made and physical, is conditioned by 'ifs.' Suppose your super cats have learned to use their paws and are awaiting us. But this is romancing," he laughed. "Let us hope that what lies there is a world upon which intelligent life has never come into existence at all. If we are lucky—"

Kimber scowled at the screen. "Luck has ridden on our jets all the way. Sometimes I wonder if we have been a little too lucky and there's a rather nasty pay-off waiting for us right at the end of this voyage. But we can at least choose our landing place and I intend to set us down as far from any signs of civilization—if there is a civilization—as I can. Say in a desert or—"

"We shall leave the selection of the spot to you, Sim. And now, Dard, if you have finished your meal, you will please come with me. There is work to be done."

Dard's attempt to get to his feet unbalanced him and he would have fallen had it not been for the First Scientist.

"These cabins have some gravity," Kordov explained. "But not as much as we knew on Terra. Hold on and move slowly until you learn how to keep your feet"

Dard did as he advised, clutching at the chairs and anything within reach until he came to the round opening of the door. Beyond that was a much smaller cabin with two built-in bunks and a series of supply cupboards.

"This is pilot's quarters during an interplanetary run." Kordov crossed to the center of the room where a well-shaped opening gave access to the ship below. "Come on down—"

Dard gingerly descended the steep stair, coming into the section where he had been stored away for the cold sleep. And Kordov was going into that very cabin. The three boxes on the far rack were open. On the other rack the coffins were solidly white as if they had been carved from virgin snow.

Kordov pressed a button and the topmost box came down to the floor. He freed it from the arms which had lowered it and trundled his prize to the door with Dard's help. Together they brought the coffin into a second chamber which was a miniature laboratory. Kordov went down on his knees to read the dials. After a minute inspection he sighed with relief. "It is well. Now we shall open—"

The lid resisted as if ages of time had applied a stiff glue. But under continued pressure it gave at last with a faint swish of air. Crisp cold curled up about them, bringing with it chemical scents. The First Scientist examined the stiff body in the exposed hollow.

"Yes, yes! Now we must help him to live again. First—on the cot there—"

Dard helped lift the man onto the cot in the middle of the room. Under direction he rubbed the icy flesh with oils from a bottle Kordov thrust upon him, watching the First Scientist inject various fluids over the heart and in scattered veins. Warmth was coming back into the body as they worked. And when the man had fully roused, been fed, and had fallen into the sudden second sleep, Dard aided in dressing him and helped transport the body up to the control cabin to be laid out on the accelerator mat.

"Who—oh, Cully!" Kimber identified the newly revived crewman. "That's good. Who else are you going to bring around?"

Kordov, puffing a little, took a moment to consider. "We have Santee, Rogan, and Macley there." "The ship's not Santee's sort of job, and Cully's our engineer. Wait a minute—Rogan! He's had space training—as a tel-visor expert. We'll need him—"

"Rogan it shall be then. But first we shall take a rest. We shall not need a tel-visor expert yet awhile, I believe?"

Kimber glanced at the timepiece set in the control board, "Not for about five hours at least And maybe eight—if you want to be lazy."

"I am lazy when laziness is of advantage. Much of the troubles from which we have fled have been born of too much rushing about trying to keep busy. There is a time for working as hard as a man can work, yes. But there must also be hours to sit in the sun and think long thoughts and do nothing at all. Too much rushing wears out the body—and maybe also the mind. We must make haste slowly if we would make it at all!"

Whether it was some lingering effect of the cold sleep they could not decide, but they all found themselves dropping off into sudden naps. Kordov believed that the condition would pass, but Kimber was uneasy as they approached the chosen planet and demanded a stimulant from the First Scientist.

"I want to be awake now," Dard caught a scrap of conversation as he came back from a rest on one of the bunks in the other cabin. "To go off into a dream. Just when I take the ship into atmosphere—that's not possible. We aren't out of the woods yet—not by a long margin. Cully could take the controls in a pinch, so could Rogan, when you get him out of cold storage. But neither are trained pilots, and landing on unknown terrain is no job for a beginner!"

"Very well, Sim. You shall have your pill in plenty of time. But now you are to go in, lie down, and relax, not fight sleep. I promise that I shall rouse you in plenty of time. And meanwhile Cully will take your seat and watch the course—"

The tall thin engineer, who had said very little since his awakening, only nodded as he folded with loose-limbed ease into Kimber's reluctantly vacated place. He made some small adjustment on the control board and dropped his head back on the chair rest to watch the screen.

During the past hoars the points of light had altered. The ball of flame Kimber designated as Sol II had slipped away over the edge of their narrow slice of vision. But the world they had chosen filled most of the expanse now, growing larger by seconds.

Kordov sat down in one of the other chairs to watch with Dard. The sphere on the screen now had a bluish-green tinge, with patches of other color. "Polar regions—snow," Kordov commented. Cully replied with a single, "Yeh!" "And seas—"

To which Cully added the first long speech he had yet made.

"Got a lot of water. Should be picking up all land masses soon."

"Unless it's all water," mused Kordov. "Then," he grinned at Dard over his shoulder, "we shall be forced to leave it to the fish and try again."

"One thing missing," Cully adjusted the screen control for the second time. "No moon—"

No moon! Dard watched that enlarging sphere and for the first time since his awakening the dream-mood of passive acceptance of events cracked. To live under a sky where no silver globe ever hung. The moon gone! All the old songs men had sung, the old legends they had told and retold, the bit of history they cherished, that the moon was their first step into space, all gone. No moon—ever again!

"Then what will future poets find to rhyme with 'June' in all their effusions?" rumbled Kordov. "And our nights to come—they will be dark ones. But one can not have everything—even another stepping stone to space. That was how our moon served us—a way station, a beckoning sign post which lured us on and out If there is or ever was intelligent life down there—they lacked that"

"No sign of space travel?" Cully wanted to know with a spark of interest.

"None. But of course, we can in no way be sure. Just because nothing has registered on our screens we can not say that it does not exist. If we were but a fraction off a well-traveled space lane we would not know it! And now, Dard, we have Rogan to rouse. I promised Sim that he would be on hand to share duty."

Again they made that trip below, lifted out the proper box and brought back to life the man who slumbered in it.

"That is the last one," stated Kordov when they had established Rogan, in the control cabin. "No more until after we land. Hah!"

He had turned to look at the screen and the exclamation was jolted out of him by what he saw there. Land masses, mottled green-blue-red against which seas of a brighter hue washed.

"So we do not join fish. Instead you, Dard; must go and shake Sim back to life. Now is the time for him to be on duty!"

Shortly afterward Dard crouched on one of the acceleration mats beside the unconscious Rogan while the others occupied the chairs before the controls. The atmosphere within the cabin was tense and yet Kimber alone was at ease.

"Rogan come to yet?" he asked without turning his head.

Dard gently shook the shoulder of the man on the next mat. He stirred, muttered. Then his eyes opened and he scowled up at the roof of the cabin. A second later he sat up.

"We made it!" he shouted.

"That we did!" Kordov answered cheerfully. "And now—"

"Now there's a job waiting for you, fella," broke in Kimber. "Come up and tell us what you think of this."

Kordov spilled out of the third chair and helped Rogan into it. Holding tightly to the arms of the seat as if he feared any moment to be tossed out of it, Rogan gave his full attention to the screen. He drew a deep breath of pure wonder.

"It's—it's beautiful!"

Dard agreed with that. The mingling of color was working on him—just as sunsets back on Terra had been able to do. There were no words he knew to describe what he now saw. But he didn't have a chance to watch long.

"Better strap down," came the suggestion from the pilot. "We're going in—"

Kordov plumped down on one of the acceleration mats, pulling the harness which flanked it up over his body, and Dard did the same. He was flat on his back against the spongy stuff of the pad with his head at an angle from which he could not see the screen. They bored into atmosphere and he must have blacked out, for he never afterward remembered the last part of the furious descent.

The ship shuddered, pushing up—or was it down—upon him. He had a misty idea that this must be full gravity returning. Then there was a shock which tore at the webs holding his body and he gasped, fighting for breath. But his hands were already at the buckles which fastened him down as he heard a voice say:

"End of the line! All out!"

And another replied—in Cully's dry tone: "Neat, Sim, nice and neat."

—❋2❋—
NEW WORLD

"ROGAN?" THE TEL-VISOR EXPERT had spun his seat around and was facing another section of the control panel, his fingers flying across the buttons there. Needles spun on dials, indicators moved, and Rogan's lips shaped words silently. When he had done Kimber flicked the control of the visa-screen which had gone dead at their landing.

Slowly pictures of the immediate surroundings of the ship unrolled before their fascinated eyes.

"Late afternoon," Rogan commented, "by the length of the shadows."

The ship had planted in the middle of an expanse of gray-blue gravel or sand—backed at a distance by perpendicular cliffs of reddish rock layered by strata of blue, yellow and white. As the scene changed, those in the control room saw the cliffs give way to the month of a long valley down the center of which carved a stream.

"That water's red!" Dard's surprise joited the words out of him.

The red river was hemmed in by blue-green, low-growing vegetation which cloaked the ground within the valley itself and ran in tongues along the water into the semi-arid stretch of sand. Their viewing device was across the river picking up more cliffs and sand. Then they were fronted by ocean shore and vivid aquamarine waves tipped with white key foam. Into this emptied the river, staining the sea red for some distance. Sea, air, cliffs, river—but no living creature!

"Wait!" Kimber's order sent Rogan's finger down on a button and the picture on the screen became fixed. Thought I saw something—flying in the air. But guess I was wrong."

The scene changed until they were looking at the same spot where it had begun. Kimber stretched.

"This part of the country appears unoccupied. And, Tas, we didn't sight any signs of civilization when we came in either. Maybe our luck's held and we have an empty world."

"Hmm. But is it one we can venture into?" The First Scientist squeezed over to Cully's side of the cabin. "Atmosphere, temperature—within a fraction of Terra's. Yet, we can live and breathe here."

Kimber freed himself from the pilot's straps. "Suppose we have a look—see in person then."

Dard was the last to leave the cabin. He was still a little drunk with that riot of color on the visa-screen. After the remembered drabness of his home section of Terra this was overpowering. He was halfway down the ladder when he heard that clang which announced the opening of the hatch and the emergence of the ramp that would carry them safely over ground super-heated by their jets.

When he came out the others were strung along the ramp, breathing the warm air that was pungent with a fresh tang. The breeze pulled at Dard's hair, whipping a lock across his forehead, singing in his ears. Clean air—with none of the chemical taint which clung in the ship. Around the fins of their ship the sand had been fused into a curdled milky glass which they avoided by leaping from the end of the ramp to the dunes.

Kimber and Kordov plowed straight ahead to the wave-smoothed shore. Cully merely dropped in the soft grit of the beach, lying full length, his hands pressed tight to the earth, staring bemusedly up at the sky, while Rogan was pivoting slowly, as if to verify the scene the visa-screen had shown them.

Dard made his way to the sand. The redness of the river occupied him. Red water—why? The sea was normal enough except where it was colored by the river. He wanted to know what painted the stream and he started off determinedly to its bank.

The sand was softer, more powdery than any he had known on Terra. It shifted into his boot packs, arose in puffs and covered all but the faintest outline where he had stepped. He stooped and sifted the stuff through his fingers, knowing a strange tingle as the earth of this new world drifted away from his palm—blue sand—red river—red, yellow and white striped cliffs—color everywhere about him! Overhead that arch of cloud studded blue—or was it blue at all? Didn't it have just the faintest shading of green? Turquoise rather than true blue! Now that he was becoming accustomed to the color he could distinguish more subtle shades among the glows of brighter tones—shades he could not name—like that pale violet which streaked the sand.

Dard went on until he was in the stone-and-pebble-strewn border of the river. It was not a large stream, four strides might take him across it. There was a ripple of current but the water was opaque, dull rusty red, and it left a reddish rim about every stone it lipped in passage. He went down on one knee and was about to dip in a cautious exploratory finger when a voice called a warning;

"Don't try that, kid. Might not be healthy," Rogan came down the stony bank to join him. "Better be safe than sorry. Learned that myself on Venus—the hard way. See a piece of drift wood anywhere about?"

Dard searched among the rocks and found what appeared to be a very ordinary stick. But Rogan inspected it carefully before he picked it up. The stick was lowered into the flood and as cautiously withdrawn, an inch or so of a now dyed red. Together they held a close for examination.

"It's alive!" If he had been holding that test branch, Dard thought later, he might have dropped it at the realization of what the red stain was. But Rogan kept a tight grip.

"Lively little beggars, aren't they?" he asked. "Look like spiders. Do they float—or swim? And why so thick in the water. Now let's just see." He knelt and using the stick along the surface of the water skimmed off a good portion of what Dard secretly considered the extremely repulsive travelers. With the layer of "spiders" removed the water changed color becoming a clearer brownish fluid.

"So they can be scraped off," Rogan observed cheerfully. "With a strainer we may be able to get a drink—if this stuff is drinkable."

Dard swallowed hastily as Rogan tapped off on a convenient boulder the greater number of creatures he had fished out of the stream; and then together they followed the water to the sea. Several times they detoured, quite widely on Dard's part, to escape contact with patches of red marooned on share. Not that the "spiders" appeared uncomfortable on the firmer element for they made no attempt to move away from the spots where some sudden eddy had deposited them.

A stiff breeze came in over the waves. It was heavy with the tang Rogan now identified for Dard.

"Natural sea—that's salt air!" What he might have added was drowned out by a hideous screech.

Close on its dying echo came a very human shout. Kimber and Kordov were running along the beach just beyond the water's edge. And above their heads twisted and darted a nightmare, a small nightmare to be sure, but still one horrible enough to have winged out of an evil dream.—

If a Terran snake had been equipped with bat wings, two clawed legs, a barbed tail, and a wide fanged mouth, it might have approached in general this horror. The whole thing could not have been more than eighteen or twenty inches long, but its snapping fury was several times larger than its body and it was making power dives at the running men.

Rogan dropped his spider stick as Dard's hand flew inside his blouse to claim the only possession he had brought from Terra. He threw a hunting knife and by some incredible luck clipped a wing, not only breaking the dragon's dive, but sending it fluttering down, end over end, screeching. It flapped and beat with the good wing, squirming across the sand until Kimber and Kordov pinned it to the shingle with hastily flung stones.

Its eyes gleamed with red hate as they gathered in a circle around it, avoiding the snapping jaws and the flipping of the barbed tail which now dripped oily yellow drops.

"Bet that's poison," suggested Rogan. "Nice critter— hope they don't grow any bigger."

"What's the matter?" Cully came tearing down the slope, one of the green ray guns in his hand. "What's making all that racket?"

Rogan moved aside to display the injured dragon. "Native telling us off."

"Usually," Kimber broke in, "I don't believe in shooting first and investigating afterward. But this thing certainly hasn't any better nature to appeal to—nearly stripped the ear off my head before I knew he was around. Can you shoot it, Jorge, without messing it up too much? Tas, here, probably will want to take it apart later to see what makes it tick"

The biologist was squatting at a safe distance watching the convulsive struggles of the dragon with fascinated eyes.

"Yes, please do not destroy it utterly. A snake—a flying snake! But that is not possible!"

"Maybe not on Terra," Kimber reminded him. "What can we say is possible or impossible here? Jorge, put it out of its misery!"

The green ray clipped the top of the creature's head and it went limp on the sand. Tas approached it gingerly, keeping as far as he could from the tail barb still exuding the yellow venom. Rogan went back down the beach to retrieve his spider collection, and Dard picked up and wiped his knife clean.

"Flying snakes and swimming spiders," the communications techneer held out his stick for their appraisal. "I'm going to be afraid to sit down out here—anything may pop up now."

Tas was plainly torn between the now tractable dragon and the water dwellers Rogan had brought him. "All this"—his pudgy hands indicated the world of cliffs, sand and sea—"new, unclassified."

Cully bolstered his gun. He was frowning at the ceaseless waves.

"What do you make of those, Sim?" he demanded of the pilot, pointing to a low bank of clouds slowly expanding up the rim of the sky.

"On earth, I'd say a storm."

"Might be a bad one, too," Rogan commented. "And we have no shelter but the ship. At least this summer—we're warm enough."

"You think so?" asked Dard with some reason. The sea wind was rising, to become a wet lash with an icy bite in its flail. The temperature was dropping fast.

Kimber studied the clouds. "I'd say we better get back."

But when he turned inland his gasp brought them all around.

They had left the star ship on an even keel. Now it listed so that its nose pointed down the valley away from the sea.

A good half hour later Kimber got to his feet, relief mirrored on his face. One of the fins had broken through the fused coating the jet heat had put on the beach. But beneath the splintered glass crust it had found rock support—it would slip no farther. The scarred sides towering above them were no longer mirror bright as they had been in the Cleft, she had too many years, too long a voyage behind her. But she was not going to fail them.

"Rock all right," Kimber repeated the statement he had made so Joyfully a few minutes before. "The ledge slants a little, which is why she canted that way. But she'll stand. And," he did not need to draw their attention to the darkness closing in, "maybe it's some more luck at work again. With her nose pointing away from this breeze, she's less likely to come a cropper, even if it turns out to be a full-sized blow."

Dard held on to the rail of the ramp. The wind screamed around them, stirring up devils born of the powdery sand, which filled unwary eyes and any mouth that had the misfortune to be open. The dust had already driven Kordov inside, his precious dragon in a pair of forceps. He was more interested in that and Rogan's spiders than he now was in the ship.

"Full-sized blow?" drawled Rogan. "This has the makings of a hurricane if I'm any judge. And unless you fellas want to be buried alive in these marching sand dunes, you'd better run for cover. As long as you're sure we're not going to land bottom side up, I think it's time to adjourn."

Dard followed him up the ramp test in time to escape a miniature sandstorm through which the other two had to fight their way. There was a brushing-off party in the air lock, but, as they climbed back to the crew's quarters Dard could still taste grit in his mouth and hear it crunch under his feet.

Kordov was not to be found in the control cabin or bunk room when Kimber and the other two sat on the bunks and Dard dropped down cross-legged on the floor. The ship was vibrating under him. Could the wind have risen to that pitch already? It was Rogan who answered that.

"Like to see what's happening out there?" He got up and went into the control cabin.

Kimber and Dard got up to follow, but Cully shook his head.

"What you don't know, doesn't hurt you much," he remarked. "And I don't see anything exciting about a sandstorm."

It was true that when Rogan adjusted the visa-screen there was little for them to see. The storm had brought night and obscurity. With an exclamation of annoyance the techneer clicked off the viewer and they drifted back to find Cully asleep and Kordov climbing up to join them.

"Your 'spiders,'" he burst out as soon as he sighted Rogan, "are plants!"

"But they moved!" protested Dard. "They had legs."

Kordov shook his head. "Roots, not legs. And plants they are in spite of being mobile. Some form of aquatic fungi!"

"Toadstools with legs yet!" Rogan laughed. "Next, trees with arms, I suppose. What about the dragon—was he a flying cabbage?"

Kordov did not need any urging to discuss the dragon. "Poisonous reptile—and carnivorous. We shall have to beware of them. But it was full grown, we need not worry."

"About their coming in larger sizes?" asked the relaxed Kimber in a lazy voice. "Let us be thankful for small favors and hope that they do a lot of screeching when they go ahunting. But now—let us think about tomorrow."

"And tomorrow—and tomorrow—" Rogan repeated sleepily but Cully sat up thoroughly aroused.

"When do we wake up the others?" he wanted to know. "And are we going to stay right here?"

Kordov locked his fingers behind his head and leaned back against the wall of the cabin. "I will revive Dr. Skort—Carlee—in the morning. She can help me with the others. Do you intend to explore the immediate terrain then? We should decide soon whether to stay here or try to find semipermanent headquarters elsewhere."

"There is just one thing," said Kimber. "I can lift ship again, yes. But I can't guarantee another safe landing. The fuel—" he shrugged. "I don't know how long our voyage here lasted, but if we hadn't made this landfall when we did, we might not have been able to come in at all."

"So?" Kordov's lips shaped a soundless whistle. "Then we had better be very sure before we think of a move. What about taking out the 'sled'?"

"I'll break it out first thing tomorrow. That is, I will if this storm blows itself out by then. I don't propose to take that contraption up in a high wind—the bugs aren't out of it yet," Kimber retorted.

—✻—

"And how about food?" Cully asked. "Specifically here and now for us, and objectively for the rest when they wake up."

"Specifically," Kordov opened one of the storage cabinets and took out five small packages which he tossed around to the company. "Concentrates. But, you're right, supplies are not going to last forever. We shall not be able to awaken all our company until we are reasonably sure of food and shelter. But—we'll get Harmon out of storage and have him investigate the soil up river where the vegetation is so thick. The exploration party might also hunt."

"Not dragons, I hope," Rogan mumbled through a mouthful of the dry concentrate cake. "I have a distinct feeling dragons will not agree with my internal arrangements! Or traveling fungi either—"

For the first time Dard ventured to break in upon his elders. "Some fungi—mushrooms—are good." He had no desire to lunch off red spiders, but he knew what real hunger meant and if it were a question of being hungry or eating swimming mushrooms, he could close his eyes and eat.

"Just so," Kordov beamed at him. "And we shall investigate the food value of these. I shall get the hamsters out of cold storage and try the local products on them."

"So if they don't curl up and go blue in the face we feast," Kimber stretched and yawned. "Since we have quite a full day before us tomorrow, suppose we hit the sack now. Toss for the bunks and the acceleration pads." They solemnly tossed a coin—one with a hole in it which Kimber wore on a chain about his neck as a lucky piece.

Dard found that Fortune relegated him to one of the acceleration pads and did not care. To his mind the soft sponge of that support was infinitely more comfortable than any bed he could remember.

But when he curled up on it he found that he could not sleep. All the wonders of the new world whirled through his mind in a mad dance. And behind him lurked fear. Lui Skort had been a strong young man but he had not survived the passage. How many more of the boxes housed below in the star ship held death instead of life? What about Dessie?

Now that there was nothing to distract him, nothing he could give attention to, he remembered only her—the tight yellow braids sticking out at sharp angles, how she had been able to sit so quietly in the grass that birds and little animals accepted her as part of their world and had been entirely unafraid—how good and patient she had always been. Dessie!

He sat up. To lie there and sleep when Dessie might never wake to see this new land! He couldn't!

On his hands and knees Dard crawled out of the control cabin and between the bunks. Kimber was carted in a ball on one, but the other, which had fallen to Kordov, was empty. Dard started down the stair.

The deck below showed a patch of strong light and he could hear someone moving. He ventured to the door of the laboratory where he had helped to revive Cully and Rogan. The First Scientist was busy there, setting out instruments and bottles. He looked up as Dard's shadow fell into the room.

"What is it?"

"Dessie!" the boy blurted out "I've got to know about Dessie!"

"Ah, so? But it is for their own comfort and protection that our companions must continue to sleep until we are sure of food and shelter."

"I know that." But the desperation in Dard could not be so sensibly silenced. "But—isn't there any way at all of telling? I have to know about Dessie—I just have to!"

Tas Kordov pulled out his lower lip with thumb and forefinger and allowed it to snap back into place with a soft smacking sound.

"That is a thought, my boy. We can tell whether the mechanism has in any way failed. And perhaps—just perhaps we can have other assurances. I must open that particular compartment in the morning anyway to bring out Carlee Skort. Carlee—" his face puckered with the misery of an unhappy child. "And then I must be the one to tell her about Lui. That will be a very hard thing to do. Well, we do not escape the hard things in this life. Come along."

They went down five levels in the ship. Here the few lights were very dim, and the force of the wind against the hull could be more strongly felt. Kordov verified markings on the sealed door and at last released the fastening of a portal which came open with a faint sigh of displaced air. The chill of the room fed Dard's unease. He edged along after Kordov, between doubled racks of the coffin boxes to the final set. The First Scientist dropped to his knees and snapped on a hand torch to read dials.

"Dessie and Lara Skort are in this one together, they were so small they could share a compartment." The light in Kordov's hand flashed from one dial to the next, and the next. Then he smiled up at Dard.

"These are all as they should be, son. There has been no organic or chemical change inside since this was sealed. To my honest belief they are alive and well. Soon they will be out to run about as little girls should. They shall be free—as they never could have been on Terra. Do not worry. Your Dessie shall share this world with you!"

Dard had himself under control now and he was able to answer quite levelly:

"Thanks—thanks a lot, sir."

But Kordov had moved to another box and was reading more dials. He gave that case a slap of approbation as he straightened to his full height again.

"Carlee, too—we have been so very lucky."

—3—
STORM WRACK

"GOOD LORD!" The tone rather than the words of that horrified exclamation awoke Dard and brought him up on the acceleration pad. Kimber, Rogan, and Cutty were crowded together before the visa-screen. The hour might have been in the middle of the night, or late in the morning, for inside the ship day and night had no division. But on the screen it was day.

A gray sky was patched by ragged drifts of cloud. And as Dard leaned over the back of the pilot's seat, he saw what had so startled the others.

Where the day before there had stretched that smooth sweep of blue sand, forming a carpet clear to the base of the colorful cliffs, there was now only water, a sheet of it. Rogan set the viewer to turning so that they could see the flood completely surrounded the ship. Even the river had been swallowed up without any red stain left to betray its flow.

As the scene reached the seaside Rogan pushed the button which held it there. The beach was gone, it was the sea which had come in to enclose them.

"Surprise, surprise!" that was Rogan. "Do we now swim ashore?"

"I don't think that it is that deep," answered Kimber. "The water may come in this way during every hard storm. Switch over to the cliffs again, Les."

The picture whizzed with a dizzy speed back to the cliff. Kimber was right, already there was a stretch of sand showing at the base of that rock escarpment. The water was draining away.

They clattered down through the quiet ship, sending out the ramp so that they could venture to the water's swirl. A weak current swilled around the fins and the bare sand at the cliff grew wider as they watched.

The flood was not clear, and caught around the fins of the ship were huge loops of weed. Some variety of fish had been beached close to the foot of the ramp, and a scaled tail beat waves as the stranded monster fought for life. Other debris showed tantalizingly now and again as the water was sullenly sucked away from the sand.

"What the—!" Cully's start was near to a jump. "Over—over to the right! What is that?"

Something was venturing out on the still-wet sand, following the retreating line of the sea. But, what it was, none of them dared guess. Kimber ran back into the ship while the rest tried vainly to see it better. The color was queer, a pale green, hardly to be distinguished from the sea water as it scurried along on four thin legs. But the outline of its head!

"Here!" Kimber skidded down the ramp, keeping himself out of the sea by a quick grab for the rail. He carried a pair of field glasses. "Is it still there—yes, I see it!" He focused the lenses in the right direction. "Great guns!"

"What is it?" demanded Rogan, plainly doing his best to keep from snatching the glasses away from the pilot.

"Yeah." Cully, too, was shaken out of his usual calm, "pass those along, fella! We all want a look-see!"

Dard squinted, trying to make natural sight serve as well as the lenses Kimber was now passing to Rogan. At least the thing on the sand did not appear to be alarmed either by the ship or the men watching it. Maybe it would stay in sight until he, as the very junior member of the party, had the right to use the lenses too.

It stayed, digging in the wet sand, until Cully did pass the glasses. Dard adjusted them feverishly. Having met the fungi spiders and a flying dragon, he could hardly be surprised by the weird beast he saw now. Its pale green skin was entirely hairless, nor was that skin scaled— instead it resembled to a marked degree his own smooth flesh. The creature's head was pear-shaped with ears which were hardly more than holes and large eyes set far apart so that the range of vision was probably wider than that of any Terran animal. But that pear head ended in what could only be described as a broad, duck's bill or hard blackish substance. And just as Dard trained the glasses upon it, it folded its hind legs neatly under it, to sit up in a doglike stance and gaze mildly across the dwindling tongue of sea straight at the star ship. Sand clung to its bill and it absent-mindedly brushed that off with a foreleg.

"Duck-dog," Kimber named it. "Doesn't look dangerous, does it? I'll be—! Just look at that!"

"That" was a short procession of more duck-dogs

emerging from a dark crevice in the cliff to join the first. One of them, about three-quarters the size of the first, was the same pale green, but the three others were yellow, the exact yellow, Dard noted, of the strata in the cliff. In fact as they marched by a projection of that particular stratum, they faded from sight. Two of the yellow beasts were full grown but the third was very small And halfway along the path it sat down, refusing to move on until one of the larger animals returned to butt it ahead.

"Family party," suggested Dard, not daring to hold the glasses away from Kimber's impatient reach any longer.

"But harmless," the pilot suggested for the second time. "Do you suppose they'd let us near them? The water's gone down a lot."

"Nothing like trying. Just let Jorge be ready with that ray gun, then if they do turn out to be first-class menaces, we'll be prepared." The communications techneer lowered himself cautiously into the flood, which was at knee level.

He detoured to avoid the floating weed and paused when he reached the fish still beating the air with a frenzied tail. Dard caught up with him at that point.

Save for a curiously flattened head and a huge, paunchy middle, the stranded fish was the first living thing they had seen here which did resemble a Terran product. It was a good five feet long and displayed murderous teeth. The powerful tail beat the receding water into froth but it was beyond hope of escape. Dard spoke impulsively:

"Can't—can't you shoot it? It won't be able to get away and I think it knows that."

"Unhuh." That was Cully and as usual he wasted no words. He snapped the ray at that writhing head. With a last convulsion the fish flopped completely out of the water, to float with its huge belly up when it fell back. "Maybe breakfast?" Rogan asked. "Looks a little bit like a tuna—might even taste like one. We'll let Kordov get it and see if it's fit for us to bury the teeth in. I could do with a steak—maybe two of them! Hello—the fireworks didn't send our duck-dogs running. I'd say they were enjoying the show."

Rogan was right The duck-dog family party sat in a line along the crest of the fast drying sand ridge, appreciably closer to the ship, their attention all for the men and the now limp fish.

But as Dard tentatively splashed another step in the direction of that sand bank, the yellow members of the clan retreated, one of them nudging the smallest one in front of it. The green ones continued to stand their ground, the half-grown one running along the water's edge hissing. Dard stopped, the flood swishing about his legs.

Cully looped a cord about the tail of the dead fish and fastened it to the ramp rail. Perhaps overcome by the sight of so much meat the smallest duck-dog gave a tiny whimpering cry and ran between the legs of its guardian to the water. Resignedly the larger yellow beast followed the cub, turning over the loose sand with large blunt claws of a forepaw to dig out a squirming red creature which the baby pounced upon to swallow greedily. But the green boss of the party hissed angrily at the hunter and sent both scuttling back.

Then he withdrew also, with his head turned toward the men, facing the danger represented by the Terrans bravely, hissing a stern warning. When the last of the smaller duck-dogs had dodged into the break in the cliff, he disappeared there also leaving only scuffed tracks in the sand to mark their trail. But Dard sighted the tip of a dark bill still protruding from the crack.

"It's still watching us."

"Wary," mused the pilot. "Which suggests that it has enemies—enemies which may look like us. But it's curious, too. If we ignore it—maybe"

He was interrupted by a shout from the ship. Kordov had come out on the ramp and was waving vigorously to the explorers. As the others sloshed back he pulled on the cord, reeling in the fish.

"What's your verdict?" Rogan wanted to know when they joined him bending over their capture. "Do we eat that, or don't we?"

"Give me but a few minutes and some aid in the laboratory and I shall have an answer to that. But this is close to Terran life. So it may be edible. And what were you watching by the cliffs—more dragons?"

"Just passing the time of day with another breakfasting party," Rogan told him, and went on to explain about the duck-dogs.

It was worth waiting for Kordov's verdict, Dard thought later, as he savored the fine white flakes of meat, grilled under Kordov's supervision, and portioned out to the hungry and none-too-patient crew.

"At least we can chalk old pot-belly up on our bill of fare," observed Rogan.

"But finding this one may only be a fluke. It's a deep-water fish, and we won't have storms to drive such ashore every day," Kimber pointed out.

He explored his lips with his tongue and then studied the empty plastic plate he held wistfully. "We can, however, look around for another stranded one."

Cully unfolded long legs. "We'll take out the sled now?"

"The wind has died down—I'd say it was safe. And," the pilot turned to Kordov, "how about rousing Santee and Harmon—we're going to need them."

The First Scientist agreed. "But first Carlee, as a doctor. And then we shall bring out the others. You are leaving soon?"

"We'll tell you before we go. And we don't intend to go far. Maybe a turn into that valley up ahead, and then along the shore line for a mile or so. We may have landed in a wilderness—indications point to that—but I want to be sure."

Until a sun breaking through the clouds overhead said it was noon they were hard at work. The sled, Dard discovered, was just what its name implied, a flat vehicle possessing two seats each wide enough for two passengers, with a space behind for supplies. He helped to assemble the larger sections while Kimber and Cully sweated and swore over the business of installing the engine.

It was a flying craft Dard realized, but totally unlike a 'copter or rocket, and he did not see what would make it air borne without blades or tubes. When he said as much to Rogan the techneer leaned back against a convenient sand dune to combine rest and explanation.

"I can't tell you how it works, kid. The principle's something really new. They whipped that engine together during the last months we were in the Cleft. But it's some sort of anti-gravity. Takes you up and keeps you there until you shut it off. Broadcasts a beam which sends you along by pushing against the earth. If they had had the time they might have powered the ship with it But there was only this one experimental sled built and we had to depend upon power we knew more about. How about it, Sim? Getting her together?"

The pilot smiled through a streak of grease which turned his brown skin black.

"Tighten that one bolt, Cully," he pointed out the necessary adjustment, "and, she's ready to lift! Or at least she should be. We'll try her."

He boarded the shallow craft and settled himself behind the controls, buckling a safety belt around his hips before he triggered the motor. The sled zoomed straight up with a speed which sent the spectators sprawling and tore an exclamation from the pilot. Then, under Kimber's expert hand, it leveled off and swung in a wide circle about the star ship. Finishing off the test flight with a figure eight, Kimber brought the sled back to a slow and studied landing on the now dry sand at the foot of the ramp.

"Bravo!"

That encouraging cheer came from the open hatch. Kordov beamed down at them and with him, one hand on the rail, her head lifted so that the sun made a red-glory of the braids wreathing it, was a woman. Dard stared up at her with no thought of rudeness. This was the Carlee who had taken care of Dessie.

But she was younger than he had expected, younger and somehow fragile. There were dark shadows beneath her eyes, and when she smiled at them, it was with a patient acceptance which hurt. Kimber broke the silence as she joined the party below.

"What do you think, Carlee?" he asked matter-of-factly, as if they had parted only the hour before and no tragedy lay between. "Would you trust yourself to this crazy flyer?"

"With the right pilot at the controls, yes." And then looking at each one she spoke their names slowly as if reassuring herself that they were really there. "Les Rogan, Jorge Cully and—" She reached Dard, hesitated, before her smile brightened—"why, you must be Dessie's Dard, Dard Nordis! Oh, this is good—so good—" She looked beyond the men at the cliffs, the sea, the blue-green sky arching over them.

"Now—before you start off, explorers," Kordov announced, "there is food to be eaten."

The food was fish again, together with quarter portions of the concentrate cakes and some capsules Kordov insisted they take. When they were finished the First Scientist turned to Kimber.

"Now that you have that sky-buggy of yours put together you will be off?"

"Yes. There are four, maybe five hours of daylight left. I think that a survey from the air would show us more in that length of time than a trip on foot"

"You say 'us.' Whom do you take with you?" asked Carlee.

"Rogan—he's had experience on Venus. And—"

Dard held his tongue. He could not beg to go. Kimber would choose Cully, of course. The pilot didn't want a green hand. He was so sure of that choice that he could hardly believe it when he heard Kimber say:

"And the kid—he's light weight. We don't want to overload if we haul back game or specimens, too. Cully's a crack shot and I'll feel safer to leave him on guard here."

"Good enough!" Kordov agreed. "Just do not voyage too far, and do not fall off that silly ship of yours—to land on your heads. We have no time to waste patching up explorers who do not know enough to keep themselves right side up!"

Thus Dard found himself sharing the pilot's seat on the sled with Rogan crawling in behind. Kimber insisted that they buckle their safety belts under his supervision and he tested their fastenings before they took off. The rise of the light craft was not so abrupt as the first time and Kimber did not try to get much above the level of the cliff tops. They skimmed along only a few feet above the rock as they flashed north, the curving shoreline as their guide. From this height he had a good view to the west, seeing most of the wide valley through which the red river flowed. The low vegetation they sighted from the ship thickened into clumps of good-sized trees. And among these were flying things which did not appear to be dragons.

Along the edge of the sea the cliff rose in an unbroken perpendicular wall. Apparently the star ship had earthed in the only opening in it for from the elevation of the sled they could sight nothing but that barrier of brilliantly hued stone dividing vegetation and low land from the beating sea.

Rogan cried out and a moment later Dard, too, cringed as a ray of light struck painfully into his eyes. It flashed up from sea level, as if a mirror had been used to direct the sunlight straight at them. Kimber brought the sled around and ventured out over the water in a sweep designed to bring them to the source of that light.

There was a scrap of beach, a few feet of sand across which the weed, driven up by the storm, lay. Kimber, with infinite caution, maneuvered to set them down there.

When the sled jolted to earth its occupants stared in open amazement at the source of the mirrored ray.

Protruding from the face of the cliff, as if from a pocket or hollow especially fashioned to contain it, was a coneshaped section of metal. And not metal in a crude, un-worked state, but of a finely fashioned and refined alloy!

Dard split a fingernail on the buckle which fastened his belt in his haste to get to the find. But Kimber was already halfway across the sand before he gained his feet. The three, not quite daring to touch, studied the peculiar object. Kimber squatted down to peer under it There was a thin ring of similar metal encircling the widest part of the cone, as if it rested within a tube.

"A—bullet in a rifle barrel!" Rogan found a comparison which was none too reassuring. "This a shell?"

"I don't think so." Kimber pulled gently at the tip. "Let's see if we can work it out." From the sled he brought an assortment of tools.

"Take it easy," Rogan eyed these preparations askance. "If it is an explosive, and we do the wrong thing—we're apt to finish up in pieces."

"It isn't a shell," Kimber repeated stubbornly. "And it's been here a long time. See that?" He pointed to fresh scars on the cliff face. "That's a recent break. Maybe the storm tore that down and uncovered this. Now—a little probing."

They worked gingerly at first and then, when nothing happened, with more confidence—until they had it out far enough to see that the cone was only the tip of a long cylinder. Finally they hooked a chain to it and used the power of the sled to draw it completely free of the tube.

Six feet long, it lay half in, half out of the water, a sealed opening showing midway in its length. Kimber knelt down before the tube and flashed his hand-light inside. As far as they could see ran a tunnel lined with seamless metal.

"What in the name of Space is it, anyway?" Rogan wondered.

"Some form of transportation, I would say." Kimber still held the light inside as if by wishing alone he could deduce the destination of their discovery.

Rogan prodded the cylinder with his foot and it rolled slightly. The techneer stooped and tagged at the end in the sand. To his astonishment he was able to lift it several inches above the beach.

"A whole lot lighter than you'd think! I believe we could take it back on the sled!"

"Hmm . . ." Kimber took Rogan's place and hoisted. "We might at that. No harm in trying."

The three of them manhandled the cylinder on board the sled and lashed it into place—though both ends projected over the sides of the craft.

Kimber was doubly careful in his take-off. He brought them up with much room to spare away from the cliff side and circled back toward the valley.

"This answers one question," Rogan leaned forward. "We aren't the first intelligent life here."

"Yes." the pilot added nothing to that bare assent He was intent on reaching the star ship.

Dard squirmed in his seat. He did not need to turn to see that smooth piece of metal, he could feel its presence—and what its presence meant to all of them.

Only intelligence, a high standard of intelligence could have fashioned it. And where was that intelligent life now? Watching and waiting for the Terrans to make the first fatal move?

⊸4⊷
THOSE OTHERS!

"EASY DOES IT NOW." Cully laid down the chisel he had been using delicately and applied pressure with the flat of his hand.

The others weren't really breathing down his neck. But they did struggle against the curiosity which made them crowd about the engineer as he worked to open the cylinder.

"It's too light for an explosive," Rogan repeated for about the fiftieth time since they had unloaded their find before the star ship.

At a good vantage point up on the ramp Carlee Skort and Trade Harmon sat together while the men below tried to hand Cully tools he didn't need and generally got in each other's way. But now they had come to the last moment of suspense. After more than an hour's work the engineer had been able to force open the small seal hatch.

Cully bumped heads with Kimber and Kordov as he flashed a torch beam into the interior. Then, with infinite care, he began to hand out to eager assistants a series of boxes, small round containers and a larger, ornamented chest All these were fashioned of the same lightweight alloy as the large carrier and they appeared unmarked by time.

"Cargo carrier," Kimber decided. "What can be in these?" He held one of the smallest boxes to his ear and shook it cautiously, but there was no answering rattle.

Kordov picked up the chest, examining its fastening carefully. At last he shook his head and brought out a pocket knife, working the blade into the crevice between lid and side, using it to lever up the cover.

Soft creamy stuff puffed up as the pressure of the lid was removed, fluffing over the rim. The First Scientist plucked it carefully away in strips. As the late afternoon sun struck full on the contents which had been protected by that packing, there was a concerted gasp from the Terrans.

"What are they?" someone demanded.

Kordov picked up a fine intwisted strand, dangling its length in the light.

"Opals?" he suggested. "No, these are too hard, cut in facets. Diamonds—? I don't think so. I confess I have never seen anything like them before." "A world's ransom," Dard did not know he had spoken aloud. The wild beauty swinging from Kordov's hand drew him as no man-fashioned thing had done before.

"Any more in there?" asked Kimber. "That's a large box to hold only one item."

"We shall see. Girls," Kordov held out the rope of strange Jewels to the two women, "hang on to that."

Another layer of the packing was pulled out to display

a pair of bracelets. This time red stones which Santee identified.

"Them's rubies! I prospected in the Lunar mountains and found some Just like 'em. Good color. What else you got there, Tas?"

A third layer of packing led to the last and greatest wonder of all—a belt, five inches wide, with a clasp so set in gems as to be just an oval glitter—the belt itself fashioned of rows of tiny crystalline chains.

Trade Harmon tried to clasp it about her waist to discover it would not meet by inches. Nor was Carlee able to wear it either.

"Must have been mighty slim, the girl what wore that!" Harmon commented.

"Maybe she wasn't a girl at all," Carlee said.

And there was something daunting in that thought Carlee had been the first to put into words their lurking fear, that those who had packed the carrier had been nonhuman.

"Well, bracelets argue arms," Rogan pointed out "And that necklace went around a neck. A belt suggests a waist—even if it is smaller than yours, girls. I think we can believe that the lady those were meant for wasn't too far removed from our norm."

Santee pawed another box away from the pile. "Let's see the rest."

The boxes were sealed with a strip of softer metal which had to be peeled from around the edge. And the first three they forced contained unidentifiable contents. Two held packages of dried twigs and leaves, the third vials filled with various powders and a dark scum which might have been the remains of liquid. These were turned over to Kordov for further investigation.

Of the remaining boxes three were larger and heavier. Dard broke the end of the sealing strip on one and rolled it away. Under the lid was a square of coarse woven stuff folded over several times to serve as protective padding. Since this was like the jewel case the others stopped their own delving and gathered around as he pulled the stuff loose. What he found beneath was almost as precious in its way as the gems.

He dared not put his fingers on it, but worked it out of the container gently by the end of the metal rod on which it was wound in a bolt. For here was a length of fabric. But none of them—not even those who could remember the wonders of the pre-Burn cities—had ever seen any thing such as this. It was opalescent, fiery color rippled along every crease and fold as Dard turned it around in the sunlight. It might have been spun from the substance of those same jewels which formed the necklace.

Carlee almost snatched it from him and Trade Harmon inserted a timid finger under the edge.

"It's a veil!" she cried "How wonderful!"

"Open the rest of those!" Carlee pointed to the two similar boxes, "Maybe there's more of this."

There was more fabric, not so sheer and not opalescent, but woven of changing colors in delicate subtle shades the Terrans could not put names to. Inspired by this find they plunged into a frenzy of opening until Kordov called them to order.

"These," he indicated the wealth from the plundered boxes, "can't be anything but luxury goods, luxury goods of a civilization far more advanced than ours. I'm inclined to believe that this was a shipment which never reached its destination."

"That tube we found the carrier in," mused Kimber. "Suppose they shot such containers through tubes for long distances. Even across the sea. We didn't transport goods that way, but we can't judge this world by Terra. And they have no high tides here."

"Tas, Sim," Carlee turned one of the bracelets around in hands which bore the scars of the hardworking Cleft life, "could they—are they still here? Those Others—?"

Kimber got to his feet, brushing the sand from his breeches.

"That's what we'll have to find out—and soon!" He squinted at the sun. "Too late to do anything more today. But tomorrow—"

"Hey!" Rogan balanced on his palm a tiny roll of black staff he had Just pried out of a pencil-slim container. "I think that this is some kind of microfilm. Maybe we can check on that—if we can rig up a viewer which will take it"

Kordov was instantly alert "How many of those things in there?"

Rogan took them one at a time from the box he had opened. "I see twenty."

"Can you rig a viewer?" was Kordov's next question.

The techneer shrugged. "I can try. But I'll have to get at machines we packed in the bottom storeroom—and that will take some doing."

"And"—Cully had been poking in the interior of the now empty carrier—"there's an engine in here—must have supplied the motive power. I'd like to dig it out and see what makes it tick."

Kimber ran his hands over the tight cap of his hair. "And you'll need a machine shop to do that in, I suppose?" He was very close to sarcasm. "There's the problem of those still in the ship—what will we do?"

Carlee broke in. "You haven't found any signs of civilization yet—except this. And you don't know how long this could have lain where you discovered it We can't hold off settlement until we are sure. The cities, or centers of civilization—if there are any—may be hundreds of miles away. Suppose a space ship had landed on Terra in a center section of the Canadian northwest, on the steppes of Central Asia, or in the middle of Australia—any thinly populated district It would have been months, perhaps years, before its arrival became known—especially since Pax forbade travel There may exist a similar situation here. Our landing may go undiscovered for a long time— if we do share this world."

"And that, you know," Kordov added, "is common sense. Let us explore the valley—if it is promising, make a place there for our people. But at the same time an exploring team can operate to map the district. Only, let us not make contact with any race we find, until we know its attitude."

"Or what manner of creature," Carlee said softly to herself.

"What manner of creature" Dard had caught that. Carlee most likely believed that the intelligence which might share this world was nonhuman. Man's old fear of the unknown, the not-understood, would again haunt them. This was an alien world, could they ever make it home?

"These—these are beautiful!" Trude Harmon had knelt beside him in the sand to see the small carvings he was mechanically unwrapping.

The one he held represented an animal which was a weird cross between horse and deer—possessing flowing mane, tail and horns. Presented as rearing, with snorting nostrils, it was a miniature of savage fury. Tiny gems were set in the eye sockets and the hooves were plated with a contrasting metal. Some master-craftsman had endowed it with life.

"All these things—they are so wonderful!"

"They loved beauty," Dard answered her. "But I think that these"—he picked up a second carving, representing quite a different creature—a manikin with webbed feet, a monkey face and hands lacking a thumb—"are all pieces to be used in a game. See; here's another, horned horse, but made of a different color, and another webfooted monkey. Chessmen?"

"And a little tree!" She freed a third piece from its wrappings. "A tree of golden apples!"

True enough, on the branches of the cone shaped tree there were round gems of a glowing yellow. Golden apples! That story Lars used to tell Dessie about the apples of the sun!

"Huh!" Harmon squatted down by his wife to see what held her attention. "Apples? What's that about apples, Trude?"

She held out her hand with the small tree standing on its flattened palm. "Golden apples! See, Tim?"

"Looks more like some kind of a pine to me." But he took the tree gently. "Fruit—that's what those are supposed to be all right." His eyes went past the star ship to the open mouth of the valley where the blue-green of growing things beckoned. "Might find us a pine growin' apples at that, Trude. After them there flyin' snakes, and floatin' spider-plants, and them green and yellow duck-dogs what keep peekin' at us from holes yonder—well, I can believe that we're gonna pick us apples offa pine trees, too. Only we'd better get about the business of goin' to hunt them trees pretty soon."

The business of hunting their future settlement began the next morning. Somber with Rogan and Santee took off in the sled to make a circuit of the inner valley. When they signaled that they viewed nothing disturbing there, a second exploring party set off on foot. Cully, Harmon and Dard, with packets of supplies, stun rifles and water-filled canteens progressed slowly up the river.

At the entrance to the inner valley the sand was broken by patches of soil shading from red-yellow to a dark brown. In this earth grew tufts and clumps of thin-bladed, very tough-stemmed grass which in its turn gave way to small bushes, clothed with ragged blue-green leaves.

All three of the explorers stopped short as the grass before them swayed, masking the progress of some living thing. Dard was the first to move forward with his silent woodsman's tread. Cautiously he parted the tall stalks to see below him a real path, as well marked as a Terran game trail, but in miniature. As the swaying still continued he stood waiting, hardly daring to breathe.

Around the roots of a low bush a small red-brown

head, almost indistinguishable from the bare earth of the trail, showed. Dard waited. With a hop the traveler came into plain sight.

Close to the size of a Terran rat it hopped on large, overdeveloped hind legs, between which bobbed a fluff of tail. Small handlike paws hung down across fits darker belly fur. The ears were large, fan shaped, and fringed with the same fluff as the tail. Black buttons of eyes showed neither pupil nor iris, and a rounded muzzle ended in a rodent's prominent teeth. But Dard did not have long to catalogue such physical points, It sighted him. Then it gave a wild bound, making an about-face turn while in the air—disappearing in a second. Dard was left to pick up from the center of the trail the object it had just dropped in its flight.

"Rabbit?" Harmon wondered, "or squirrel or rat? How're we gonna know? What did that critter drop, boy?"

Dard held a pod about three inches long, dark blue and shiny. He surrendered it to Harmon who slit the outer covering with thumbnail and shook out a dozen dark-blue seeds.

"Pears, beans, wheat?" Harmon's bewilderment showed signs of irritation. "It grows, ripens this way, and it may be good to eat. But," he turned to his companions and ended with an explosive, "how're we gonna know?"

"Take 'em back and try 'em on the hamsters,'" Cully returned laconically. "But that hopper sure could go, couldn't he?" Thus he unconsciously christened the third type of fauna they had discovered in the new world.

Harmon stowed seeds and pod away in a zipper closed pocket, before they moved on through grass which arose waist high about them. Here and there in it they spotted more of the seed pods.

In fact shortly, the pod-headed plants were so thick around them that they might have been swishing through a field of ripened grain. Harmon broke silences:

"This remind you of anything?"

They regarded the expanse of blue doubtfully and shook their heads.

"Well, it does me. This here looks jus' like a wheatfield all ready t' be reaped! I tell you I'm athinkin' we're walkin' over somebody's farm!"

"But there's no fences," protested Dard.

"No, but you take a farm that's not been touched for a good long time—this stuff coulda jus' kept seedin' itself and spread out a lot I gotta feelin' this is part of a farm!"

With that Harmon took the lead, cutting across the narrowest section of the ripe crop to a line of bushes. Now that his attention had been stimulated by Harmon's theory Dard thought that that clump of taller vegetation was strung out as if it might provide a barrier for the grain, a fence for the field.

They worked their way around this line of brush to discover Harmon's instinct right For there was no disguising the artificiality of the large dome flanked by several smaller ones which stood surmounted and surrounded by rank vines, tall grass and long unpruned shrubbery.

But it was not those domes which held the explorers' attention. A constant murmur of sound and a flash of flying things drew them to a tree standing in what once must have been the front yard—if Those Others cultivated front yards.

"The golden apples!" Dard identified the tree from the carved piece he had seen the night before.

Its symmetrical cone shape of blue-green provided the right background for the yellow globes which dragged down branches with their weight. And the air and grass about the tree were alive with feasters.

The Terrans watched the wheeling birds—or were they oversized butterflies?—that settled and squabbled for a chance to sink beaks into those ripened orbs. While, on the ground, there was a steady coming and going of hoppers harvesting the soft fallen fruit And from that scene of activity the breeze wafted a scent which set the watchers' mouths watering—semi-intoxicating with its promise of juicy delights.

As the men advanced, the busy feeders displayed no signs of alarm. One hopper ran straight between Cully's feet, a quarter section of dripping fruit clasped in its arms. And a bird-butterfly skimmed Dard's head on its way to the banquet.

"Wel—for—!" Cully caught himself in midstride to avoid stepping on a furry red-brown mass. He picked up one of the hoppers in a completely comatose state. Harmon gave a bark of laughter.

"Dead drunk." he commented. "Seen chickens—pigs, too—get that way on cider leavin's. Lookit here—this bird can't fly straight neither!"

He was right. A lavender creature, whose wings were banded with pale green and gray, flapped an erratic course to a nearby bush and clung there as if it did not trust its powers for a farther flight.

Cully laid down the limp hopper and picked one of the

golden apples. It snapped away easily, and he held it out for their closer examination. The skin was firm over the pulp, and radiating out from the stem were tiny rosy freckles. And the enticing scent was a temptation hard to withstand. Dard wanted to snatch the fruit from the engineer, to sink his teeth in that smooth skin and prove to himself that it tasted as good as it smelled.

"Pity we ain't got a hamster with us to try it on. But we can take some back. Iffen they're good," Harmon swallowed visibly, "we can have us some real eatin! Needn't let the critters take 'em all. The fella what lived here. I bet he set a store by them there things. Golden apples, yeah, that's jus' what they be. But they ain't gonna run away, and me, I'd kinda like to see the house and barns."

The house and barns, if those were the correct designations for the domes, were half buried in twisting vines and rank growth. When they broke their way through to what must have been the front door of the largest dome, Gully let out his breath in a low whistle.

"Fight here. This door was smashed in from the outside."

Dard, accustomed to the violence of the raiding parties of Pax, noted the broken scraps of metal on the portal and agreed. They edged into a scene of desolation. The place had been looted long ago, tough grass grew through a crack in the wall, and the litter underfoot went to powder when their boots touched it Dard picked up a shred of golden glass which held a fairy tracery of white pattern. But there was nothing whole left.

"Raiding party, all right," Harmon agreed, conditioned by his Terran past. "Could be that they had them some

Peacemen here too. But it was a long time ago. We'd better let Kordov and the brains prospect around in here. Maybe they can learn what really happened. Wonder if the barn took a beatin'."

But what they did discover in the larger of the two remaining domes brought a steady stream of curses from Harmon and made Dard's skin crawl with its suggestion of wanton and horrible rapine. A line of white skeletons lay along the wall, each in what seemed a stall Harmon tried to pick up an oddly shaped skull which went to dust in his fingers.

"Left 'em to die of thirst, and starvation!" gritted the farmer. "Knocked off the people and jus' left the rest. They—they were worse'n Peacemen—them what did this!"

"And they must have been the winners, too," observed Cully. "Not too pleasant to think about"

All three started at a shout, and Dard swung his stun rifle around at the entrance of that tragic barn. What if "they" were returning? Then he forced imagination under control. This horror had occurred years ago—its perpetrators were long since dead. But had they left descendants—with the same characteristics?

Kimber came into the dome. "What're you doing in here?" he wanted to know. "We've been watching you from the sled. What—what in blue blazes is this?"

"Warning left by some very nasty people," Dard spoke up. "This farm was raided and whoever did it left the animals penned up to starve to death!"

Kimber walked slowly along that pitiful line of bones. His face was very sober indeed.

"It's been a long time since this happened." It appeared to Dard that the pilot was reassuring himself by that statement.

"Yeah," Harmon agreed. "A good long time. And they ain't bin back since. Guess we can move down here and take over, Sim. This was a good farm once, no reason why it can't be one agin."

— 5 —
WAR RUIN

FOR THE NEXT five days they were well occupied. An extensive exploration of the inner valley, on foot and in the air, revealed no other evidences of the former civilization.— And the Terrans decided against inhabiting the farm. About those domes there clung the shreds of ancient fear and disaster, and Dard was not the only one to feel uneasy within their walls.

The tree of golden apples was one of their best finds. The hamsters relished the fruit and, so encouraged, the humans raided along with the valley's furred and feathered inhabitants, because the globes were as good as they looked and smelled—though their intoxicating effect did not hold with the Terrans. The grain also proved to be useful, and Harmon took the risk of rousing one of the two heifer calves, carried in the ship, and feeding it in the forsaken fields where it lived and grew fat.

On the other hand a bright green berry with a purplish blush was almost fatal to a hamster and had to be shunned by the Terrans, although the hoppers and the birds gorged upon it.

Quarters were established, not outside the cliffs which walled the valley, but within them. The second day's exploration had located a cave which led in turn to an inner system of galleries, through one of which the rivers wove a way. Habituated to such a dwelling from their years in the Cleft, they seized upon this discovery eagerly. More of the adult passengers were awakened and put to work assembling machines, laboring to make the caves into a new home which could not be easily detected. For the threat kept before them by the ruined farm was always in their minds.

Three more bodies were carried from the star ship to be interred beside Lui Skort, still encased in the boxes which had held them during the voyage. But Kordov continued to insist that they had been very lucky. There were fifteen men at work now, and ten women added their strength to harvesting the strange grain and making habitable the cave dwelling.

"Blast it!" Kimber drew out of the motor section of the sled and made a grab at thin air.

"What's the matter?" Dard began. Then he caught sight of what had brought the pilot to the exploding point.

A hopper bounded toward the tall grass, something shiny between its front paws. Stealing again! Dard dived, and his fingers closed about the small, frantically kicking body, while a squeak which approached a scream rent the quiet of their outdoor workshop. The boy freed his captive to nurse a bitten hand, but the hopper had also dropped the bolt it hand stolen. Now it retired empty pawed into the bushes uttering impolite remarks concerning Dard's destination and ancestry.

"Better go and have that bite looked after," Kimber ordered with resignation as he accepted the rescued bolt "I don't know what we are going to do about those little beasts. They'd carry off everything they could lug if we didn't watch them all the time. Regular pack rats."

Dard cradled the bitten hand in the other. "I'd like to find one of their burrows, or nests, or whatever they build to keep their loot in. It should be a regular curiosity shop."

"If any one can—you will," Cully spoke from the cylinder he was dismantling. "Ever notice, Sim," he continued, "how this kid gets around? I'll wager he could walk through the grain field and not make a sound or leave a trail another could follow. How'd you ever learn that useful trick, fella?"

Dard was sober. "The hard way, living as an outlaw. You know, those hoppers are awful pests, but I can't help admiring them."

Kimber snorted. "Why? Because they know what they want and go after it? They are single-minded aren't they? Only I wish they were a little more timid. They should be more like the duck-dogs, willing to watch us, but keeping their distance. Cut along, kid, and get that finger seen to right away. Working hours aren't over yet."

Dard traced Carlee Skort to where she was busy fitting up the small dispensary, a niche in the wall of the second cave, and had his bite sterilized and bandaged with plasta-skin.

"Hoppers!" She shook her head. "I don't know what

we're going to do to discourage them. They stole Trade's little paring knife yesterday and three spools of thread."

He could understand her dismay over these losses. Little things, yes—but articles which could not be replaced.

"Luckily they appear to be afraid to come into the caves. So far we haven't caught any of them inside. But they are the most persistent and accomplished thieves I have ever seen. Dard, when you go out, stop in the kitchen and pick up a lunch for your working crew. Trude should have the packets made up by now."

He obediently made his way past work gangs into the other small cave room where Trude Harmon with an assistant was setting out stacks of plastic containers. The rich scent which filled the air tickled Dard's nose and made him very aware of hunger. It had been hours and hours since breakfast!

"Oh, it's you," Trude greeted him. "How many in your gang?"

"Three."

Her lips moved, counting silently, as she apportioned the containers and set them in a carrier.

"Mind you bring those back. And don't, don't you dare leave them where any hoppers can put paw on them!"

"No, ma'am. Something sure smells good."

She smiled proudly. "Those golden apples. We stewed some up into a kind of pudding. Just you wait 'til you taste it, young man. Which reminds me—where is that queer leaf, Petra?"

The dark-haired girl who had been stirring the largest pot on the stove pulled a glossy green leaf from one of her

pockets. It was an almost perfect triangle in shape—
green, threaded by bright red and yellow veins. "Ever see
one like that before, Dard?" Trade asked. He took it and
examined it curiously before he answered with a shake of
his head.

"Pinch it and give a sniff!" Trude suggested. He did
and the good odor of cooking was nullified by another
aromatic, clean fragrance, a mixture of herb and flower—
of all the pleasant scents he had ever known.

"You can rub it on skin or hair and the scent lingers,"
Petra told him eagerly.

"And you'll never guess where we got that one," Trude
broke in. "Tell him."

"I saw a hopper carrying it out in the grain field when
I was gleaning yesterday. I thought it had been stealing
from our food and chased it Then when it wriggled
through a hole in the brush fence it dropped the leaf. I
picked it up and at first we thought it might be good to eat
because the hopper wanted it But it is just nice perfume."

"Sure, and if you want to get on the good side of the
kitchen detail," Trade twinkled at him, "you just find out
where you can get about a peck of those, Dard. We ain't got
the smell of that ship off us yet—nasty chemicals. And we'd
admire a chance to get some perfume. You do a little looking around when you're off on this jaunt of yours and see
what you can find us. Now—clear out. Take your lunch."

Dard gave the leaf back to Petra and picked up the
carrier. But he went out of the kitchen puzzled. What had
Trade meant by "this jaunt of yours?" As far as he knew he
was not intending to leave the valley. Had some other
plans been made?

— ✿ —

He started back to Kimber, determined to have an explanation.

"Lunch, huh?" Cully crawled out from under the cylinder as Dard sat the carrier on the ground.

The engineer wiped his hands on the grass and then on a piece of waste. "What do they have for us this time?"

"Stew of apples for one thing," Dard returned impatiently. "Listen, Kimber, Mrs. Harmon said something about my going on an expedition."

Sim Kimber pried the lid off a container of stew and poked into the depths of the savory mixture before he replied.

"We have to earn our keep, kid. And not being specialists in anything but woodcraft and transportation, it's up to us to do what we can along those lines. You knew the woods and mountains back on earth, and you have a feeling for animals. So Kordov assigned you to the exploration department."

Dard sat very still, afraid to answer, afraid to burst out with the wild exultation which surged in him now. He had tried, tried so hard these past few days to follow Harmon's overpowering interest in the land, to be another, if unskilled, pair of hands in the work about the cave. But the machines they were assembling at top speed were totally unknown to him. The men who worked on them lapsed into a jargon of functions he knew nothing about, until it seemed that they jabbered a foreign tongue.

For so long he had been responsible for others—for Lars and Dessie, for their food, their shelter, even their safety. And now he was not even responsible for himself

He was beginning to feel useless, for here he knew so little that was of any account.

All his training had been slanted toward keeping alive, at a minimum level of existence, in a hostile world. With that pressure removed he believed he had nothing to offer the colonists.

What he had dreamed and longed to do was to leave this compact group where he was the outsider, to go on into this new world, searching out its wonders, whether that meant trailing a hopper to its mysterious lair or flying above the cliffs into the unknown country beyond. Exploration was what he wanted, wanted so badly that sometimes just thinking about it hurt.

And here was Kimber offering him that very thing! Dard could not say anything. But maybe his eyes, his rapturous face answered for him, as the pilot glanced up, met Dard's wide happy eyes, and quickly looked away. When the boy's feelings were under control again, and he was able to say, in what he believed was a level and unmoved voice: "But what are you planning?"

"Go up and over." It was Cully who answered that before Kimber could swallow his mouthful of stew. "We load up this old bus," the engineer patted the sled affectionately, "and take off to see what lies on the other side of the cliffs. Mainly to discover whether we need expect any visitors."

"We—who?"

Kimber named those who would share in the adventure. "I'll pilot. Cully goes along to keep the sled ticking. And Santee is to provide the strong right arm."

"To fight—?" But Dard didn't complete that question before Kimber had an answer.

"Killing," he said, staring thoughtfully down at the full spoon he balanced on its way to his mouth, "is not on the program if we can help it Even such pests as—Cully! Behind you!"

The engineer slowed around just in time to snatch up a small wrench and so baffle the furry thief that tried to seize it.

"Even those pests are safe from us," Kimber continued before he added to the swearing engineer, "Why don't you sit on everything, Jorge? That's what I am doing." He moved to let them see that all the smaller tools he had been using were now covered by his body. "It may not be comfortable, but they'll still be here when I need them!"

"No," he returned to his earlier theme, "we're not going to kill anything if we can help it. To save our lives— for food, if it is absolutely necessary. But not for sport—or because we are unsure!" His lips twisted in a sneer. "Sport! The greatest sport of all is the hunting of man! As man finally discovered, having terrorized all of the rest of the living earth. Our species killed wantonly—now we have a second choice and chance. Maybe we can be saner this time. So—Santee is a crack shot—but that does not mean he is going to use the rifle."

Dard had only one more question. "When do we go?"

"Tomorrow morning, early. On our last swing around the cliffs two days ago we sighted indications of a road leading eastward from the other side. It could be the guide we want."

They finished their work upon the sled in mid-afternoon and the remaining hours of work time stowing away supplies and equipment Kimber made preparations for five days' absence from the valley—flying east to the interior of the land mass on which the star ship had earthed.

"That tube we found pointed in that direction. If it was a freight carrier for some city—and I am of the opinion that it was—that's where we may find the remains of civilization." Kimber's voice came muffled as he checked dials behind the wind screen of the aircraft.

"Yeah." Santee added a small bag of his own to the supplies. "But—after what we seen at that there farmhouse—they played rough around here once upon a time. Better watch out that we don't get shot down before we make peace signs."

"It's been a long time since the farm was looted," Dard ventured to point out "And why didn't. the looters return—if they were the winners in some war. Harmon says this land is rich, that any farmer would settle here."

"Soldiers ain't farmers, "said Santee. 'Me, I'd say this was lootin' done by an army or somebody like them blasted Peacemen. They was out to smash and grab and run. Land don't mean nothin', to them kinda guys. But I se. what Harmon means. If the war ended why didn't somebody come back here to rebuild? Yeah, that's sense."

"Maybe there was no one left," Dard said.

"Blew themselves up?" Kimber's expressive eyebrows rose as he considered that. "Kind of wholesale, even for a big time war. The burn-off took most of Terra's cities and the purge killed off the people who could rebuild them. But there were still plenty of men kicking around afterward. Of course, they were ahead of us technically here—those things in the carrier point to that. Which argues that—if they were like us—they were way ahead in the production of bigger and more lethal weapons, too. Well, I have a feeling that tomorrow or the next day we're going to learn about it"

The light was that gray wash which preceded sunrise when Dard sat up in his bedroll to answer the shadowy figure who roused him. He shivered, more with excitement than the morning chill, as he rolled his bag together and stole after Cully out of the cave to the sled.

There the four explorers made a hasty breakfast on cold scraps while Kimber talked disjointedly with Kordov, Harmond and Rogan.

"We'll say five days," he said. "But it may be longer. Give us a good margin for error. And don't send out after us if we don't make it back. Just take precautions."

Kordov shook his head. "No man is expendable here, Sim, not any more. But why should we borrow trouble in such large handfuls? I will not believe that you won't return! You have the list of plants, of things you are to look for?

Simba Kimber touched a breast pocket in answer. Cully took his place in the second seat of the sled and beckoned Dard to Join him. When Kimber was behind the control Santee scrambled in, a stun rifle across his big knees.

"I'll listen for any broadcast," Rogan promised. And Harmond mouthed something which might have been either reminder or farewell as Kimber took them up into the crisp air of the dawn.

Dard was too excited to waste any time waving good-bye or looking back into the safety of the valley. Instead he was leaning forward, his body tense, as if by the sheer power of his will he could speed their flight into the unknown.

They kept to a speed about equal to that of a running man as they followed the cliffs along to the narrow upper end of the valley. Close packed below to the edge of those stone walls was the woods the exploring parties had located earlier, only to be kept from penetration by the density of the growth.

"Queer stuff," Cully remarked now as they soared over the tree tops. "A limb grows long, bends over to the ground touches, then takes root and another tree starts to grow out right there. That whole mass down there may have started with just one tree. And you cant break or hack through it!"

The sky before them was bannered with pink streamers. A flight of the delicately hued butterfly-birds circled them and then flew as escort until they were just beyond the valley wall What the explorers saw beneath them now was a somber earth-covering blanket of blue-green, vaguely dismal and depressing with its unchanging darkness. Another collection of the self-planting trees made an effective barrier along the eastern side of the cliffs, and this was not a small wood but a far-stretching forest.

"There!" Santee pointed downward "That there's it! Them trees cover it some, but I say it's a road!"

A narrow ribbon of a light-colored substance, hidden for long distances by the invading trees ran due east. Kimber brought the sled into line over it.

But it was a full hour before they reached the end of the forest and saw clearly the cracked and broken highway which was their guide. It threaded across open plains where now and again they sighted more of the dome dwellings standing alone and deserted, wreathed with masses of greenery.

"No people—the land is empty," Dard commented as the sled crossed the fourth of these.

"War," Kimber wondered, "or diseases. . . . Must have made a clean sweep in this section. And a long time ago— by the growth of the bushes and the appearance of the road."

It was more than two hours after they left the valley that they came upon what had been a village. And here was the first clue to the type of disaster which had struck the land. One vast pit was the center of the clustered domes. Crushed and shattered buildings ringed it bearing the stains and melted smears of intense heat.

"Air raid?" Cully asked of the silence. "They got it good—and for keeps; it was war then."

Kimber did not circle the damage. Instead he stepped up the speed of the sled, driven by the same desire that possessed them all, the longing to know what lay beyond the broken horizon.

A second town, larger, brutally treated, its remaining structures half melted, its heart a crater, passed under them. Then again open country, beaded by deserted farms. The road ended at last in a city, shattered, smashed. A city planted on the shore of a bay, for here the sea curved in from the northwest to meet them once more.

There were towers, snapped, torn, twisted, until those in the sled could not be sure of their original shape, looming beside dark sores of craters. And at the waterside there was literally nothing but a slick expanse of crystalline slag reflecting the sun's rays.

Sea waves lipped that slag, but its edges remained unworn by the touch of water and time alike. And beyond, in the bay, the waves also curled restlessly about other wreckage—ships? Or parts of the buildings blown there?

Kimber cruised slowly across the spiderweb map of the ancient streets. But the wreckage was so complete they could only guess at the use or meaning of what they saw. Mounds of disintegrating metal might mark the residue of ground transportation devices, their weathered erosion testifying in part to the age of the disaster. And from the sled the explorers sighted nothing at all which might mark the remains of those who had lived there.

They landed on a patch of grassy ground before a huge pile of masonry which had three walls still standing. The ruined farmhouse had pictured for them tragedy, fear and cruelty. But this whole city—it was impersonal, too much. Such complete wreckage was closer to a dream.

"Atom bomb, H-bomb, Null-bomb." Cully recited the list of the worst Terra had known. "They must have had them here—all of them!"

"And they were certainly men—for they used them!" Kimber added savagely. He climbed out of the sled and faced the building. Its walls reflected the sun as if they were of some metallic substance but softly, with a glow of green-blue—as if the blocks used in building had been quarried of sea water. A flight of twelve steps, as wide as a Terran city block, led up to a mighty portal through which they could see the sun glow bright in the roofless interior.

Around that portal ran a band of colors, blending and

contrasting in a queer way which might have had meaning and yet did not—for Terran eyes. As he studied the hues Dard thought he had a half-hint. Perhaps those colors did have a deliberate sequence—perhaps they were more than just decoration.

—6—
DISASTER

THEIR ATTEMPTS to explore on foot were frustrated by the mounds of debris and danger from falling rubble. Cully jumped to safety from the top of a mound which caved in under his weight, and so escaped a dangerous slide into one of the pits. Those pits were everywhere, dug so deeply into the foundations of the city that the Terrans, huddling on the ruins, could look down past several underground levels to a darkness uncut by the sun.

A little shaken by the engineer's narrow escape, they retired to the sled and made an unappetizing meal on concentrates.

"No birds," Dard suddenly realized that fact. "Nothing alive."

"Uhhuh." Santee dug his heel into the grass and earth. "No bugs either. And there're enough of them back in the valley!"

"No birds, no insects," Kimber said slowly. "The place is dead. I don't know how the rest of you feel, but I've had just about enough."

They did agree with that. The brooding stillness, broken only when debris crashed or rolled, rasped their nerves.

Dard swallowed his last bit of concentrate and turned to the pilot

"Do we have any microfilm we can use?"

"For what—a lot of broken buildings?" Cully wanted to know.

"I'd like one of those bands of color around that doorway," Dard answered. His idea that the bands had a meaning was perhaps silly but he could not push it away.

"All right, kid." Kimber unpacked the small recorder and focused it on a place where the sun was strong. "No pattern I can see. But, it just might mean something at that." That was the only picture they took when on the ground. But once again in the air Gully ran the machine for a bird's-eye view of as much of the ruined area as could be recorded.

They were approaching the outer reaches of the city to the east when Santee gave an exclamation and touched Kimber's arm. They were over a street less cumbered with rubble than any they had yet crossed, and there was a flicker of movement there.

As the sled coasted down they disturbed a pack of grayish, four-footed things that streaked away into the ruins leaving their meal behind them on the blood-smeared pavement.

"Whew!" Cully coughed and Dard gagged at the stench the wind carried in their direction. They left the sled to gather around the tangle of stripped bones and rotting flesh.

"That wasn't killed today," Kimber observed unnecessarily.

Dard rounded the stained area. The dead thing had been large, perhaps the size of a Terran draft horse, and the skeleton—tumbled as the bones now were—suggested that it was four-footed and hooved. But that skull, to which ragged and blood-clotted hair still clung, was what he had moved to see. He had been right—two horns sprouted above the eye sockets. This was the horned horse of the game set!

"A duocorn?" mused the pilot.

"A what?" Santee wanted to know.

"There was a fabled animal mentioned in some of the old books on Terra. Had a single horn in the middle of the forehead, but the rest was all horse. Well, here's a horse with two horns—a duocorn instead of a unicorn. But those things we saw feeding here—they were pretty small to bring down an animal of this size."

"Unless they carry a burper, they didn't!" Dard, in spite of the odor, leaned down to inspect that stretch of spine beyond the loose skull. A section of vertebra had been smashed just as if a giant vise had been applied to the nape of the duocorn's neck.

"Crushed!" Kimber agreed. "But whatever could do that?"

Cully studied the body. "Mighty big for a horse."

"There were breeds on earth which were seventeen to twenty hands high at the shoulder and weighed close to a ton," returned Kimber. "This fellow must have been about that size."

"And what is big enough to crunch through a spine

supporting a ton of meat?" Santee wanted to know. He went back to the sled and picked up the rifle.

Dard back-trailed from the evil-smelling bones. Several paces farther on he discovered what he was looking for, marks which proved that the body had been dragged and worried for almost half of a city block. And also, plain to reach in a drift of soil across the street, prints. The marks cut deeply by the hooves of the duocorn were half blotted out in places by another spoor—three long-clawed toes, with faint scuffed spaces between, as if they were united by a webbed membrane. Dard went down on one knee and flexed his own hand over the clearest of those prints. With his fingers spread to the fullest extent he could just span it.

"Looks like a chicken track." Santee had come up behind him.

"More likely a reptile. I've seen a field lizard leave a spoor such as this—except for the size."

"Another dragon—large size?" Cully suggested.

Dard shook his head as he got to his feet and started along that back trail. "This one runs, not flies. But I'm sure it's a nasty customer."

There was a scuttling to their left Santee whirled, rifle ready. A small stone rolled from the top of the nearest pile of rubbish and thudded home against the yellow teeth of the skull.

"Somebody's getting impatient over an interrupted dinner." Cully ended with a laugh which sounded unnaturally loud in these surroundings.

Kimber went back to the sled. "We might as well let him—or her—or it—come back to the table. There are," he glanced around at the ruins, "altogether too many good lurking places here. I'll feel safe out in open country where I can see any lizard that big—before it sees me!"

But when they were air borne Kimber did not turn inland, instead he followed the curve of the bay on to the northwest. The ruins beneath them dwindled to isolated houses—domed or towered—in better repair than those situated in the heart of the city. Beneath them now were brilliant patches of flowers long since returned to the wild. Little streams made graceful curves through what Dard was sure had been pleasure gardens. Fairy towers, which appeared too delicate to withstand the pull of the planet's gravity, pointed useless fingers up at the cruising sled.

Once they flew for almost half a mile above a palace. But here again a curdled crystalline blotch cut the building in two. None of what they saw gave them any desire to descend and explore. Here the trees grew too high, there were too many shadows. The tangled pleasure gardens and wild grounds were good lurking places for terror to stalk the unwary.

The broken city faded into the green of the rolling country and the aquamarine of the sea. Fewer and fewer domed houses broke the green—and those were probably farms. Here were birds as if the haunted horror of the city was gone. The seashore curved again but Kimber did not follow it west. He veered to the east to cross fields of which the old regular patterns were marked by bushy hedgerows. It was in one of these that they sighted the first living duocorns, four adults and two colts, but all four well under the size of the monster whose skeleton had attracted their attention in the city.

These animals were uniform in color, showing none of the variations in marking possessed by Terran horses. Their coats were a slaty blue-gray, their unkempt manes and tails black, and their bellies and the under portions of their legs silver. The horns were silver with the real sheen of the precious metal.

As the sled droned over them, the largest flung up its head to issue a trumpeting scream. Then, herding its companions before it, it settled into a rocking gallop up the sloping field to the hedge at the far side beyond which was a grove of trees. With graceful ease all of the fleeing animals leaped the hedge and disappeared under those trees, nor did they come out on the other side of the grove.

"Good runners," Cully gave credit. "Do you suppose they were always wild—or the descendants of domestic stock? Bet Harmon'd like to have a couple of them. He was pretty fed up when he found we couldn't bring those two colts he had picked out."

"The big one was a fighter! D'yuh see him shake them horns?" demanded Santee. "I wouldn't want him to catch me out in the open walkin'."

"Odd." Dard had been watching the far end of the grove and was now puzzled. "You'd think they'd keep on running. But they're staying in there."

"Under cover. Safe from any menace from the air," Kimber said. "Which suggests some unpleasant possibilities."

"A large flying danger!" Dard whistled as he caught Kimber's idea. "A thing maybe as big as this sled. But it would be too big to fly on its own power!"

"Bigger things than this have flown in Terra's past," the

pilot reminded him. "And it may not be a living thing they fear—but a machine. Either way—we'd better watch out."

"But those flying things were far back in our history," protested the boy. "Could such primitive things exist along with man—or whatever built that city?"

"How can we say what may or may not have survived here? Or—if that city was destroyed by radioactive missiles—what may have mutated? Or what may fly machines?" Since the duocorns remained stubbornly in hiding, the sled gave up investigation and flew east, the setting sun behind them and long afternoon shadows stretching to point their path.

"Where we gonna camp?" Santee wanted to know. "Out here somewheres?"

"I'd say yes," Kimber said. "There's a river over there. Might find a good place somewhere along it"

The river was shallow and its waters were clear enough for them to be able to sight from the air the rough stones which paved its bed. An uneven fringe of water plants cloaked the shore line until climbing ground provided bluffs. The sparkle of sun on ripples flashed up from a wider expanse as the sled reached a place where the graveled bed flattened out into a round lake. The stream spattered down from heights to feed this, forming a miniature waterfall, and there was a level stretch of sand unencumbered by rocks which made a good landing for the sled.

Cully stretched and grinned. "Good enough. You know how to pick 'em, Sim. Even a cave to sleep in!"

The space he pointed to was not a real cave, rather a semiprotected hollow beneath an overhang of rock. But it gave them a vague sense of security when they unrolled their sleeping bags against its back wall.

This was the first night Dard had spent in the open under a moonless sky and he found the darkness discomforting—though stars made new crystal patterns across the heavens. They had a fire of river drift, but beyond that the darkness was thick enough to be smooth between thumb and forefinger.

The fire had died down to gleaming coals when Dard was shocked awake by a howling wail. The sound was repeated, to be either echoed or answered from down river. Above the ramble of the fall he was sure he caught the clink of disturbed gravel. Another ear-splitting shriek made his heart jump as Kimber flashed on the beam of a pocket torch without moving from beside him.

Pinned in that beam hunched a weird biped. About four feet tall, its body was completely covered with fine silky hair which arose in a fluff along its back and limbs, roughened by its astonished fright. The face was three-quarters eyes, round, staring, with no discernible lids. There was no apparent nose above an animal's sharply fanged muzzle. Four-digit hands went up to shield those eyes and the thing gave a moan which arose to a howl. But it made no attempt to flee, as if the strange light held it prisoner.

"Monkey!" that was Santee. "A night runnin' monkey!"

Into that beam from the torch, insects began to gather—great feathery-winged moth things, some as large as birds. And, at their appearance, the night howler came to life. With a feline's lithe grace it leaped and captured two of the moths and then scurried into the darkness where a low snarl suggested that it was now disputing possession of these prizes with another. Kimber held the torch steady and the moths came in, a drifting cloud, coasting along that ray toward the explorers. Round eyeballs of phosphorescence glittered just on the border of that light. And furry paws clawed through it at the flying things. Triumphant squeaks heralded captures and the howling arose in a triumphant chorus as if others were being summoned to this lucky hunting. Kimber snapped off the light just before the first wave of moths reached the Terrans.

The whisper of wings was drowned out by several shrill cries. But when the light was not turned on again the four heard the rattle of gravel and a fading wailing as the "monkeys" withdrew down river.

"Show's over for this night—I hope," Cully grunted sleepily. "Bet some wise guy could make a fortune selling torches to those boys as moth lures."

Dard allowed his head to drop back on the padded end of the sleeping bag. Suppose those "monkeys" were intelligent enough to enable the Terrans to establish trade relations. Could one make contact with them? To the human eye their manlike stance and the way they used their hands made them appear more approachable than any other native creatures of this world which the Terrans had so far sighted. Surely these creatures had not built the city. But they walked erect and had been quick enough to evaluate the use of light for attracting their food supply. If they were wholly night creatures, as their large eyes and ease in traveling through the dark suggested, would the Terrans ever see them again?

Dard was still puzzling that out when he slipped into a dream in which he again stood before the ruined building within the city and studied those baffling lines of color. But this time those bands held a meaning, and he had almost grasped it when he heard a sound behind him. Not daring to turn his head—for he knew that death sniffed his trail—he began to run with dragging, leaden feet. And, behind him, death pounded relentlessly. With bursting lungs he turned the corner into another cluttered, half-blocked street and saw before him blood and bones from which gray things ran. He slipped, went down. . . . He awoke, his heart pounding wildly, his body slippery with a dank, chill sweat. It was gray light. He could see the moving water, the remains of the previous night's fire. Stealthily he wriggled out of his sleeping bag and crawled in to the open.

Then he went to the water and splashed it over head and forearms, until its clear chill washed out of him the fear the nightmare had left. Gasping a little from the chill he tramped along to the rising cliffs beside the falls.

Vines ran down the shiny black of this stone, clinging to its uneven surface with tiny sucker feet. The lianas themselves were a gray-white and bare of leaves except for a few which grew in tight bunches near the top of the cliff. Clusters of ropy creepers dangled in a limp fringe along each main stem.

In a pocket formed by the crossing of several lianas he sighted a find. Surely that brighter green marked one of the perfume plants Trude Harmon wanted! The triangular leaves, glossy and colorful against such a drab background, bobbed from scarlet stems. And there were seed pods also! They hung, red and yellow, pulled down by the weight of their contents, within his reach. He snapped off three and stretched to reach a fourth.

It was just then he caught sight of the twitching close to the ground, where something struggled hopelessly. Two of the creepers, about the size of his little finger, were holding in a throttling grip the writhing body of a hopper. The small animal's eyes protruded agonizingly and a bloody froth ringed its gasping mouth. Dard drew his knife and slashed at the white-cords. But the steel did not cut through them. It rebounded as if he had tried to sever rubber with a dull edge. Before he could raise it for a second blow, a larger creeper flicked out and encircled his wrist, pulling him off balance against the cliff. With lightning speed the ropy fringe dangling there came to life, those near enough whipping over his body, those too far away straining toward the struggle until they were stretched in straight lines. And, as each tie fell about him, he discovered that it was equipped with small thorns which tore his skin in red-hot torment. He shouted and fought, but all his struggles seemed to carry him closer to other suckers and they were fast winding him helpless when he heard the excited cries of the others and saw them racing for him.

Before they were close enough to help he was able to tear his knife arm free, to slash and score the mass of weaving tendrils which enclosed him. Then he paused— the things were falling away of their own accord. Within another minute the last and largest sullenly relinquished its hold.

"What happened?" yelled Santee. "What did you do to make those things let go?"

Wherever the plants had met his flesh they had left their brand in pin-point dots of oozing blood which trickled down his arms, throat and one cheek. But those lianas which had fallen away from him—they were turning black, shriveling, rotting away in pieces! The thing had tasted his blood and it was poisoned!

"Poisoned! I poisoned it!"

"Be glad that you did," snapped Kimber. "You're in luck. These weren't!" He kicked up the gravel below the vines with the toe of his boot and plowed up brittle bones and small skulls.

The pilot as he treated Dard's slight wounds was emphatic:

"Hereafter we stay together. It worked out all right this time. But again it might not. Stick together and distrust everything unless you have already seen it in action!" But they were all together and apparently in no danger when disaster struck them a back-handed blow that same day. They had been using the sleepy stream as a guide back into a range of hills and by midmorning had sighted in the northeast what could only be a chain of mountains, purple-blue against the sky. These ran from north to south as far as those in the sled could see.

Perhaps if the Terrans had not been so intent upon those distant peaks they might have seen something below which would have warned them. Probably not. Man, when he goes to war, displays the deepest depths of cunning.

The first intimation of danger arrived simultaneously with the blow that smashed them out of the sky. A sharp burst of sound and the sled bucked—as if batted by a giant club. The craft fluttered into a falling twirl while

Kimber fought the controls, trying to pull out of the spin. If the passengers had not been strapped in they would have plunged earthward in the first three seconds of that wild descent.

While Dard was trying to understand what had happened a burst of brilliant light temporarily blinded him. More sound, bracketing them, and someone cried out in pain. Then he knew that they were falling out of control, and by some instinct he flung up his arms to shield his head just before they struck and he blacked out.

He couldn't have been unconscious long, because when he raised his head Cully was still dazedly fumbling to free himself from the safety straps. Dard spat to clear a full mouth and saw a blob of blood and a tooth strike the ground. He loosened the belt and lurched out of the sled after Cully. In front Santee bent over a limp Kimber on whose face blood trickled from a cut just below the hair line.

"What happened?" Dard wiped his chin and took away a bloody hand. His lips hurt and his jaw ached.

Kimber's dark eyes opened and stared up at them bemusedly. Then comprehension came back and he demanded:

"Who shot us down?"

Santee had his rifle in his hands.

"That's what I'm gonna see, right now!"

Before the rest could protest, he darted away, back down the valley where they had landed, zigzagging into cover as he neared its mouth. There was a final boom of an exploding shell from that direction and then silence.

Dard and Cully got Kimber free of the sled. The pilot's

right arm was bleeding from a ragged wound near the shoulder. They broke open the medical kit and the engineer went competently to work so that Dard had nothing to do. When Kimber was stretched out on a bedroll Cully returned to examine the sled itself. He took up the cover of the motor and squirmed half into the space which enclosed it, ordering Dard to hold the torch for him. When he crawled back his face was very sober.

"How bad?" asked Kimber. There was more color in his dark face and he levered himself up on an elbow.

"Not the worst—but about as near to that as we can get." Cully was interrupted by a shout from the trees where Santee had disappeared.

The big man returned walking in the open, his rifle cradled in the crook of his arm—as if they had nothing to fear.

"Fellas, this here's plain crazy! There's a nest of guns down there all hidden away. Little stuff—light field pieces. But there's not a livin' critter in the place. Them there guns fired at us their ownselves!"

"A robot control triggered when we flew over a certain point!" exploded Cully. "Some kind of radar, I'll bet. Rogan ought to be here."

"First," Kimber reminded him grimly, "we've got to get back to tell him about them."

A broken sled with which to cross several hundred miles of unknown country. They were going to have quite a hike, thought Dard. But he did not comment upon that aloud.

⇥7⇤
RETURN JOURNEY

"WONDER HOW MANY more booby traps such as that are hidden around?" Cully glanced down the valley with open suspicion.

"Not many, I'd say," Kimber answered weakly. "It must have been only a fluke that those guns were still able to fire—"

His voice was swallowed by an explosion severe enough to rock the ground under them. Dard saw earth, trees and debris rise into the air far down the valley as an acrid white-yellow smoke fouled the air in drifting wisps.

"That," Kimber said into the ensuing silence, "was probably the end of the guns. They've blown themselves up."

"Shoulda done that sooner!" growled Santee. "A lot sooner! How about us gettin' away from here?" He turned to Cully who had been blasted loose from his work on the sled.

"That's going to be a problem. She'll get into the air

again, yes. But not with a full load. Stripped down she may be able to carry two—flying with a list."

Santee grinned at his follow castaways. "All right. Two of us'll hike and pack some stuff. The other two'll ride."

Kimber frowned as he agreed reluctantly. "I suppose we'll have to do that. Those in the sled can make a camp a half day's march ahead and wait for the others to catch up. We mustn't lose contact. Do you think you can raise Rogan in the valley?"

Cully brought out the small vedio. And Kimber, using his left hand awkwardly, made the proper adjustment. But there was no answering spark. The engineer raised the box; and shook it gently. They all heard that faint answering rattle which put an end to their hopes of a message to those they had left by the sea.

Camp was made that night just where the fortunes of that long ago war had marooned them. Santee and Dard undertook another visit to the hidden emplacement. Two of the strange guns were tilted at a crazy angle, their loading mechanism ripped wide open, behind them a pit newly hollowed and still cloudy with fumes.

Keeping away from that the two Terrans prowled about the installation. If man or any other intelligent life had been there before them, it had been many years in the past. But Dard, knowing very little of mechanics, believed that it had been robot controlled. Perhaps lack of manpower had made the last war a purely push-button affair.

"Now here's somethin'!"

Santee's shout brought him to an opening in the ground. The cover had been wrenched loose by the explosion and its clever camouflage no longer hid the steps leading down into the dark. Santee flashed a beam ahead and started to descend. The steps were very narrow and shallow as if those who had used them had had feet not quite the same shape or size of a Terran's. But once down, the explorers found themselves in a square box of a metal-walled chamber. Along one entire wall was a control panel and facing it a small table and a single backless bench. Otherwise the room was empty.

"Musta jus' set them robots goin' and left. This metal ain't rusted none. But it was left a long time ago. . . ."

As Santee swept the light across that control board Dard saw an object lying on the table. He picked up his find just as the big man started up the stairs to the outer and fresher air.

What he held was four sheets of a crystalline substance, fastened together at the upper left-hand corner. Running through each sheet, as if they had been embedded when the stuff was made, were lines of shaded colors in combinations not unlike those he had seen about the city door. Instruction book? Orders? Did Those Others express their thoughts in color patterns? He thrust the find into his safest pocket, determined to compare it with the microfilm of the doorway.

The next morning they followed Santee's plan. The pilot, handicapped by a stiff shoulder, went in the sled along with Cully who was able to take the controls. Their supplies pared to the minimum were shared between the sled and two packs for Dard and Santee.

When the sled took off, due south, it cruised just above tree-top level. It would fly at lowest speed on that same course until noon when its crew would camp, waiting for the two on foot to join them.

Dard shouldered his pack, setting it into place with a weight, and picked up their compass. Santee followed with pack and rifle, and they went forward at a ground-eating pace Dard had learned in the woods of Terra, as the sled vanished over the rise.

For the most part they found the going through this rolling country easy. There were no wooded stretches to form impassable barriers, and they soon struck an old road running in the right direction to provide footing good enough to allow a faster pace. Insects spun out of the tall grass to blunder past them and hoppers spied them constantly.

Shortly before noon the road made a sharp curve west toward the distant sea, and the Terrans had to strike away across fields again. They had the good luck to stumble on a farm where not only one but two of the golden apple trees bent under the weight of ripe fruit. Pushing through the mob of semidrunk birds, insects, and hoppers, including a new and larger variety of the latter, they secured fruit which was not only food but drink, filling an unprovided bag for the sake of the sled riders.

Sentee bit into the fragrant pulp with a sigh of pleasure. "D'yuh know—I wonder a lot—where did all the people go? They had a bad war—sure. But there must have been some survivors. Everybody couldn't have been killed!"

"What if they used gas, or a germ—certain kinds of infective radiation?" questioned Dard. "There are no traces of any survivors, in the city ruins, around farms."

"It looks to me jus' as if"—the big rifleman licked his fingers carefully—"they all packed up and got out together, the way we left the Cleft."

When they left the farm the character of the country began to change. Here the soil was spotted with patches of sandy gravel which grew larger. The clumps of trees dwindled to thickets of wiry thorn bushes, and there were outcroppings of the same shiny black rock which had nursed the killing vines by the river. Santee shot a long survey about as they halted on the top of a steep hill.

"This's kinda like a desert. Glad we brought them apples—we might not hit water here."

It was hot, hotter than it had seemed back when they were in the blue-green fields, for this sun-baked red-brown earth and blue sand reflected the heat. Dard's skin, chafed by the pack straps, smarted when moisture trickled down between his shoulder blades. He licked his lips and tasted salt. Santee's comment concerning lack of water had aroused his thirst.

Below them was a gorge. Dard blinked and rubbed his eyes with the back of his hand. No, that was no trick of shimmering heat—there was a bright gleaming line straight across the floor of the valley. He called it to Santee's attention and the other focused the field glasses on it.

"A rail! But why only one?"

"We can get down over there," Dard pointed. "Let's see what it is."

They made the hard climb down to verify the fact that a single metal rail did reach from one tunnel hole in the gorge wall to another tunnel directly across. Unable to discover anything else, they pulled themselves up the opposite cliff to continue the southward march.

It was midafternoon when they saw, rising into a cloudless sky, the smoke signal of the sled. And their strides became a trot until they panted up the side of a small mesa-plateau to the camp.

"How long," Santee wanted to know later as they sucked appreciatively on golden apples, "is this trip gonna last?"

"Another full day's journey for you two, and maybe half the next. At this speed we can't expect to cut it any shorter," Kimber replied. "Jorge's been working on the engine again. But there isn't much he can do without other tools."

The big man grinned. "Well, these here plasta-boots of our'n are holdin' up pretty well. We can keep sloggin' a while longer. And there's nothin' to be afraid of."

"Don't be too sure of that," cautioned the pilot. "Keep your eyes open, you two. There may have been other booby traps scattered around. Since we were shot down, I don't trust even a clear sky!"

The second day's routine followed the first. Except, in the arid desert land, it was tougher going and they did not make time.

Dard's head went up and his nostrils expanded as he started to pick his way down a series of ledges into a sandy-floored ravine. There was a musky, highly repellent stench arising from below. And he had sniffed something very much like it before! The putrescent remains of fee duocorn! Below, an organic thing was very dead! Santee worked along to join him.

"What're you stoppin' for?"

"Smell that?"

Santee's bearded face wrinkled. "Yah, a big stink! Somethin' dead!"

Dard studied the ground before them carefully. If they, tried to double back on their trail through this up and down country they were going to lose hours of time. After all, what had made that kill below—if it were a kill— might have been gone for days. He decided to leave it up to Santee.

"Shall we go down?"

"We'll lose a lotta time back trailin' from here. I'd say keep on."

But they continued the descent cautiously and when Dard disturbed a small stone, which dropped noistly over the edge, he stiffened for several listening seconds. There was no sound from below—nothing but that terrible stomach-disturbing odor.

Santee unslung the rifle, and Card's hand went to his own belt. That morning Cully had given him the ray gun, suggesting that it could be of more use to the foot travelers. Now, as his hand closed around the butt, Dard was very glad that he held it. There was something about this ill-omened place—something in the very silence which brooded there—that hinted of danger.

A screen of stubby thorn bushes masked the far end of the narrow ravine, hinting at the presence of moisture, although the prickly leaves had a grayish, unhealthy cast.

The two worked their way through these as carefully and noiselessly as possible and found a seeping spring. Minerals salted the lip of the water-filled depression, and a greenish powder was dry along the banks of the rivulet which trickled on down the valley.

Chemical fumes from the water scented the air, but not heavy enough to cover the other sickish effuvium.

They should have beaten their way through the brush to the other side of the valley and climbed out of that tainted hole. But no broken ledges hung over there to furnish climbing aids, and they followed the stream along in the search for an easier path.

The contaminated water spilled out into a shallow shaking pool with a broad rim of the poisonous green.

Grouped around the far perimeter of the pool, half buried in the sand, were such things as nightmares are made of!

Their dingy yellowish-green skins were scaled with the stigmata of the reptile. But the creatures drowsing in the sun were not even as wholesome as the snakes most humans shrink from with age-old inbred horror. These were true monsters—evil. Gorged, they had fallen in a stupor among the grisly fragments of their feasting, and from those fragments and the smeared sand came a stench foul enough to suggest that this was a long used lair.

Dard estimated that they were from seven to ten feet long. The hind legs, ending in huge webbed feet, mere stems of bone laced with powerful driving muscles. Short, horribly stained forearms had terrible travesties of human hands which curved over their protruding bellies, each finger a ten-inch claw. But their heads were the worst, too small for the bodies, flat of skull, they were mounted on unusually long and slender necks, giving the impression of a cobra on the shoulders of a lizard.

As the two humans halted, a flap of loose skin on the belly of the nearest nightmare was pushed aside and a small replica of the monster drew itself out of a sac and wobbled weakly down to the water, curling its neck over to suck up the liquid. After it swallowed the first mouthful, some instinct drew its attention to the watchers. With a shrill hiss it scrambled back to its parent. The head of the larger thing snapped up, swaying back and forth, a snake preparing to strike!

Dard threw himself back, carrying Santee with him. They were brought up short by the cliff wall, but they dared not turn their backs upon the aroused monster long enough to find hand and foot holds there.

The thing across the pool was on its feet, towering far over them. With a cuff of one paw it sent the infant sprawling to safety before it slewed around kicking up blood-clotted sand. The flat serpent's head went down to a level with the lizardlike shoulders, and from its fanged jaws came a hiss which gathered volume until it rivaled the piercing whistle of a steam-powered engine.

That battle cry aroused its fellow sleepers. But they arose sluggishly, too torpid from their feasting to respond.

Santee shot. The nerve-paralyzing projectile of the stun rifle struck fair between those murderous yellow, unwinking eyes. The skull shattered with a spatter of green ooze. But the thing waded the pool to rush them, tearing claws outstretched. It should have been dead. But with a broken, empty skull, blinded, it came on!

"No brain in the head!" Dard shouted. "Jump!"

They jumped apart. The advancing horror struck hard against the cliff to cling there stubbornly clawing at the rock. It continued to scream senselessly, bringing the others of its kind into full alertness.

One gave a bound, clearing the pool, to fall upon its wounded companion with tearing jaws and claws. The other three appeared undecided. Their snake heads rose and fell as they hissed. One made to join the battle on the other side of the pool and then retreated.

Daring to hesitate no longer, Dard took careful aim with the ray gun and sent a green beam straight into the distended middle of the creature that rocked from one splayed foot to another on his right. The Terrans had to clear a path past the pool, for to return near the fighters was sure death.

Screaming madly, Dard's quarry clapped both hands over the frightful gapping emptiness the ray had left and wilted forward into the water, sending up a slimy spray of blood and poisonous liquid. With the attention of its two fellows attracted to its struggles Dard darted to join Santee.

Together the humans edged along the cliff wall, their goal the valley beyond the pool. For a few minutes it seemed that they might be able to gain it undetected by the monsters. For one of the unhurt creatures had gone to work on the body in the pool. But when its smaller companion made to join it, fangs and talons threatened, forcing that other to withdraw, hissing fury. As its head swung back and forth it sighted the Terrans. An arching leap brought it after them. Both the length and speed of that bound panicked the cornered men. They scrambled into the meager protection offered by the boulders and fallen rock. Santee's second bullet tore a hole in the scaled breast of the pursuer without slowing its charge. Dard pressed the firing stud on the ray gun. But the responding beam was weak. It clipped the side of the weaving head, shearing off part of the skull and one eye, and cutting neck muscles so badly that the battered head flopped erratically.

Dard fired again—with no result. The clip left in the weapon must have been exhausted! His ears roared as Santee shot from beside him. But the bullet only nicked the shoulder of the writhing body. Despairing they scuttled and backed away, keeping in among the rough footing. But they were past the pool, in the middle of the valley, on a course which paralleled a path worn deep and smooth by the feet of the monsters.

The scream of the hunter behind them was cut by a trumpeting squeal. A second was bearing down to join in the chase.

"Ahead—three—four—yards"—Dard got out the words between tearing breaths—"hole—too—small—"

He concentrated on reaching that haven, and Santee ran beside him. The hole was a perfectly round one, and from it ran the monorail of the ancient transport system. They threw themselves into the dark, scrambling on until Dard brought up against a heavy object which gave under his weight, slipping on so suddenly that he sprawled face down, the wind driven out of him.

When he caught his breath again he sat up, still groggy. The crack of the rifle filled the tunnel with a blast of sound.

"Got one at last! And it's blocked up that hole—for a while anyways. But it ain't healthy in here—they can get in—squeeze themselves altogether and do it. What the—!" The big man ended his report with an exclamation of both outrage and fear.

Dard had breath enough to ask: "What's the matter?"

"That was the last round, I just fired. You got another clip for the ray gun?"

"No."

"Then we'd better make tracks for the other end of this here tunnel. From the sound back there they're taking the dead one out—in pieces! When they've got that done they'll be after us again'—"

"Let's have the flash. There's something ahead here. It moves—"

Dard put a tentative hand out—to encounter the smoothness of metal. And when Santee snapped on the torch beam he discovered that he was fronting a cylinder, not unlike the one they had pulled out of the seaside tube. But this one was mounted on a grooved fin made to run along the monorail. There was no way of getting past it, since its sides were within inches of the tunnel walls. They would have to push it before them if they were going to get out the other end.

That worked properly for about five minutes and then an extra hard push sent the carrier ahead to stop with a clang. All their shoving force could force it along no farther. Dard flattened himself against the wall and flashed the torch down the side of the cylinder.

"There's a cave-in!"

Santee massaged his bearded chin with a dirt-streaked hand. "Kinda bottles us up, don't it? Give us the light and let's have a look along these walls."

Several paces back he found a niche, not too roomy and still accommodating some oddly shaped tools which Santee kicked aside.

"Repairman's safety hole," he explained. "Thought maybe we might happen on one of these here. Now, suppose we work that there truck past here and get ahead to look at the damage."

Pushing the carrier before them had been an easy task. But getting it back again was another matter altogether, especially when there were no proper handholds on its smooth surface. As they worked at it, hampered by their necessarily cramped position, they broke nails and tore fingers raw. The stubborn thing moved with frustrating slowness. While, to rasp the nerves, sounds from the entrance told them that the body which had obstructed the passage there was being rapidly disposed of.

At last the car was pushed far enough along so that they could get out of the niche behind it. Without waiting to take up their packs, they ran to the cave-in, only to be met by a hard mound of earth and rock. Santee dug the barrel of his rifle into it, disturbing only a scattered clod or two. To dig a way through that they needed tools, and time—and they had neither as the big man was forced to acknowledge.

"There're two of them critters left. And if either one gets in here now it's gonna push that car right back on us. But—if there's any smashin' done—I'm gonna be the one to do it!"

He padded purposefully back to the carrier. Dard hurried after him. The picture Santee had evoked, of the lizard things pushing that car down upon them, was one he didn't want to think about. He had no idea of what Santee had in mind, but any action now was better than just waiting for such an end.

"All right," Santee put his hands on the back of the carrier, "put away that torch and start pushin'! Here's where we give them lizards a big surprise—a nasty one, too, I hope!"

Dard dropped the torch and put his hands beside Santee's. Together they set their strength against the immobility of the carrier. It moved, much more easily than it had before. There was a low hum which became a steady purr. It gathered speed—moving away from them.

"We've started it to workin'!" Santee's exultant cry arose to explain. He caught Dard and held him away from the entrance as the Carrier sped on.

There was a shock of impact followed by a hissing scream. Then they saw the clear circle of daylight marking the entrance, carrier and besiegers were both gone!

❧ 8 ❧
DESSIER'S MERMAN

WHEN NOTHING moved across that circle of light they dared to retrieve their packs and go out.

The carrier had plunged full speed ahead, leaving the curve of the monorail. Under it, but crushed legs pinned to the sand and rock of the valley floor, threshed one of the monsters, writhing over the torn remains of the one Santee had shot earlier. Leaping out of the reach of the prisoned creature's darting head the Terrans rounded its body and made for the opposite wall of the canyon.

Here the rock afforded holds and they pulled themselves up. But the lizard crashed beneath the car appeared to be alone and nothing menaced their retreat. Panting, they reached the top and dared to look back.

Below, the monster still fought insanely against the carrier which held it down. But if there were others of its fellows alive they had not joined it. Santee wiped his steaming face with the back of a hand.

"I still don't know how we got outa that one, kid. It was sure a close call."

"Too close. I want to catch up to the sled before we run into any more of those murdering devils."

"Yeah," Santee pulled ruefully at the sling of the rifle. "Next time I go walkin', I'm gonna have a lotta ammo. This here country's got too many surprises."

They set out at a sober pace, too exhausted by their exertions of the past hour to hurry. It was dusk growing into night before they found their way down a rise into another grassy plain. In the distance was a massed shadow of what could only be a wood.

Would they have to fight their way through or around that, Dard asked himself drearily. But a light reassured him. There was a campfire down there. Cully had landed the sled this side of the barrier.

As Santee and Dard dragged themselves wearily into the circle of firelight they were met with a flood of questions. Dard was too tired to try to answer. He ate and drank and crawled into his bedroll before all the tale of their adventure of the afternoon had been told. Kimber was very sober when it was complete.

"That was too close. We'll have to go better armed when we explore. But now that we know there is no civilized threat to our colony it may be some time before we return this way. Tomorrow the sled will ferry us over the forest and the cliffs and we shall be home. Those are our cliffs there."

"Home," Dard repeated that word in his mind, trying to associate it with the sea valley, with the cave house of the star voyagers. A long, long time ago "home" had had a good meaning. Before the burning, before the purge. But his memory of that halcyon time was so dim. Then "home" had meant the farm, and cold, hunger, the constant threat of danger. Now "home" would be a cell hollowed out of a colored cliff on a weird world generations of time away from Terra.

In the morning he lazed about the camp with Santee while Cully, after a last tune-up of the limping engine, lifted the sled toward the sea with Kimber as the first passenger. It was an hour before the sled returned and the engineer ordered Dard into the listing craft. They flew slowly, skimming the barrier, and Cully did not take him all the way down the sea valley to the cliff house, but dropped him with his pack at the edge of the ancient fields.

Dard swished through the tall grass. He could see people moving in the distant fields, more of them than had been about when he had left. More of the sleepers had probably been aroused.

Then a clear, lilting whistle announced the boy, some years younger than himself, who came driving before him three calves. He stopped short when he caught sight of the battered explorer and smiled.

"Hi! You're Dard Nordis, ain't you? Say, you musta had yourself a time—seein' them ruined cities and the lizards and all! I'm gonna go out and see 'em, too—when I can get Dad to let me. I'm Lanny Harmon. Can you wait 'til I stake out these critters? I'd like to go back with you."

"Sure." Dard eased his pack to the ground and watched Lanny tether the calves in the pasture.

"They sure do like this kinda grass," the farm boy explained as he came back. "Hey, let me carry that there pack for you. Mr. Kimber said you had a big fight with some giant lizards. Are they worse'n those flyin' dragons?"

"They sure are," Dard replied feelingly. "Say, is everybody awake now?"

"Everybody's that's goin' to." A shadow darkened the boy's face for a moment. "Six didn't come through. Dr. Skort—but you knew 'bout him, and Miz Winson, and Miz Grene, Looie Denton and a coupla men I didn't know. But the rest, they're all right. We were awful lucky. Whee—look out!"

Dard overbalanced as he tried to stop in mid-step and landed on the ground beside Lanny who had squatted down to sweep away the grass and display a dome of mud-plastered leaves and grass.

"What in the world?"

Lanny chuckled. "That there's a hopper house! Dessie, she found one yesterday and showed me where to look. Watch!" He rapped smartly with his knuckles on the top of the dome.

A second later a hopper's head popped out of the ground level door and the indignant beast let them know very plainly its opinion of such a disturbance of the peace.

"Dessie, she got a hopper to stand still and let her pet him. My sister Marya—now she wants a hopper—says they're like kittens. But Ma says they steal too much and we ain't gonna bring any in the cave. I'd like to try to tame one though."

They detoured around a field of the blue-pod grain, meeting the harvesters working there. Dard shook hands with strangers, bewildered by all the new faces. As he went on he asked Lanny:

"How many are there of us now?"

Lanny's lips moved as he counted. "Twenty-five

men—counting you explorers—and twenty-three women. Then there're the girls, my sisters, Marya and Martie, and Dessie and Lara Skort—they're all little. And Don Winson, he's just a baby. That's all. Most of the men are down rippin' up the ship."

"Ripping up the ship?" Why did that dismay him so?

"Sure. We ain't gonna fly again—not enough fuel. And she was made to take apart so we can use parts of her for machine shops and things like that. Well—here we are!"

They came out on what was now a well-defined path running up to the main entrance of the cave. Three men were working on a swinging platform suspended from the top of the cliff, fitting glass into a hole ready to receive it as a window.

"Dardie! Dardie! Dardie!"

A whirlwind swept down upon him, wrapping thin arms about his waist, burrowing a face against him. He went down on his knees and took Dessie into a tight hug.

"Dardie," she was sniffling a little. "They said you would come an' I've been watching all the time! Dardie," she smiled at him blissfully, "I do like this place! I do! There are lots of animals in the grass and some of them have houses just like us—and they like me! Now that you've come home, Dardie, everything is wonderful—truly it is!"

"It sure is, honey."

"So there you are, son," Trade Harmon bore down upon him. "Hungry, too, I'll wager. You come right in and rest and eat. Heard tell that you had yourselves some excitin' times."

With Dessie holding his hand tightly and Lanny

bringing up the rear still carrying his pack, Dard came into a room where there was a long table flanked by benches. Kimber was already sitting there, empty plates before him, talking to an excited Kordov.

"But where did they go—those city dwellers?" the little biologist sputtered as Dard waded into the food Trude Harmon spread before him. "They could not just vanish—pouff!" He snapped his fingers. "As if they were but puffs of smoke!"

Kimber gave the same answer to that question as Dard had made. "Say an epidemic following war—germ warfare—or radiation sickness—who can tell now? By the weathering of the city they have been gone a long time. We found no traces of anything but animal life. And nothing to fear but the lizards . . ."

"A whole world deserted!" Kordov shook his head. "It is enough to frighten one! Those Others took the wrong turning somewhere."

"It is up to us to see that we don't follow their example," Kimber cut in.

That evening the voyagers gathered about a giant camp-fire in the open space before the cliff house, while Kimber and the others in turn recited the saga of their journey into the interior. The city, the robot-controlled battery, the battle with the lizards, held their listeners enthralled. But when they had done the question came again:

"But where did they go?"

Kordov gave the suggested answers, but then he added: "It would be better if we asked ourself now why did they go and be governed by the reply to that. They have left us a deserted land in which to make a new beginning. Though we must not forget that in other continents of this world some remnants of that race may still exist. Wisdom suggests alertness in the future."

Dessie, sitting in Dard's lap, leaned her head back against his shoulder and whispered:

"I like hearing about the night monkeys, Dardie. Do you suppose they will ever come here so I can see them too? Knowing them would be fun."

"Yes, it would," he whispered back.

Maybe someday when they were sure of safety beyond the cliffs, all the Terrans could venture out and he could show Dessie the night monkeys. But not until the last of that scaled death had been found and exterminated!

Since Kimber could not use his arm until the shoulder wound healed, Dard became hands for the pilot, working with Cully on the damaged sled. Seeing that he could and did follow instructions, Cully went back to his own pet project of dismantling the engine of the carrier they had rescued from the sea tube. He intended some day, he insisted, to hunt out that second car from the lizard valley and compare the two.

Dessie kept near them as they worked. She was Dard's shadow in the waking hours, as she had always been since taking her first uncertain steps. The other children were objects to be watched with sober interest, but as yet she preferred company she knew. And, since she was perfectly content to sit quietly, absorbed in the antics of the hoppers, insects, and the butterfly-birds, they often forgot she was with them.

"No—"

Dard was startled into turning by her sudden cry. She was having a tug of war with the largest hopper he had yet seen, a grandfather of a clan at least. But Dessie's strength was superior, and she wrenched away the prize the animal had just stolen from the blouse Dard had discarded in the heat.

"He opened your pocket," she told the boy indignantly, "and he took this out, just as if it were his own! What is it? Pretty—" She crooned the word as she fingered the sheets in which colors ran in waving bands.

"Why—I'd forgotten all about that. It's a book—or I think it is, Dessie. It belonged to Those Others."

"A what!" Kimber reached for it. "Where did you get it kid?"

Dard explained how he had found it in the hidden room of the gun emplacement and of his theory that Those Others might have used the bands of color as a means of communication.

"I was going to compare it with those shots you took on microfilm of that doorway in the city. And then so much happened I forgot all about it."

"You do have a feeling for word patterns—I remember."

"Dard makes pictures out of words." Dessie answered for him. "Show how, Dardie."

Under Kimber's interested eyes Dard sketched out the pattern of a line of verse. The pilot nodded.

"Patterns for words. And that must be how you understood the importance of this. All right. Remember those rolls of some kind of recording tape we found in the first carrier? Rogan believes that they can be read by the help of our machines. You're going down to the ship right now and tell him to get out that equipment. We didn't see any use for it yet and it's been left down these. But I want to know—Yes, go right now!"

So Dard, with Dessie still in tow, set off down river to the seashore where the remains of the star ship were being dismantled as fast as they could use its materials at the cliffs. The red spider plants were again floating in wide patches on the water, but not cloaking all the river as they had on the day the ship landed.

"I haven't been down here yet," Dessie confided. "Mrs. Harmon says that there are bad dragons."

Dard was quick to underline that warning. Dessie might just try to make friends with one of the things!

"Yes, there are, Dessie. And they are not like the animals at all. Promise me that if you see one you will call me right away!"

She was apparently impressed by his gravity for she agreed at once.

"Yes, Dardie. Mr. Rogan brought me a pretty shell from the sea. Might I just go down and see if I can find another?" Dessie asked.

"Stay in sight of the ship and don't wander away," he told her, seeing no reason why she should not hunt for treasures along the water's edge.

The ship which had been so solid and secure against the dangers of outer space was but a shell of her former self. In some places she had been stripped down to the inner framework. Dard squeezed through open partitions to a storeroom where he found the techneer checking the markings on a pile of boxes. When he explained his errand Rogan was enthusiastic.

"Sure we can try reading those tapes. We'll need this, and this, and"—he pushed aside a larger container to free a third—"this. I'll go to work assembling as soon as we get this back to the cliff. Might be able to try running off one roll tonight or early tomorrow. Want to give me a hand?"

Dard took one of the boxes under his arm and hooked his fingers in the carrying handle of another before tramping back over the ramp to the sand.

"Dessie came down with me. She wanted some more sea shells. I'll have to round her up."

"Sure thing." Rogan set down his large box and came along. They were almost at the shore when the scream sent them into a run.

"Dardie! Dardie! Quick—!"

Dard's hand went to the ray gun Cully had given him after the adventure with the lizards. It had a full charge in it now. But they had seen no trace of the monsters here!

"There she is! By those rocks!"

But he didn't need Regan's direction. Dard had already righted Dessie, her back to some sea-washed rocks, shying stones at one of the flying dragons, while she continued to shout for help. To Dard's surprise she made no move to join her rescuers but stood her ground valiantly until he used the ray to slice the head of the dragon and send to body flopping into the sea.

"Come here!" he called but she shook her head. He saw tears on her cheeks.

"It's the sea baby, Dardie, the little baby out of the sea. It's so afraid! We must help it—"

Dard stopped, catching at Rogan to bring him to a halt also. He trusted Dessie's instincts. She had been protecting another creature, not herself, and he had a feeling now that her act was of vast importance to them all. He schooled his voice to a low, even level as he said: "All right, Dessie. The dragon is dead. Can you get the sea baby to come out now—or shall I come to help you?"

She smeared her hand across her wet face. "I can do it, Dard. It's so frightened and it might be more afraid of somebody as big as you."

She squatted down before a small opening between two rocks and made soft coaxing sounds. At last she turned her head.

"It's coming out. But you must stay away—please—"

Dard nodded. Dessie held out her hand to the hollow between the rocks. He was sure, he saw something hesitatingly touch that small palm. Then she wriggled back, still coaxing.

What followed her brought a gasp from Dard, even inured as he now was to the surprises this world had to offer. Some twenty slender inches tall, it walked upright, the four tiny digits of one hand confidently hooked about Dessie's fingers. In color the creature was a soft silvery gray, but when a shaft of sunlight touched the fluff of thick fur which completely covered it, rainbow lights twinkled from each hair tip.

Its head was round, with no vestige of ears, the eyes very large, turning from Dessie to the two men. When it caught sight of them it stopped short and, with a gesture which won Dard completely, put the other hand to its wide, ranged mouth, chewing on its fingertips shyly. The small feet were webbed and scaled with rainbow tints, as were the hands. He continued to examine it, puzzled. It was akin to the night-howling monkeys, but it was much smaller and plainly amphibian. And it appeared to be able to see perfectly well in the daylight.

"Where did it come from, Dessie?" he asked quietly, trying hard not to alarm the engaging little thing.

"Out of the sea," she waved her free hand at the waves. "I was hunting shells and I found a pretty one. When I went down to wash the sand off it there he was, coming out of the water to watch me. He was sleeked down with the wet then—he's a lot prettier now—" She broke off and stopped to address her companion with a series of chirrups such as Dard had heard her use with the wild things of lost Terra.

"Then," she continued, "that bad dragon came and chased him into the rocks and I called you—like you told me to, Dardie, if I saw a dragon. They are bad. The sea baby was so frightened."

"Did it tell you so?" asked Rogan eagerly.

Perhaps it was the vibration of his deeper voice in the air which sent the sea creature crowding against Dessie, half hiding its face against her.

"Please, Mr. Rogan," she shook her head reprovingly. "He's afraid when you talk. No, I don't think he talks like us. I just know what he feels—here," she touched a forefinger to her head. "He wanted to play with me so he came ashore. He's a nice baby—the nicest I ever, ever knew! Better than a fox or a bunny or even the big owl."

"Great Space! Look there—off the rocks!"

Dard's eyes followed the line of Rogan's pointing finger. Two sleek round heads bobbed out of the water, great unblinking orbs were, turned to the party on the beach. Dard's grasp on Rogan's arm tightened.

"Keep quiet! This is important!"

Dessie beamed at their interruption.

"More sea people! Look, baby!" She directed the mer-child's attention seaward.

Instantly it slipped its hand free and ran to the edge of the water. But, just as it was about to plunge into the waves, it stopped and looked back at Dessie. While it teetered there, toes in the lapping waves, the two others of its race swam into the shallows and arose to their feet to wade in. The merchild made up its mind and splashed out to meet the shorter of the two advancing figures and was gathered up in eager arms. The largest of the three—an inch or two above four feet Dard judged—moved in between its mate and child and those on shore.

"See what it's carrying!" Rogan schooled his voice with an effort.

But Dard needed no one to point out that discovery. The merman was armed with a spear, a spear with a mean looking many barbed head. And about his loins was a belt supporting a small, fastened case and a long dagger of pointed bone. This was no animal!

The merchild struggled to free itself, slipped under the reaching hand of its father, and darted back to Dessie. Grabbing again at her hand, it tugged her toward the couple in the water. Dard moved up, he didn't like the look of that spear.

But before he could get to Dessie the merman thrust that weapon at something washing along the rocks. When he raised the spear its point impaled the headless body of the dragon. With a gesture of fury the merman smashed the battered corpse down on the stone, ripping it off the barbs. Then he splashed up to Dessie and caught the merchild, giving it a smart slap across its buttocks with a very human expression of exasperation. Dard chuckled and forgot his momentary fears.

The merpeople were unhuman in appearance but they appeared to share certain emotions with the Terrans. Dard stepped cautiously into the water. The merman was instantly alert, his spear on guard, backing toward his mate and the child he had pushed out to her.

Dard held out empty hands in the gesture of good will as old as time. The merman's big eyes searched his. Then slowly that spear was lowered, to be laid on wet sand, with webbed toes curled over it to hold it safe, and the rainbow scaled paws were raised in the right answer.

—9—
TREATY AND ALLIANCE

"WHEN'S BLAST-OFF?" Cully was boring holes in the sand with one finger, restless away from his machines.

Dard glanced along the line of the six men who had accompanied him down to the shore. They sat cross-legged in the sand with strict orders to keep quiet and wait. The first meeting between the Terrans and the representatives of the merpeople had been scheduled for this afternoon—if he had been able to get the idea across in gestures alone.

Spread out on the shore several feet above the water level were those gifts the Terrans believed might please sea dwellers. Some nested plastic bowls made a bright-colored spot, a collection of empty bottles of various sizes, hastily assembled from laboratory supplies, golden apples, native grain, all there together. Objects which could be used under water had been hard to find.

"They're coming!" Dessie had been waiting impatiently by the waves' sweep, and now, heedless of the water curling about her legs, she ran forward, holding out her hands to the merchild who threshed up a fountain of spray in its eagerness to meet her. Hand in hand they pattered to dry land where the merchild shrank shyly against the little girl when it saw the men.

But Dessie was smiling and said importantly, "Ssssat and Ssssutu are coming now."

Dard hid his surprise. How could Dessie so confidently mouth those queer names—how did she know? From all his questioning—and Kimber's and Kordov's and Carlee's—last night, they had only been able to elicit that the "sea people thought into her head." They had been forced to accept the concept of telepathy—which could be possible with an undersea race.

So, deciding that Dessie's interpretation might be needed that day, they had schooled her in her part.

Ssssat and Ssssutu—if those were the proper designations of the mermen who were borne in with the next wave—came ashore. They both carried the barbed spears and wore long bone daggers at the belts which were their only articles of clothing. Without a sound they seated themselves on the seaside of the gifts, facing Dard, regarding him and the other Terrans with owlish solemnity.

"Dessie!" Dard called, and she came trotting to him.

"Do I give the presents now, Dard?"

"Yes. Try to make them understand that we want to be friends."

She picked out two of the bowls, put an apple and a handful of grain into each, and carried them over to set down before the envoys.

The one on Dard's right held out his hand and Dessie, without hesitation, laid hers, palm down, upon it. For a long moment they made contact. Then both mermen relaxed their tense watchfulness. They put their spears behind them and one ran his hands through the fur on his head and shoulders where it was fast drying into rainbow dotted fluff.

"They want to be friends, too," Bessie reported. "Dardie, if you put your hand on theirs, then they can talk to you. They don't talk with their mouths at all. This, is Ssssat—"

Dard got to his feet slowly so as not to alarm the mermen and crossed the strip of shore until he could sit face to face. Then he held out his hand. Cool and damp the scaled digits and palm of the other lay upon his warmer flesh. And, Dard almost broke the contact in his surprise and awe, for the other was talking to him! Words, ideas, swept into his mind—some concepts so alien he could not understand. But bit by bit he pieced together much of what the other was striving to tell him.

"Big ones, land dwellers, we have watched you—with fear. Fear that you have come to lead us once more into the pens of darkness—"

"Pens of darkness?" Dard echoed aloud and then shaped a mental query.

"Those who once walked the land here—they kept the pens of darkness where our fathers' fathers' fathers"—the concept of a long stretch of past time trailed through the Terran's receptive mind—"were hatched. The days of fire came and we broke forth and now we shall never return." There was stern warning, an implied threat, in that.

"We know nothing of the pens, nor do we threaten you," Dard thought slowly. "We, too, have broken out of pens of darkness," he added with sudden inspiration.

"It is true that you are not the color or shape of those who made the pens. And you have shown only friendship. Also you killed the flying death which would have slain my cub. I believe that you are good. Will you stay here?"

Dard pointed inland. "We build there."

"Do you wish the fruits of the river?" came next.

The fruits of the river?" Dard was puzzled until a clear picture of one of the red spider plants formed in his mind. Then he shook his head to reinforce his unspoken denial.

"We may then come and harvest as we have always done? And," there was a shrewd bargaining note in this, "perhaps you will see that the flying death does not attack us; since your slaying powers are greater than ours?"

"We like the dragons no better than you do. Let me speak with the others now—" Dard broke contact and reported to the Terran committee.

"Sure!" Santee's jovial boom could not be kept to a whisper and at the sound, or its vibration, both mermen started. "Let 'em come in and get their spiders. I'll watch for dragons."

"Fair enough," Kimber agreed. "We don't care for the dragons any more than they do."

Before the hour had passed cordial relations had been established, and the mermen promised to return early the next morning with their harvest crew. Carrying the gifts they waded out into the sea, Ssssat's cub riding on his father's shoulder. The little one waved back at Dessie until all three disappeared under water.

"Those pens they spoke of," Kordov mused later that night when they discussed the meeting in an open convocation of all the voyagers. "They must have been

imprisoned at one time by the city builders and escaped
during or after the war. But surely they weren't domestic
animals."

"More likely slaves," suggested Carlee Skort. "Perhaps
they were forced to do undersea work where landsmen
could not venture. They are coming tomorrow? Well, why
can't we all go down and meet them? Maybe we can help
in the harvesting and prove our good will."

The clamor which interrupted and supported her was
indicative of the enthusiasm of the rest. Dessie's merpeople
had caught the imaginations of all. And Dard believed
that the Terrans would have gone to meet them in any
case.

Early as the colonists came down to the river bank the
next morning, the merpeople were there before them,
wading along the shallows of the slowly flowing stream,
sweeping between them woven basket nets, as fine as
sieves, to skim up the red fungi. Merchildren paddled in
and out, and a line of spear-bearing males patrolled the
shoreline with attention for the cliff perches of the dragons.

They stopped all these activities as the Terrans came
into sight, and when they began again it was with a certain
self-consciousness. Dard and the others who had been on
the seashore the day before went up to meet the sea
people, their hands outstretched.

A party of the armed males split off to face them. In
the center of their group was one portly individual who,
though there was no way save by size for the humans to
guess at merman ages, gave the impression of dignity and
authority.

Dard touched palms with the leading warrior.

"This is Aaaatak, our 'Friend of Many.' He would communicate with your "Giver of Law.'"

"Giver of Law." Kordov came the nearest to being the leader of the colonists. Dard beckoned to the First Scientist.

"This is their chieftain, sir. He wants to speak to our leader."

"So? I can not call myself leader," Kordov met the hands of the older merman, "but I am honored to speak to him." As Kordov and the merchief clasped hands the rest of the colonists came up, timidly. But an hour later merpeople and humans mingled with freedom. And when the Terran party set out food, the mermen brought in their own supplies, flat baskets of fish and aquatic plants, kept in water until time to eat. They accepted the golden apples eagerly, but kept away from the fires where their hosts cooked the fish they offered in return. Although each fire had a ring of amazed spectators, standing at a safe distance to gaze at the wonder.

Three dragons that dared to invade were brought down with rays, to the savage exultation of the merpeople. They asked to inspect the weapons and returned them regretfully when they understood that such arms would not last in their water world.

"Though," Cully said thoughtfully, when this had been explained, "I don't see why they couldn't use some of the metal forged by Those Others. It seems to resist rust and erosion on land—it might in the water."

"Nordis!"

The urgency in that call brought Dard away from the engineer to the small group of Kimber, Kordov, the merchief and several others. Harmon was mere, as well as Santee, and some techneers.

"Yes, sir?"

"You've seen the lizards, ask Aaaatak if those are what he is trying to tell us about. We can't get the right impression of what he means and it seems to be vitally important." Kordov edged back for the boy to take his place. Dard clasped the readily extended claws of the merchief.

"Do you wish to tell us about—" He shut his eyes in order to concentrate better upon a mental image of the huge reptiles.

"No!" The answer was a decided negative. "Those we have seen, yes—hunting down other land dwellers. They were once subordinate to those we speak of now. These—"

Another picture indeed—a biped—humanoid in outline—but somehow all wrong. Dard had seen nothing like it. And the image was fuzzy, indistinct as if he observed it from a distance—or through water!

Through water! That was caught up eagerly by Aaaatak.

"Now you are thinking straight. We do not come out of hiding when those are about! So we see them in that fashion—"

"They live on land, men? Near here?" Dard demanded. The emotion of fear colored so strongly all the impressions he received from the merchief.

"They live on land, yes. Near here, no, or we should not be here. We hunt out shores where they do not come. Once they were very, very many, living everywhere—

here—across the sea. They were the builders of those pens where creatures of my kind were imprisoned for them to work their will upon. Then something happened. There came fire raining from the sky, and a sickness which struck them. They died, some quickly, some much more slowly, when my people burst from the pens." There was a cold and deadly satisfaction in that flash of memory. "After that we fled into the wilds of the sea where they could not find us. Even when I was but a new-hatched cub we lived in the depths. But through the years our young warriors went out to search for food and for a safer place to live—there are monsters in the deeps as horrible as the lizards of the land. And these parties discovered that those"—again Dard saw the queer biped— "were gone from long stretches among the reefs, as we had always longed to do."

"There are none of those left in this land now but—" The merchief hesitated before suddenly withdrawing his hand from Dard's and turning to his followers as if consulting them. Dard took the opportunity to translate to the others what he had learned.

"Survivors of Those Others," Kimber caught him up. "But not here?"

"No. Aaaatak says that his people will not come where they are. Wait—he has more to tell."

For Aaaatak was holding out his hand and Dard met it readily.

"My people now believe that you are not like those. You do not seem in body quite the same, your skin is of a different color," he drew his claw finger across the back of Dard's hand to emphasize his meaning, "and you have—received us as one free people greets another. This those others do not—there is much hate and bitterness between us from the far past—and they always delight in killing.

"We have watched you ever since you first came out of the sky. Those others once traveled in the sky—though of late we have not seen their bird ships—and so we thought you of the same breed. Now we know that that is untrue. But we must tell you—be on your guard! For on the other side of the sea those others still live, even if their numbers are few, and there is a blackness in their minds which leads them to raise spears against all living things!

"Now," Dard had a strong impression that the merchief was coming to the main point, "we are a people who know much about the sea, but little of the land. We have learned that you are not native of this world, having fallen from the sky—but, did you not also say that you came from a place where, you, too, were penned by enemies?"

Dard assented, remembering his statement to the first envoys.

"If you are wise you will not seek out those who would lay such bonds upon you again. For that is what those others will do. In this world they recognize no other rights or desires than are born of their own wills. We have warriors of our race who keep watch upon them secretly and bring news of their coming and going. Against their might—though they have lost much of their ancient knowledge—we have only our own cunning and knowledge of the sea. And what good is a spear against that which may kill at—a distance? But you have mightier weapons. And should we two peoples join skills and hearts against them—But do you now say this to your Giver of Laws and other Elder Ones so that they may understand." He withdrew his hand again and left Dard to interpret.

"An alliance!" Tas Kordov caught the meaning of that offer. "Hmm," he plucked his lower lip. "Better tell him— No, let me. I'll explain that we shall talk it over."

"What's all this 'bout Those Others?" Harmon demanded. "Did they," he indicated the merpeople, "say that they're still here—the ones who lived in that city?"

"Not here—across the sea," Dard was beginning when Rogan broke in.

"That chieftain doesn't think much of them, does he?"

"He says they're enemies."

"They aren't his kind," Harmon pointed out "And his people were their slaves once."

"We," Kimber said slowly, "have had some experience with slavery ourselves, haven't we? On Terra we'd have been in labor camps, if we hadn't been lucky—that is if we weren't shot down in cold blood, I have a pretty good memory of the last few years there."

Harmon sifted a palmful of sand from one hand to another. "Yeah, I know. Only we don't want to get into no local war."

That echoed after his voice died away. No entangling alliances to drag them into any war! Dard sensed the electric agreement which ran through them at that thought. Only Kimber, Santee, and maybe Kordov, did not wholly agree with Harmon.

Dard gazed down to the river bank. The merpeople had almost completed the harvest and were gathering up their possessions and slipping in family groups back to the sea. He wondered what Kordov would tell the chief.

Suddenly he could not stand the uncertainty any longer. He wanted to get away—to escape from the thought that perhaps it was going to start all over again— the insecurity—the constant guard duty against a hostile force.

According to the merchief Those Others were now across the sea—but would they remain there? Wouldn't this fertile, deserted land where they had once ruled draw them back again? And they would not accept new settlers kindly.

If the Terrans only knew more about them! Those Others had blasted their world. Dard remembered the callous cruelty of that barn in the valley. Raids, looting, the blasted city, the robot-controlled guns to shoot anything passing out of the air, the warnings of the merpeople.

He plodded across the sand to the inner valley, heading for the cliff house. Rogan had set up the projector the night before, and they had put the first of the discovered tapes in it. If something about the rulers of this world could be learned from those—this was the time to do it!

"Where're you bound for, kid?" Kimber fell into step.

"The cliffs," Dard was being pushed by the feeling that time was not his to waste, that he must know—now!

The pilot asked no more questions but followed Dard into the rock cell where Rogan had installed his machine. The boy checked the preparation made the night before. He turned off the light—the screen on the wall was a glowing square of blue-white and then the projector began to hum.

"This one of those rolls from the carrier?"

But Dard did not answer. For now the screen was in use. He began to watch. . . .

"Turn it off! Turn that off!"

His frenzied fingers found the proper button. They were surrounded by honest light, clean red-yellow walls.

Kimber's face was in his hands, the harshness of his breathing filled the room. Dard, shaken, sick, dazed not move. He gripped the edge of the shelf which supported the projector, gripped so tightly that the flesh under his nails turned dead white. He tried to concentrate upon that phenomenon—not on what he had just seen.

"What—what did you see?" he moistened his lips and asked dully. He had to know. Maybe it was only his own reaction. But—but it couldn't be! The very thought that only he had seen that led to panic—to a terror beyond bearing.

"I don't know . . ." Kimber's answer dragged out of him word by painful word. "It wasn't meant—ever meant for man—our kind of man—to see—"

Dard raised his head, made himself stare at that innocuous screen, to assure himself that there was nothing there now.

"It did something to me—inside," he half whispered.

"It was meant to, I think. But—Great Lord—what sort of minds—feelings—did they have! Not human—totally alien. We have no common meeting point—we never shall have—with that!"

"And it was all just color, twisting, turning color," Dard began.

Kimber's hand closed about his wrist with crushing intensity.

"I was right," Dard did not feel the pain of that grip, "they used color as a means of communication. But—but—"

"What they had to say with it! Yes, not for us—never for us. Keep your mind off it, Dard. Five minutes more of that and you might not have been human—ever again!"

"We couldn't establish contact with them—with—"

"Minds that could conceive that? No, we can't. So that was what brought you here—you wanted to see if Harmon was right in his neutral policy? Now you know—with that we have no common ground. And we'll have to make the others understand. If we do meet Those Others—the result will undoubtedly be war."

"Fifty-three of us—maybe a whole nation of them left."

Dard was still sick and shaken—sensing a deep inner violation.

First there had been the tyranny of Pax, which had been man-made and so understandable, in all its narrow cruelty because it had been the work of human beings. And now this—which man dared not—touch!

Kimber had regained control of himself. There was even a trace of the familiar impish grin on his face as he said:

"When the fighting is the toughest, that's when our breed digs in toes. And we needn't borrow trouble. Get Kordov and Harmon in here. If we are going to discuss the offer of the mermen we want them to know what to expect from overseas."

But—to Dard's dismay—the projection of Those Others' tapes aroused in Harmon no more than a vague uneasiness—though it shook Kordov. And, as they insisted on the rest of the men viewing it, they discovered that it varied in its effects upon different individuals. Rogan, sensitive to communication devices, almost fainted after a few moments' strict attention. Santee admitted that he did not like it but couldn't say why. But, in the end, the weight of evidence was that they could not hope to deal with Those Others.

"I'm still sayin'," Harmon insisted, "that we shouldn't get pulled into anything them seapeople has started. You say them pictures make Those Others regular devils. Well, they're still across the sea. We shouldn't go lookin' for trouble—then maybe we don't find none!"

"We're not suggesting an expeditionary force, Tim," Kimber answered mildly. "But if they are alive overseas they may just get the idea to reclaim this land—and you'd want to know about it ahead of time if they did. The mermen will keep us informed. Then we could supply them with better arms."

"Yeah, and right there you've got trouble! You make sea-goin' ray guns and the first thing you know they're gonna use 'em. They hate Those Others, don't they? Back on earth we picked off a Peaceman whenever we got the chance, didn't we? And let that happen a coupla times and Those Others are gonna come lookin' for where those new guns came from. I ain't sayin' we oughta turn our backs on the mermen—they seem peaceful. But we're plain foolish if we get mixed up in any war of theirs. I said it before and I'm gonna keep on sayin' it!"

"All right, Tim. And you're speaking the truth. But this is good land, ain't it?"

"Sure, it's good land! We're gonna have a mighty fine farm here. But farmin' and fightin' don't mix. What about that fella what lived right over there? He didn't live out the last war, did he?"

"Suppose they want this good land back? How long can we defend it?"

For the first time a shadow of doubt appeared in Tim Harmon's eyes.

"Okay!" he flung up a hand in surrender. "I'll go with you halfway. I say be friends with the mermen and help 'em—some. But I'm not gonna vote for no gangin' up with 'em in a private war!"

"That's all we want you to do, Tim. We'll ally with the mermen and make plans for defense," Kordov soothed him.

Dard smiled wryly. Inside he was amused, amused and tired. They had come across the galaxy to escape to freedom, only to live again under the shadow of fear. It was a long way to travel to come—home!

A new frontier to guard. What was that thing Kimber had once quoted while standing on a mountainside in the Terran winter?

"Frontiers of any type, physical or mental, are but a challenge to our breed. Nothing can stop the questing of men, not even Man. If we will it, not only the wonders of space, but the very stars are ours!"

They had known the wonders of space, the stars were theirs—if they could hold them! But who—or what— dared to say that they could not? Why, Dard savored the new pride growing hotly within him, they had broken the bonds of space—

There was a wide world before them, unlimited in its possibilities. On distant Terra this ill-assorted group had drawn into tight alliance because they believed alike—in what? Freedom—Man's freedom! They had faced the sterility of Pax clear-eyed and refused to be bound by it—entrusting their lives to the knowledge Pax had outlawed—and it had brought them here. They—if they willed it—worked for a united goal—they could do anything!

Dard's eyes were on the painted cliffs but inwardly he saw beyond—across the wide and waiting land. Alliance with the merpeople—taming of the land—building a new civilization—his breath came faster. Why a lifetime was not going to be time enough to do everything that even he could see had to be done.

Could their breed be defeated? He gave his answer to the uncertain future with a single word:

"NO!"

STAR BORN

"What of our children—the second and third
   generations born on this new world? They will have no
memories of Terra's green hills and blue seas. Will they be
Terrans—or something else?"
                    —Tas Kordov, Record of the First Years

⫸1⫷
SHOOTING STAR

THE TRAVELERS had sighted the cove from the sea—a narrow bite into the land, the first break in the cliff wall which protected the interior of this continent from the pounding of the ocean. And, although it was still but mid-afternoon, Dalgard pointed the outrigger into the promised shelter, the dip of his steering paddle swinging in harmony with that wielded by Sssuri in the bow of their narrow, wave-riding craft.

The two voyagers were neither of the same race nor of the same species, yet they worked together without words, as if they had established some bond which gave them a rapport transcending the need for speech.

Dalgard Nordis was a son of the Colony; his kind had not originated on this planet. He was not as tall nor as heavily built as those Terran outlaw ancestors who had fled political enemies across the Galaxy to establish a foothold on Astra, and there were other subtle differences between his generation and the parent stock.

Thin and wiry, his skin was brown from the gentle

toasting of the summer sun, making the fairness of his closely cropped hair even more noticeable. At his side was his long bow, carefully wrapped in water-resistant flying-dragon skin, and from the belt which supported his short breeches of tanned duocorn hide swung a two-foot blade—half wood-knife, half sword. To the eyes of his Terran forefathers he would have presented a barbaric picture. In his own mind he was amply clad and armed for the man-journey which was both his duty and his heritage to make before he took his place as a full adult in the Council of Free Men.

In contrast to Dalgard's smooth skin, Sssuri was covered with a fluffy pelt of rainbow-tipped gray fur. In place of the human's steel blade, he wore one of bone, barbed and ugly, as menacing as the spear now resting in the bottom of the outrigger. And his round eyes watched the sea with the familiarity of one whose natural home was beneath those same waters.

The mouth of the cove was narrow, but after they negotiated it they found themselves in a pocket of bay, sheltered and calm, into which trickled a lazy stream. The gray-blue of the seashore sand was only a fringe beyond which was turf and green stuff. Sssur's nostril flaps expanded as he tested the warm breeze, and Dalgard was busy cataloguing scents as they dragged their craft ashore. They could not have found a more perfect place for a camp site.

Once the canoe was safely beached, Sssuri picked up his spear and, without a word or backward glance, waded out into the sea, disappearing into the depths, while his companion set about his share of camp tasks. It was still early in the summer—too early to expect to find ripe fruit. But Dalgard rummaged in his voyager's bag and brought out a half-dozen crystal beads. He laid these out on a flat-topped stone by the stream, seating himself cross-legged beside it.

To the onlooker it would appear that the traveler was meditating. A wide-winged living splotch of color fanned by overhead; there was a distant yap of sound. Dalgard neither looked nor listened. But perhaps a minute later what he awaited arrived. A hopper, its red-brown fur sleek and gleaming in the sun, its eternal curiosity drawing it, peered cautiously from the bushes. Dalgard made mind touch. The hoppers did not really think—at least not on the levels where communication was possible for the colonists—but sensations of friendship and good will could be broadcast, primitive ideas exchanged.

The small animal, its humanlike front paw-hands dangling over its creamy vest, came out fully into the open, black eyes flicking from the motionless Dalgard to the bright beads on the rock. But when one of those paws shot out to snatch the treasure, the traveler's hand was already cupped protectingly over the hoard. Dalgard formed a mental picture and beamed it at the twenty-inch creature before him. The hopper's ears twitched nervously, its blunt nose wrinkled, and then it bounded back into the brush, a weaving line of moving grass marking its retreat.

Dalgard withdrew his hand from the beads. Through the years the Astran colonists had come to recognize the virtues of patience. Perhaps the mutation had begun before they left their native world. Or perhaps the change in temperament and nature had occurred in the minds and bodies of that determined handful of refugees as they rested in the frozen cold sleep while their ship bore them through the wide, uncharted reaches of deep space for centuries of Terran time. How long that sleep had lasted the survivors had never known. But those who had awakened on Astra were different.

And their sons and daughters, and the sons and daughters of two more generations were warmed by a new sun, nourished by food grown in alien soil, taught the mind contact by the amphibian mermen with whom the space voyagers had made an early friendship—each succeeding child more attuned to the new home, less tied to the far-off world he had never seen or would see. The colonists were not of the same breed as their fathers, their grandfathers, or great-grandfathers. So, with other gifts, they had also a vast, time-consuming patience, which could be a weapon or a tool, as they pleased—not forgetting the instantaneous call to action which was their older heritage.

The hopper returned. On the rock beside the shining things it coveted, it dropped dried and shriveled fruit. Dalgard's fingers separated two of the gleaming marbles, rolled them toward the animal, who scooped them up with a chirp of delight. But it did not leave. Instead it peered intently at the rest of the beads. Hoppers had their own form of intelligence, though it might not compare with that of humans. And this one was enterprising. In the end it delivered three more loads of fruit from its burrow and took away all the beads, both parties well pleased with their bargains.

Sssuri splashed out of the sea with as little ado as he had entered. On the end of his spear twisted a fish. His fur, slicked flat to his strongly muscled body, began to dry in the air and fluff out while the sun awoke prismatic lights on the scales which covered his hands and feet. He dispatched the fish and cleaned it neatly, tossing the offal back into the water, where some shadowy things arose to tear at the unusual bounty.

"This is not hunting ground." His message formed in Dalgard's mind. "That finned one had no fear of me."

"We were right then in heading north; this is new land." Dalgard got to his feet.

On either side, the cliffs, with their alternate bands of red, blue, yellow, and white strata, walled in this pocket. They would make far better time keeping to the sea lanes, where it was not necessary to climb. And it was Dalgard's cherished plan to add more than just an inch or two to the explorers' map in the Council Hall.

Each of the colony males was expected to make his man-journey of discovery some time between his eighteenth and twentieth year. He went alone or, if he formed an attachment with one of the mermen near his own age, accompanied only by his knife brother. And from knowledge so gained the still-small group of exiles added to and expanded their information about their new home.

Caution was drilled into them. For they were not the first masters of Astra, nor were they the masters now. There were the ruins left by Those Others, the race who had populated this planet until their own wars had completed their downfall. And the mermen, with their traditions of slavery and dark beginnings in the experimental pens of the older race, continued to insist that across the sea— on the unknown western continent—Those Others still held onto the remnants of a degenerate civilization. Thus the explorers from Homeport went out by ones and twos and used the fauna of the land as a means of gathering information.

Hoppers could remember yesterday only dimly, and instinct took care of tomorrow. But what happened today sped from hopper to hopper and could warn by mind touch both merman and human. If one of the dread snake-devils of the interior was on the hunting trail, the hoppers sped the warning. Their vast curiosity brought them to the fringe of any disturbance, and they passed the reason for it along. Dalgard knew there were a thousand eyes at his service whenever he wanted them. There was little chance of being taken by surprise, no matter how dangerous this journey north might be.

"The city—" He formed the words in his mind even as he spoke them aloud. "How far are we from it?"

The merman hunched his slim shoulders in the shrug of his race. "Three days' travel, maybe five. And it"— though his furred face displayed no readable emotion, the sensation of distaste was plain—"was one of the accursed ones. To such we have not returned since the days of falling fire—"

Dalgard was well acquainted with the ruins which lay not many miles from Homeport. And he knew that that sprawling, devastated metropolis was not taboo to the merman. But this other mysterious settlement he had recently heard of was still shunned by the sea people. Only Sssuri and a few others of youthful years would consider a journey to explore the long-forbidden section their traditions labeled as dangerous land.

The belief that he was about to venture into questionable territory had made Dalgard evasive when he reported his plans to the Elders three days earlier. But since such trips were, by tradition, always thrusts into the unknown, they had not questioned him too much. All in all, Dalgard thought, watching Sssuri flake the firm pink flesh from the fish, he might deem himself lucky and this quest ordained. He went off to hack out armloads of grass and fashion the sleep mats for the sun-warmed ground.

They had eaten and were lounging in content on the soft sand just beyond the curl of the waves when Sssuri lifted his head from his folded arms as if he listened. Like all those of his species, his vestigial ears were hidden deep in his fur and no longer served any real purpose; the mind touch served him in their stead. Dalgard caught his thought, though what had aroused his companion was too rare a thread to trouble his less acute senses.

"Runners in the dark—"

Dalgard frowned. "It is still sun time. What disturbs them?"

To the eye Sssuri was still listening to that which his friend could not hear.

"They come from afar. They are on the move to find new hunting grounds."

Dalgard sat up. To each and every scout from Homeport the unusual was a warning, a signal to alert mind and body. The runners in the night—that furred monkey race of hunters who combed the moonless dark of Astra when most of the higher fauna were asleep—were very distantly related to Sssuri's species, though the gap between them was that between highly civilized man and the jungle ape. The runners were harmless and shy, but they were noted also for clinging stubbornly to one particular district generation after generation. To find such a clan on the move into new territory was to be fronted with a puzzle it might be well to investigate.

"A snake-devil—" he suggested tentatively, forming a mind picture of the vicious reptilian danger which the colonists tried to kill on sight whenever and wherever encountered. His hand went to the knife at his belt. One met with weapons only that hissing hatred motivated by a brainless ferocity which did not know fear.

But Sssuri did not accept that explanation. He was sitting up, facing inland where the thread of valley met the cliff wall. And seeing his absorption, Dalgard asked no distracting questions.

"No, no snake-devil—" after long moments came the answer. He got to his feet, shuffling through the sand in the curious little half dance which betrayed his agitation more strongly than his thoughts had done.

"The hoppers have no news," Dalgard said.

Sssuri gestured impatiently with one outflung hand. "Do the hoppers wander far from their own nest mounds? Somewhere there—" he pointed to the left and north, "there is trouble, bad trouble. Tonight we shall speak with the runners and discover what it may be."

Dalgard glanced about the camp with regret. But he made no protest as he reached for his bow and stripped off its protective casing. With the quiver of heavy-duty arrows slung across his shoulder he was ready to go, following Sssuri inland.

The easy valley path ended less than a quarter of a

mile from the sea, and they were fronted by a wall of rock with no other option than to climb. But the westering sun made plain every possible hand and foot hold on its surface.

When they stood at last on the heights and looked ahead, it was across a broken stretch of bare rock with the green of vegetation beckoning from at least a mile beyond. Sssuri hesitated for only a moment or two, his round, almost featureless head turning slowly, until he fixed on a northeasterly course—striking out unerringly as if he could already sight the goal. Dalgard fell in behind, looking over the country with a wary eye. This was just the type of land to harbor flying dragons. And while those pests were small, their lightning-swift attack from above made them foes not to be disregarded. But all the flying things he saw were two moth birds of delicate hues engaging far over the sun-baked rock in one of their graceful winged dances.

They crossed the heights and came to the inland slope, a drop toward the central interior plains of the continent. As they plowed through the high grasses Dalgard knew they were under observation. Hoppers watched them. And once through a break in a line of trees he saw a small herd of duocorns race into the shelter of a wood. The presence of those two-horned creatures, so like the pictures he had seen of Terran horses, was insurance that the snake-devils did not hunt in this district, for the swift-footed duocorns were never found within a day's journey of their archenemies.

Late afternoon faded into the long summer twilight and still Sssuri kept on. As yet they had come across no traces of Those Others. Here were none of the domed farm buildings, the monorail tracks, the other relics one could find about Homeport. This wide-open land could have been always a wilderness, left to the animals of Astra for their own. Dalgard speculated upon that, his busy imagination supplying various reasons for such tract. Then the voiceless communication of his companion provided an explanation.

"This was barrier land."

"What?"

Sssuri turned his head. His round eyes which blinked so seldom stared into Dalgard's as if by the intensity of that gaze he could drive home deeper his point.

"What lies to the north was protected in the days before the falling fire. Even Those"—the distorted mermen symbol for Those Others was sharpened by the very hatred of all Sssuri's kind, which had not paled during the generations since their escape from slavery to Astra's one-time masters—"could not venture into some of their own private places without special leave. It is perhaps true that the city we are seeking is one of those restricted ones and that this wilderness is a boundary for it."

Dalgard's pace slowed. To venture into a section of land which had been used as a barrier to protect some secret of Those Others was a highly risky affair. The first expedition sent out from Homeport after the landing of the Terran refugee ship had been shot down by robot-controlled guns still set against some long-dead invader. Would this territory be so guarded? If so they had better go carefully now—

Sssuri suddenly struck off at an angle, heading not

northeast now, but directly north. The brush lands along the foot of the cliffs gave way to open fields, bare except for the grass rippled by the wind. It was not the type of country to attract the night runners, and Dalgard wondered a little. They should discover water, preferably a shallow stream, if they wanted to find what the monkey creatures liked best.

Within a quarter-hour he knew that Sssuri was not going wrong. Cradled in a sudden dip in the land was the stream Dalgard had been looking for. A hopper lifted a dripping muzzle from the shore ripples and stared at them. Dalgard contacted the animal. It was its usual curious self, nothing had alarmed or excited its interest. And he did not try to establish more than a casual contact as they made their way down the bank to the edge of the stream, Sssuri splashing in ankle-deep for the sheer pleasure of feeling liquid curl about his feet and legs once more.

Water dwellers fled from their passing and insects buzzed and hovered. Otherwise they moved through a deserted world. The stream bed widened and small islands of gravel, swept together in untidy piles by the spring floods, arose dry topped, some already showing the green of venturesome plants.

"Here—" Sssuri stopped, thrusting the butt of his spear into the shore of one such islet. He dropped cross-legged on his choice, there to remain patiently until those he sought would come with the dark. Dalgard withdrew a little way downstream and took up a similar post. The runners were shy, not easy to approach. And they would come more readily if Sssuri were alone.

Here the murmur of the stream was loud, rising above

the rustle of the wind-driven grass. And the night was coming fast as the sun, hidden by the cliff wall, sank into the sea. Dalgard, knowing that his night sight was far inferior to that of the native Astran fauna, resignedly settled himself for an all-night stay, not without a second regretful memory of the snug camp by the shore.

Twilight and then night. How long before the runners would make their appearance? He could pick up the sparks of thought which marked the coming and going of hoppers, most hurrying off to their mud-plastered nests, and sometimes a flicker from the mind of some other night creature. Once he was sure he touched the avid, raging hunger which marked a flying dragon, though they were not naturally hunters by darkness.

Dalgard made no move to contact Sssuri. The merman must be left undisturbed in his mental quest for the runners.

The scout lay back on his miniature island and stared up into the sky, trying to sort out all the myriad impressions of life about him. It was then that he saw it. . . .

An arrow of fire streaking across the black bowl of Astra's night sky. A light so vivid, so alien, that it brought him to his feet with a chill prickle of apprehension along his spine. In all his years as a scout and woodsman, in all the stories of his fellows and his elders at Homeport—he had never seen, never heard of the like of that!

And through his own wonder and alert alarm, he caught Sssuri's added puzzlement.

"Danger—" The merman's verdict fed his own unease.

Danger had crossed the night, from east to west. And to the west lay what they had always feared. What was going to happen now?

⫸ 2 ⫷
PLANEFALL

RAF KURBI, flitter pilot and techneer, lay on the padded shock cushion of his assigned bunk and stared with wide, disillusioned eyes at the stretch of stark, gray metal directly overhead. He tried to close his ears to the mutter of meaningless words coming from across the narrow cabin. Raf had known from the moment his name had been drawn as crew member that the whole trip would be a gamble, a wild gamble with the odds all against them. RS 10—those very numbers on the nose of the ship told part of the story. Ten exploring fingers thrust in turn out into the blackness of space. RS 3's fate was known—she had blossomed into a pinpoint of flame within the orbit of Mars. And RS 7 had clearly gone out of control while instruments on Terra could still pick up her broadcasts. Of the rest—well, none had returned.

But the ships were built, manned by lot from the trainees, and sent out, one every five years, with all that had been learned from the previous job, each refinement the engineers could discover incorporated into the latest to rise from the launching cradle.

RS 10—Raf closed his eyes with weary distaste. After months of being trapped inside her ever-vibrating shell, he felt that he knew each and every rivet, seam, and plate in her only too well. And there was no reason yet to believe that the voyage would ever end. They would just go on and on through empty space until dead men manned a drifting hulk—

There—to picture that was a danger signal. Whenever his thoughts reached that particular point, Raf tried to think of something else, to break the chain of dismal foreboding. How? By joining in Wonstead's monologue of complaint and regret? Raf had heard the same words over and over so often that they no longer had any meaning— except as a series of sounds he might miss if the man who shared this pocket were suddenly stricken dumb.

"Should never have put in for training—" Wonstead's whine went up the scale.

That was unoriginal enough. They had all had that idea the minute after the sorter had plucked their names for crew inclusion. No matter what motive had led them into the stiff course of training—the fabulous pay, a real interest in the project, the exploring fever—Raf did not believe that there was a single man whose heart had not sunk when he had been selected for flight. Even he, who had dreamed all his life of the stars and the wonders which might lie just beyond the big jump, had been honestly sick on the day he had shouldered his bag aboard and had first taken his place on this mat and waited, dry mouthed and shivering, for blast-off.

One lost all sense of time out here. They are sparingly, slept when they could, tried to while away the endless hours artificially divided into set periods. But still weeks might be months, or months weeks. They could have been years in space—or only days. All they knew was the unending monotony which dragged upon a man until he either lapsed into a dreamy rejection of his surroundings, as had Hamp and Floy, or flew into murderous rages, such as kept Morris in solitary confinement at present. And no foreseeable end to the flight—

Raf breathed shallowly. The air was stale, he could almost taste it. It was difficult now to remember being in the open air under a sky, with fresh winds blowing about one. He tried to picture on that dull strip of metal overhead a stretch of green grass, a tree, even the blue sky and floating white clouds. But the patch remained stubbornly gray, the murmur of Wonstead went on and on, a drone in his aching ears, the throb of the ship's life beat through his own thin body.

What had it been like on those legendary early flights, when the secret of the overdrive had not yet been discovered, when any who dared the path between star and star had surrendered to sleep, perhaps to wake again generations later, perhaps never to rouse again? He had seen the few documents discovered four or five hundred years ago in the raided headquarters of the scientific outlaws who had fled the regimented world government of Pax and dared space on the single hope of surviving such a journey in cold sleep, the secret of which had been lost. At least, Raf thought, they had escaped the actual discomfort of the voyage.

Had they found their new world or worlds? The end of their ventures had been debated thousands of times since those documents had been made public, after the downfall of Pax and the coming into power of the Federation of Free Men.

In fact it was the publication of the papers which had given the additional spur to the building of the RS armada. What man had dared once he could dare anew. And the pursuit of knowledge which had been so long forbidden under Pax was heady excitement for the world. Research and discovery became feverish avenues of endeavor. Even the slim hope of a successful star voyage and the return to Terra with such rich spoils of information was enough to harness three quarters of the planet's energy for close to a hundred years.

And if the RS 10 was not successful, there would be 11, 12, more—flaming into the sky and out into the void, unless some newer and more intriguing experiment developed to center public imagination in another direction.

Raf's eyes closed wearily. Soon the gong would sound and this period of rest would be officially ended. But it was hardly worth rising. He was not in the least hungry for the concentrated food. He could repeat the information tapes they carried dull word for dull word.

"Nothing to see—nothing but these blasted walls!" Again Wonstead's voice arose in querulous protest.

Yes, while in overdrive there was nothing to see. The ports of the ship would be sealed until they were in normal space once more. That is, if it worked and they were not caught up forever within this thick trap where there was no time, light or distance.

The gong sounded, but Raf made no move to rise. He

heard Wonstead move, saw from the corner of his eye the other's bulk heave up obediently from the pad.

"Hey—mess gong!" He pointed out the obvious to Raf.

With a sigh the other levered himself up on his elbows. If he did not move, Wonstead was capable of reporting him to the captain for strange behavior, and they were all too alert to a divagation which might mean trouble. He had no desire to end in confinement with Morris.

"I'm coming," Raf said sullenly. But he remained sitting on the edge of the pad until Wonstead left the cabin, and he followed as slowly as he could.

So he was not with the others when a new sound tore through the constant vibrating hum which filled the narrow corridors of the ship. Raf stiffened, the icy touch of fear tensing his muscles. Was that the red alarm of disaster?

His eyes went to the light at the end of the short passage. But no blink of warning red shown there. Not danger—then what—?

It took him a full moment to realize what he had heard, not the signal of doom, but the sound which was to herald the accomplishment of their mission—the sound which unconsciously they had all given up any hope of ever hearing. They had made it!

The pilot leaned weakly against the wall, and his eyes smarted, his hands were trembling. In that moment he knew that he had never really, honestly, believed that they would succeed. But they had! RS 10 had reached the stars!

"Strap down for turnout—strap down for turnout—!" The disembodied voice screaming through the ship's speedier was that of Captain Hobart, but it was almost unrecognizable with emotion. Raf turned and stumbled back to his cabin, staggered to throw himself once more on his pad as he fumbled with the straps he must buckle over him.

He heard rather than saw Wonstead blunder in to follow his example, and for the first time in months the other was dumb, not uttering a word as he stowed away for the breakthrough which should take them back into normal space and the star worlds. Raf tore a nail on a fastening, muttered.

"Condition red—condition red—Strap down for breakthrough—" Hobart chanted at them from the walls. "One, two, three"—the count swung on numeral by numeral; then—"ten—Stand by—"

Raf had forgotten what breakthrough was like. He had gone through it the first time when still under take-off sedation. But this was worse than he remembered, so much worse. He tried to scream out his protest against the torture which twisted mind and body, but he could not utter even a weak cry. This, this was unbearable—a man could go mad or die—die—die . . .

He aroused with the flat sweetness of blood on his tongue, a splitting pain behind the eyes he tried to focus on the too familiar scrap of wall. A voice boomed, receded, and boomed again, filling the air and at last making sense, in it a ring of wild triumph!

"Made it! This is it, men, we've made it; Sol-class sun—three planets. We'll set an orbit in—"

Raf licked his lips. It was still too much to swallow in one mental gulp. So, they had made it—half of their venture was accomplished. They had broken out of their own solar system, made the big jump, and before them lay the unknown. Now it was within their reach.

"D' you hear that, kid?" demanded Wonstead, his voice no longer an accusing whine, more steady than Raf ever remembered hearing it. "We got through! We'll hit dirt again! Dirt—" his words trailed away as if he were sinking into some blissful daydream.

There was a different feeling to the ship herself. The steady drone which had ached in their ears, their bones, as she bored her way through the alien hyper-space had changed to a purr as if she, too, were rejoicing at the success of their desperate try. For the first time in weary weeks Raf remembered his own duties which would begin when the RS 10 came in to a flame-cushioned landing on a new world. He was to assemble and ready the small exploration flyer, to man its controls and take it up and out. Frowning, he began to run over in his mind each step in the preparations he must make as soon as they planeted.

Information came down from control, where now the ports were open on normal space and the engines were under control of the spacer's pilot. Their goal was to be the third planet, one which showed signs of atmosphere, of water and earth ready and waiting.

Those who were not on flight duty crowded into the tiny central cabin, where they elbowed each other before the viewer. The ball of alien earth grew from a pinpoint to the size of an orange. They forgot time in the wonder which none had ever thought in his heart he would see on the screen. Raf knew that in control every second of this was being recorded as they began to establish a braking orbit, which with luck would bring them down on the surface of the new world.

"Cities—those must be cities!" Those in the cabin studied the plate with awe as the information filtered through the crew. Lablet, their xenobiologist, sat with his fingers rigid on the lower bar of the visa plate, so intent that nothing could break his vigil, while the rest speculated wildly. Had they really seen cities?

Raf went down the corridor to the door of the sealed compartment that held the machine and the supplies for which he was responsible. These last hours of waiting were worse with their nagging suspense than all the time which had gone before. If they could only set down!

He had, on training trips which now seemed very far in the past, trod the rust-red desert country of Mars, waddled in a bulky protective suit across the peaked ranges of the dead Moon, known something of the larger asteroids. But how would it feel to tread ground warmed by the rays of another sun? Imagination with which his superiors did not credit him began to stir. Traits inherited from a mixture of races were there to be summoned. Raf retreated once more into his cabin and sat on his bunk pad, staring down at his own capable mechanic's hands without seeing them, picturing instead all the wonders which might lie just beyond the next few hours' imprisonment in this metallic shell he had grown to hate with a dull but abiding hatred.

Although he knew that Hobart must be fully as eager as any of them to land, it seemed to Raf, and the other impatient crew members, that they were very long in entering the atmosphere of the chosen world. It was only when the order came to strap down for deceleration that they were in a measure satisfied. Pull of gravity, ship beaming in at an angle which swept it from night to day or night again as it encircled that unknown globe. They could not watch their objective any longer. The future depended entirely upon the skill of the three men in control—and last of all upon Hobart's judgment and skill.

The captain brought them down, riding the flaming counter-blasts from the ship's tail to set her on her fins in an expert point landing, so that the RS 10 was a finger of light into the sky, amid wisps of smoke from brush ignited by her landing.

There was another wait which seemed endless to the restless men within, a wait until the air was analyzed, the coutryside surveyed. But when the go-ahead signal was given and the ramp swung out, those first at the hatch still hesitated for an instant or so, though the way before them was open.

Beyond the burnt ground about the ship was a rolling plain covered with tall grass which rippled under the wind. And the freshness of that wind cleansed their lungs of the taint of the ship.

Raf pulled off his helmet, held his head high in that breeze. It was like bathing in air, washing away the smog of those long days of imprisonment. He ran down the ramp, past the little group of those who had preceded him, and fell on his knees in the grass, catching at it with his hands, a little over-awed at the wonder of it all.

The wide sweep of sky above them was not entirely blue, he noted. There was the faintest suggestion of green, and across it moved clouds of silver. But, save for the grass, they might be in a dead and empty world. Where were the cities? Or had those been born of imagination?

After a while, when the wonder of this landing had somewhat worn away, Hobart summoned them back to the prosaic business of setting up base. And Raf went to work at his own task. The sealed storeroom was opened, the supplies slung by crane down from the ship. The compact assembly, streamlined for this purpose, was all ready for the morrow.

They spent the night within the ship, much against their will. After the taste of freedom they had been given, the cramped interior weighed upon them, closing like a prison. Raf lay on his pad unable to sleep. It seemed to him that he could hear, even through the heavy plates, the sigh of that refreshing wind, the call of the open world lying ready for them. Step by step in his mind, he went through the process for which he would be responsible the next day. The uncrating of the small flyer, the assembling of frame and motor. And sometime in the midst of that survey he did fall asleep, so deeply that Wonstead had to shake him awake in the morning.

He bolted his food and was out at his job before it was far past dawn. But eager as he was to get to work, he paused just to look at the earth scuffed up by his boots, to stare for along moment at a stalk of tough grass and remember with a thrill which never lessened that this was not native earth or grass, that he stood where none of his race, or even of his kind, had stood before—on a new planet in a new solar system.

Raf's expert training and instruction paid off. By evening he had the flitter assembled save for the motor which still reposed on the turning block. One party had gone questing out into the grass and returned with the story of a stream hidden in a gash in the plain, and Wonstead carried the limp body of a rabbit-sized furred creature he had knocked over at the waterside.

"Acted tame." Wonstead was proud of his kill. "Stupid thing just stood and watched me while I let fly with a stone."

Raf picked up the little body. Its fur was red-brown, plush-thick and very soft to the touch. The breast was creamy white and the forepaws curiously short with an uncanny resemblance to his own hands. Suddenly he wished that Wonstead had not killed it, though he supposed that Chow, their biologist, would be grateful. But the animal looked particularly defenseless. It would have been better not to mark their first day on this new world with a killing—even if it were the knocking over of a stupid rabbit thing. The pilot was glad when Chow bore it off and he no longer had to look at it.

It was after the evening meal that Raf was called into consultation by the officers to receive his orders. When he reported that the flitter, barring unexpected accidents, would be air-borne by the following afternoon, he was shown an enlarged picture from the records made during the descent of the RS 10.

There was a city, right enough—showing up well from the air. Hobart stabbed a finger down into the heart of it.

"This lies south from here. We'll cruise in that direction."

Raf would have liked to ask some questions of his own. The city photographed was a sizable one. Why then this deserted land here? Why hadn't the inhabitants been out to investigate the puzzle of the space ship's landing? He said slowly. "I've mounted one gun, sir. Do you want the other installed? It will mean that the flitter can only carry three instead of four—"

Hobart pulled his lower lip between his thumb and forefinger. He glanced at his lieutenant then to Lab-let, sitting quietly to one side. It was the latter who spoke first.

"I'd say this shows definite traces of retrogression." He touched the photograph. "The place may even be only a ruin."

"Very well. Leave off the other gun." Hobart ordered crisply. "And be ready to fly at dawn day after tomorrow with full field kit. You're sure she'll have at least a thousand-mile cruising radius?"

Raf suppressed a shrug. How could you tell what any machine would do under new conditions? The flitter had been put through every possible test in his home world. Whether she would perform as perfectly here was another matter.

"They thought she would, sir," he replied. "I'll take her up for a shakedown run tomorrow after the motor is installed.

Captain Hobart dismissed him with a nod, and Raf was glad to clatter down ladders into the cool of the evening once more. Flying high in a formation of two lanes were some distant birds, at least he supposed they were birds. But he did not call attention to them. Instead he watched them out of sight, lingering alone with no desire to join those crew members who had built a campfire a little distance from the ship. The flames were familiar and cheerful, a portion, somehow, of their native world transported to the new.

Raf could hear the murmur of voices. But he turned and went to the flitter. Taking his hand torch, he checked the work he had done during the day. Tomorrow—tomorrow he could take her up into the blue-green sky, circle out over the sea of grass for a short testing flight. That much he wanted to do.

But the thought of the cruise south, venturing toward that sprawling splotch Hobart and Lablet identified as a city was somehow distasteful, and he was reluctant to think about it.

⊸3⊹
SNAKE-DEVIL'S TRAIL

DALGARD drew the waterproof covering back over his brow, making a cheerful job of it, preparatory to their pushing out to sea once more. But he was as intent upon what Sssuri had to tell as he was on his occupation of the moment.

"But that is not even a hopper rumor," he was protesting, breaking into his companion's flow of thought.

"No. But, remember, to the runners yesterday is very far away. One night is like another; they do not reckon time as we do, nor lay up memories for future guidance. They left their native hunting grounds and are drifting south. And only a very great peril would lead the runners into such a break. It is against all their instincts!"

"So, long ago—which may be months, weeks, or just days—there came death out of the sea, and those who lived past its coming fled—" Dalgard repeated the scanty information Sssuri had won for them the night before by patient hour-long coaxing. "What kind of death?"

Sssuri's great eyes, sombre and a little tired, met his.

289

"To us there is only one kind of death to be greatly feared."

"But there are the snake-devils—" protested the colony scout.

"To be hunted down by snake-devils is death, yes. But it is a quick death, a death which can come to any living thing that is not swift or wary enough. For to the snake-devils all things that live and move are merely meat to fill the aching pit in their swollen bellies. But there were in the old days other deaths, far worse than what one meets under a snake-devil's claws and fangs. And those are the deaths we fear." He was running the smooth haft of his spear back and forth through his fingers as if testing the balance of the weapon because the time was not far away when he must rely upon it.

"Those Others!" Dalgard shaped the words with his lips as well as in his mind.

"Just so." Sssuri did not nod, but his thought was in complete agreement.

"Yet they have not come before—not since the ship of my fathers landed here," Dalgard protested, not against Sssuri's judgment but against the whole idea.

The merman got to his feet, sweeping his arm to indicate not only the cove where they now sheltered but the continent behind it.

"Once they held all this. Then they warred and killed, until a handful lay in cover to lick their wounds and wait. It has been many threes of seasons since they left that cover. But now they come again—to loot their place of secrets—Perhaps in the time past they have forgotten much so that now they must renew their knowledge."

Dalgard stowed the bow in the bottom of the outrigger. "I think we had better go and see," he commented, "so that we may report true tidings to our Elders—something more than rumors learned from night runners."

"That is so."

They paddled out to sea and turned the prow of the light craft north. The character of the land did not change. Cliffs still walled the coast, in some places rising sheer from the water, in others broken by a footing of coarse beach. Only flying things were to be sighted over their rocky crowns.

But by midday there was an abrupt alteration in the scene. A wide river cut through the heights and gave birth to a fan-shaped delta thickly covered with vegetation. Half hidden by the riot of growing things was a building of the dome shape Dalgard knew so well. Its windowless, doorless surface reflected the sunlight with a glassy sheen, and to casual inspection it was as untouched as it had been on the day its masters had either died within it or left it for the last time, perhaps centuries before.

"This is one way into the forbidden city," Sssuri announced. "Once they stationed guards here."

Dalgard had been about to suggest a closer inspection of the dome but that remark made him hesitate. If it had been one of the fortifications rimming in a forbidden ground, there was more than an even chance that unwary invaders, even this long after, might stumble into some trap still working automatically.

"Do we go upriver?" He left it to Sssuri, who had the traditions of his people to guide him, to make the decision.

The merman looked at the dome; it was evident from his attitude that he had no wish to examine it more closely. "They had machines which fought for them, and sometimes those machines still fight. This river is the natural entrance for an enemy. Therefore it would have been well defended."

Under the sun the green reach of the delta had a most peaceful appearance. There was a family of duckdogs fishing from the beach, scooping their broad bills into the mud to locate water worms. And moth birds danced in the air currents overhead. Yet Dalgard was ready to agree with his companion—beware the easy way. They dipped their paddles deep and cut across the river current toward the cliffs to the north.

Two days of steady coastwise traveling brought them to a great bay. And Dalgard gasped as the full sight of the port confronting them burst into view.

Tiers of ledges had been cut and blasted in the native rock, extending from the sea back into the land in a series of giant steps. Each of them was covered with buildings and here the ancient war had left its mark. The rock itself had been brought to a bubbling boil and sent in now-frozen rivers down that stairway in a half-dozen places, overwhelming all structures in its path, and leaving crystallized streams to reflect the sun blindingly.

"So this is your secret city!"

But Sssuri shook his round head. "This is but the sea entrance to the country," he corrected. "Here struck the day of fire, and we need not fear the machines which doubtless lie in wait elsewhere."

They beached the outrigger and hid it in the shell of

one of the ruined buildings on the lowest level. Dalgard sent out a questing thought, hoping to contact a hopper or even a duck-dog. But seemingly the ruins were bare of animal life, as was true in most of the other towns and cities he had explored in the past. The fauna of Astra was shy of any holding built by Those Others, no matter how long it may have been left to the wind, and cleansing rain.

With difficulty and detours to avoid the rivers of once-molten rock, they made their way slowly from ledge to ledge up that giant's staircase, not stopping to explore any of the buildings as they passed. There was a taint of alien age about the city which repelled Dalgard, and he was eager to get out of it into the clean countryside once more. Sssuri sped on silent feet, his shoulders hunched, his distaste for the structures to be read in every line of his supple body.

When they reached the top, Dalgard turned to gaze down to the restless sea. What a prospect! Perhaps Those Others had built thus for reasons of defense, but surely they, too, must have paused now and then to be proud of such a feat. It was the most impressive site he had yet seen, and his report of it would be a worthy addition to the Homeport records.

A road ran straight from the top of the stair, stabbing inland without taking any notice of the difficulties of the terrain, after the usual arrogant manner of the alien engineers. But Sssuri did not follow it. Instead he struck off to the left, avoiding that easy path, choosing to cross through tangles which had once been gardens or through open fields.

They were well out of the sight of the city before they

flushed their first hopper, a full-grown adult with oddly pale fur. Instead of displaying the usual fearless interest in strangers, the animal took one swift look at them and fled as if a snake-devil had snorted at its thumping heels. And Dalgard received a sharp impression of terror, as if the hopper saw in him some frightening menace.

"What—?" Honestly astounded, he looked to Sssuri for enlightenment.

The hoppers could be pests. They stole any small bright object which aroused their interest. But they could also be persuaded to trade, and they usually had no fear of either colonist or merman.

Sssuri's furred face might not convey much emotion, but by all the signs Dalgard could read he knew that the merman was as startled as he by the strange behavior of the grass dweller.

"He is afraid of those who walk erect as we do," he made answer.

Those who walk erect—Dalgard was quick to interpret that.

He knew that Those Others were biped, quasi-human in form, closer in physical appearance to the colonists than to the mermen. And since none of Dalgard's people had penetrated this far to the north, nor had the mermen invaded this taboo territory until Sssuri had agreed to come, that left only the aliens. Those strange people whom the colonists feared without knowing why they feared them, whom the mermen hated with a hatred which had not lessened with the years of freedom. The faint rumor carried by the migrating runners must be true, for here was a hopper afraid of bipeds. And it must have been recently provided with a reason for such fear, since hoppers' memories were very short and such terror would have faded from its mind in a matter of weeks.

Sssuri halted in a patch of grass which reached to his waist belt. "It is best to wait until the hours of dark."

But Dalgard could not agree. "Better for you with your night sight," he objected, "but I do not have your eyes in my head."

Sssuri had to admit the justice of that. He could travel under the moonless sky as sure-footed as under broad sunlight. But to guide a blundering Dalgard through unknown country was not practical. However, they could take to cover and that they did as speedily as possible, using a zigzag tactic which delayed their advance but took them from one bit of protecting brush or grove of trees to the next, keeping to the fields well away from the road.

They camped that night without fire in a pocket near a spring. And while Dalgard was alert to all about them, he knew that Sssuri was mind questing in a far wider circle, trying to contact a hopper, a runner, any animal that could answer in part the inquiries they had. When Dalgard could no longer hold open weary eyes, his last waking memory was that of his companion sitting statue-still, his spear across his knees, his head leaning a trifle forward as if what he listened to was as vocal as the hum of night insects.

When the colony scout roused in the morning, his companion was stretched full length on the other side of the spring, but his head came up as Dalgard moved.

"We may go forward without fear," he shaped the assurance. "What has troubled this land has gone."

"A long time ago?"

Dalgard was not surprised at Sssuri's negative answer. "Within days they have been here. But they have gone once more. It will be wise for us to learn what they wanted here."

"Have they come to establish a base here once more?" Dalgard brought into the open the one threat which had hung over his own clan since they first learned that a few of Those Others still lived—even if overseas.

"If that is their plan, they have not yet done it." Sssuri rolled over on his back and stretched. He had lost that tenseness of a hound in leash which had marked him the night before. "This was one of their secret places, holding much of their knowledge. They may return here on quest for that learning."

All at once Dalgard was conscious of a sense of urgency. Suppose that what Sssuri suggested was the truth, that Those Others were attempting to recover the skills which had brought on the devastating war that had turned this whole eastern continent into a wilderness? Equipped with even the crumbs of such discoveries, they would be enemies against which the Terran colonists could not hope to stand. The few weapons their outlaw ancestors had brought with them on their desperate flight to the stars were long since useless, and they had had no way of duplicating them. Since childhood Dalgard had seen no arms except the bows and the sword-knives carried by all venturing away from Homeport. And what use would a bow or a foot or two of sharpened metal be against things which could kill from a distance or turn rock itself into a flowing, molten river?

He was impatient to move on, to reach this city of forgotten knowledge which Sssuri was sure lay before them. Perhaps the colonists could draw upon what was stored there as well as Those Others could.

Then he remembered—not only remembered but was corrected by Sssuri. "Think not of taking their weapons into your hands." Sssuri did not look up as he gave that warning. "Long ago your fathers' fathers knew that the knowledge of Those Others was not for their taking."

A dimly remembered story, a warning impressed upon him during his first guided trips into the ruins near Homeport flashed into Dalgard's mind. Yes, he knew that some things had been forbidden to his kind. For one, it was best not to examine too closely the bands of color patterns which served Those Others as a means of written record. Tapes of the aliens' records had been found and stored at Homeport. But not one of the colonists had ventured to try to break the color code and learn what lay locked in those bands. Once long ago such an experiment had led to the brink of disaster, and such delvings were now considered too dangerous to be allowed.

But there was no harm in visiting this city, and certainly he must make some report to the Council about what might be taking place here, especially if Those Others were in residence or visited the site.

Sssuri still kept to the fields, avoiding the highway, until mid-morning, and then he made an abrupt turn and brought them out on the soil-drifted surface of the road. The land here was seemingly deserted. No moth birds performed their air ballets overhead, and they did not see a single hopper. That is, they did not until the road dipped before them and they started down into a cupped hollow filled with buildings. The river, whose delta they had earlier seen, made a half loop about the city, lacing it in. And here were no signs of the warfare which had ruined the port.

But in the middle of the road lay a bloody bunch of fur and splintered bone, insects busy about it. Sssuri used the point of his spear to straighten out the small corpse, displaying its headlessness. And before they reached the outer buildings of the city they found four more hoppers all mangled.

"Not a snake-devil," Dalgard deduced. As far as he knew only the huge reptiles or their smaller flying-dragon cousins preyed upon animals. But a snake-devil would have left no remains of anything as small as a hopper, one mouthful which could not satisfy its gnawing hunger. And a flying dragon would have picked the bones clean.

"Them!" Sssuri's reply was clipped. "They hunt for sport."

Dalgard felt a little sick. To his mind, hoppers were to be treated with friendship. Only against the snake-devils and the flying dragons were the colonists ever at war. No wonder that hopper had run from them back on the plain during yesterday's journey!

The buildings before them were not the rounded domes of the isolated farms, but a series of upward-pointing shafts. They walked through a tall gap which must have supported a now-disappeared barrier gate, and their passing was signaled by a whispering sound as they shuffled through the loose sand and soil drifted there in a miniature dune.

This city was in a better state of preservation than any Dalgard had previously visited. But he had no desire to enter any of the gaping doorways. It was as if the city rejected him and his kind, as if to the past that brooded here he was no more than a curious hopper or a fluttering, short-lived moth bird.

"Old—old and with wisdom hidden in it—" he caught the trail of thought from Sssuri. And he was certain that the merman was no more at ease here than he himself was.

As the street they followed brought them into an open space surrounded by more imposing buildings, they, made another discovery which blotted out all thoughts of forbidden knowledge and awakened them to a more normal and everyday danger.

A fountain which no longer played but gave birth to a crooked stream of water, was in the center. And in the muddy verge of the stream, pressed deep, was the fresh track of a snake-devil. Almost full grown, Dalgard estimated, measuring the print with his fingers. Sssuri pivoted slowly, studying the circle of buildings about them.

"An hour—maybe two—" Dalgard gave a hunter's verdict on the age of the print. He, too, eyed those buildings. To meet a snake-devil in the open was one thing, to play hide-and-seek with the cunning monster in a warren such as this was something else again. He hoped that the reptile had been heading for the open, but he doubted it. This mass of buildings would provide just the type of shelter which would appeal to it for a lair. And snake-devils did not den alone!

"Try by the river," Sssuri gave advice. Like Dalgard, he

accepted the necessity of the chase. No intelligent creature
ever lost the chance to kill a snake-devil when fortune
offered it. And he and the scout had hunted together on
such trails before. Now they slipped into familiar roles
from long practice.

They took a route which should lead them to the river,
and within a matter of yards, came across evidence proving
that the merman had guessed correctly; a second claw
print was pressed deep in a patch of drifted soil.

Here the buildings were of a new type, window-less,
perhaps storehouses. But what pleased Dalgard most was
the fact that most of them showed tightly closed doors.
There was no chance for their prey to lurk in wait.

"We should smell it." Sssuri picked that worry out of
the scout's mind and had a ready answer for it.

Sure—they should smell the lair; nothing could cloak
the horrible odor of a snake-devil's home. Dalgard sniffed
vigorously as he padded along. Though odd smells clung
to the strange buildings none of them were actively
obnoxious—yet.

"River—"

There was the river at the end of the way they had
been following, a way which ended in a wharf built out
over the oily flow of water. Blank walls were on either
side. If the snake-devil had come this way, he had found
no hiding place.

"Across the river—"

Dalgard gave a resigned grunt. For some reason he
disliked the thought of swimming that stream, of having
his skin laved by the turgid water with its brown sheen.

"There is no need to swim."

Dalgard's gaze followed Sssuri's pointing finger. But what he saw bobbing up and down, pulled a little downstream by the current, did not particularly reassure him. It was manifestly a boat, but the form was as alien as the city around them.

━━4━━
CIVILIZATION

RAF SURVEYED the wide sweep of prairie where dawn gave a gray tinge to soften the distance and mark the rounded billows of the ever-rippling grass. He tried to analyze what it was about this world which made it seem so untouched, so fresh and new. There were large sections of his own Terra which had been abandoned after the Big Burn-Off and the atomic wars, or later after the counter-revolution which had defeated the empire of Pax, during which mankind had slipped far back on the road to civilization. But he had never experienced this same feeling when he had ventured into those wildernesses. Almost he could believe that the records Hobart had showed him were false, that this world had never known intelligent life herding together in cities.

He walked slowly down the ramp, drawing deep breaths of the crisp air. The day would grow warmer with the rising sun. But now it was just the sort of morning which led him to be glad he was alive—and young! Maybe part of it was because he was free of the ship and at last not just excess baggage but a man with a definite job before him.

Spacemen tended to be young. But until this moment Raf had never felt the real careless freedom of youth. Now he was moved by a desire to disobey orders—to take the flitter up by himself and head off into the blue of the brightening sky for more than just a test flight, not to explore Hobart's city but to cruise over the vast sea of grass and find out its wonders for himself.

But the discipline which had shaped him almost since birth sent him now to check the flyer and wait, inwardly impatient, for Hobart, Lablet, and Soriki, the com-tech, to join him.

The wait was not a long one since the three others, with equipment hung about, tramped down the ramp as Raf settled himself behind the control board of the flyer. He triggered the shield which snapped over them for a windbreak and brought the flitter up into the spreading color of the morning. Beside him Hobart pressed the button of the automatic recorder, and in the seat behind, Soriki had the headset of the com clamped over his ears. They were not only making a record of their trip, they were continuing in constant communication with the ship—now already a silver pencil far to the rear.

It was some two hours later that they discovered what was perhaps one reason for the isolation of the district in which the RS 10 had set down. Rolling foothills rose beneath them and miles ahead the white-capped peaks of a mountain range made a broken outline against the turquoise sky. The broken lands would be a formidable barrier for any foot travelers: there were no easy roads through that series of sharp lifts and narrow valleys. And the one stream they followed for a short space descended from the heights in spectacular falls. Twice they skimmed thick growths of trees, so tightly packed that from the air they resembled a matted carpet of green-blue. And to cut through such a forest would be an impossible task.

The four in the flitter seldom spoke. Raf kept his attention on the controls. Sudden currents of air were tricky here, and he had to be constantly alert to hold the small flyer on an even keel. His glimpses of what lay below were only snatched ones.

At last it was necessary to zoom far above the vegetation of the lower slopes, to reach an altitude safe enough to clear the peaks ahead. Since the air supply within the windshield was constant they need not fear lack of oxygen. But Raf was privately convinced, as they soared, that the range might well compare in height with those Asian mountains which dominated all the upflung reaches of his native world.

When they were over the sharp points of that chain disaster almost overtook them. A freakish air current caught the flitter as if in a giant hand, and Raf fought for control as they lost altitude past the margin of safety. Had he not allowed for just such a happening they might have been smashed against one of the rock tips over which they skimmed to a precarious safety. Raf, his mouth dry, his hands sweating on the controls, took them up—higher than was necessary—to coast above the last of that rocky spine to see below the beginning of the downslopes leading to the plains the range cut in half. He heard Hobart draw a hissing breath.

"That was a close call." Lablet's precise, lecturer's voice cut through the drone of the motor.

"Yeah," Soriki echoed, "looked like we might be sandwich meat there for a while. The kid knows his stuff after all."

Raf grinned a little sourly, but he did not answer that. He ought to know his trade. Why else would he be along? They were each specialists in one or two fields. But he had good sense enough to keep his mouth shut. That way the less one had to regret minutes—or hours—later.

The land on the south side of the mountains was different in character to the wild northern plains.

"Fields!"

It did not require that identification from Lablet to point out what they had already seen. The section below was artificially divided into long narrow strips. But the vegetation growing on those strips was no different from the northern grass they had seen about the spacer.

"Not cultivated now," the scientist amended his first report. "It's reverting to grassland—"

Raf brought the flitter closer to the ground so that when a domed structure arose out of a tangle of overgrown shurbs and trees they were not more than fifty feet above it. There was no sign of life about the dwelling, if dwelling it was, and the unkempt straggle of growing things suggested that it had been left to itself through more than one season. Lablet wanted to set down and explore, but the captain was intent upon reaching the city. A solitary farm was of little value compared with what they might learn from a metropolis. So, rather to Raf's relief, he was ordered on.

He could not have explained why he shrank from

such investigation. Where earlier that morning he had
wanted to take the flitter and go off by himself to explore
the world which seemed so bright and new, now he was
glad that he was only the pilot of the flyer and that the
others were not only in his company but ready to make
the decisions. He had a queer distaste for the countryside,
a disinclination to land near that dome.

Beyond the first of the deserted farms they came to
the highway and, since the buckled and half-buried roadway
ran south, Hobart suggested that they use it as a visible
guide. More isolated dome houses showed in the course
of an hour. And their fields were easy to map from the air.
But nowhere did the Terrans see any indication that those
fields were in use. Nor were there any signs of animal or
bird life. The weird desolation of the landscape began to
work its spell on the men in the flitter. There was something unnatural about the country, and with every mile the
flyer clocked off, Raf longed to be heading in the opposite
direction.

The domes drew closer together, made a cluster at
crossroads, gathered into a town in which all the buildings
were the same shape and size, like the cells of a wasp nest.
Raf wondered if those who had built them had not been
humanoid at all, but perhaps insects with a hive mind.
And because that thought was unpleasant he resolutely
turned his attention to the machine he piloted.

They passed over four such towns, all marking inter-
sections of roads running east and west, north and south,
with precise exactness. The sun was at noon or a little past
that mark when Captain Hobart gave the order to set
down so that they could break out rations and eat.

Raf brought the flitter down on the cracked surface of the road, mistrusting what might lie hidden in the field grass. They got out and walked for a space along pavement which had once been smooth.

"High-powered traffic—" That was Lablet. He had gone down on one knee and was tracing a finger along the substance.

"Straight—" Soriki squinted against the sun. "Nothing stopped them, did it? We want a road here and we'll get it! That sort of thing. Must have been master engineers."

To Raf the straight highways suggested something else. Master engineering, certainly. But a ruthlessness too, as if the builders, who refused to accept any modifications of their original plans from nature, might be as arrogant and self-assured in other ways. He did not admire this relic of civilization; in fact it added to his vague uneasiness.

The land was so still, under the whisper of the wind. He discovered that he was listening—listening for the buzz of an insect, the squeak of some grass dweller, anything which would mean that there was life about them. As he chewed on the ration concentrate and drank sparingly from his canteen, Raf continued to listen. Without result.

Hobart and Lablet were engrossed in speculation about what might lie ahead. Soriki had gone back to the flitter to make his report to the ship. The pilot sat where he was, content to be forgotten, but eager to see an animal peering at him from cover, a bird winging through the air.

"—if we don't hit it by nightfall—But we can't be that far away! I'll stay out and try tomorrow." That was Hobart.

And since he was captain what he said was probably what they would do. Raf shied away from the thought of spending the night in this haunted land. Though, on the other hand, he would be utterly opposed to lifting the flitter over those mountains again except in broad daylight.

But the problem did not arise, for they found their city in the midafternoon, the road bringing them straight to an amazing collection of buildings, which appeared doubly alien to their eyes since it did not include any of the low domes they had seen heretofore.

Here were towers of needle slimness, solid blocks of almost, windowless masonry looking twice as bulky beside those same towers, archways stringing at dizzy heights above the ground from one skyscraper to the next. And here time and nature had been at work. Some of the towers were broken off, a causeway displayed a gap—Once it had been a breathtaking feat of engineering, far more impressive than the highway, now it was a slowly collapsing ruin.

But before they had time to take it all in Soriki gave an exclamation. "Something coming through on our wave band, sir!" He leaned forward to dig fingers into Hobart's shoulder. "Message of some kind—I'd swear to it!"

Hobart snapped into action. "Kurbi—set down—there!"

His choice of a landing place was the flat top of a near-by building, one which stood a little apart from its neighbors and, as Raf could see, was not overlooked except by a ruined tower. He circled the flitter. The machine had been specially designed to land and take off in confined spaces, and he knew all there was possible to learn about its handling on his home world. But he had never tried to bring it down on a roof, and he was very sure that now he had no margin for error left him, not with Hobart breathing impatiently beside him, his hands moving as if, as a pilot of a spacer, he could well take over the controls here.

Raf circled twice, eyeing the surface of the roof in search of any break which could mean a crack-up at landing. And then, though he refused to be hurried by the urgency of the men with him, he came in, cutting speed, bringing them down with only a slight jar.

Hobart twisted around to face Soriki. "Still getting it?"

The other, cupping his earphones to his head with his hands, nodded. "Give me a minute or two," he told them, "and I'll have a fix. They're excited about something—the way this jabber-jabber is coming through—"

"About us," Raf thought. The ruined tower topped them to the south. And to the east and west there were buildings as high as the one they were perched on. But the town he had seen as he maneuvered for a landing had held no signs of life. Around them were only signs of decay.

Lablet got out of the flitter and walked to the edge of the roof, leaning against the parapet to focus his vision glasses on what lay below. After a moment Raf followed his example.

Silence and desolation, windows like the eye pits in bone-picked skulls. There were even some small patches of vegetation rooted and growing in pockets erosion had carved in the walls. To the pilot's uninformed eyes the city looked wholly dead.

—◈—

"Got it!" Soriki's exultant cry brought them back to the flitter. As if his body was the indicator, he had pivoted until his outstretched hand pointed south-west. "About a quarter of a mile that way."

They shielded their eyes against the westering sun. A block of solid masonry loomed high in the sky, dwarfing not only the building they were standing on but all the towers around it. Its imposing lines made clear its one-time importance.

"Palace," mused Lablet, "or capitol. I'd say it was just about the heart of the city."

He dropped his glasses to swing on their cord, his eyes glistening as he spoke directly to Raf.

"Can you set us down on that?"

The pilot measured the curving roof of the structure. A crazy fool might try to make a landing there. But he was no crazy fool. "Not on that roof!" he spoke with decision.

To his relief the captain confirmed his verdict with a slow nod. "Better find out more first." Hobart could be cautious when he wanted to. "Are they still broadcasting, Soriki?"

The com-tech had stripped the earphones from his head and was rubbing one ear. "Are they!" he exploded. "I'd think you could hear them clear over there, sir!"

And they could. The gabble-gabble which bore no resemblance to any language Terra knew boiled out of the phones.

"Someone's excited," Lablet commented in his usual mild tone.

"Maybe they've discovered us." Hobart's hand went to the weapon at his belt. "We must make peaceful contact—if we can."

Lablet took off his helmet and ran his fingers through the scrappy ginger-and-gray fringe receding from his forehead. "Yes—contact will be necessary—" he said thoughtfully.

Well, he was supposed to be their expert on that. Raf watched the older man with something akin to amusement. The pilot had a suspicion that none of the other three, Lablet included, was in any great hurry to push through contact with unknown aliens. It was a case of dancing along on shore before having to plunge into the chill of autumn sea waves. Terrans had explored their own solar system, and they had speculated learnedly for generations on the problem of intelligent alien life. There had been all kinds of reports by experts and would-be experts, But the stark fact remained that heretofore mankind as born on the third planet of Sol had not encountered intelligent alien life. And just how far did speculations, reports, and arguments go when one was faced with the problem to be solved practically—and speedily?

Raf's own solution would have been to proceed with caution and yet more caution. Under his technical training he had far more imagination than any of his officers had ever realized. And now he was certain that the best course of action was swift retreat until they knew more about what was to be faced.

But in the end the decision was taken out of their hands. A muffled exclamation from Lablet brought them all around to see that distant curving roof crack wide open. From the shadows within, a flyer spiraled up into the late afternoon sky.

Raf reached the flitter in two leaps. Without orders he had the spray gun ready for action, on point and aimed at the bobbing machine heading toward them. From the earphones Soriki had left on the seat the gabble had risen to a screech and one part of Raf's brain noted that the sounds were repetitious: was an order to surrender being broadcast? His thumb was firm on the firing button of the gun and he was about to send a warning burst to the right of the alien when an order from Hobart stopped him cold.

"Take it easy, Kurbi."

Soriki said something about a "gun-happy flitter pilot," but, Raf noted with bleak eyes, the com-tech kept his own hand close to his belt arm. Only Lablet stood watching the oncoming alien ship with placidity. But then, as Raf had learned through the long voyage of the spacer, a period of time which had left few character traits of any of the crew hidden from their fellows, the xenobiologist was a fatalist and strictly averse to personal combat.

The pilot did not leave his seat at the gun. But within seconds he knew that they had lost the initial advantage. As the tongue-shaped stranger thrust at them and then swept on to glide above their heads so that the weird shadow of the ship licked them from light to dark and then to light again, Raf was certain mat his superiors had made the wrong decision. They should have left the city as soon as they picked up those signals—if they could have gone then. He studied the other flyer. Its lines suggested speed as well as mobility, and he began to doubt if they could have escaped with that craft tailing them.

Well, what would they do now? The alien flyer could not land here, not without coming down flat upon the flitter. Maybe it would cruise overhead as a warning threat until the city dwellers were able to reach the Terrans in some other manner. Tense, the four spacemen stood watching the graceful movements of the flyer. There were no visible portholes or openings anywhere along its ovoid sides. It might be a robot-controlled ship, it might be anything, Raf thought, even a bomb of sorts. If it were being flown by some human—or nonhuman—flyer, he was a master pilot.

"I don't understand," Soriki moved impatiently. "They're just shuttling around up there. What do we do now?"

Lablet turned his head. He was smiling faintly. "We wait," he told the com-tech. "I should imagine it takes time to climb twenty flights of stairs—if they have stairs—"

Soriki's attention fell from the flyer hovering over their heads to the surface of the roof. Raf had already looked that over without seeing any opening. But he did not doubt the truth of Lablet's surmise. Sooner or later the aliens were going to reappear. And it did not greatly matter to the marooned Terrans whether they would drop from the sky or rise from below.

— 5 —
BANDED DEVIL

FAMILIAR only with the wave-riding outriggers, Dalgard took his seat in the alien craft with misgivings. And oddly enough it also bothered him to occupy a post which earlier had served not a nonhuman such as Sssuri, whom he admired, but a humanoid whom he had been taught from childhood to avoid—if not fear.

The skiff was rounded at bow and stern with very shallows sides and displayed a tendency to whirl about in the current, until Sssuri, with his instinctive knowledge of watercraft, used one of the queerly shaped paddles tucked away in the bottom to both steer and propel them. They did not strike directly across the river but allowed the current to carry them in a diagonal path so that they came out on the opposite bank some distance to the west.

Sssuri brought them ashore with masterly skill where a strip of sod angled down to the edge of the water, marking, Dalgard decided, what had once been a garden. The buildings on this side of the river were not set so closely

315

together. Each, standing some two or three stories high, was encircled by green, as if this had been a section of private dwellings.

They pulled the light boat out of the water and Sssuri pointed at the open door of the nearest house. "In there—"

Dalgard agreed that it might be well to hide the craft against their return. Although as yet they had found no physical evidence, other than the dead hoppers, that they might not be alone in the city, he wanted a means of escape ready if such a flight would be necessary. In the meantime there was the snake-devil to track, and that wily creature, if it had swum the river, might be lurking at present in the next silent street—or miles away.

Sssuri, spear ready, was trotting along the paved lane, his head up as he thought-quested for any hint of life about them. Dalgard tried to follow that lead. But he knew that it would be Sssuri's stronger power which would warn them first.

They cast east from where they had landed, studying the soil of each garden spot, hunting for the unmistakable spoor of the giant reptile. And within a matter of minutes they found it, the mud still moist as Dalgard proved with an exploring fingertip. At the same time Sssuri twirled his spear significantly. Before them the lane ran on between two walls without any breaks. Dalgard uncased his bow and strung it. From his quiver he chose one of the powerful arrows, the points of which were kept capped until use.

A snake-devil, with its nervous system controlled not from the tiny, brainless head but from a series of auxilliary "brains" at points along its powerful spine, could and would go on fighting even after that head was shorn away, as the first colonists had discovered when they depended on the deadly ray guns fatal to any Terran life. But the poison-tipped arrow Dalgard now handled, with confidence in its complete efficiency, paralyzed within moments and killed in a quarter-hour one of the scaled monstrosities.

"Lair—"

Dalgard did not need that warning thought from his companion. There was no mistaking that sickly sweet stench born of decaying animal matter, which was the betraying effluvium of a snake-devil's lair. He turned to the right-hand wall and with a running leap reached its broad top. The lane curved to end in an archway cut through another wall, which was higher than Dalgard's head even when he stood on his present elevation. But bands of ornamental patterning ran along the taller barrier, and he was certain that it could be climbed. He lowered a hand to Sssuri and hoisted the merman up to join him.

But Sssuri stood for a long moment looking ahead, and Dalgard knew that the merman was disturbed, that the wall before them had some terrifying meaning for the native Astran. So vivid was the impression of what could only be termed horror that Dalgard dared to ask a question:

"What is it?"

The merman's yellow eyes turned from the wall to his companion. Behind his hatred of this place there was another emotion Dalgard could not read.

"This is the place of sorrow, the place of separation. But they paid—oh, how they paid—after that day when the fire fell from the sky." His scaled and taloned feet moved in a little shuffling war dance, and his spear spun and quivered in the sunlight, as Dalgard had seen the spears of the mer-warriors move in the mock combats of their unexplained, and to his kind unexplainable, rituals. "Then did our spears drink, and knives eat!" Sssuri's fingers brushed the hilt of the wicked blade swinging from his belt. "Then did the People make separations and sorrows for them! And it was accomplished that we went forth into the sea to be no longer bond but free. And they went down into the darkness and were no more—" In Dalgard's head the chant of his friend skirled up in a paean of exultation. Sssuri shook his spear at the wall.

"No more the beast and the death," his thoughts swelled, a shout of victory. "For where are they who sat and watched many deaths? They are gone as the wave smashes itself upon the coast rocks and is no more. But the People are free and never more shall Those Others put bonds upon them! Therefore do I say that this is a place of nothing, where evil has turned in upon itself and come to nothing. Just as Those Others will come to nothing since their own evil will in the end eat them up!"

He strode forward along the wall until he came to the barrier, seemingly oblivious of the carrion reek which told of a snake-devil's den somewhere about. And he raised his arm high, bringing the point of his spear gratingly along the carved surface. Nor did it seem to Dalgard a futile gesture, for Sssuri lived and breathed, stood free and armed in the city of his enemies—and the city was dead.

Together they climbed the barrier, and then Dalgard discovered that it was the rim of an arena which must have seated close to a thousand in the days of its use. It was a perfect oval in shape with tiers of seats now forming a staircase down to the center, where was a section ringed about by a series of archways. A high stone grille walled this portion away from the seats as if to protect the spectators from what might enter through those portals.

Dalgard noted all this only in passing, for the arena was occupied, very much occupied. And he knew the occupiers only too well.

Three full-grown snake-devils were stretched at pulpy ease, their filled bellies obscenely round, their long necks crowned with their tiny heads flat on the sand as they napped. A pair of half-grown monsters, not yet past the six-foot stage, tore at some indescribable remnants of their elders' feasting, hissing at each other and aiming vicious blows whenever they came within possible fighting distance. Three more, not long out of their mothers' pouches scrabbled in the earth about the sleeping adults.

"A good catch," Dalgard signaled Sssuri, and the merman nodded.

They climbed down from seat to seat. This could not rightfully be termed hunting when the quarry might be picked off so easily without risk to the archer. But as Dalgard notched his first arrow, he sighted something so surprising that he did not let the poisoned dart fly.

The nearest sleeping reptile which he had selected as his mark stretched lazily without raising its head or opening its small eyes. And the sun caught on a glistening band about its short foreleg just beneath the joint of the taloned pawhands. No natural scales could reflect the light with such a brilliant glare. It could be only one thing—metal! A metal bracelet about the tearing arm of a snake-devil!

Dalgard looked at the other two sleepers. One was lying on its belly with its forearms gathered under it so that he could not see if it, also, were so equipped. But the other—yes, it was banded!

Sssuri stood at the grille, one hand on its stone divisions. His surprise equaled Dalgard's. It was not in his experience either that the untamed snake-devils, regarded by merman and human alike as so dangerous as to be killed on sight, could be banded—as if they were personal pets!

For a moment or two a wild idea crossed Dalgard's mind. How long was the natural life span of a snake-devil? Until the coming of the colonists they had been the undisputed rulers of the deserted continent, stupid as they were, simply because of their strength and ferocity. A twelve-foot, scale-armored monster, that could tear apart a duocorn with ease, might not be successfully vanquished by any of the fauna of Astra. And since the monsters did not venture into the sea, contact between them and the mermen had been limited to casual encounters at rare intervals. So, how long did a snake-devil live? Were these creatures sprawled here in sleep ones that had known the domination of Those Others—though the fall of the master race of Astra must have occurred generations, hundreds of years in the past?

"No," Sssuri's denial cut through that. "The smaller one is not yet full-grown. It lacks the second neck ring. Yet it is banded."

The merman was right. That unpleasant wattle of armored flesh which necklaced the serpent throat of the devil Dalgard had picked as his target was thin, not the thick roll of fat such as distinguished its two companions.

It was not fully adult, yet the band was plain to see on the foreleg now stretched to its full length as the sun bored down to supply the heavy heat the snake-devils relished next to food.

"Then—" Dalgard did not like to think of what might be the answer to that "then."

Sssuri shrugged. "It is plain that these are not wild roamers. They are here for a purpose. And that purpose—" Suddenly his arm shot out so that his fingers protruded through the slits in the stone grille, "See?"

Dalgard had already seen, in seeing he knew hot and terrible anger. Out of the filthy mess in which the snake-devils wallowed, something had rolled, perhaps thrown about in play by the unspeakable offspring. A skull, dried scraps of fur and flesh still clinging to it, stared hollow-eyed up at them. At least one merman had fallen prey to the nightmares who ruled the arena.

Sssuri hissed and the red range in his mind was plain to Dalgard. "Once more they deal death here—" His eyes went from the skull to the monsters. "Kill!" The command was imperative and sharp.

Dalgard had qualified as a master bowman before he had first gone roving. And the killing of snake-devils was a task which had been set every colonist since their first brush with the creatures.

He snapped the cap off the glass splinter point, designed to pin and then break off in the hide so that any clawing foot which tore out an arrow could not rid the victim of the poisonous head. The archer's mark was under the throat where the scales were soft and there was a chance of piercing the skin with the first shot.

The growls of the two feeding youngsters covered the snap of the bow cord as Dalgard shot. And he did not miss. The brilliant scarlet feather of the arrow quivered in the baggy roll of flesh.

With a scream which tore at the human's eardrums, the snake-devil reared to its hind feet. It made a tearing motion with the banded forearm which scraped across the back of one of its companions. And then it fell back to the blood-stained sand, limp, a greenish foam drooling from its fangs.

As the monster that the dead devil had raked roused, Dalgard had his chance for another good mark. And the second scarlet shaft sped straight to the target.

But the third creature which had been sleeping belly down on the sand presented only its armored back, a hopeless surface for an arrow to pierce. It had opened its eyes and was watching the now motionless bodies of its fellows. But it showed no disposition to move. It was almost as if it somehow understood that as long as it remained in its present position it was safe.

"The small ones—"

Dalgard needed no prompting. He picked off easily enough the two half-grown ones. The infants were another problem. Far less sluggish than their huge elders they sensed that they were in danger and fled. One took refuge in the pouch of its now-dead parent, and the others moved so fast that Dalgard found them difficult targets. He killed one which had almost reached an archway and at length nicked the second in the foot, knowing that, while the poison would be slower in acting, it would be as sure.

Through all of this the third adult devil continued to

lie motionless, only its wicked eyes giving any indication that it was alive. Dalgard watched it impatiently. Unless it would move, allow him a chance to aim at the soft underparts, there was little chance of killing it.

What followed startled both hunters, versed as they were in the usual mechanics of killing snake-devils. It had been an accepted premise, through the years since the colonists had known of the monsters, that the creatures were relatively brainless, mere machines which fought, ate and killed, incapable of any intelligent reasoning, and therefore only dangerous when one was surprised by them or when the hunter was forced to face them inadequately armed.

This snake-devil was different, as it became increasingly plain to the two behind the grille. It had remained safe during the slaughter of its companions because it had not moved, almost as if it had wit enough not to move. And now, when it did change position, its maneuvers, simple as they were, underlined the fact that this one creature appeared to have thought out a solution to its situation—as rational a solution as Dalgard might have produced had it been his problem.

Still keeping its soft underparts covered, it edged about in the sand until its back, with the impenetrable armor plates, was facing the grille behind which the hunters stood. Retracting its neck between its shoulders and hunching its powerful back limbs under it, it rushed from that point of danger straight for one of the archways.

Dalgard sent an arrow after it. Only to see the shaft scrape along the heavy scales and bounce to the sand. Then the snake-devil was gone.

"Banded—" The word reached Dalgard. Sssuri had been cool enough to note that while the human hunter had been only bewildered by the untypical actions of his quarry.

"It must be intelligent." The scout's statement was more than half protest.

"Where they are concerned, one may expect many evil wonders."

"We've got to get that devil!" Dalgard was determined on that. Though to run down, through this maze of deserted city, an enraged snake-devil—above all, a snake-devil which appeared to have some reasoning powers—was not a prospect to arouse any emotion except grim devotion to duty.

"It goes for help."

Dalgard, startled, stared at his companion. Sssuri was still by the grille, watching that archway through which the devil had disappeared.

"What kind of help?" For a moment Dalgard pictured the monster returning at the head of a regiment of its kind, able to tear out this grille and get at their soft-fleshed enemies behind it.

"Safety—protection," Sssuri told him. "And I think that the place to which it now flees is one we should know."

"Those Others?" The sun had not clouded, it still streamed down in the torrid heat of the early afternoon, warm on their heads and shoulders. Yet Dalgard felt as chill as if some autumn wind had laid its lash across the small of his back.

—❖—

"They are not here. But they have been—and it is possible that they return. The devil goes to where it expects to find them."

Sssuri was already on his way, running about the arena's curve to reach the point above the archway through which the snake-devil had raced. Dalgard padded after him, bow in hand. He trusted Sssuri implicitly when it came to tracking. If the merman said that the snake-devil had a definite goal in view, he was right. But the scout was still a little bemused by a monster who was able to have any goal except the hunting and devouring of meat. Either the one who fled was a freak among its kind or—There were several possibilities which could answer that "or," and none of them were very pleasant to consider.

They reached the section above the archway and climbed the tiers of seat benches to the top of the wall. Only to see no exit below them. In fact nothing but a wide sweep of crushed brown tangle which had once been vegetation. It was apparent that there was no door below.

Sssuri sped down again. He climbed the grille and was on his way to the sand when Dalgard caught up with him. Together they ventured into the underground passage which the snake-devil had chosen.

The stench of the lair was thick about them. Dalgard coughed, sickened by the foul odor. He was reluctant to advance. But, to his growing relief, he discovered that it was not entirely dark. Set in the roof at intervals were plates which gave out a violet light, making a dim twilight which was better than total darkness.

It was a straight passage without any turns or openings. But the horrible odor was constant, and Dalgard began to think that they might be running head-on into another lair, perhaps one as well populated as that they had left behind them. It was against nature for the snake-devils he had known to lair under cover, they preferred narrow rocky places where they could bask in the sun. But then the devil they now pursued was no ordinary one.

Sssuri reassured him. "There is no lair, only the smell because they have come this way for many years."

The passage opened into a wide room and here the violet light was stronger, bright enough to make plain the fact that alcoves opened off it, each and every one with a barred grille for a door. There was no mistaking that once this had been a prison of sorts.

Sssuri did no exploring but crossed the room at his shuffling trot, which Dalgard matched. The way leading out on the opposite side slanted up, and he judged it might bring them out at ground level.

"The devil waits," Sssuri warned, "because it fears. It will turn on us when we come. Be ready—"

They were at another door, and before them was a long corridor with tall window openings near the ceiling which gave admittance to the sunlight. After the gloom of the tunnel, Dalgard blinked. But he was aware of movement at the far end, just as he heard the hissing scream of the monster they trailed.

~6~
TREASURE HUNT

RAF, SQUATTING on a small, padded platform raised some six inches from the floor, tried to study the inhabitants of the room without staring offensively. At the first glance, in spite of their strange clothing and their odd habit of painting their faces with weird designs, the city people might have been of his own species. Until one saw their too slender hands with the three equal-length fingers and thumb, or caught a glimpse, under the elaborate head coverings, of the stiff, spiky substance which served them for hair.

At least they did not appear to be antagonistic. When they had reached the roof top where the Terrans had landed their flitter, they had come with empty hands, making gestures of good will and welcome. And they had had no difficulty in persuading at least three of the exploring party to accompany them to their own quarters, though Raf had been separated from the flyer only by the direct order of Captain Hobart, an order he still resented and wanted to disobey.

The Terrans had been offered refreshment—food and drink. But knowing the first rule of stellar exploration, they had refused, which did not mean that the hosts must abstain. In fact, Raf thought, watching the aliens about him, they ate as if such a feast were novel. His two neighbors had quickly divided his portion between them and made it disappear as fast, if not faster, than their own small servings.

At the other end of the room Lablet and Hobart were trying to communicate with the nobles about them, while Soriki, a small palm recorder in his hand, was making a tape strip of the proceedings.

Raf glanced from one of his neighbors to the other. The one on his right had chosen to wear a sight-torturing shade of crimson, and the material was wound in strips about his body as if he were engulfed in an endless bandage. Only his fluttering hands, his three-toed feet and his head were free of the supple rolls. Having selected red for his clothing, he had picked a brilliant yellow paint for his facial makeup, and it was difficult for the uninitiated to trace what must be his normal features under that thick coating of stuff which fashioned a masklike strip across his eyes and a series of circles outlining his mouth, circles which almost completely covered his beardless cheeks. More twists of woven fabric, opalescent and changing color as his head moved, made a turban for his head.

Most of the aliens about the room wore some variation of the same bandage dress, face paint, and turban. An exception, one of three such, was the feaster on Raf's left.

His face paint was confined to a conservative set of bars on each cheek, those a stark black and white. His sinewy arms were bare to the shoulder, and he wore a shell of some metallic substance as a breast-and back-plate, not unlike the very ancient body armor of Raf's own world. The rest of his body was covered by the bandage strips, but they were of a dead black, which, because of the natural thinness of his limbs, gave him a rather unpleasant resemblance to a spider. Various sheaths and pockets hung from a belt pulled tight about his wasp middle, and a helmet of the metal covered his head. Soldier? Raf was sure his guess was correct.

The officer, if officer he was, caught Raf's gaze. His small round mouth gaped, and then his hands, with a few quick movements which Raf followed, fascinated, pantomimed a flyer in the air. With those talking fingers, he was able to make plain a question: was Raf the pilot of the flitter?

The pilot nodded. Then he pointed to the officer and forced as inquiring an expression as he could command.

The answer was sketched quickly and readably: the alien, too, was either a pilot or had some authority over flyers. For the first time since he had entered this building, Raf knew a slight degree of relaxation.

The wrinkleless, too smooth skin of the alien was a darkish yellow. His painted face was a mask to frighten any sensible Terran child; his general appearance was not attractive. But he was a flyer, and he wanted to talk shop, as well as they could with no common speech. Since the scarlet-wound nobleman on Raf's right was completely engrossed in the feast, pursuing a few scraps, avidly about the dish, the Terran gave all his attention to the officer.

Twittering words poured in a stream from the warrior's lips. Raf shook his head regretfully, and the other jerked his shoulders in almost human impatience. Somehow that heartened Raf.

With many guesses to cover gaps, probably more than half of which were wrong, Raf gathered that the officer was one of a very few who still retained the almost forgotten knowledge of how to pilot the remaining airworthy craft in this crumbling city. On their way to the building with the curved roof, Raf had noted the evidences that the inhabitants of this metropolis could not be reckoned as more than a handful and that most of these now lived either within the central building or close to it. A pitiful collection of survivors lingering on in the ruins of their past greatness.

Yet he was impressed now by no feeling that the officer, eagerly trying to make contact, was a degenerate member of a dying race. In fact, as Raf glanced at the aliens about the room, he was conscious of an alertness, of a suppressed energy which suggested a young and vigorous people.

The officer was now urging him to go some place, and Raf, his dislike for being in the heart of the strangers' territory once more aroused, was about to shake his head in a firm negative when a second idea stopped him. He had resisted separation from the flitter. Perhaps he could persuade the alien, under the excuse of inspecting a strange machine, to take him back to the flyer. Once there he would stay. He did not know what Captain Hobart and Lablet thought they could accomplish here. But, as for himself, Raf was sure that he was not going to feel easy again until he was across the northern mountain chain and coming in for a landing close by the RS 10.

It was as if the alien officer had read his thoughts, for

the warrior uncrossed his black legs, and got nimbly to his feet with a lithe movement, which Raf, cramped by sitting in the unfamiliar posture, could not emulate. No one appeared to notice their withdrawal. And when Raf hesitated, trying to catch Hobart's eye and make some explanation, the alien touched his arm lightly and motioned toward one of the curtained doorways. Conscious that he could not withdraw from the venture now, Raf reluctantly went out.

They were in a hall where bold bands of color interwove in patterns impossible for Terran eyes to study. Raf lowered his gaze hurriedly to the gray floor under his boots. He had discovered earlier that to try to trace any thread of that wild splashing did weird things to his eyesight and awakened inside him a sick panic. His space boots, with the metal, magnetic plates set in the soles, clicked loudly on the pavement where his companion's bare feet made no whisper of sound.

The hall gave upon a ramp leading down, and Raf recognized this. His confidence arose. They were on their way out of the building. Here the murals were missing so that he could look about him for reference points.

He was sure that the banquet hall was some ten stories above street level. But they did not go down ten ramps now. At the foot of the third the officer turned abruptly to the left, beckoning Raf along. When the Terran remained stubbornly where he was, pointing in the direction which, to him, meant return to the flitter, the other made gestures describing an aircraft in flight. His own probably.

Raf sighed. He could see no way out unless he cut and ran. And long before he reached the street from this warren they could pick him up. Also, in spite of all the precautions he had taken to memorize their way here, he was not sure he could find his path back to the flyer, even if he were free to go. Giving in, he went after the officer.

Their way led out on one of the spider-web bridges which tied building and tower into the complicated web which was the city. Raf, as pilot of a flitter, had always believed that he had no fear of heights. But he discovered that to coast above the ground in a flyer was far different than to hurry at the pace his companion now set across one of these narrow bridges suspended high above the street. And he was sure that the surface under them vibrated as if the slightest extra poundage would separate it from its supports and send it, and them, crashing down.

Luckily the distance they had to cover was relatively short, but Raf swallowed a sigh of relief as they reached the door at the other end. They were now in a tower which, unluckily, proved to be only a way station before another swing out over empty space on a span which sloped down! Raf clutched at the guide rail, the presence of which suggested that not all the users of this road were as nonchalant as the officer who tripped lightly ahead. This must explain the other's bare feet—on such paths they were infinitely safer than his own boots.

The downward sloping bridge brought them to a square building which somehow had an inhabited look which those crowding around it lacked. Raf gained its door to become aware of a hum, a vibration in the wall he touched to steady himself, hinting at the drive of motors, the throb of machinery inside the structure. But within, the officer passed along a corridor to a ramp which brought them out, after what was for Raf a steep climb, upon the roof. Here was not one of the tongue-shaped craft such as had first met them in the city, but a gleaming glove. The officer stopped, his eyes moving from the Terran to the machine, as if inviting Raf to share in his own pride. To the pilot's mind it bore little resemblance to any form of aircraft past or present with which he had had experience in his own world. But he did not doubt that it was the present acme of alien construction, and he was eager to see it perform.

He followed the officer through a hatch at the bottom of the globe, only to be confronted by a ladder he thought at first he could not climb, for the steps were merely toe holds made to accommodate the long, bare feet of the crew. By snapping on the magnetic power of his space boots, Raf was able to get up, although at a far slower speed than his guide. They passed several levels of cabins before coming out in what was clearly the control cabin of the craft.

To Raf the bank of unfamiliar levers and buttons had no meaning, but he paid strict attention to the gestures of his companion. This was not a space ship he gathered. And he doubted whether the aliens had ever lifted from their own planet to their neighbors in this solar system. But it was a long-range ship with greater cruising power than the other flyer he had seen. And it was being readied now for a voyage of some length.

The Terran pilot squatted down on the small stool before the controls. Before him a visa plate provided a clear view of the sky without and the gathering clouds of evening. Raf shifted uncomfortably. That signal of the passing of time triggered his impatience to be away—back to the RS 10. He did not want to spend the night in this city. Somehow he must get the officer to take him back to the flitter—to be there would be better than shut up in one of the alien dwellings.

Meanwhile he studied the scene on the visa plate, trying to find the roof on which they had left the flitter. But there was no point he was able to recognize.

Raf turned to the officer and tried to make clear the idea of returning to his own ship. Either he was not as clever at the sign language as the other, or the alien did not wish to understand. For when they left the control cabin, it was only to make an inspection tour of the other parts of the globe, including the space which held the motors of the craft and which, at another time, would have kept Raf fascinated for hours.

In the end the Terran broke away and climbed down the thread of ladder to stand on the roof under the twilight sky. Slowly he walked about the broad expanse of the platform, attempting to pick out some landmark. The central building of the city loomed high, and there were any number of towers about it. But which was the one that guarded the roof where the flitter rested? Raf's determination to get back to his ship was a driving force.

The alien officer had watched him, and now a three-fingered hand was laid on Raf's sleeve while its owner looked into Raf's face and mouthed a trilling question.

Without much hope the pilot sketched the set of gestures he had used before. And he was surprised when the other led the way down into the building. This time they did not go back to the bridge, which had brought them across the canyons of streets, but kept on down ramps within the building.

There was a hum of activity in the place. Aliens, all in tight black wrappings and burnished metal breastplates, their faces barred with black and white paint, went on errands through the halls or labored at tasks Raf could not understand. It now seemed as if his guide were eager to get him away.

It was when they reached the street level mat the officer did pause by one door, beckoning Raf imperiously to join him. The Terran obeyed reluctantly—and was almost sick.

He was staring down at a dead, very dead body. By the stained rags still clinging to it, it was one of the aliens, a noble, not one of the black-clad warriors. The gaping wounds which had almost torn the unfortunate apart were like nothing Raf had ever seen.

With a guttural sound which expressed his feelings as well as any words, the officer picked up from the floor a broken spear, the barbed head of which was dyed the same reddish yellow as the blood still seeping from the torn body. Swinging the weapon so close to Raf that the Terran was forced to retreat a step of two to escape contact with the grisly relic, the officer burst into an impassioned speech. Then he went back to the gestures which were easier for the spaceman to understand.

This was the work of a deadly enemy, Raf gathered. And such a fate awaited any one of them who ventured beyond certain bounds of safety. Unless this enemy were destroyed, the city—life itself—was no longer theirs—

Seeing those savage wounds which suggested that an

insane fury had driven the attacker, Raf could believe that. But surely a primitive spear was no equal to the weapons his guide could command.

When he tried to suggest that, the other shook his head as if despairing of making plain his real message, and again beckoned Raf to come with him. They were out on the littered street, heading away from the central building where the rest of the Terran party must still be. And Raf, seeing the lengthening shadows, the pools of dusk gathering, and remembering that spear, could not resist glancing back over his shoulder now and then. He wondered if the metallic click of his boot soles on the pavement might not draw attention to them, attention they would not care to meet. His hand was on his stun gun. But the officer gave no sign of being worried; he walked along with the assurance of one who has nothing to fear.

Then Raf caught sight of a patch of color he had seen before and relaxed. They were on their way back to the flitter! He had come down this very street earlier. And he did not mind the long climb back, ramp by steep ramp, which brought him out at last beside the flyer. His relief was so great that he put out his hand to draw it along the sleek side of the craft as he might have caressed a well-loved pet.

"Kurbi?"

At Hobart's bark he stiffened. "Yes, sir!"

"We camp here tonight. Have to make some plans."

"Yes, sir." He agreed with that. To attempt passage of the mountains in the dark was a suicide mission which he would have refused. On the other hand, to his mind, they would sleep more soundly if they were out of the city. He speculated whether he dared suggest that they use the few remaining moments of twilight to head into the open and establish a camp somewhere in the countryside.

The alien officer made some comment in his slurred speech and faded away into the shadows. Raf saw that the others had already dragged out their blanket rolls and were spreading them in the shelter of the flitter while Soriki busied himself at the com, sending back a message to the RS 10.

" . . . should not be too difficult to establish a common speech form," Lablet was saying as Raf climbed into the flitter to tug loose his own roll. "Color and pitch both seem to carry meaning. But the basic pattern is there to study. And with the scanner to sort out those record strips—did you adjust them, Soriki?"

"They're all ready for you to push the button. If the scanner can read them, it will. I got all that speech the chief, or king, or whatever he was, made just before we left."

"Good, very good!" In the light of the portable lamp by Soriki's com, Lablet settled down, plugged the scanner tubes in his ears, absently accepting a ration bar the captain handed him to chew on while he listened to the playback of the record the com-tech had made that afternoon.

Hobart turned to Raf. "You went off with that officer. What did he have to show you?"

The pilot described the globe and the body he had been shown and then added what he had deduced from the sketchy explanations he had been given. The captain nodded.

"Yes, they have aircraft, have been using them, too.

But I think that there's only one of the big ones. And they're fighting a war all right. We didn't see the whole colony, but I'll wager that there are only a handful of them left. They're holed up here, and they need help or the barbarians will finish them off. They talked a lot about that."

Lablet pulled the ear plugs from his ears. In the lamplight there was an excited expression on his face. "You were entirely right, Captain! They were offering us a bargain there at the last! They are offering us the accumulated scientific knowledge of this world!"

"What?" Hobart sounded bewildered.

"Over there"—Lablet made a sweep with his arm which might indicate any point to the east—"there is a storehouse of the original learning of their race. It's in the heart of the enemy country. But the enemy as yet do not know of it. They've made two trips over to bring back material and their ship can only go once more. They offer us an equal share if we'll make the next trip in their company and help them clean out the storage place—"

Hobart's answer was a whistle. There was an avid hunger on Lablet's lean face. No more potent bribe could have been devised to entice him. But Raf, remembering the spear-torn body, wondered.

In the heart of the enemy country, he repeated to himself.

Lablet added another piece of information. "After all, the enemy they face is only dangerous because of superior numbers. They are only animals—"

"Animals don't carry spears!" Raf protested.

"Experimental animals that escaped during a worldwide

war generations ago," reported the other, "It seems that the species have evolved to a semi-intelligent level. I must see them!"

Hobart was not to be hurried. "We'll think it over," he decided. "This needs a little time for consideration."

—7—
MANY EYES, MANY EARS

THIS WAS NOT the first time Dalgard had faced the raging fury of a snake-devil thirsting for a kill. The slaying he had done in the arena was an exception to the rule, not the usual hunter's luck. And now that he saw the creature crouched at the far end of the hall he was ready. Sssuri, also, followed their familiar pattern, separating from his companion and slipping along the wall toward the monster, ready to attract its attention at the proper moment.

Only one doubt remained in Dalgard's mind. This devil had not acted in the normal brainless fashion of its kin. What if it was able to assess the very simple maneuvers, which always before had completely baffled its species, and attacked not the moving merman but the waiting archer?

It was backed against another door, a closed one, as if it had fled for refuge to some aid it had expected and did not find. But as Sssuri moved, its long neck straightened until it was almost at right angles with its narrow shoulders, and from its snake's jaws proceeded a horrific hissing

341

which arose to a scream as its leg muscles tensed for a spring.

At just the right moment Sssuri's arm went back, his spear sang through the air. And the snake-devil, with an incredible twist of its neck, caught the haft of the weapon between its teeth, crunching the iron-hard substance into powder. But with that move it exposed its throat, and the arrow from Dalgard's bow was buried head-deep in the soft inner flesh.

The snake-devil spat out the spear and tried to raise its head. But the muscles were already weakening. It fought the poison long enough to take a single step forward, its small red eyes alight with brainless hate. Then it crashed and lay twisting. Dalgard lowered his bow. There was no need for a second shot.

Sssuri regarded the remains of his spear unhappily. Not only was it the product of long hours of work, but no merman ever felt fully equipped to face the world without such a weapon to hand. He salvaged the barbed head and broke it free of the shred of haft the snake-devil had left. Knotting it at his belt he turned to Dalgard.

"Shall we see what lies beyond?"

Dalgard crossed the hall to test the door. It did not yield to an inward push, but rolled far enough into the wall to allow them through.

On the other side was a room which amazed the scout. The colonists had their laboratory, their workshops, in which they experimented and tried to reserve the remnants of knowledge their forefathers had brought across space, as well as to discover new. But the extent of this storehouse with its bewildering mass of odd machines, tanks, bales, and stocked shelves and tables, was too much to be taken in without a careful and minute examination.

"We are not the first to walk here." Sssuri had given little attention to what was stacked about him. Instead he bent over the disturbed dust in one aisle. Dalgard noted as he went to join the merman that there were gaps on those tables which ran the full length of the room, lines left in the grimy deposit of years which told of things recently moved. And then he saw what had interested Sssuri: tracks, some resembling those which his own bare feet might leave, except that there were only three toes!

"They."

Dalgard who had been a hunter and a tracker before he was an explorer crouched for a clearer view. Yes, they were recent, yet not made today or even yesterday; there was a thin film of dust resettled in each.

"Some days ago. They are not in the city how," the merman declared with certainty. "But they will come again."

"How do you know that?"

Sssuri's hand swept about to include the wealth around them. "They have taken some, perhaps to them the most needful. But they will not be able to resist garnering the rest. Surely they will return, perhaps not once but many times. Until—"

"Until they come to stay." Dalgard was grim as he completed that sentence for the other.

"That is what they will work for. This land was once under their mastery. This world was theirs before they threw it away warring among themselves. Yes, they dream of holding all once more. But—" Sssuri's yellow eyes took on some of the fire which had shone in those of the snake-devil during its last seconds of life—"that must not be so!"

"If they take the land, you have the sea," Dalgard pointed out. The mermen had means of escape. But what of his own clansmen? Large families were unknown among the Terran colonists. In the little more than a century they had been on this planet their numbers, from the forty-five survivors of the voyage, had grown to only some two hundred and fifty, of which only a hundred and twenty were old enough or young enough to fight. And for them there was no retreat or hiding place.

"We do not go back to the depths!" There was stern determination in that declaration from Sssuri. His tribe had been long hunted, and it wasn't until they had made a loose alliance with the Terran colonists that they had dared to leave the dangerous ocean depths, where they were the prey of monsters more ferocious and cunning than any snake-devil, to house their families in the coast caves and on the small islands offshore, to increase in numbers and develop new skills of civilization. No, knowing the stubbornness which was bred into their small, furry bodies, Dalgard did not believe that many of the sea people would willingly go back into the sunless depths. They would not surrender tamely to the rulership of the loathed race.

"I don't see," Dalgard spoke aloud, half to himself, as he studied the tables closely packed, the machines standing on bases about the walls, the wealth of alien technology, "what we can do to stop them."

The restriction drilled into him from early childhood, that the knowledge of Those Others was not for his race and in some way dangerous, gave him an uneasy feeling of guilt to be standing there. Danger, danger which was far worse than physical, lurked there. And he could bring it to life by merely putting out his hand and picking up any one of those fascinating objects which lay only inches away. For the pull of curiosity was warring inside him against the stern warnings of his Elders.

Once when Dalgard had been very small he had raided his father's trip bag after the next to the last exploring journey the elder Nordis had made. And he had found a clear block of some kind of greenish crystal, in the heart of which threadlike lines of color wove patterns which were utterly strange. When he had turned the block in his hand, those lines had whirled and changed to form new and intricate designs. And when he had watched them intently it had seemed that something happened inside his mind and he knew, here and there, a word, a fragment of alien thought—just as he normally communicated with the cub who was Sssuri or the hoppers of the field. And his surprise had been so great that he had gone running to his father with the cube and the story of what happened when one watched it.

But there had been no praise for his discovery. Instead he had been hurried off to the chamber where an old, old man, the son of the Great Man who had planned to bring them across space, lay in his bed. And Forken Kordov himself had talked to Dalgard in his old voice, a voice as withered and thin as the hands crossed helplessly on his shrunken body, explaining in simple, kindly words that the knowledge which lay in the cubes, in the oddly shaped books which the Terrans sometimes came across in the

ruins, was not for them. That his own great-grandfather
Dard Nordis, who had been one of the first of the mutant
line of sensitives, had discovered that. And Dalgard,
impressed by Forken, by his father's concern, and by all
the circumstances of that day, had never forgotten nor lost
that warning.

"We cannot hope to stop them," Sssuri pointed out.
"But we must learn when they will come again and be
waiting for them—with your people and mine. For I tell
you now, brother of the knife, they must not be allowed to
rise once more!"

"And how can we foretell their coming?" Dalgard
wanted to know.

"Perhaps that alone we cannot do. But when they
come they will not leave speedily. They have stayed here
before without harm, and their distrust has been lulled.
When next they come, it will be only according to their
natures that they will wish to stay longer. Not snatching up
the closest to hand of these treasures of theirs, but choosing
out with care those things which will give them the best
results. Therefore they may make a camp, and we can
summon others to aid us."

"To return to Homeport will take several days even if
we push," pointed out the scout.

"Word can pass swifter than man," the merman
returned, with confidence in his own plan of action. "We
shall put other eyes, other ears, many eyes, many ears, to
service for us. Be assured we are not the only ones to fear
the return of Those Others from overseas."

Dalgard caught his meaning. Yes, it would not be the
first time the hoppers and other small animals living in the

grasslands, the runners and even the moth birds that only the mermen could mind touch, would relay a message across the land. It might not be an accurate message—to transmit that by small animal brains was impossible—but the meaning would reach both merman and colony Elders: trouble in the north, help needed there. And since Dalgard was the only explorer at present who had chosen the northern trails, his people would know that he had sent that warning and would act upon it, as Sssuri's message would in turn be heeded by the warriors of his tribe.

Yes, it could be done. But what of the traces they had left here—the slaughtered snake-devils—?

Sssuri had an answer for that also. "Let them believe that one of my race came here, or that a party of us ventured to explore inland. We can make it appear that way. But they must not know of you. I do not believe that they ever learned of you or how your fathers came, from the sky. And so that may swing the battle in our favor if it comes to open warfare."

What the merman said was sensible enough, and Dalgard was willing to obey orders. As he left the store-house, Sssuri trailed him, scuffling each dusty print the scout left. Perhaps a master of trailcraft could unravel that spoor, but the colonist was ready to believe that no such master existed in the ranks of Those Others.

In the outer hall the merman approached the now dead snake-devil and jerked from its loose skin the arrow which had killed it. Loosing the head of his ruined spear from his belt, he dug and gouged at the small wound, tearing it so that it's original nature was concealed forever. Then they retraced their way through the underground passages until they reached the sanded arena. Already insects buzzed hungrily about the hulks of the dead monsters.

There was a shrill squeal as the remaining infant reptile fled from the pouch where it had hidden. Sssuri hurled his knife, and the blade caught the small devil above the shoulder line, half cutting, half snapping its tender neck, so that it bounded aimlessly on to crash against the wall and fall back squirming feebly.

They collected the darts which had killed the others. Dalgard took the opportunity to study those bands on the forearms of the adults. To his touch they had the slick smoothness of metal, yet he was unfamiliar with the material. It possessed the ruddy fire of copper, but through it ran small black veins. He would have liked to have taken one with him for investigation, but it was out of the question to pry it off that scaled limb.

Sssuri straightened up from his last gruesome bit of stage setting with a sigh of relief. "Go ahead." He pointed to one of the other archways. "I will confuse the trail."

Dalgard obeyed, treading as lightly as he could, avoiding all stretches in which he could leave a clear print. Sssuri ran lightly back and forth mixing the few impressions to the best of his ability.

They backtracked to the river, retrieved the boat and recrossed, to leave the city behind and strike into the open country beyond its sinister walls. Night was falling, and Dalgard was very glad that he was not to spend the time of darkness within those haunted buildings. But he knew that it was more than a dislike for being shut up in the alien dwellings which had brought Sssuri out into the fields. The second part of their plan must be put into operation.

While Dalgard willed his body motionless, the merman lay relaxed upon the ground before him as he might have floated upon his beloved waves in some secluded cove. His brilliant eyes were closed. Yet Dalgard knew that Sssuri was far from asleep, and with all his own power he tried to join in the broadcast: that urgency which should send some hopper, some night runner, on to spread the rumor that there was trouble in the north, that danger existed and must be investigated. They had already met one colony of runners ranging southward to escape. But if they could send another such tribe traveling, arouse and aim south a hopper exodus, the story would spread until the fringe would reach the animals who lived in peace within touch of Homeport.

The sun was gone, the dark gathered fast. Dalgard could not even see the clustered buildings of the city now. And since he lacked Sssuri's range and staying power, he had no idea whether their efforts had met with even a shadow of success. He shivered in the bite of the wind and dared to lay his hand on Sssuri's shoulder, feeling anew the electric shock of warmth and bursting life which was always there.

Having so broken the other's absorption he asked a question: "Would it not be well, brother of the knife, if with the rising sun you returned to the sea and struck out to join your tribesmen, leaving me here to watch until your return?"

Sssuri's answer came with a speed which suggested that he, too, had been considering that problem. "We shall see what happens with the sun's rising. It is true that in the sea I can travel with greater speed, that there are hunting parties of my people striking into these waters. But they will not come to this city without good reason. It is an accursed place."

With the early morning the city drew them once more. Dalgard's curiosity pulled him to that storehouse. He could not stifle the hope that with luck he might find something there which would solve their problem for them. If there could only be a way to avoid open conflict with Those Others, some solution whereby the aliens need never know of the existence of the Colony. For so many generations, even centuries, the aliens had been confined, or had confined themselves, safely overseas on the western continent. Perhaps if now they were faced by some new catastrophe, they would never attempt to come east again. He had visions of discovering and activating some trap set to protect their treasures which could be turned against them. But he realized that he lacked the technical knowledge which would have aided him in the search for such a weapon.

The remnants of Terran science and mechanics, which the outlaws had brought with them from their native world, had been handed on; the experiments they had managed since with crude equipment had been carefully recorded, and he was acquainted with the outlines of most of them. But the few destructive arms they had imported were long since worn out or lacked charges, and they had not been able to duplicate them. Just as they had torn asunder the ship in which they had crossed space, to use its parts for the building of Homeport, so had they hoarded all else they had brought. But they were limited by lack of materials on Astra, and their fear of the knowledge of the aliens had kept them from experimenting with things found in the ruins.

There might be hundreds of objects on the shelves of that storage place, which, properly used, would reduce not only just the room and its contents to glowing slag, but take half the city with it. But he had no idea which, or which combination, would do it.

And here Sssuri could be no help. The mermen had made great strides forward in biological and mental sciences, but mechanics was a closed section of learning because of their enforced habitat under the sea, and of machines they knew less than the colonists.

"I have been thinking—" Sssuri broke into his companion's chain of reasoning, "of what we may do. And perhaps there is a way to reach the sea more swiftly than by returning overland."

"Downriver? But you said that way may have its watching devices."

"Which would be centered on objects coming upstream, not down. But in this city there should be yet another way—"

He did not enlarge upon that, but since he apparently knew what he was doing, Dalgard let him play guide once more. They recrossed the sluggish river, the scout looking into its murky depths with little relish for it as a means of transportation. Though it had an oily, flowing current, there was a suggestion of stagnant water with unpleasant surprises waiting beneath its turgid surface.

For the second time they entered the arena. Avoiding

the bodies, Sssuri made a circuit of the sanded floor. He did not turn in at the archway which led to the storage place, but paused before another as if there lay what he had been searching for.

Dalgard's less sensitive nostrils picked up a new scent, the not-to-be-missed fetor of damp underground ways where water stood. The merman edged around a barred gate as Dalgard sniffed again. The smell of damp was crossed by other and even less appetizing odors, but he did not catch the stench of the snake-devils. And, relying on Sssuri's judgment, he followed the merman into the dark.

Once again patches of violet light glimmered over their heads as the passage narrowed and sloped downward. Dalgard tried to remember the general geography of the section which was above them now. He had assumed that this way with its dank chill must give on the river. But when they had pattered on for a long distance, he knew that either they had passed beneath the stream or that he was totally lost as to direction.

As their eyes adjusted to the gloom of the passage the violet light grew stronger. So Dalgard saw clearly when Sssuri whirled and faced back along the way they had come, his body in a half crouch, his knife ready in his hand.

Dalgard, his bow useless in the damp, drew his own sword-Knife, But, though his mind probed and he listened, he could sense or hear nothing on their trail.

⫸8⫷
AIRLIFT

THEY WERE air-borne once more, but Raf was not pleased. In the seat beside him, which Captain Hobart should be occupying, there now squirmed an alien warrior who apparently was uncomfortable in the chair-like depression so different from the low stools he was accustomed to. Soriki was still in the second passenger place, but he, too, shared that with another of the men from the city who rested across bony knees a strange weapon rather like a Terran rifle.

No, the spacemen were not prisoners. According to the official statement they were allies. But, Raf wondered, as against his will he followed the globe in a northeastern course, how long would that fiction last if they refused to fall in with any suggestions the aliens might make? He did not doubt that there was on board the globe some surprise which could shoot the flitter out of the air, if, for example, he adjusted the controls before him and bore west toward the mountains and the safety of the space ship. Either of the aliens he now transported could bring him under control by using those weapons, which might do anything from boiling a man in some unknown ray to smothering him in gas. He had not seen the arms in action, and he did not want to.

Yet Hobart and Lablet did not, as far as he could tell, share his suspicions. Lablet was eager to see the mysterious storehouse, and the captain was either moved by the same desire or else had long since deduced the folly of trying to make a break for it. Thus they were now heading seaward with the captain and Lablet sharing quarters with the leaders of the expedition on board the globe, and Raf and the com-tech, with companions—or guards—bringing up the rear. The aliens had even insisted on stripping the flitter of much of its Terran equipment before they left the city, pointing out that the cleared storage space would be filled with salvage when they made the return voyage.

The globe had been trailing along the coastline, and now it angled out to glide over a long finger of cape, rocky and waterworn, which pointed at almost a right angle into the sea. This dwindled into a reef of rock, like the nail on a finger. The sea ahead was no unbroken expanse. Instead there was a series of islands, some merely tops of reefs over which the waves broke, others more substantial, rising well above the threatening water, and one or two showing the green of vegetation.

The chain of islets extended so far out that when the flitter passed over the last one the main continent was out of sight. Now only water stretched beneath them. The globe skidded on as if its pilot had given it an extra burst of power, and Raf accelerated in turn, having no desire to lose his guide. But they were not to make the ocean-wide trip in one jump.

At midday he saw again a break in the smooth carpet of waves, another island, or perhaps the southern tip of a northern continent for the land swept in that direction as far as he could see. The globe spiraled down to make a neat landing on a flat plateau, and Raf prepared to join it. When the undercarriage of the flitter jarred lightly on the rock, he saw signs that this was a man—or alien—fashioned place which must have had much use in the dim past when his new companions ruled all their native world.

The rock had been smoothed off to a flat surface, and at its perimeter were several small domed buildings. Yet, as there had been in the countryside and in the city, except at its very heart, there was an aura of desertion at the site.

Both his alien passengers jumped out of the flitter, as if only too pleased at their release from the Terran flyer. For the first time Raf was shaken out of his own preoccupation with his dislike for the aliens to wonder if they could be moved by a similar distaste for Terrans. Lablet might be interested in that as a scientific problem—the pilot only knew how he felt and that was not comfortable.

Soriki got out and walked across the rock, stretching. But for a long moment Raf remained where he was, behind the controls of the flyer. He was as cramped and tired of travel as the com-tech, perhaps even more so since the responsibility of the flight had been his. And had they landed in open country he would have liked to have thrown himself down on the ground, taking off his helmet and unhooking his tunic collar to let the fresh wind blow through his hair and across his skin. Perhaps that would take away the arid dust of centuries, which, to his mind, had grimed him since their hours in the city. But here was no open country, only a landing space which reminded him too much of the roof of the building in the metropolis.

A half-dozen of the breastplated warriors filed out of the globe and went to the nearest dome, returning with heavy boxes. Fuel—supplies—Raf shrugged off the problem. The pilot was secretly relieved when Captain Hobart dropped out of the hatch in the globe and made his way over to the flitter.

"Everything running smoothly?" he asked with a glance at the two aliens who were Raf's passengers.

"Yes sir, Any idea how much farther—?" Raf questioned.

Hobart shrugged. "Until we work out basic language difficulties," he muttered, "who knows anything? There is at least one more of these way stations. They don't run on atomics, need some kind of fuel, and they have to have new supplies every so often. Their head man can't understand why it isn't necessary for us to do the same."

"Has he suggested that his techneers want a look at our motors, sir?"

Hobart unbent a little. It was as if in the question he had read something which pleased him. "So far we've managed not to understand that. And if anyone tries it on his own, refer him to me—understand?"

"Yes, sir!" Some of the relief in Raf's tone came through, and he saw the captain was watching him narrowly.

"You don't like these people, Kurbi?"

The pilot replied with the truth. "I don't feel easy with them, sir. Not that they've shown any unfriendliness. Maybe it's because they're alien—"

He had said the wrong thing and knew it immediately.

"That sounds like prejudice, Kurbi!" Hobart's voice carried the snap of reprimand.

"Yes, sir," Raf said woodenly. That had done it as far as the captain was concerned. The fierce racial and economical prejudices which had been the keystones of the structure of Pax had left their shadow on Terra's thinking. Nowadays a man would better be condemned for murder than for prejudice against another—it was the unforgivable crime. And in that unconsidered answer Raf had rendered unreliable in the eyes of authority any future report on the aliens which he might be forced to make.

Silently cursing his lack of judgment, Raf made a careful check of the flyer, which might not be necessary but going through the motions of doing his duty gave him some relief. Once the idea struck him of claiming some trouble that would take them back to the spacer for repairs. But Hobart was too good a mechanic himself not to see through that.

They covered the second stage of their flight by evening, this time putting down on an island where, by some ancient and titanic feat of labor, the top had been sheared off a central mountain to make a base. A ring of reefs cut off the land from the action of the waves. At once a party of aliens left the main company and made their way down the mountain to prowl along the shore. They made a discovery of sorts, for Raf saw them ring in some object they had pulled up on the sand. What it was and what meaning it had for them they did not try to explain to the Terrans.

The party spent the night there, the four spacemen wrapped in their sleeping rolls by the flitter, the aliens in their globe ship. The Terrans did not miss the fact that the others had unobtrusively posted guards at the only two places where the mountain could be climbed. And each of those guards cradled in the crook of his arm one of the rifle weapons.

They were aroused shortly after dawn. As far as Raf could see the island was barren of life, or else any creature native to it kept prudently out of the way while the flyers were there. They took off, the globe rising like a balloon into the morning sky, the flitter waiting until it was air-borne before scaling after it.

The mountainous island where they had based was the sea sentinel of an archipelago, which they saw spread out below them as if someone had flung a handful of pebbles into a shallow pool. Most of the islands were merely rocky crags. But there were two which showed the green of small open fields, and Raf thought he caught a glimpse of a dome house on the last.

They were now over a region thick with islands, the first collection giving way to a second and then a third. Raf, expecting no sudden move on the part of the globe he trailed, was startled when the alien ship made a downward swoop. At the same time the warrior seated beside him tugged at the sleeve of his tunic and jabbed a finger toward the ground, clearly an order to follow. Raf cut speed and cautiously lost altitude, determined that he was not going to be rushed into any move for which he did not know the reason.

The globe was hovering over a small island set a little apart from the others. A moment later Soriki's excited voice drew Raf's attention from his controls to what was going on below.

"There's people down there! Look at them run!"

They were too far away to be sure of the nature of the brown-gray things so close to the color of the seawashed rock that they could only be detected when they moved. But it was evident that they were alive, and as Raf brought the flitter closer, he was also certain that they ran on their two hind feet instead of on an animal's four pads.

From the under part of the globe ship licked a tongue of fire. With the force of a whiplash it coursed across the rock and in its passing embrace, the creatures below writhed and withered to charred heaps. They had no chance under that methodical blasting. The alien beside Raf signaled again for a drop. He patted the weapon that he held and motioned for Raf to release the covering of the windshield. But the pilot shook his head firmly.

This might be war. The aliens could have a very good reason for their deadly attack on the creatures surprised below. But he wanted no part of it, nor did he want to get any closer to the scene of slaughter. And he made an emphatic gesture that the windshield could not be opened while the flitter was air-borne.

But as he did so they glided down, and he caught a single good look at what was going on on the rock—a look which remained to haunt his dreams for long years to come. For now he saw clearly the creatures who ran fruitlessly for safety. Some reached the edge of the cliff and leaped to what was an easier death in the sea. But too many others could not make it and died in flaming agony. And they were not all of one size!

Children! There was no mistaking the infant in its mother's arms, the two small ones who fled hand in hand until one stumbled and the burning lash caught them both as the other strove to pull the fallen to its feet. Raf gagged. He triggered the controls and soared up and away, fighting the heaving in his middle, shaking off with one savage jerk the insistent pawing hand of the alien who wanted to join in the fun.

"Did you see that?" he demanded of Soriki.

For once the com-tech sounded subdued. "Yes," he replied shortly.

"Those were children," Raf hammered home the point.

"Young ones anyway," the com-tech conceded. "Maybe they aren't people. They had fur all over them—"

Raf grinned mirthlessly. Should he now accuse Soriki of prejudice? What did it matter if a thinking creature was clothed in a space suit, silken bandages, or natural fur—it was still a thinking creature. And he was sure that those had been intelligent creatures he had just seen blasted without a chance to fight back. If these were the enemy the aliens feared, he could understand the vicious cruelty of the attack which had killed the man he had been shown back in the city. Fire against primitive spears was not equal, and when the spears got their chance they must make up for much to balance the scales of justice.

He did not even wonder why his emotions were so

wholeheartedly enlisted upon the side of the furred people. Nor did he try to analyze his feelings. He was only sure that more than ever he wanted to be free of the aliens and out of this whole venture.

The warrior sharing his seat was sulking now, twisting about to look back at the island as Raf circled in ever-widening glides to get away from the site and yet not lose track of the globe when it would have finished its dirty business and take once more to the air. But the alien ship was in no hurry to leave.

"They are making sure," Soriki reported. "Giving the whole island a fire bath. I wonder what that stuff is—"

"I'd just as soon not know," Raf returned from between set teeth. "If that is one of their pieces of precious knowledge, we're as well off without it—" he stopped short. Perhaps he had said too much. But Terra had been racked by the torrid horror of atomic war, until all his kind had been so revolted that it was bred into them not to meddle again with such weapons. And war by fire aroused in them that old horror. Surely Soriki must feel it too, and when the com-tech did not comment, Raf was sure of that. He hoped that the slaughter had made some impression on the captain and on Lablet into the bargain.

But when, as if sated with killing, the globe rose again from its position over the island, moving almost sluggishly into the fresh sky, he had to follow it on. More islands were below, and he feared that each one might show some sign of life and tempt the killers to a second hunting.

Luckily that did not happen. The chains of islands became a cape as they had on the coast of the western continent. And now the globe swung to the south, trailing the shore line. Forests made green splotches with bluish overtones running from the sea cliffs back to carpet the land. So far no signs of civilization were to be seen. This land was as untouched as that where the spacer had landed.

Then they saw the bay, stretching out wide arms to engulf the sea. It could have harbored a whole fleet. And marching down to its waters were broad levels of buildings, a giant's staircase leading from sea to cliff tops.

"They had it here—!"

Raf saw what Soriki meant by that outburst. Destruction had struck. He had seen the atomic ruins of his own world, those which were free enough from radiation to explore. But he had never seen anything like these chilling scars. In long strips the very stone which provided foundation for the tiered city had been churned and boiled, had run in rivulets of lava down to the sea, enclosing narrow tongues of still untouched structures. The fire whip the globe had used, magnified to some infinitely greater extent—? It could be.

The alien at his side pressed tightly against the windshield gazing down at the ruins. And now he mouthed a gabble of words which was echoed by his fellow sitting with Soriki. Their excitement must mean that this was their goal. Raf slacked speed, waiting for the globe to point a way to a landing.

But to his surprise the alien ship shot forward inland. The long day was almost over as they came to a second city with a river knotting a ribbon through its middle. Here were no traces of the fury which had laded the seaport with havoc. This collection of buildings seemed whole and perfect.

There was, oddly enough, no landing strip within the

city. The globe coasted over the rough oval and came down in open fields to the west. It was a maneuver which Raf copied, though he first dropped a flare as a precaution and brought the flier down in its red glare, with the warrior expressing shrill disapproval:

"I don't think they like fireworks," Soriki remarked.

Raf snorted. "So they don't like fireworks! Well, I don't like crack-ups, and I'm the pilot!" But he didn't believe that the com-tech was really protesting. Soriki had been very quiet since they had witnessed the attack on the island.

"Grim-looking place," was his second comment as they touched ground.

Since Raf privately had held that opinion of all the alien settlements he had so far seen, he agreed. Their two alien passengers were out of the flitter as soon as he opened the bubble shield. And as they stood by the Terran flyer, they held their weapons ready, facing out into the dusk as if they half expected trouble. After the earlier episode that day, Raf did not wonder at their preparedness. Terror begets terror, and ruthlessness arouses retaliation in kind.

"Kurbi! Soriki!" Hobart's voice sounded out of the shadows. "Stay where you are for the present."

Soriki settled deeper in his seat. "He doesn't have to tell me to brake jets," he muttered. "I like it here—"

Raf did not need to echo that. He had a strong surmise that had he been tempted to roam away from the flitter the move would not have been encouraged by the alien guardsmen. If this was their treasure city, they would not welcome any independent investigation by strangers.

When the captain joined them, he was accompanied

by the officer who had first shown Raf the globe. And the warrior was either disturbed or angry, for he was talking in a steady stream and his hands were whirling in explanatory gestures.

"They didn't like that flare," Hobart remarked. But there was no reproof in his words. As a spacer pilot he knew that Raf had only done what duty demanded. "We're to remain here—for the night."

"Where's Lablet?" Soriki wanted to know.

"He's staying with Yussoz, the alien commander. He thinks he has the language problem about solved.

"Good enough." Soriki pulled out his bed roll. "We're out of touch with the ship—"

There was a second of silence, unduly prolonged it seemed to Raf. Then Hobart spoke:

"We couldn't expect to keep in call forever. The best com has its range. When did you lose contact?"

"Just before these wrapped-up heroes played with fire back there. I gave the boys all I knew up until then. They know we were headed west, and they had us beamed as long as they could."

So it wasn't too bad, thought Raf. But he didn't like it, even with that mitigating factor. To all purposes the four Terrans were now surrounded by some twenty times their number, in an unknown country, out of all communication with the rest of their kind. It could add up to disaster.

—9—
SEA GATE

"WHAT IS IT?" Dalgard asked his question as Sssuri, his attention still on their back trail, stole along cautiously on a retracing of their path.

But that retreat ended abruptly with the merman plastered against the wall, his whole shadowy form a tense warning which stopped Dalgard short. In that moment the answer flashed from mind to mind.

"There are those which follow—"

"Snake-devils? Those Others?" The colony scout supplied the only two explanations he had, sending his own thought out questing. But as usual he could not hope to equal the more sensitive merman whose race had always used that form of communication.

"Those who have long haunted the darkness," was the only reply he could get.

But Sssuri's actions were far more indicative of danger. For the merman turned and caught at Dalgard, pulling the larger colonist along a step or two with the urgency of his grip.

"We cannot return this way—and we must travel fast!"

For Sssuri who would face and had faced up to a snake-devil with a spear his sole weapon, this timidity was new. Dalgard was wise enough to accept his verdict of the wisdom of flight. Together they ran along the underground corridor, soon putting a mile between them and the point where the merman had first taken alarm.

"From what do we flee?" As the merman began to slacken pace, Dalgard sent that query.

"There are those who live in this darkness. By one, or by two, we could speedily remove them from life. But they hunt in packs and they are as greedy for the kill as are the snake-devils scenting meat. Also they are intelligent. Once, long before the days of burning, they served Those Others as hunters of game. And Those Others tried to make them ever more intelligent and crafty so they might be sent to hunt without a huntsman. At last they grew too knowing for their masters. Then Those Others, realizing their menace, tried to kill them all with traps and tricks. But only the most stupid and the slowest were so disposed of. The others withdrew into underground ways such as this, venturing form only in the dark of night."

"But if they are intelligent," countered the scout, "why can they not be reached by the mind touch?"

"Through the years they have developed their own ways of thought. And these are not the simple creatures of the sun, or such as the runners. Once they were taught to answer only to Those Others. Now they answer only to each other. But—" he spread out his hands in one of his quick, nervous gestures—"to those who are cornered by one of their packs, they are sudden death!"

Since they could not, by Sssuri's reckoning, turn back, there was only one course before them, to follow the passage they had chanced upon. The merman was certain that it underran the river and that eventually they would reach the sea—unless some side turn before that point would make them free in the countryside once more.

Dalgard doubted if it had ever been a well-used way. And the presence of earth falls here and there, over which they stumbled and clawed their way, led him to consider the wisdom of keeping on to what might be a dead end. But his trust in Sssuri's judgment was great, and as the merman plowed forward with every appearance of confidence, he continued to trot along without complaint.

They snatched moments of rest, taking turns at guard. But the walls about them were so unchanging that it was hard to measure time or distance. Dalgard chewed at his emergency rations, a block of dried meat and fruit pounded together to an almost rocklike consistency, and tried to make the crumbs he sucked loose satisfy his growing hunger.

The passageway was growing damper; water trickled down the walls and gathered in fetid pools on the floor. Dalgard's dislike of the place grew. His shoulders hunched involuntarily as he strode along, for his imagination pictured the rock above them giving away to dump tons of the oily river water down to engulf them. But though Sssuri avoided splashing through the pools wherever he might, he did not appear to find anything upsetting about the moisture.

At last the human could stand it no longer. "How much farther to the sea?" he asked without any hope of a real answer.

As he had expected him to do, Sssuri shrugged. "We should be close. But having never trod this way before, how can I tell you?"

Once more they rested, choosing a stretch which was reasonably dry, munching their dried food and drinking sparingly from the stoppered duocorn horns which swung from their belts. A man would have to be dying of thirst, Dalgard thought, before he would palm up any of the stagnant water from the passage pools.

He drifted off into a troubled sleep in which he fled beneath a sky which was a giant lid in the hand of an unseen enemy, a lid which was slowly lowered to crush him flat. He awoke with a start to find Sssuri's cool, scaled fingers stroking his shoulder.

"Dream demons walk these roads." The words drifted into his half-awake mind.

"They do indeed," he roused to answer.

"It is always so where Those Others have been. They leave behind them the thoughts which breed such dreams to trouble the sleep of those who are not of their kind. Let us go. I would like to be out of this place under the clean sky, where no ancient wickedness hangs to poison the air and thought."

Either the merman had miscalculated the direction of their route or the river mouth was much farther from the inland city than they had believed, for, though they pushed on for what seemed like weary hours, they came to no upward slope, no exit to the world they knew.

Instead Dalgard began to realize that just the opposite was true. At last he could stand it no longer and broke out with what he feared, hoping that Sssuri would deny that fear.

"We are going downhill!"

To his disappointment the merman agreed. "It has been so for the last thousand of our paces. It is my belief that this leads not to the sun but out under the sea."

Dalgard missed a step. To Sssuri the sea was home and perhaps the thought of being under its floor was not disturbing. The land-born human was not so prepared. If he had experienced discomfort under the river, what would it be like under the ocean? His terrifying dream of a lid being pressed down upon him flashed back into his mind. But his companion was continuing:

"There will be doors, perhaps into the sea itself."

"For you," Dalgard pointed out, "but I am no dweller in the depths."

"Neither were Those Others, yet they used these ways. And I tell you—" in his earnestness the merman laid his hand once more on Dalgard's arm—"to turn back now is out of the question. The death which haunts the darkness is still sniffing out our trail."

Dalgard glanced involuntarily over his shoulder. By the faint and limited light of the purple disks he could see little or nothing. An army might creep there undetected.

"But—" His protest was in answer to the merman's seeming unconcern.

Sssuri at the first intimation that the hunters were behind them had shown wariness. Now he did not appear to care.

"They had fed," he replied. "Scouts follow because we are something new and thus suspect. When hunger rises once more in them, and their scouts report that we are meat, then is the time to draw knives and prepare for battle. But before that hour we may have won free. Let us search for the gate we now need."

However confident the merman might be, Dalgard could not match that confidence. In the open air he would have faced a snake-devil four times his size without any more emotion than a hunter's instinctive caution. But here in the dark, unable to rid himself of the belief that thousands of tons of sea water hung over his head, he found himself starting at any sound, his knife bare and ready in his sweating hand.

He noted that Sssuri had stepped up the pace, passing into his sure-footed glide which made Dalgard exert himself to keep up. Before them the corridor stretched without a break. The merman's promised exit, if it existed, was still out of sight.

It was difficult to gauge time in this dark hall, but Dalgard thought that they were at least an hour farther on their way when Sssuri paused abruptly once more, his head cocked in a listening attitude, as if he caught some whisper of sound too rarefied for his human companion.

"Now—" the thought hissed as if he spat the words, "they hunger—and they hunt!"

He bounded forward with a spurt, which Dalgard copied, and they ran lightly, the dust undisturbed in years puffing up beneath the merman's bare, scaled feet and Dalgard's hide boots. Still the unbroken walls, the feeble patches of violet in the ceiling. But no exit. And what good would any exit do him, Dalgard thought, if it opened under the sea?

"There are islands off the coast—many islands—"

Sssuri caught him up. "It is in my mind that we shall find our door on one of those. But—run now, knife brother, for those at our heels awake and thirst for flesh and blood. They have decided that we are not to be feared but may be run down for their pleasure."

Dalgard weighed his knife in his hand. "They shall find us with fangs," he promised grimly.

"It will be better if they do not find us at all," returned Sssuri.

A burning arch of pain encased Dalgard's lower ribs, and his breath came in gusts of hastily sucked air as their flight kept on, down the endless corridor. Sssuri was also showing signs of the grueling pace, his round head bent forward, his furred legs pumping as if only his iron will kept them moving. And the determination which kept him going was communicated to the scout as a graver warning than any thought message of fear.

They were passing under one of the infrequent violet lights when Dalgard got something else—a mental thrust so quick and sharp it was as if a sword had cut through the daze of fatigue to reach his brain. Yet that had not come from Sssuri, for it was totally alien, wavering on a band so near the extreme edge of his consciousness that it pricked, receded, and pricked again as a needle might.

This was no message of fear or warning, but of implacable stubbornness and ravening hunger. And in that instant Dalgard knew that it came from what was sniffing out their trail, and he no longer wondered that the hunters were immune to other mental contact. One could not reason with—that!

He spurted forward, matching the merman's acceleration

of speed. But to Dalgard's horror he saw that his companion now ran with one hand brushing along the wall, as if he needed that support.

"Sssuri!"

His thought met a wall of concentration through which he could not break. In a way he was reassured—for a moment, until another of those stabs from their pursuers struck him. He longed to look back, to see what hunted them. But he dared not break stride to do that.

"Ahhhh!" The welcoming cry from Sssuri brought his attention back to his companion as the merman broke into a wild run.

Dalgard summoned up his last rags of energy and coursed after him. Sssuri had halted before a dark lump which protruded from the side of the corridor.

"A sea lock!" Sssuri's claws were clicking over the surface of the hatch, seeking the secret of its latch.

Panting, Dalgard leaned against the opposite wall. Just as a protest formed in his mind he heard something else, the pad of feet, many feet, echoing down the corridor. And somehow he was able now to look.

Round spots of light, dull, greenish, close to the ground, as if someone had flung a handful of phosphorescence into the dark. But this was no phosphorescence! Eyes! Eyes—he tried to count and knew it was impossible to so reckon the number of the pack that ran mute but ready. Nor could he distinguish more than a very shadowy glimpse of forms which glided close to the ground with an unpleasant sinuosity.

"Ahhhhh!" Again Sssuri's paean of triumph.

There was the grate of unwilling metal forced to move,

a puff of air redolent with the sea striking their bodies in chill threat, the brightness of violet light stepped up to a point far beyond the lamps in the corridor.

With it came no rush of drowning water as Dalgard had half expected, and when the merman clambered through the hatch he prepared to follow, well aware that the eyes, and the pattering of feet which bore them, were now almost within range.

There was a snarl from the passage, and a black thing sprang at the scout. Without clear sight of what he was fighting, he struck down with his knife and felt it slit flesh. The snarl was a scream of rage as the creature twisted in midair for a second try at him. In that instant Sssuri, leaning halfway out of the hatch, struck in his turn, thrusting his bone knife into shadows which now boiled with life.

Dalgard leaped for the lock door, kicking out swiftly and feeling the toe of his boot contact with a crunch against one of those darting shades, sending it back end over end into the press where its fellows turned snapping upon it. Then Sssuri grabbed at him, bringing him in, and together they slammed the hatch, feeling it shake with the shock of thudding bodies as the pack outside went mad in their frustration.

While the merman fastened the locking bar, bringing out of the long-motionless metal another protesting screech, Dalgard had a chance to look about him. They were in a room some eight or nine feet long, the violet light showing up well tangles of equipment hanging from pegs on the walls, a pile of small cylinders on the floor. At the far end of the chamber was another hatch door, locked with the same type of bar as Sssuri had just lowered to seal the inner one. The merman nodded to it.

"The sea—"

Dalgard slid his knife back into its sheath. So the sea lay beyond. He did not welcome the thought of passing through that door. Like all of his race he could swim—perhaps his feats in the water would have astonished the men of the planet from which his tribe had emigrated. But unlike the mermen, he was not sea-born, nor equipped by nature with a secondary breathing apparatus to make him as free in the world of water as he was on land. Sssuri might crawl through that hatch without fear. For Dalgard it was as big a test as to turn and face what now raged in the corridor on the inner side.

"There is no hope that they will go now," Sssuri answered his vague question. "They are stubborn. And hours—or even days—will mean nothing. Also they can leave a guard there and rove at will, to return upon signal. That is their way."

This left only the sea door. Sssuri padded across the chamber and reached up to free one of the strange objects dangling from the wall pegs. Like all things made of the marvelous substance used by Those Others for any article which might be exposed to the elements, it seemed as perfect as on the day it had first been hung there, though that date might be a hundred or more Astran years earlier. The merman uncoiled a length of thin, flexible piping which joined a two-foot canister with a flat piece of metallic fabric.

"Those Others could not breathe under the water, as you cannot," he explained as he worked deftly and swiftly.

"Within my own memory we have trapped their scouts wearing aids such as these so that they might spy upon our safe places. But their last foray was some years ago and at that time we taught them such a lesson that they have not dared to return. Since they are not unlike you in body and since you breathe the same air above ground, there is no reason why this should not take you out of here."

Dalgard accepted the apparatus. A couple of elastic metal bands fastened the canister to the chest of the wearer. The fabric molded into a perfect, tight face mask as it touched the skin.

Sssuri went to the pile of cylinders. Choosing one he tinkered with its pointed cone, to be rewarded with a thin hiss.

"Ahhhh—" again his recognition of the rightness of things. "These still contain air." He tested two more and then brought all three back to where Dalgard stood, the canister strapped into place, the mask ready in his hand. With infinite care the merman fitted two of the cylinders into the canister and then was forced to set the other aside.

"We could not change them while under water anyway," he explained. "So it will do little good to take extra supplies with us."

Trying not to speculate on the amount of air he could carry in the cylinders, Dalgard fastened on the mask, adjusted the air tube, and sucked. Air flowed—he could breathe! Only—for how long?

Sssuri, seeing that his companion was fully provided for, worked at the bar locking the sea hatch. But in the end it took their combined strength to spring that barrier and win through to a small cubby which was the actual sea lock.

Dalgard knew one moment of resistance as the merman closed the hatch behind them. For an instant it seemed that the dubious safety of the dressing chamber and a faint hope of the hunters' giving up their vigil was better than what might lie before them now. But Sssuri pushed shut the hatch, and Dalgard stood quietly, without offering any visible protest.

He tried to draw even breaths—slowly—as the merman activated the lock. When the water curled in from hidden openings, rising from ankle to calf and then to knee, its chill striking through flesh to bone, he kept to the same stolid waiting, though this seemed almost worse than a sudden gush of water sweeping them out in its embrace.

The liquid swirled about Dalgard's waist now, tugging at his belt, his arrow quiver, tapping on the bottom of the canister which held his precious air supply. His brow, shielded from the wet by its casing, was swallowed up inch by inch.

As the water lapped at his chin, the outer door opened with a slow inward push which suggested that the machinery controlling it had grown sluggish with the years. Sssuri, perfectly at home, darted out as soon as the opening was large enough to afford him an exit. And his thought came back to reassure the more clumsy landsman.

"We are in the shallows—land rises ahead. The roots of an island. There is nothing to fear—" The word ended abruptly in what was like a mental gasp of either astonishment or fear.

Knowing all the menaces which might lie in wait, even

n the shallows of the sea, Dalgard drew his knife once
nore as he plowed through water—ready to rescue or at
east to offer what aid he could.

~10~
THE DEAD GUARDIANS

THE SPACEMEN spent a cramped and almost sleepless night. Although in his training on Terra, on his trial trips to Mars and the harsh Lunar valleys, Raf had known weird surroundings, and climates, inimical to his kind, he had always been able to rest almost by the exercise of his will. But now, curled in his roll, he was alert to every sound out of the moonless night, finding himself listening—for what he did not know.

Though there were sounds in plenty. The whistling call of some night bird, the distant lap, lap of water which he associated with the river curving through the long-deserted city, the rustle of grass as either the wind or some passing animal disturbed it.

"Not the best place in the world for a nap," Soriki observed out of the dark as Raf wriggled, trying to find a more comfortable position. "I'll be glad to see these band-aged boys on the ground waving good-bye as we head away from them—fast—"

"Those weren't animals they killed—back on that

island." Raf brought out what was at the heart of his trouble.

"They wore fur instead of clothing." Soriki's reply was delivered in a colorless, even voice. "We have apes on Terra, but they are not men."

Raf stared up at the sky in which stars were sprinkled like carelessly flung dust motes. "What is a 'man'?" he returned, repeating the classical question which was a debating point in all the space training centers.

For so long his kind had wondered that. Was a "man" a biped with certain easily recognized physical characteristics? Well, by that ruling the furry things which had fled fruitlessly from the flames of the globe might well qualify. Or was "man" a certain level of intelligence, no matter what form housed that intelligence? They were supposed to accept the latter definition. Though, in spite of the horror of prejudice, Raf could not help but believe that too many Terrans secretly thought of "man" only as a creature in their own general image. By that prejudiced rule it was correct to accept the aliens as "men" with whom they could ally themselves, to condemn the furry people because they were not smooth-skinned, did not wear clothing, nor ride in mechanical transportation.

Yet somewhere within Raf at that moment was the nagging feeling mat this was all utterly wrong, that the Terrans had not made the right choice. And that now "men" were not standing together. But he had no intention of spilling that out to Soriki.

"Man is intelligence." The com-tech was answering the question Raf had almost forgotten that he had asked the moment before. Yes, the proper conventional reply.

Soriki was not going to be caught out with any claim of prejudice.

Odd—when Pax had ruled, there were thought police and the cardinal sin was to be a liberal, to experiment, to seek knowledge. Now the wheel had turned—to be conservative was suspect. To suggest that some old ways were better was to exhibit the evil signs of prejudice. Raf grinned wryly. Sure, he had wanted to reach the stars, had fought doggedly to come to the very spot where he now was. So why was he tormented now with all these second thoughts? Why did he feel every day less akin to the men with whom he had shared the voyage? He had had wit enough to keep his semirebellion under cover, but since he had taken the flitter into the morning sky above the landing place of the spacer, that task of self-discipline was becoming more and more difficult.

"Did you notice," the com-tech said, going off on a new track, "that these painted boys were not too quick about blasting along to their strongbox? I'd say that they thought some bright rocket jockey might have rigged a surprise for them somewhere in there—"

Now that Soriki mentioned it, Raf remembered that the alien party who had gone into the city hail huddled together, and that several of the black-and-white warriors had fanned out ahead as scouts might in enemy territory.

"They didn't go any farther than that building to the west either."

That Raf had not noticed, but he was willing to accept Soriki's observation. The com-tech had a ready eye for details. He'd better pay closer attention himself. This was no time to explore the why and wherefore of his present position. So, if they went no farther than that building, it would argue that the aliens themselves didn't care to go about here after nightfall. For he was certain that the isolated structure Soriki had pointed out was not the treasure house they had come to loot.

The night wore on and sometime during it Raf fell asleep. But the two or three hours of restless, dream-filled unconsciousness was not what he needed, and he blinked in the dawn with eyes which felt as if they were filled with hot sand. In the first gray light a covey of winged things, which might or might not have been birds, arose from some roosting place within the city, wheeled three times over the building, and then vanished out over the countryside.

Raf pulled himself out of his roll, made a sketchy toilet with the preparations in a belt kit, and looked about with little favor for either the scene or his part in it. The globe, sealed as if ready for a take-off, was some distance away, but installed about halfway between it and the flitter were two of the alien warriors. Perhaps they had changed watches during the night. If they had not, they could go without sleep to an amazing degree, for as Raf walked in a circle about the flyer to limber up, they watched him closely, nor did their grips on their odd weapons loosen. And he had a very clear idea that if he stepped over some invisible boundary he would be in for trouble.

When he came back to the flitter, Soriki was awake and stretching.

"Another day," the com-tech drawled. "And I could do with something besides field rations." He made a face at the small tin of concentrates he had dug out of the supply compartment.

"We'd do well to be headed west," Raf ventured.

"Now you can come in with that on the com again!" Soriki answered with unwonted emphasis. "The sooner I see the old girl standing on her pins in the middle distance, the better I'll feel. You know—" he looked up from his preoccupation with the ration package and gazed out over the city—"this place gives me the shivers. That other town was bad enough. But at least there were people living there. Here's nothing at all—at least nothing I want to see."

"What about all the wonders they've promised to show us?" countered Raf.

Soriki grinned. "And how much do we understand of their mouth-and-hand talk? Maybe they were promising us wonders, maybe they were offering to take us to where we could have our throats cut more conveniently—for them! I tell you, if I go for a walk with any of these painted faces, I'm going to have at least three of my fingers resting on the grip of my stun gun. And I'd advise you to do the same—if I didn't know that you were already watching these blast-happy harpies out of the corner of your eye. Ha—company. Oh, it's the captain—"

The hatch of the globe had opened, and a small party was descending the ladder, conspicuous among them the form and uniform of Captain Hobart. The aliens remained in a cluster at the foot of the ladder while the Terran commander crossed to the flitter.

"You"—he pointed to Raf—"are to come along with us."

"Why, sir?" "What about me, Sir?" The questions from the two at the flitter came together.

"I said that one of you had to remain by the machine. Then they said that you, in particular, must come along, Kurbi."

"But I'm the pilot—" Raf bagan and then realized that it was just that fact which had made the aliens attach him to the exploring party. If they believed that the Terran flitter was immobilized when he, and he alone, was not behind its controls, this was just the move they would make. But there they were wrong. Soriki might not be able to repair or service the motor, but in a pinch he could take it up, send it westward and land it beside the spacer. Each and every man about the RS 10 had that much training.

Now the com-tech was scowling. He had grasped the significance of that arrangement as quickly as Raf. "How long do I wait for you, sir?" he asked in a voice which had lost its usual good-humored drawl.

And at that inquiry Captain Hobart showed signs of irritation. "Your suspicions are not founded on facts," he stated firmly. "These people have displayed no signs of wanting to harm us. And an attitude of distrust at this point might be fatal for future friendly contact. Lablet is sure that they have a highly complex society, probably advanced beyond Terran standards, and that their technical skills will be of vast benefit to us. As it happens we have come at just the right moment in their history, when they are striving to get back on their feet after a disastrous series of wars. It is as if a group of off-world explorers had allied themselves with us after the Burn-Off. We can exhange information which will be of mutual benefit."

"If any off-world explorers had set down on Terra after the Burn-Off," observed Soriki softly, "they would have come up against Pax. And just how long would they have lasted?"

Hobart had turned away. If he heard that half-whisper, he did not choose to acknowledge it. But the truth in the com-tech's words made an impression on Raf, a crew of aliens who had been misguided enough to seek out and try to establish friendly relations with the officials of Pax would have had a short and most unhappy shrift. If all the accounts of that dark dictatorship were true, they would have vanished from Terra, and not in their ships either. What if something like Pax ruled here? They had no way of knowing for sure.

Raf's eyes met Soriki's, and the com-tech's hand dropped to hook fingers in his belt within touching distance of his side arm. The flitter pilot nodded.

"Kurbi!" Hobart's impatient call sent him on his way. But there was some measure of relief in knowing that Soriki was left behind and that they had this slender link with escape.

He had tramped the streets of that other alien city. There there had been some semblance of habitation; here was abandonment. Earth drifted in dunes to half block the lanes, and here and there climbing vines had broken down masonry and had dislodged blocks of the paved sideways and courtyards.

The party threaded their way from one narrow lane to another, seeming to avoid the wider open stretches of the principal thoroughfares. Raf became aware of an unpleasant odor in the air which he vaguely associated with water, and a few minutes afterward he caught glimpses of the river between the buildings which fronted on it. Here the party turned abruptly at a right angle, heading westward once more, passing vast, blank-walled structures which might have been warehouses.

One of the aliens just ahead of Raf in the line of march suddenly swung around, his weapon pointing up, and from its nose shot a beam of red-yellow light which brought an answering shrill scream as a large, winged creature came fluttering down. The killer kicked at the crumpled thing as he passed. As far as Raf could see there had been no reason for that wanton staying.

The head of the party had reached a doorway, sealed shut by what looked like a solid slab of material. He placed both palms flat down on its surface at shoulder height and leaned forward against it, almost as if he were whispering some secret formula. Raf watched the muscles stand up on his slender arms as he exerted strength. And then the door split in two, and his fellows helped him push the separate halves back into the wall.

Lablet, Hobart, and Raf were among the last to enter. It was as if their companions had now forgotten them, for the aliens were pushing on at a pace which took them down an empty corridor at a quickening trot.

The corridor ended in a ramp which did not slope in one straight reach but curled around itself, so that in some places only the presence of a handrail, to which they all clung, kept them from losing balance. Then they gathered in a vaulted room, on which opened a complete circle of closed doors.

There was some argument among the aliens, a dispute of sorts over which of those doors was to be opened first, and the Terrans drew a little apart, unable to follow the twittering words and lightning swift gestures.

Raf tried to work out the patterns of color which swirled and looped over each door and around the walls, only to discover that too long an examination of any one band, or an attempt to trace its beginning or end, awoke a sick sensation which approached inner turmoil the longer he looked. At last he had to rest his eyes by studying the gray flooring under his boots.

The aliens finally made up their minds, or else one group was able to outargue the other, for they converged upon a door directly opposite the ramp. Once more they went through the process of unsealing the panels, while the Terrans, drawn by curiosity, were close behind them as they entered the long room beyond. Here were shelves in solid tiers along the walls, crowded with such an array of strange objects that Raf, after one mystified took, thought that it might well take months to sort them all out.

In addition, long tables divided the chamber into aisles. Halfway down one of these narrow passageways the aliens had gathered in a group as silent and intent now as they had been noisy outside. Raf could see nothing to so rivet their attention but a series of scuffed marks in the dust which covered the floor. But an alien, whom he recognized as the officer who had taken him to inspect the globe, moved carefully along that trail, following it to a second door. And as Raf pushed down another aisle, paralleling his course, he was conscious of a sickly sweet, stomach-churning stench. Something was very, very dead and not too far away.

The officer must have come to the same conclusion, for he hurried to open the other door. Before them now was a narrow hall broken by slit windows, near the roof, through which entered sunlight. And one such beam fully illuminated a carcass as large as that of a small elephant, or so it seemed to Raf's startled gaze.

It was difficult to make out the true appearance of the creature, though guessing from the scaled strips of skin it had been reptilian, for the body had been found by scavengers and feasting had been in progress.

The alien officer skirted the corpse gingerly. Raf thought that he would like to investigate the body closely but could not force himself to that highly disagreeable task. There was a chorus of excited exclamation from the doorway as others crowded there.

But the officer, having circled the carcass, turned his attention to the dusty floor again. If there had been any trail there, it was now muddled past their reading, for remnants of the grisly meal had been dragged back and forth. The alien picked his way fastidiously through the noxious debris to the end of the long room. Raf, with the same care, toured the edge of the chamber in his wake.

They were out in a smaller passageway, which was taking them underground, the Terran estimated. Then there was a large space with barred cells about it and a second corridor. The stench of the death chamber either clung to them, or was wafted from another point, and Raf gagged as an especially foul blast caught him full in the face. He kept a sharp look about him for signs of those feasters. The feast had not been finished—it might have been that their entrance into the storeroom had disturbed the scavengers. And things formidable enough to drag down that scaled horror were not foes he would choose to meet in these unlighted ways.

The passage began to slope upward once more, and Raf saw a half-moon of light ahead, brilliant light which could only come from the sun. The alien was outlined there as he went out; then he himself was scuffing through sand close upon another death scene. The dead monster had had its counterparts, and here they were, sprawled out, mangled, and torn. Raf remained by the archway, for even the open air and the morning winds could not destroy the reek which seemed as deadly as a gas attack.

It must have disturbed the officer too, for he hesitated. Then with visible effort he advanced toward the hunks of flesh, casting back and forth as if to find some clue to the manner of their death. He was still so engaged when a second alien burst out of the archway, a splintered length of white held out before him as if he had made some important discovery.

The officer grabbed that shaft away from him, turning it around in his hands. And though expression was hard to read on those thin features under the masking face paint, the emotion his whole attitude expressed was surprise tinged with unbelief—as if the object his subordinate had brought was the last he expected to find in that place.

Raf longed to inspect it, but both aliens brushed by him and pattered back down the corridor, the discoverer pouring forth a volume of words to which the officer listened with great intentness. And the Terran pilot had to hurry to keep up with them.

Something he had seen just before he had left the arena remained in his mind: a forearm flung out from the supine body of what appeared to be the largest of the dead things—and on that forearm a bracelet of metal. Were those things pets! Watchdogs? Surely they were not intelligent beings able to forge and wear such ornaments of their own accord. And if they were watchdogs—whom did they serve? He was inclined to believe that the aliens must be their masters, that the monsters had been guardians of the treasure, perhaps. But dead guardians suggested a rifled treasure house. Who and what—?

His mind filled with speculations and questions, Raf trotted behind the others back to the chamber where they had found the first reptile. The alien who had brought the discovery to his commander stepped gingerly through the litter and laid the white rod in a special spot, apparently the place where it had been found.

At a barked order from the officer, two of the others came forward and tugged at the creature's mangled head, which had been freed from the serpent neck; rolling it over to expose the underparts. There was a broad tear there in the flesh, but Raf could see little difference between it and those left by the feasters. However the officer, holding a strip of cloth over his nose, bent stiffly above it for a closer look and then made some statement which sent his command into a babbling clamor.

Four of the lower ranks separated from the group and, with their hand weapons at alert, swung into action, retracing the way back toward the arena. It looked to Raf as if they now expected an attack from that direction.

Under a volley of orders the rest went back to the storeroom, and the officer, noting that Raf still lingered, waved him impatiently after them.

Inside the men spread out, going from shelf to table, selecting things with a speed which suggested that they had been rehearsed in this task and had only a limited time in which to accomplish it. Some took piles of boxes or other containers which were so light that they could manage a half-dozen in an armload, while two or three others struggled pantingly to move a single piece of weird machinery from its bed to the wheeled trolley they had brought. There was to be no lingering on this job—that was certain.

—❚11❚—
ESPIONAGE

INTENT UPON joining Sssuri, Dalgard left the lock, forgetting his earlier unwillingness, stepping from the small chamber down to the sea bottom, or endeavoring to, although instinctively he had begun to swim and so forge ahead at a different rate of speed.

Waving fronds of giant water plants, such as were found only in the coastal shallows, grew forest fashion but did not hide rocks which stretched up in a sharp rise not too far ahead. The scout could not see the merman, but as he held onto one of those fronds he caught the other's summons:

"Here—by the rocks—!"

Pushing his way through the drifting foliage, Dalgard swam ahead to the foot of the rocky escarpment. And there he saw what had so excited his companion.

Sssuri had just driven away an encircling collection of sand-dwelling scavengers, and what he was on his knees studying intently was an almost clean-picked skeleton of one of his own race. But there was something odd—

Dalgard brushed aside a tendril of weed which cut his line of vision and so was able to see clearly.

White and clean most of those bones were, but the skull was blackened, and similar charring existed down one arm and shoulder. That merman had not died from any mishap in the sea!

"It is so," Sssuri replied to his thought. "They have come once more to give the flaming death—"

Dalgard, startled, looked up that slope which must lead to the island top above the waves.

"Long dead?" he asked tentatively, already guessing what the other's answer would be.

"The pickers move fast," Sssuri indicated the sand dwellers. "Perhaps yesterday, perhaps the day before— but no longer than that."

"And they are up there now?"

"Who can tell? However, they do not know the sea, nor the islands—"

It was plain that the merman intended to climb to investigate what might be happening above. Dalgard had no choice but to follow. And it was true that the merpeople had no peers or equals when it came to finding their ways about the sea and the coasts. He was confident that Sssuri could get to the island top and discover just what he wished to learn without a single sentry above, if they had stationed sentries, being the wiser. Whether he himself could operate as efficiently was another matter.

In the end they half climbed, half swam upward, detouring swiftly once to avoid the darting attack of a rock hornet, harmless as soon as they moved out of the reach of its questing stinger, for it was anchored for its short life to the rough hollow in which it had been hatched.

Dalgard's head broke water as he rolled through the surf onto a scrap of beach in the lee of a row of tooth-pointed outcrops. It was late evening by the light, and he clawed the mask of his face to draw thankful lungfuls of the good outer air. Sssuri, his fur sleeked tight to his body, waded ashore, shook himself free of excess water, and turned immediately to study the wall of the cliff which guarded the interior of the island.

This was one of a chain of such isles, Dalgard noted, now that he had had time to look about him. And with their many-creviced walls they were just the type of habitations which appealed most strongly to the merpeople. Here could be found the dry inner caves with underwater entrances, which they favored for their group homes. And in the sea were kelp beds for harvesting.

The cliffs did not present too much of a climbing problem. Dalgard divested himself of the diving equipment, tucking it into a hollow which he walled up with stones that he thought the waves would not scour out in a hurry. He might need it again. Then, hitching his belt tighter, pressing what water he could out of his clothing, and settling his bow and quiver to the best advantage at his back, he crossed to where Sssuri was already marking claw holds.

"We may be seen—" Dalgard craned his neck, trying to make out details of what might be waiting above.

The merman shook his head with a quick jerk of negation. "They are gone. Behind them remains only death—much death—" And the bleakness of his thoughts reached the scout.

Dalgard had known Sssuri since he was a toddler and the other a cub coming to see the wonders of dry land for the first time. Never, during all their years of close association since, had he felt in the other a desolation so great. And to that emotional blast he could make no answer.

In the twilight, with the last red banners across the sky at their back, they made the climb. And it was as if the merman had closed off his mind to his companion. Flesh fingers touched scaled ones as they moved from one hold to the next, but Sssuri might have been half a world away for all the communication between them. Never had Dalgard been so shut out and with that his sensitivity to the night, to the world about him, was doubly acute.

He realized—and it worried him—that perhaps he had come to depend too much on Sssuri's superior faculty of communication. It was time that he tried to use his own weaker powers to the utmost extent. So, while he climbed, Dalgard sent questing thoughts into the gloom. He located a nest of duck-dogs, those shy waterline fishers living in cliff holes. They were harmless and just settling down for the night. But of higher types of animals from which something might be learned—hoppers, runners— there were no traces. For all he was able to pick up, they might be climbing into blank nothingness.

And that in itself was ominous. Normally he should have been able to mind touch more than duck-dogs. The merpeople lived in peace with most of the higher fauna of their world, and a colony of hoppers, even a covey of moth birds, would settle in close by a mer tribe to garner in the remnants of feasts and for protection from the flying dragons and the other dangers they must face.

"They hunt all life," the first break in Sssuri's self-absorption came. "Where they walk the little harmless peoples face only death. And so it has been here." He had pulled himself over the rim of the cliff, and through the dark Dalgard could hear him panting with the same effort which made his own lungs labor.

Just as the stench of the snake-devil's lair had betrayed its site, here disaster and death had an odor of its own. Dalgard retched before he could control throat and stomach muscles. But Sssuri was unmoved, as if he had expected this.

Then, to Dalgard's surprise the merman set up the first real call he had ever heard issue from that furred throat, a plaintive whistle which had a crooning, summoning note in it, akin to the mind touch in an odd fashion, yet audible. They sat in silence for a long moment, the human's ears as keen for any sound out of the night as those of his companion. Why did Sssuri not use the customary noise-less greeting of his race? When he beamed that inquiry, he met once again that strange, solid wall of non-acceptance which had enclosed the merman as they climbed. As if now there was danger to be feared from following the normal ways.

Again Sssuri whistled, and in that cry Dalgard heard a close resemblance to the flute tone of the night moth birds. Up the scale the notes ran with mournful persistence. When the answer came, the scout at first thought that the imitation had lured a moth bird, for the reply seemed to ripple right above their heads.

Sssuri stood up, and his hand dropped on Dalgard's shoulder, applying pressure which was both a warning and a summons, bringing the scout to his feet with as little noise as possible. The horrible smell caught at his throat, and he was glad when the merman did not head inland toward the source of that odor, but started off along the edge of the cliff, one hand in Dalgard's to draw him along.

Twice more Sssuri paused to whistle, and each time he was answered by a sighing note or two which seemed to reassure him.

Against the lighter expanse which was the sea, Dalgard saw the loom of a peak which projected above the general level of the island. Though he knew that the merpeople did not build aboveground, being adept in turning natural caves and crevices into the kind of living quarters they found most satisfactory, the barrenness of this particular rock top was forbidding.

Led by Sssuri, he threaded a tangled patch among outcrops, once squeezing through a gap which scraped the flesh on his arms as he wriggled. Then the sky was blotted out, the last winking star disappeared, and he realized that he must have entered a cave of sorts, or was at least under an overhang.

The merman did not pause but padded on, tugging Dalgard along, the scout's boots scraping on the rough footing. The colonist was conscious now that they were on an incline, heading down into the heart of the island. They came to a stretch where Sssuri set his hands on holds, patiently shoved his feet into hollowed places, finding for him the ladder stops he could not see, which took him through a sweating, fearful journey of yards to another level, another sloping, downward way.

Here at long last was a fraction of light, not the violet

glimmer which had illuminated the underground ways of
Those Others, but a ghostly radiance which he recognized
as the lamps of the mermen—living creatures from the
sea depths imprisoned in laboriously fashioned globes of
crystal and kept in the caves for the light they yielded.

But still no mind touch! Never had Dalgard penetrated
into the cave cities of the sea folk before without inquiries
and open welcome lapping about him. Were they entering
a place of massacre where no living merman remained?
Yet there was that whistling which had led Sssuri to this
place . . .

And at that moment a shrill keening note arose from
the depths to ring in Dalgard's ears, startling him so that
he almost lost his footing. Once again Sssuri made answer
vocally—but no mind touch.

Then they rounded a curve, and the scout was able to
see into the heart of the amphibian territory. This was a
natural cave, as were all the merman's dwellings, but its
walls had been smoothed and hung with the garlands
of shells which they wove in their leisure into strange
pictures. Silver-gray sand, smooth and dust-fine, covered
the floor to the depth of a foot or more. And opening off
the main chamnber were small nooks, each marking the
private storage place and holding of some family clan. It
was a large place, and with a quick estimate Dalgard
thought that it had been fashioned to harbor close to a
hundred inhabitants, at least the nooks suggested mat
many. But gathered at the foot of the ledge they were
descending, spears poised, were perhaps ten males, some
hardly past cubhood, others showing the snowy shine of
fur which was the badge of age. And behind them, drawn

knives in their ready hands, were half again as many merwomen, forming a protecting wall before a crouching group of cubs.

Sssuri spoke to Dalgard, "Spread out your hands— empty—so that they may see them clearly!"

The scout obeyed. In the limited light his ten fingers were fans, and it was then that he understood the reason for such a move. If these mermen had not seen a colonist before, he might resemble Those Others in their eyes. But only his species on all Astra had five fingers, five toes, and that physical evidence might insure his safety now.

"Why do you bring a destroyer among us? Or do you offer him for our punishment, so that we can lay upon him the doom that his kind have earned?"

The question came with arrow force, and Dalgard held out his hands, hoping they would see the difference before one of those spears from below tore through his flesh.

"Look upon the hands of this—my knife brother— look upon his face. He is not of the race of those you hate, but rather one from the south. Have you of the northern reaches not heard of Those-Who-Help, Those-Who-Came-From-the-Stars?"

"We have heard." But there was no relaxing of tension, not a spear point wavered.

"Look upon his hands," Sssuri insisted. "Come into his mind, for he speaks with us so. And do they do that?"

Dalgard tried to throw open his mind, awaiting the trial. It came quickly, traces of inimical, alien thought, which changed as they touched his mind, reading there only all the friendliness he and his held for the sea people.

"He is not of them." The admission was grudging. As if

they did not want to believe that. "Why comes one from the south to this place—now?"

There was an inflection to that "now" which was disturbing.

"After the manner of his people he seeks new things so that he may return and report to his Elders. Then he will receive the spear of manhood and be ready for the choosing of mates," Sssuri translated the reason for Dalgard's quest into the terms of his own people. "He has been my knife brother since we were cubs together, and so I journey with him. But here in the north we have found evil—"

His flow of thought was submerged by a band of hate so red that its impact upon the mind was almost a blow. Dalgard shook his head. He had known that the merpeople, aroused, were deadly fighters, fearless and crafty, and with a staying power beyond that of any human. But their rage was something he had not met before.

"They come once again—they burn with the fire— They are among our islands—"

A cub whimpered and a merwoman stooped to pat it to silence.

"Here they have killed with the fire—"

They did not elaborate upon that statement, and Dalgard had no wish for them to do so. He was still very glad that it had been dark when he had climbed to the top of that cliff, that he had not been able to see what his imagination told him lay there.

"Do they stay?" That was Sssuri.

"Not so. In their sky traveler they go to the land where lies the dark city. There they make much evil against the day when this shall be their land once more."

"But these lie if they think that." Another strong thought broke across the current of communication. "We are not now penned for their pleasure. We may flee into me sea once more, and there live as did our fathers' fathers, and they dare not follow us there—"

"Who knows?" It was Sssuri who raised that objection. "With their ancient knowledge once more theirs, even the depths of the sea may not be ours much longer. Do they not know how to ride upon the air?"

The knot of mer-warriors stirred. Several spears thudded butt down into the sand. And Sssuri accepted that as an invitation to descend, summoning Dalgard after him with a beckoning finger.

Later they sat in a circle in the cushioning gray powder, the two from the south eating dried fish and sea kelp, while Sssuri related, between mouthfuls, their recent adventures.

"Three times have they flown across these islands on their way to that city," the Elder of the pitifully decimated merman tribe told the explorers.

"But this time," broke in one of his companions, "they had with them a new ship—"

"A new ship?" Sssuri pounced upon that scrap of information.

"Yes. The ships of the air in which they travel are fashioned so"—with his knife point he drew a circle in the sand—" but this one was smaller and more in the likeness of a spear with a heavy point—thus"—he made a second sketch beside the first, and Dalgard and Sssuri leaned over to study it.

"That is unlike any of their ships that I have heard of,"

Sssuri agreed. "Even in the old tales of the Days Before the Burning there is nothing spoken of like that."

"It is true. Therefore we wait now for the coming of our scouts, who were set in hiding upon their sea rock of resting, that they may tell us more concerning this new ship. They should be here within this time of sleeping. Now, go you to rest, which you plainly have need of and we shall call you when they come."

Dalgard was willing enough to stretch out in the sand in the shadows of the far end of the cave. Beyond him three cubs slumbered together, their arms about each other, and a feeling of peace was there such as he had not known since he left the stronghold of Homeport.

The weird glow of the imprisoned sea monsters gave light to the main part of the cave, and it might still have been night when the scout was shaken awake once more. A group of the merpeople were sitting together, and their thoughts interrupted each other as their excitement arose. Their spies must have returned.

Dalgard crossed to join the group, but it seemed to him that his welcome was not unqualified, and that some of the openness of the early hours of the night was lacking. He might have been once more under suspicion.

"Knife brother"—to Dalgard's sensitive mind that form of address from Sssuri was used for a special purpose: to underline the close bond between them—"listen to the words of Sssim who is a Hider-to-Watch on the island where they rest their ships during the voyage from one land to another." He drew Dalgard down beside him to face a young merman who was staring round-eyed at the colony scout.

"He is like—yet unlike"—his first wisp of thought meant nothing to the scout. "The strangers wear many coverings on their bodies as do they, and they had also coverings upon their heads. They were bigger. Also from their minds I learned that they are not of this world—"

"Not of this world!" Dalgard burst out in his own speech.

"There!" The spy was triumphant. "So did they talk to one another, not with the mind but by making mouth noises, different mouth noises from those that they make. Yes, they are like—but unlike this one."

"And these strangers flew the ship we have not seen before?"

"It is so. But they did not know the way and were guided by the globe. And at least one among them was distrustful of those and wished to be free to return to his own place. He walked by the rocks near my hiding place, and I read his thoughts. No, they were with them, but they are not them!"

"And now they have gone on to the city?" Sssuri probed.

"It was the way their ship flew."

"Like me," Dalgard repeated, and then the truth which might lie behind that exploded within his brain. "Terrans!" he breathed the word. Men of Pax perhaps who had come to hunt down the outlaws who had successfully eluded their rule on earth? But how had the colonist been traced? And why? Or were they other fugitives like themselves? So much, so very much of what the colonist should know of their past had been erased during the time of the Great Sickness twenty years after their landing. Then three fourths of the original immigrants had died. Only the children of the second generation and a handful of weakened Elders had remained. Knowledge was lost and some distorted by failing memories, old skills were gone. But if the new Terrans were in that city . . . He had to know—to know and be able to warn his people. For the darkness of Pax was a memory they had not lost!

"I must see them," he said.

"That is true. And only you can tell us what manner of folk these strangers be," the merman chief agreed. "Therefore you shall go ashore with my warriors and look upon them—to tell us the truth. Also we must learn what they do here."

It was decided that using waterways known to the merpeople, one which Dalgard could also take wearing the diving equipment, a scouting party would head shoreward the next day, with the river itself providing the entrance into the heart of the forbidden territory.

—12—
ALIEN PATROL

RAF LEANED back against the wall. Long since the actions of the aliens in the storage house had ceased to interest him, since they would not allow any of the Terrans to approach their plunder and he could not ask questions. Lablet continued to follow the officer about, vainly trying to understand his speech. And Hobart had taken his place by the upper entrance, his hand held stiffly across his body. The pilot knew that the captain was engaged in photographing all this activity with a wristband camera, hoping to make something of it later.

But Raf's own inclination was to slip out and do some exploring in those underground corridors beyond. Having remained where he was for a wearisome time, he noticed that his presence was now taken for granted by the hurrying aliens who brushed about him intent upon their assignments. And slowly he began to edge along the wall toward the other doorway. Once he froze as the officer strode by, Lablet in attendance. But what the painted warrior was looking for was a crystal box on a shelf to Raf's left. When he had pointed that out to an underling he was off again, and Raf was free to continue his crab's progress.

Luck favored him, for, as he reached the moment when he must duck out the portal, there was a sudden flurry at the other end of the chamber where four of the aliens, under a volley of orders, strove to move an unwieldy piece of intricate machinery.

Raf dodged around the door and flattened back against the wall of the room beyond. The moving bars of sun said that it was midday. But the room was empty save for the despoiled carcass, and there was no sign of the aliens who had been sent out to scout.

The Terran ran lightly down the narrow room to the second door, which gave on the lower pits beneath and the way to the arena. As he took that dark way, he drew his stun gun. Its bolt was intended to render the victim unconscious, not to kill. But what effect it might have on the giant reptiles was a question he hoped he would not be forced to answer, and he paused now and then to listen.

There were sounds, deceptive sounds. Noises as regular as footfalls, like distant padded running. The aliens returning? Or the things they had gone to hunt? Raf crept on—out into the sunshine which filled the arena.

For the first time he studied the enclosure and recognized it for what it was—a place in which savage and bloody entertainments could be provided for the population of the city—and it merely confirmed his opinion of the aliens and all their ways.

The temptation to explore the city was strong. He eyed

the grilles speculatively. They could be climbed—he was sure of that. Or he could try some other of the various openings about the sanded area. But as he hesitated over his choice, he heard something from behind. This was no unidentifiable noise, but a scream which held both terror and pain. It jerked him around, sent him running back almost before he thought.

But the scream did not come again. However there were other sounds—snuffing whines—a scrabbling—

Raf found himself in the round room walled by the old prison cells. Stabs of light shot through the gloom, thrusting into a roiling black mass which had erupted through one of the entrances and now held at bay one of the alien warriors. Three or four of the black creatures ringed the alien in, moving with speed that eluded the bolts of light he shot from his weapon, keeping him cornered and from escape, while their fellows worried another alien limp and defenseless on the floor.

It was impossible to align the sights of his stun gun with any of those flitting shadows, Raf discovered. They moved as quickly as a ripple across a pond. He snapped the button on the hand grip to "spray" and proceeded to use the full strength of the charge across the group on the floor.

For several seconds he was afraid that the stun ray would prove to have no effect on the alien metabolism of the creatures, for their weaving, tearing activity did not cease. Then one after another dropped away from the center mass and lay unmoving on the floor. Seeing that he could control them, Raf turned his attention to the others about the standing warrior.

Again he sent the spray wide, and they subsided. As the last curled on the pavement, the alien moved forward and, with a snarl, deliberately turned the full force of his beam weapon on each of the attackers. But Raf plowed on through the limp pile to the warrior they had pulled down.

There was no hope of helping him—death had come with a wide tear in his throat. Raf averted his eyes from the body. The other warrior was methodically killing the stunned animals. And his action held such vicious cruelty that Raf did not want to watch.

When he looked again at the scene, it was to find the narrow barrel of the strange weapon pointed at him. Paying no attention to his dead comrade, the alien was advancing on the Terran as if in Raf he saw only another enemy to be burned down.

Moves drilled in him by long hours of weary practice came almost automatically to the pilot. The stun gun faced the alien rifle sight to sight. And it seemed that the warrior had developed a hearty respect for the Terran arm during the past few minutes, for he slipped his weapon back to the crook of his arm, as if he did not wish Raf to guess he had used it to threaten.

The pilot had no idea what to do now. He did not wish to return to the storehouse. And he believed that the alien was not going to let him go off alone. The ferocity of the creatures now heaped about them had been sobering, an effective warning against venturing alone in these underground ways.

His dilemma was solved by the entrance of a party of aliens from another doorway. They stopped short at the sight of the battlefield, and their leader descended upon the surviving scout for an explanation which was made with gestures Raf was able to translate in part.

The alien had been far down one of the neighboring corridors with his dead companion when they had been tracked by the pack and had managed to reach this point before they were attacked. For some reason Raf could not understand, the aliens had preferred to flee rather than to face the menace of the hunters. But they had not been fast enough and had been trapped here. The gesturing hands then indicated Raf, acted out the battle which had ensued.

Crossing to the Terran pilot, the alien officer held out his hand and motioned for Raf to surrender his weapon. The pilot shook his head. Did they think him so simple that he would disarm himself at the mere asking? Especially since the warrior had rounded on him like that only a few moments before? Nor did he holster his gun. If they wanted to take it by force just let them try such a move!

His determination to resist must have gotten across to the leader, for he did not urge obedience to his orders. Instead he waved the Terran to join his own party. And since Raf had no reason not to, he did. Leaving the dead, both alien and enemy, where they had fallen, the warriors took another way out of the underground maze, a way which brought them out into a street running to the river.

Here the party spread out, paying close attention to the pavement, as if they were engaged in tracking something. Raf saw impressed in one patch of earth a print dried by the sun, left by one of the reptiles. And there were smaller tracks he could not identify. All were inspected carefully, but none of them appeared to be what his companions sought.

They trotted up and down along the river bank, and from what he had already observed concerning the aliens, Raf thought that the leader, at least, was showing exasperation and irritation. They expected to find something—it was not there—but it had to be! And they were fast reaching the point where they wanted to produce it themselves to justify the time spent in hunting for it.

Ruthlessly they rayed to death any creature their dragnet drove into the open, leaving feebly kicking bodies of the furry, long-legged beasts Raf had first seen after the landing of the spacer. He could not understand the reason for such wholesale extermination, since certainly the rabbitlike rodents were harmless.

In the end they gave up their quest and circled back to come out near the field where the flitter and the globe rested. When the Terran flyer came into sight, Raf left the party and hurried toward it. Soriki waved a welcoming hand.

"'Bout time one of you showed up. What are they doing—toting half the city here to load into that thing?"

Raf looked along the other's pointing finger. A party of aliens towing a loaded dolly were headed for the gaping hatch of the globe, while a second party and an empty conveyance passed them on the way back to the storehouse.

"They are emptying a warehouse, or trying to."

"Well, they act as if Old Time himself was heating their tails with a rocket flare. What's the big hurry?"

"Somebody's been here." Swiftly Raf outlined what he

had seen in the city, and ended by describing the hunt in which he had taken an unwilling part. "I'm hungry," he ended and went to burrow for a ration pack.

"So," mused Soriki as Raf chewed the stuff which never had the flavor of fresh provisions, "somebody's been trying to beat the painted lads to it. The furry people?"

"It was a spear shaft they found broken with the dead lizard thing," Raf commented. "And some of those on the island were armed with spears—"

"Must be good fighters if, armed with spears, they brought down a reptile as big as you say. It was big, wasn't it?"

Raf stared at the city, a square of half-eaten concentrate in his fingers. Yes, that was a puzzler. The dead monster would be more than he would care to tackle without a blaster. And yet it was dead, with a smashed spear for evidence as to the manner of killing. All those others dead in the arena, too. How large a party had invaded the city? Where were they now?

"I'd like to know," he was speaking more to himself than to the com-tech, "how they did do it. No other bodies—"

"Those could have been taken away by their friends," Soriki suggested. "But if they're still hanging about, I hope they won't believe that we're bigger and better editions of the painted lads. I don't want a spear through me!"

Raf, remembering the maze of lanes and street—bordered by buildings which could provide hundreds of lurking places for attackers—which he had threaded with the confidence of ignorance earlier that day, began to realize why the aliens had been so nervous. Had a sniper with a blast rifle been stationed at a vantage point somewhere on the roofs today none of them would ever have returned to this field. And even a few spacemen with good cover and accurate throwing aim could have cut down their number a quarter or a third. He was developing a strong distaste for those structures. And he had no intention of returning to the city again.

He lounged about with Soriki for the rest of the afternoon, watching the ceaseless activity of the aliens. It was plain that they were intent upon packing into the cargo hold of their ship everything they could wrest from the storage house. As if they must make this trip count double. Was that because they had discovered that their treasure house was no longer inviolate?

In the late afternoon Hobart and Lablet came back with one of the work teams. Lablet was still excited, full of what he had seen, deduced, or guessed during the day. But the captain was very quiet and sober, and he unstrapped the wrist camera as soon as he reached the flitter, turning it over to Soriki.

"Run that through the ditto," he ordered. "I want two records as soon as we can get them!"

The com-tech's eyebrows slid up, "Think you might lose one, sir?"

"I don't know. Anyway we'll play it safe with double records." He accepted the ration pack Raf had brought out for him. But he did not unwrap it at once; instead he stared at the globe, digging the toe of his space boot into the soil as if he were grinding something to powder.

"They're operating under full jets," he commented. "As if they were about due to be jumped—"

"They told us that this was territory now held by their enemies," Lablet reminded him.

"And who are these mysterious enemies?" the captain wanted to know. "Those animals back on that island?"

Raf wanted to say yes, but Lablet broke in with a question concerning what had happened to him, and the pilot outlined his adventures of the day, not forgetting to give emphasis to the incident in the celled room when the newly rescued alien had turned upon him.

"Naturally they are suspicious," Lablet countered, "but for a people who lack space flight, I find them unusually open-minded and ready to accept us, strange as we must seem to them."

"Ditto done, Captain." Soriki stepped out of the flitter, the wrist camera dangling from his fingers.

"Good," But Hobart did not buckle the strap about his arm once more, neither did he pay any attention to Lablet. Instead, apparently coming to some decision, he swung around to face Raf.

"You went out with that scouting party today. Think you could join them again, if you see them moving for another foray?"

"I could try."

"Sure," Soriki chuckled, "they couldn't do any more than pop him back at us. What do you think about them, sir? Are they fixing to blast us?"

But the captain refused to be drawn. "I'd just like to have a record of any more trips they make." He handed the camera to Raf. "Put that on and don't forget to trigger it if you do go. I don't believe they'll go out tonight. They aren't too fond of being out in the open in darkness.

We saw that last night. But keep an eye on them in the morning—"

"Yes, sir." Raf buckled on the wristband. He wished that Hobart would explain just what he was to look for, but the captain appeared to think that he had made everything perfectly plain. And he walked off with Lablet, heading to the globe, as if there was nothing more to be said.

Soriki stretched. "I'd say we'd better take it watch and watch," he said slowly. "The captain may think that they won't go off in the dark, but we don't know everything about them. Suppose we just keep an eye on them, and then you'll be ready to tail—"

Raf laughed. "Tailing would be it. I don't think I'll have a second invitation and if I get lost—"

But Soriki shook his head. "That you won't. At least if you do—I'm going to make a homer out of you. Just tune in your helmet buzzer."

It needed a com-tech to think of a thing like that! A small adjustment to the earphones built into his helmet, and Soriki, operating the flitter com, could give him a guide as efficient as the spacer's radar! He need not fear being lost in the streets should he lose touch with those he was spying upon.

"You're on course!" He pulled off his helmet and then glanced up to find Soriki smiling at him.

"Oh, we're not such a bad collection of space bums. Maybe you'll find that out someday, boy? They breezed you into this flight right out of training, didn't they?"

"Just about," Raf admitted cautiously, on guard as ever against revealing too much of himself. After all, his experience was part of his record, which was open to any-one on board the spacer. Yes, he was not a veteran; they must all know that.

"Someday you'll lose a little of that suspicion," the com-tech continued, "and find out it isn't such a bad old world after all. Here, let's see if you're on the beam." He took the helmet out of Raf's hands and, drawing a small case of delicate instruments from his belt pouch, unscrewed the ear plates of the com device and made some adjustments. "Now that will keep you on the buzzer without bursting your eardrums. Try it."

Raf listened on the helmet and started away from the flitter. The buzzer which he had expected to roar in his ears was only a faint drone, and above it he could easily hear other sounds. Yet it was there, and he tested it by a series of loops away from the flyer. Each time as he came on the true beam he was rewarded by a deepening of the muted note. Yes, he could be a homer with that, and at the same time be alert to any other noise in his vicinity.

"That's it!" He paid credit where it was due. But he was unable to break his long habit of silence. Something within him still kept him wary of the com-tech's open friendliness.

None of the aliens approached the flitter as the shadows began to draw in. The procession of moving teams stopped, and most of the burden-bearing warriors withdrew to the globe and stayed there. Soriki pointed this out.

"They're none too sure, themselves. Looks as if they are closing up for the night."

Indeed it did. The painted men had hauled up their

ramp, the hatch in the globe closed with a definite snap. Seeing that, the com-tech laughed.

"We have a double reason for a strict watch. Suppose whatever they've been looking for jumps us? They're not worrying over that it now appears."

So they took watch and watch, three hours on and three hours in rest. When it came Raf's turn he did not remain sitting in the flitter, listening to the com-tech's heavy breathing, but walked a circular beat which took him into the darkness of the night in a path about the flyer. Overhead the stars were sharp and clear, glittering gem points. But in the dead city no light showed, and he was sure that no aliens camped there tonight.

He was sleeping when Soriki's grasp on his shoulder brought him to that instant alertness he had learned on field maneuvers half the Galaxy away.

"Business," the com-tech's voice was not above a whisper as he leaned over the pilot. "I think they are on the move."

The light was the pale gray of pre-dawn. Raf pulled himself up with caution to look at the globe. The com-tech was right. A dark opening showed on the alien ship; they had released their hatch. He fastened his tunic, buckled on his equipment belt and helmet, strapped his boots.

"Here they come!" Soriki reported. "One—two—five—no, six of them. And they're heading for the city. No dollies with them, but they're all armed."

Together the Terrans watched that patrol of alien warriors, their attitude suggesting that they hoped to pass unseen, hurry toward the city. Then Raf slipped out of the flyer. His dark clothing in this light should render him largely invisible.

Soriki waved encouragingly and the pilot answered with a quick salute before he sped after his quarry.

—13—
A HOUND IS LOOSED

DALGARD'S FEET touched gravel; he waded cautiously to the bank, where a bridge across the river made a concealing shadow on the water. None of the mermen had accompanied him this far. Sssuri, as soon as his human comrade had started for the storage city, had turned south to warn and rally tribes. And the merpeople of the islands had instituted a loose chain of communication, which led from a clump of water reeds some two miles back to the seashore, and so out to the islands. Better than any of the now legendary coms of his Terran forefathers were these minds of the spies in hiding, who could pick up the racing thoughts beamed to them and pass them on to their fellows.

Although there were no signs of life about the city, Dalgard moved with the same care that he would have used in penetrating a snake-devil's lair. In the first hour of dawn he had contacted a hopper. The small beast had been frightened almost out of coherent thought, and Dalgard had had to spend some time in allaying that terror to get a fractional idea of what might be going on in this countryside.

Death—the hopper's terror had come close to insanity. Killers had come out of the sky, and they were burning—burning—All living things were fleeing before them. And in that moment Dalgard had been forced to give up his plan for an unseen spy ring, which would depend upon the assistance of the animals. His information must come via his own eyes and ears.

So he kept on, posting the last of the mermen in his mental relay well away from the city, but swimming upstream himself. Now that he was here, he could see no traces of the invaders. Since they could not have landed their sky ships in the thickly built-up section about the river, it must follow that their camp lay on the outskirts of the metropolis.

He pulled himself out of the water. Bow and arrows had been left behind with the last merman; he had only his sword-knife for protection. But he was not there to fight, only to watch and wait. Pressing the excess moisture out of his scant clothing, he crept along the shore. If the strangers were using the streets, it might be well to get above them. Speculatively he eyed the buildings about him as he entered the city.

Dalgard continued to keep at street level for two blocks, darting from doorway to shadowed doorway, alert not only to any sound but to any flicker of thought. He was reasonably sure, however, that the aliens would be watching and seeking only for the merpeople. Though they were not telepathic as their former slaves, Those Others were able to sense the near presence of a merman, so that the sea people dared not communicate while within danger range of the aliens without betraying themselves. It was the fact that he was of a different species, therefore possibly immune to such detection, which had brought Dalgard into the city.

He studied the buildings ahead. Among them was a cone-shaped structure which might have been the base of a tower that had had all stories above the third summarily amputated. It was ornamented with a series of bands in high relief, bands being the color script of the aliens. This was the nearest answer to his problem. However the scout did not move toward it until after a long moment of both visual and mental inspection of his surroundings. But that inspection did not reach some twelve streets away where another crouched to watch. Dalgard ran lightly to the tower at the same moment that Raf shifted his weight from one foot to the other behind a parapet as he spied upon the knot of aliens gathered below him in the street. . . .

The pilot had followed them since that early morning hour when Soriki had awakened him. Not that the chase had led him far in distance. Most of the time he had spent in waiting just as he was doing now. At first he had believed that they were searching for something, for they had ventured into several buildings, each time to emerge conferring, only to hunt out another and invade it. Since they always returned with empty hands, he could not believe that they were out for further loot. Also they moved with more confidence than they had shown the day before. That confidence led Raf to climb above them so that he could watch them with less chance of being seen in return.

It had been almost noon when they had at last come into this section. If two of them had not remained idling on the street as the long moments crept by, he would have believed that they had given him the slip, that he was now a cat watching a deserted mouse hole. But at the moment they were coming back, carrying something.

Raf leaned as far over the parapet as he dared. Trying to catch a better look at that flat, boxlike object two of them had deposited on the pavement. Whatever it was either needed some adjustment or they were attempting to open it with poor success, for they had been busied about it for what seemed an unusually long time. The pilot licked dry lips and wondered what would happen if he swung down there and just walked in for a look-see. That idea was hardening into resolution when suddenly the group below drew quickly apart, leaving the box sitting alone as they formed a circle about it.

There was a puff of white vapor, a protesting squawk, and the thing began to rise in jerks as if some giant in the sky was pulling at it spasmodically. Raf jumped back. Before he could return to his vantage point, he saw it rise above the edge of the parapet, reach a level five or six feet above his head, hovering there. It no longer climbed; instead it began to swing back and forth, describing in each swing a wider stretch of space.

Back and forth—watching it closely made him almost dizzy. What was its purpose? Was it a detection device, to locate him? Raf's hand went to his stun gun. What effect its rays might have on the box he had no way of knowing, but at that moment he was sorely tempted to try the beam out, with the oscillating machine as his target.

The motion of the floating black thing became less violent, its swoop smoother as if some long-idle motor was now working more as its builders had intended it to perform. The swing made wide circles, graceful glides as the thing explored the air currents.

Searching—it was plainly searching for something. Just as plainly it could not be hunting for him, for his presence on that roof would have been uncovered at once. But the machine was—it must be—out of sight of the warriors in the street. How could they keep in touch with it if it located what they sought? Unless it had some built-in signaling device.

Determined to keep it in sight, Raf risked a jump from the parapet of the building where he had taken cover to another roof beyond, running lightly across mat as the hound bobbed and twisted, away from its masters, out across the city in pursuit of some mysterious quarry. . . .

The climb which had looked so easy from the street proved to be more difficult when Dalgard actually made it. His hours of swimming in the river, the night of broken rest, had drained his strength more man he had known. He was panting as he flattened himself against the wall, his feet on one of the protruding bands of colored carving, content to rest before reaching for another hold. To all appearances the city about him was empty of life and, except for the certainty of the merpeople that the alien ship and its strange companion had landed here, he would have believed that he was on a fruitless quest.

Grimly, his lower lip caught between his teeth, the scout began to climb once more, the sun hot on his body, drawing sweat to dampen his forehead and his hands. He did not pause again but kept on until he stood on the top of the shortened tower. The roof here was not flat but sloped inward to a cuplike depression, where he could see the outline of a round opening, perhaps a door of sorts. But at that moment he was too winded to do more than rest.

There was a drowsiness in that air. He was tempted to curl up where he sat and turn his rest into the sleep his body craved. It was in that second or so of time when he was beginning to relax, to forget the tenseness which had gripped him since his return to this ill-omened place that he touched—

Dalgard stiffened as if one of his own poisoned arrows had pricked his skin. Rapport with the merpeople, with the hoppers and the runners, was easy, familiar. But this was no such touch. It was like contacting something which was icy cold, inimical from birth, something which he could never meet on a plain of understanding. He snapped off mind questing at that instant and huddled where he was, staring up into the blank turquoise of the sky, waiting—for what he did not know. Unless it was for that other mind to follow and ferret out his hiding place, to turn him inside out and wring from him everything he ever knew or hoped to learn.

As time passed in long breaths, and he was not so invaded, he began to think that while he had been aware of contact, the other had not. And, embolded, he sent out a tracer. Unconsciously, as the tracer groped, he pivoted his body. It lay—there!

At the second touch he withdrew in the same second,

afraid of revelation. But as he returned to probe delicately,
ready to flee at the first hint that the other suspected, his
belief in temporary safety grew. To his disappointment he
could not pierce beyond the outer wall of identity. There
was a living creature of a high rate of intelligence, a creature
alien to his own thought processes, not too far away. And
though his attempts to enter into closer communication
grew bolder, he could not crack the barrier which kept
them apart. He had long known that contact with the
merpeople was on a lower, a far lower, band than they
used when among themselves, and that they were only
able to "talk" with the colonists because for generations
they had exchanged thought symbols with the hoppers and
other unlike species. They had been frank in admitting
that while Those Others could be aware of their presence
through telepathic means, they could not exchange
thought. So now, his own band, basically strange to this
planet, might well go unnoticed by the once dominant
race of Astra.

They—or him—or it—were over in that direction,
Dalgard was sure of that. He faced northwest and saw for
the first time, about a mile away, the swelling of the globe.
If the strange flyer reported by the merpeople was beside
it, he could not distinguish it from this distance. Yet he
was sure the mind he had located was closer to him than
that ship.

Then he saw it—a black object rising by stiff jerks
into the air as if it were being dragged upward against
its inclination. It was too small to be a flyer of any sort.
Long ago the colonists had patched together a physical
description of Those Others which had assured them that

the aliens were close to them in general characteristics and size. No, that couldn't be carrying a passenger. Then what—or why?

The object swung out in a gradually widening circle. Dalgard held to the walled edge of the roof. Something within him suggested that it would be wiser to seek some less open space, that there was danger in that flying box. He released his hold and went to the trap door. It took only a minute to fit his fingers into round holes and tug. Its stubborn resistance gave, and stale air whooshed out in his face as it opened.

In his battle with the door Dalgard had ignored the box, so he was startled when, with a piercing whistle, almost too high on the scale for his ears to catch, the thing suddenly swooped into a screaming dive, apparently heading straight for him. Dalgard flung himself through the trap door, luckily landing on one of the steep, curved ramps. He lost his balance and slid down into the dark, trying to brake his descent with his hands, the eerie screech of the box trumpeting in his ears.

There was little light in this section of the cone building, and he was brought up with bruising force against a blank wall two floors below where he had so unceremoniously entered. As he lay in the dark trying to gasp some breath into his lungs, he could still hear the squeal. Was it summoning? There was no time to be lost in getting away.

On his hands and knees the scout crept along what must have been a short hall until he found a second descending ramp, this one less steep than the first, so that he was able to keep to his feet while using it. And the gloom of the next floor was broken by odd scraps of light which showed through pierced portions of the decorative bands. The door was there, a locking bar across it.

Dalgard did not try to shift that at once, although he laid his hands upon it. If the box was a hound for hunters, had it already drawn its masters to this building? Would he open the door only to be faced by the danger he wished most to avoid? Desperately he tried to probe with the mind touch. But he could not find the alien band. Was that because the hunters could control their minds as they crept up? His kind knew so little of Those Others, and the merpeople's hatred of their ancient masters was so great that they tended to avoid rather than study them.

The scout's sixth sense told him that nothing waited outside. But the longer he lingered with that beacon overhead the slimmer his chances would be. He must move and quickly. Sliding back the bar, he opened the door a crack and looked out into a deserted street. There was another doorway to take shelter in some ten feet or so farther along, beyond that an alley wall overhung by a balcony. He marked these refuges and went out to make his first dash to safety.

Nothing stirred, and he sprinted. There came again that piercing shriek to tear his ears as the floating box dived at him. He swerved away from the doorway to dart on under the balcony, sure now that he must keep moving, but under cover so that the black thing could not pounce. If he could find some entrance into the underground ways such as those that ran from the arena—But now he was not even sure in which direction the arena stood, and he dared no longer climb to look over the surrounding territory.

He touched the alien mind! They were moving in, following the lead of their hound. He must not allow himself to be cornered. The scout fought down a surge of panic, attempted to battle the tenseness which tied his nerves. He must not run mindlessly either. That was probably just what they wanted him to do. So he stood under the balcony and tried not to listen to the shrilling box as he studied the strip of alley.

This was a narrow side way, and he had not made the wisest of choices in entering it, for not much farther ahead it was bordered with smooth walls protecting what had once been gardens. He had no way of telling whether the box would actually track him if he were caught in the open—to put that to the test was foolhardy—nor could he judge its speed of movement.

The walls . . . A breeze which blew up the lane carried with it the smell of the river. There was a slim chance that it might end in water, and he had a feeling that if he could reach the stream he would be able to baffle the hunters. He did not have long to make up his mind—the aliens were closer.

Lightly Dalgard ran under the length of the balcony, turned sharply as he reached the end of its protecting cover, and leaped. His fingers gripped the ornamental grill work, and he was able to pull himself up and over to the narrow runway. A canopy was still over his head, and there came a bump against it as the baffled box thumped. So it would try to knock him off if it could get the chance! That was worth knowing.

He looked over the walls. They guarded masses of tangled vegetation grown through years of neglect into thick mats. And those promised a way of escape, if he could reach them. He studied the windows, the door opening onto the balcony, with the hilt of his sword-knife he smashed his way into the house, to course swiftly through the rooms to the lower floor, and find the entrance to the garden.

Facing that briary jungle on the ground level was a little daunting. To get through it would be a matter of cutting his way. Could he do it and escape that bobbing, shrilling thing in the air? A trace of pebbled path gave him a ghost of a chance, and he knew that these shrubs tended to grow upward and not mass until they were several feet above the ground.

Trusting to luck, Dalgard burrowed into the green mass, slashing with his knife at anything which denied him entrance. He was swallowed up in a strange dim world wherein dead shrubs and living were twined together to form a roof, cutting off the light and heat of the sun. From the sour earth, sliming his hands and knees, arose an overpowering stench of decay and disturbed mold. In the dusk he had to wait for his eyes to adjust before he could mark the tine of the old path he had taken for his guide.

Fortunately, after the first few feet, he discovered that the tunneled path was less obstructed than he had feared. The thick mat overhead had kept the sun from the ground and killed off all the lesser plants so that it was possible to creep along a fairly open strip. He was conscious of the chitter of insects, but no animals lingered here. Under him the ground grew more moist and the mold was close to mud in consistency. He dared to hope that this meant he was either approaching the river or some garden stream feeding into the larger flood.

Somewhere the squeal of the hunter kept up a steady cry, but, unless the foliage above him was distorting that sound, Dalgard believed that the box was no longer directly above him. Had he in some way thrown it off his trail?

He found his stream, a thread of water, hardly more than a series of scummy pools with the vegetation still meeting almost solidly over it. And it brought him to a wall with a drain through which he was sure he could crawl. Disliking to venture into that cramped darkness, but seeing no other way out, the scout squirmed forward in slime and muck, feeling the rasp of rough stone on his shoulders as he made his worm's progress into the unknown.

Once he was forced to halt and, in the dark, loosen and pick out stones embedded in the mud bottom narrowing the passage. On the other side of that danger point, he was free to wriggle on. Could the box trace him now? He had no idea of the principle on which it operated; he could only hope.

Then before him he saw the ghostly gray of light and squirmed with renewed vigor—to be faced then by a grille, beyond which was the open world. Once more his knife came into use as he pried and dug at the barrier. He worked for long moments until the grille splashed out into the sluggish current a foot or so below, and then he made ready to lower himself into the same flood.

It was only because he was a trained hunter that he avoided death in that moment. Some instinct made him dodge even as he slipped through, and the hurtling black box did not strike true at the base of his brain but raked along his scalp, tearing the flesh and sending him tumbling unconscious into the brown water.

—14—
THE PRISONER

RAF WAS TWO streets away from the circling box but still able to keep it in sight when its easy glide stopped, and, in a straight line, it swooped toward a roof emitting a shrill, rising whistle. It rose again a few seconds later as if baffled, but it continued to hover at that point, keening forth its warning. The pilot reached the next building, but a street still kept him away from the conical structure above which the box now hung.

Undecided, he stayed where he was. Should he go down to street level and investigate? Before he had quite made up his mind he saw the foremost of the alien scouting party round into the thoroughfare below and move purposefully at the cone tower, weapons to the fore. Judging by their attitude, the box had run to earth there the prey they had been searching for.

But it wasn't to be so easy. With another eerie howl the machine soared once more and bobbed completely over the cone to the street which must lie beyond it. Raf knew that he could not miss the end of the chase and started on a detour along the roof tops which should bring him to a vantage point. By the time he had made that journey he found himself on a warehouse roof which projected over the edge of the river.

From a point farther downstream, a small boat was putting out. Two of the aliens paddled while a third crouched in the bow. A second party was picking its way along the bank some distance away, both groups seemingly heading toward a point a building or two to the left of the one where Raf had taken cover.

He heard the shrilling of the box, saw it bobbing along a line toward the river. But in that direction there was only a mass of green. The end to the weird chase came so suddenly that he was not prepared and it was over before he caught a good look at the quarry. Something moved down on the river bank and in that same instant the box hurtled earthward as might a spear. It struck, and the creature who had just crawled out—out of the ground as far as Raf could see—toppled into the stream. As the waters closed over the body, the box slued around and came to rest on the bank. The party in the boat sent their small craft flying toward the spot where the crawler had sunk.

One of the paddlers abandoned his post and slipped over the side, diving into the oily water. He made two tries before he was successful and came to the surface with the other in tow. They did not try to heave the unconscious captive into the boat, merely kept the lolling head above water as they turned downstream once more and vanished from Raf's sight around the end of a pier, while the second party on the bank reclaimed the now quiet box and went off.

But Raf had seen enough to freeze him where he was for a moment. The creature which had popped out of the ground only to be struck by the box and knocked into the river—he would take oath on the fact that it was not one of the furred animals he had seen on the sea island. Surely it had been smooth-skinned, not unlike the aliens in conformation—one of their own kind they had been hunting down, a criminal or a rebel?

Puzzled, the pilot moved along from roof to roof, trying to pick up the trail of the party in the boat, but as far as he could now see, the river was bare. If they had come ashore anywhere along here, they had simply melted into the city. At last he was forced to use the homing beam, and it guided him back across the deserted metropolis to the field.

There was still activity about the globe; they were bringing in the loot from the warehouse, but Lablet and Hobart stood by the flitter. As the pilot came up to them, the captain looked up eagerly.

"What happened?"

Raf sensed that there had been some change during his absence, that Hobart was looking to him for an explanation to make clear happenings here. He told his story of the hunt and its ending, the capture of the stranger. Lablet nodded as he finished.

"That is the reason for this, you may depend upon it, Captain. One of their own people is at the bottom of it."

"Of what?" Raf wanted to ask, but Soriki did it for him.

Hobart smiled grimly. "We are all traveling back together. Take off in the early morning. For some reason they wanted us out of the globe in a hurry—practically shoved us out half an hour ago."

Though the Terrans kept a watch on the larger ship as long as the light lasted, the darkness defeated them. They did not see the prisoner being taken aboard. Yet none of them doubted that sometime during the dusky hours it had been done.

It was barely dawn when the globe took off the next day, and Raf brought the flitter up on its trail, heading westward into the sea wind. Below them the land held no signs of life. They swept over the deserted, terraced city that was the gateway to the guarded interior, flew back over the line of sea islands. Raf climbed higher, not caring to go too near the island where the aliens had wrought their terrible vengeance on the trip out. And all four of the Terrans knew relief, though they might not admit it to each other, when once more Soriki was able to establish contact with the distant spacer.

"Turn north, sir?" the pilot suggested. "I could ride her beam in from here—we don't have to follow them home." He wanted to do that so badly it was almost a compulsion to make his hand move on the controls. And when Hobart did not answer at once, he was sure that the captain would give that very order, taking them out of the company of those he had never trusted.

But Lablet spoiled that. "We have their word, Captain. That anti-grav unit that they showed us last night alone—"

So Hobart shook his head, and they meekly continued on the path set by the globe across the ocean.

As the hours passed Raf's inner uneasiness grew. For some queer reason which he could not define to himself or explain to anyone else, he was now possessed by an urgency to trail the globe which transcended and then erased his dislike of the aliens. It was as if some appeal for help was being broadcast from the other ship, drawing him on. It was then that he began to question his assumption that the prisoner was one of them.

Over and over again in his mind he tried to repicture the capture as he had witnessed it from the building just too far away and at slightly the wrong angle for a clear view. He would swear that the body he had seen tumble into the flood had not been furred, that much he was sure of. But clothing, yes, there had been clothing. Not—his mind suddenly produced that one scrap of memory—not the bandage windings of the aliens. And hadn't the skin been fairer? Was there another race on this continent, one they had not been told about?

When they at last reached the shore of the western continent and finally the home city of the aliens, the globe headed back to its berth, not in the roof cradle from which it had arisen, but sinking into the building itself. Raf brought the flitter down on a roof as close to the main holding of the painted people as he could get. None of the aliens came near them. It seemed that they were to be ignored. Hobart paced along the flat roof, and Soriki sat in the flyer, nursing his com, intent upon the slender thread of beam which tied them to the parent ship so many miles away.

"I don't understand it." Lablet's voice arose almost plaintively. "They were so very persuasive about our accompanying them. They were eager to have us see their treasures—"

Hobart swung around. "Somehow the balance of

power has changed," he observed, "in their favor. I'd give anything to know more about that prisoner of theirs. You're sure it wasn't one of the furry people?" he asked Raf, as if hoping against hope that the pilot would reply in doubt.

"Yes, sir." Raf hesitated. Should he air his suspicions, that the captive was not of the same race as his captors either? But what proof had he beyond a growing conviction that he could not substantiate?

"A rebel, a thief—" Lablet was ready to dismiss it as immaterial. "Naturally they would be upset if they were having trouble with one of their own men. But to leave now, just when we are on the verge of new discoveries— That anti-gravity unit alone is worth our whole trip! Imagine being able to return to earth with the principle of that!"

"Imagine being able to return to earth with our skins on our backs," was Soriki's whispered contribution. "if we had the sense of a Venusian water nit, we'd blast out of here so quick our tail fumes'd take off with us!"

Privately Raf concurred, but the urge to know more about the mysterious prisoner was still pricking at him, until he, contrary to his usual detachment, felt driven to discover all that he could. It was almost, but Raf shied away from the wild idea, it was almost as if he were hearing a voiceless cry for aid, as if his mind was one of Soriki's corns tuned in on an unknown wave length. He was angrily impatient with himself for that fantastic supposition. At the same time, another part of his mind, as he walked to the edge of the roof and looked out at the buildings he knew were occupied by the aliens, was busy examining the scene as if he intended to crawl about on roof tops on a second scouting expedition.

Finally the rest decided that Lablet and Hobart were to try to establish contact with the aliens once more. After they had gone, Raf opened a compartment in the flitter, the contents of which were his particular care. He squatted on his heels and surveyed the neatly stowed objects inside thoughtfully. A survival kit depended a great deal on the type of terrain in which the user was planning to survive—an aquatic world would require certain basic elements, a frozen tundra others—but there were a few items common to every emergency, and those were now at Raf's fingertips. The blast bombs, sealed into their pexilod cases, guaranteed to stop all the attackers that Terran explorers had so far met on and off worlds, a coil of rope hardly thicker than a strand of knitting yarn but of inconceivable toughness and flexibility, an aid kit with endurance drugs and pep pills which could keep a man on his feet and going long after food and water failed. He had put them all in their separate compartments.

For a long moment he hunkered there, studying the assortment. And then, almost as if some will other than his own was making a choice, he reached out. The rope curled about his waist under his tunic so tautly that its presence could not be detected without a search, blast bombs went into the sealed seam pocket on his breast, and two flat containers with their capsules were tucked away in his belt pouch. He snapped the door shut and got to his feet to discover Soriki watching him. Only for a moment was Raf disconcerted. He knew that he would not be able to explain why he must do what he was going

to do. There was no reason why he should. Soriki, except
for being a few years his senior, had no authority over him
He was not under the com-tech's orders.

"Another trip into the blue?"

The pilot replied to that with a nod.

"Somehow, boy, I don't think anything's going to stop
you, so why waste my breath? But use your homer—and
your eyes!"

Raf paused. There was an unmistakable note of friendliness in the com-tech's warning. Almost he was tempted
to try and explain. But how could one make plain feelings
for which there was no sensible reason? Sometimes it was
better to be quiet.

"Don't dig up more than you can rebury." That warning
in the slang current when they had left Terra, was reassuring
simply because it was of the earth he knew. Raf grinned
But he did not head toward the roof opening and the
ramp inside the building. Instead he set a course he had
learned in the other city, swinging down to the roof of the
neighboring structure, intent on working away from the
inhabited section of the town before he went into the
streets.

Either the aliens had not set any watch on the
Terrans or else all their interest was momentarily
engaged elsewhere. Raf, having gone three or four blocks
in the opposite direction to his goal, made his way through
a silent, long-deserted building to the street without
seeing any of the painted people. In his ear buzzed the
comforting hum of the com, tying him with the flitter and
so, in a manner, to safety.

He knew that the alien community had gathered in

and around the central building they had visited. To his mind the prisoner was now either in the headquarters of the warriors, where the globe had been berthed, or had been taken to the administration building. Whether he could penetrate either stronghold was a question Raf did not yet face squarely.

But the odd something which tugged at him was as persistent as the buzz in his earphones. And an idea came. If he were obeying some strange call for assistance, couldn't that in some way lead him to what he sought? The only difficulty was that he had no way of being more receptive to the impulse than he now was. He could not use it as a compass bearing.

In the end he chose the Center as his goal, reasoning that if the prisoner were to be interviewed by the leaders of the aliens, he would be taken to those rulers, they would not go to him. From a concealed place across from the open square on which the building fronted, the pilot studied it carefully. It towered several stories above the surrounding structures, to some of which it was tied by the ways above the streets. To use one of those bridges as a means of entering the headquarters would be entirely too conspicuous.

As far as the pilot was able to judge, there was only one entrance on the ground level, the wide front door with the imposing picture-covered gates. Had he had free use of the flitter he might have tried to swing down from the hovering machine after dark. But he was sure that Captain Hobart would not welcome the suggestion.

Underground? There had been those ways in that other city, a city which, though built on a much smaller scale, was not too different in general outline from this one. The idea was worth investigation.

The doorway, which had afforded him a shelter from which to spy out the land, yielded to his push, and he went through three large rooms on the ground floor, paying no attention to the strange groups of furnishings, but seeking something else, which he had luck to find in the last room, a ramp leading down.

It was in the underground that he made his first important find. They had seen ground vehicles in the city, a few still in operation, but Raf had gathered that the fuel and extra parts for the machines were now so scarce that they were only used in emergencies. Here, however, was a means of transportation quite different, a tunnel through which ran a ribbon of belt, wide enough to accommodate three or four passengers at once. It did not move, but when Raf dared to step out upon its surface, it swung under his weight. Since it ran in the general direction of the Center he decided to use it. It trembled under his tread, but he found that he could run along it making no sound.

The tunnel was not in darkness, for square plates set in the roof gave a diffused violet light. However, not too far ahead, the light was brighter, and it came from one side, not the roof. Another station on this abandoned way? The pilot approached it with caution. If his bump of direction was not altogether off, this must be either below the Center or very close to it.

The second station proved to be a junction where more than one of the elastic paths met. Though he crouched to listen for a long moment before venturing out into that open space, he could hear or see nothing which

uggested that the aliens ever came down now to these
evels.

They had provided an upward ramp, and Raf climbed
t, only to meet his first defeat at its top. For here was no
opening to admit him to the ground floor of what he
hoped was the Center. Baffled by the smooth surface over
which he vainly ran his hands seeking for some clue to the
door, he decided that the aliens had, for some purpose of
their own, walled off the lower regions. Discouraged, he
returned to the junction level. But he was not content to
surrender his plans so easily. Slowly he made a circuit of
the platform, examining the walls and ceiling. He found
an air shaft, a wide opening striking up into the heart of
the building above.

It was covered with a grille and it was above his reach
but . . .

Raf measured distances and planned his effort. The
mouth of a junction tunnel ran less than two feet away
from that grille. The opening was outlined with a ledge,
which made a complete arch from the floor. He stopped
and triggered the gravity plates in his space boots. Made
to give freedom of action when the ship was in free fall,
they might just provide a weak suction here. And they
did! He was able to climb that arch and, standing on it,
work loose the grille which had been fashioned to open.
Now . . .

The pilot flashed his hand torch up into that dark well.
He had been right—and lucky! There were holds at regular
intervals, something must have been serviced by workmen
in here. This was going to be easy. His fingers found the
first hold, and he wormed his way into the shaft.

It was not a difficult climb, for there were niches along the way where the alien mechanics who had once made repairs had either rested or done some of their work. And there were also grilles on each level which gave him at least a partial view of what lay beyond.

His guess was right; he recognized the main hall of the Center as he climbed past the grid there, heading up toward those levels where he was sure the leaders of the aliens had their private quarters. Twice he paused to look in upon conferences of the gaudily wrapped and painted civilians, but, since he could not understand what they were saying, it was a waste of time to linger.

He was some eight floors up when chance, luck, or that mysterious something which had brought him into this venture, led him to the right place at the right time. There was one of those niches, and he had just settled into it, peering out through the grid, when he saw the door at the opposite end of the room open and in marched a party of warriors with a prisoner in their midst;

Raf's eyes went wide. It was the captive he sought; he had no doubt of that. But who—what—was that prisoner?

This was no fur-covered half-animal, nor was it one of the delicate-boned, decadent, painted creatures such as those who now ringed in their captive. Though the man had been roughly handled and now reeled rather than walked, Raf thought for one wild instant that it was one of the crew from the spacer. The light hair, showing rings of curl, the tanned face which, beneath dirt and bruises, displayed a very familiar cast of features, the body hardly covered by rags of clothing—they were all so like those of his own kind that his mind at first refused to believe that this was not someone he knew. Yet as the party moved toward his hiding place he knew that he was facing a total stranger.

Stranger or no, Raf was sure that he saw a Terran. Had another ship made a landing on this planet? One of those earlier ships whose fate had been mystery on their home world? Who—and when—and why? He huddled as close to the grid as he could get, alert to the slightest movement below as the prisoner faced his captors.

—15—
ARENA

THE DULL pain which throbbed through Dalgard's skull with every beat of his heart was confusing, and it was hard to think clearly. But the colony scout, soon after he had fought his way back to consciousness, had learned that he was imprisoned somewhere in the globe ship. Just as he now knew that he had been brought across the sea from the continent on which Homeport was situated and that he had no hope of rescue.

He had seen little of his captors, and the guards, who had hustled him from one place of imprisonment to another, had not spoken to him, nor had he tried to communicate with them. At first he had been too sick and confused, then too wary. These were clearly Those Others and the conditioning which had surrounded him from birth had instilled in him a deep distrust of the former masters of Astra.

Now Dalgard was more alert, and his being brought to this room in what was certainly the center of the alien civilization made him believe that he was about to meet the rulers of the enemy. So he stared curiously about him as the guards jostled him through the door.

On a dais fashioned of heaped-up rainbow-colored pads were three aliens, their legs folded under them at what seemed impossible angles. One wore the black wrappings, the breastplate of the guards, but the other two had indulged their love of color in weird, eye-disturbing combinations of shades in the bandages wrapping the thin limbs and paunchy bodies. They were, as far as he could see through the thick layers of paint overlaying their skins, older than their officer companion. But nothing in their attitude suggested that age had mellowed them.

Dalgard was brought to stand before the trio as before a tribunal of judges. His sword-knife had been taken from his belt before he had regained his senses, his hands were twisted behind his back and locked together in a bar and hoop arrangement. He certainly could offer little threat to the company, yet they ringed him in, weapons ready, watching his every move. The scout licked cracked lips. There was one thing they could not control, could not prevent him from doing. Somewhere, not too far away, was help . . .

Not from the merpeople, but he was sure that he had been in contact with another friendly mind.

Since the hour of his awakening on board the globe ship, when he had half-consciously sent out an appeal for aid over the band which united him with Sssuri's race, and had touched that other consciousness—not the cold alien stream about him—he had been sure that somewhere within the enemy throng there was a potential savior. Was it among those who manned the strange flyer, those the merpeople had spied upon but whom he had not yet seen?

Dalgard had striven since that moment of contact to keep in touch with the nebulous other mind, to project his need for help. But he had been unable to enter in freely as he could with his own kind, or with Sssuri and the sea people. Now, even as he stood in the heart of the enemy territory completely at the mercy of the aliens, he felt, more strongly than ever before, that another, whose mind he could not enter and yet who was in some queer way sensitive to his appeal, was close at hand. He searched the painted faces before him trying to probe behind each locked mask, but he was certain that the one he sought was not there. Only—he must be! The contact was so strong—Dalgard's startled eyes went to the wall behind the dais, tried vainly to trace what could only be felt. He would be willing to give a knife oath that the stranger was within seeing, listening distance at mis minute!

While he was so engrossed in his own problem, the guard had moved. The hooped bar which locked his wrists was loosened, and his arms, each tight in the grip of one of the warriors, were brought out before him. The officer on the dais tossed a metal ring to one of the guards.

Roughly the warrior holding Dalgard's left arm forced the band over his hand and jerked it up his forearm as far as it would go. As it winked in the light the scout was reminded of a similar bracelet he had seen—where? On the front leg of the snake-devil he had shot!

The officer produced a second ring, slipping it smoothly over his own arm, adjusting it to touch bare skin and not the wrappings which served him as a sleeve.

Dalgard thought he understood. A device to facilitate communication. And straightway he was wary. When his ancestors had first met the merpeople, they had established a means of speech through touch, the palm of one resting against the palm of the other. In later generations, when they had developed their new senses, physical contact had not been necessary. However, here—Dalgard's eyes narrowed, the line along his jaw was hard.

He had always accepted the merpeople's estimate of Those Others, that their ancient enemies were all-seeing and all-knowing, with mental powers far beyond their own definition or description. Now he half expected to be ruthlessly mind-invaded, stripped of everything the enemy desired to know.

So he was astonished when the words which formed in his thoughts were simple, almost childish. And while he prepared to answer them, another part of him watched and listened, waiting for the attack he was sure would come.

"You—are—who—what?"

He forced a look of astonishment. Nor did he make the mistake of answering that mentally. If Those Others did not know he could use the mind speech, why betray his power?

"I am of the stars," he answered slowly, aloud, using the speech of Homeport. He had so little occasion to talk lately that his voice sounded curiously rusty and harsh in his own ears. Nor had he the least idea of the impression those few archaically accented words would have on one who heard them.

To Dalgard's inner surprise the answer did not astonish

his interrogator. The alien officer might well have been expecting to hear just that. But he pulled off his own arm band before he turned to his fellows with a spurt of the twittering speech they used among themselves. While the two civilians were still trilling, the officer edged forward an inch or so and stared at Dalgard intently as he replaced the band.

"You not look—same—as others—"

"I do not know what you mean. Here are not others like me."

One of the civilians twitched at the officer's sleeve, apparently demanding a translation, but the other shook him off impatiently.

"You come from sky—now?"

Dalgard shook his head, then realized that gesture might not mean anything to his audience. "Long ago before I was, my people came."

The alien digested that, then again took off his band before he relayed it to his companions. The excited twitter of their speech scaled, up.

"You travel with the beasts—" the alien's accusation came crisply while the others gabbled. "That which hunts could not have tracked you had not the stink of the beast things been on you."

"I know no beasts." Dalgard faced up to that squarely. "The sea people are my friends!"

It was hard to read any emotion on these lacquered and bedaubed faces, but before the officer once more broke bracelet contact, Dalgard did sense the other's almost hysterical aversion. The scout might just have admitted to the most revolting practices as far as the alien was concerned. After he had translated, all three of those on the dais were silent. Even the guards edged away from the captive as if in some manner they might be defiled by proximity. One of the civilians made an emphatic statement, got creakily to his feet, and walked away as if he would have nothing more to do with this matter. After a second or two of hesitation his fellow followed his example.

The dark officer turned the bracelet around in his fingers, his dark eyes with their slitted pupils never leaving Dalgard's face. Then he came to a decision. He pushed the ring up his arm, and the words which reached the prisoner were coldly remote, as if the captive were no longer judged an intelligent living creature but something which had no right of existence in a well-ordered universe.

"Beast friends with beast. As the beasts—so shall you end. It is spoken."

One of the guards tore the bracelet from Dalgard's arm, trying not to touch the scout's flesh in the process. And those who once more shackled his wrists ostentatiously wiped their hands up and down the wrappings on their thighs afterwards.

But before they jabbed him into movement with the muzzles of their weapons, Dalgard located at last the source of that disturbing mental touch, not only located it, but in some manner broke through the existing barrier between the strange mind and his and communicated as clearly with it as he might have with Sssuri. And the excitement of his discovery almost led to self-betrayal!

Terran! One of those who traveled with the aliens? Yet he read clearly the other's distrust of that company, the fact that he lay in concealment here without their knowledge. And he was not unfriendly—surely he could not be a Peaceman of Pax! Another fugitive from a newly-come colony ship—? Dalgard beamed a warning to the other. If he who was free could only reach the merpeople! It might mean the turning point in their whole venture!

Dalgard was furiously planning, simplifying, trying to impress the most imperative message on that other mind as he stumbled away in the midst of the guards. The stranger was confused, apparently Dalgard's arrival, his use of the mind touch, had been an overwhelming surprise. But if he could only make the right move—would make it—The scout from Homeport had no idea what was in store for him, but with one of his own breed here and suspicious of the aliens he had at least a slim chance. He snapped the thread of communication. Now he must be ready for any opportunity—

Raf watched that amazing apparition go out of the room below. He was shaking with a chill born of no outside cold. First the shock of hearing that language, queerly accented as the words were, then that sharp contact, mind to mind. He was being clearly warned against revealing himself. The stranger was a Terran, Raf would swear to that. So somewhere on this world there was a Terran colony! One of those legendary ships of outlaws, who had taken to space during the rule of Pax, had made the crossing safely and had here established a foothold.

While one part of Raf's brain fitted together the jigsaw of bits and patches of information, the other section dealt with that message of warning the other had beamed to him. The pilot knew that the captive must be in immediate danger. He could not understand all that had happened in that interview with the aliens, but he was left with the impression that the prisoner had been not only tried but condemned. And it was up to him to help.

But how? By the time he got back to the flitter or was able to find Hobart and the others, it might already be too late. He must make the move, and soon, for there had been unmistakable urgency in the captive's message. Raf's hands fumbled at the grid before him, and then he realized that the opening was far too small to admit him to the room on the other side of the wall.

To return to the underground ways might be a waste of time, but he could see no other course open to him. What if he could not find the captive later? Where in the maze of the half-deserted city could he hope to come across the trail again? Even as he sorted out all the points which could defeat him, Raf's hands and feet felt for the notched steps which would take him down. He had gone only two floors when he was faced with a grille opening which was much larger. On impulse he stopped to measure it, sure he could squeeze through here, if he could work loose the grid.

Prying with one hand and a tool from his belt pouch, he struggled not only against the stubborn metal but against time. That strange mental communication had ceased. Though he was sure that he still received a trace of it from time to time, just enough to reassure him that the prisoner was still alive. And each time it touched him Raf redoubled his efforts on the metal clasps of the grid.

At last his determination triumphed, and the grille swung out, to fail with an appalling clatter to the floor.

The pilot thrust his feet through the opening and wriggled desperately, expecting any moment to confront a reception committee drawn by the noise. But when he reached the floor, the hallway was still vacant. In fact, he was conscious of a hush in the whole building, as if those who made their homes within its walls were elsewhere. That silence acted on him as a spur.

Raf ran along the corridor, trying to subdue the clatter of his space boots, coming to a downward ramp. There he paused, unable to decide whether to go down—until he caught sight of a party of aliens below, walking swiftly enough to suggest that they too were in a hurry.

This small group was apparently on its way to some gathering. And in it for the first time the Terran saw the women of the aliens, or at least the fully veiled, gliding creatures he guessed were the females of the painted people. There were four of them in the group ahead, escorted by two of the males, and the high fluting of their voices resounded along the corridor as might the cheeping of birds. If the males were colorful in their choice of body wrappings, the females were gorgeous beyond belief, as cloudy stuff which had the changing hues of Terran opals frothed about them to completely conceal their figures.

The harsher twittering of the men had an impatient note, and the whole party quickened pace until their glide was close to an undignified trot. Raf, forced to keep well behind lest his boots betray him, fumed.

They did not go into the open, but took another way which sloped down once more. Luckily the journey was

not a long one. Ahead was light which suggested the
outdoors.

Raf sucked in his breath as he came out a goodly
distance behind the aliens. Established in what was once
a court surrounded by the towers and buildings of the city
was a miniature of that other arena where he had seen the
dead lizard things. The glittering, gayly dressed aliens
were taking their places on the tiers of seats. But the place
which had been built to accommodate at least a thousand
spectators now housed less than half the number. If this
was the extent of the alien nation, it was the dregs of a
dwindling race.

Directly below where Raf lingered in an aisle dividing
the tiers of seats, there was a manhole opening with a
barred gate across it, an entrance to the sandcovered
enclosure. And fortunately the aliens were all clustered
close to the oval far from that spot.

Also the attention of the audience was firmly riveted
on events below. A door at the sand level had been flung
open, and through it was now hustled the prisoner. Either
the aliens still possessed some idea of fair play or they
hoped to prolong a contest to satisfy their own pleasure,
for the captive's hands were unbound and he clutched a
spear.

Remembering far-off legends of earlier and more savage
civilizations on his own world, Raf was now sure that the
lone man below was about to fight for his life. The question
was, against what?

Another of the mouthlike openings around the edge of
the arena opened, and one of the furry people shambled
out, weaving weakly from side to side as he came, a spear

in his scaled paws. He halted a step or two into the open, his round head swinging from side to side, spittle drooling from his gaping mouth. His body was covered with raw sores and bare patches from which the fur had been torn away, and it was apparent that he had long been the victim of ill-usage, if not torture.

Shrill cries arose from the alien spectators as the furred one blinked in the light and then sighted the man some feet away. He stiffened, his arm drew back, the spear poised. Then as suddenly it dropped to his side, and he fell on his knees before wriggling across the sand, his paws held out imploringly to his fellow captive.

The cries from the watching aliens were threatening. Several rose in their seats gesturing to the two below. And Raf, thankful for their absorption, sped down to the manhole, discovering to his delight it could be readily opened from his side. As he edged it around there was another sound below. This was no high-pitched fluting from the aliens deprived of their sport, but a hissing nightmare cry.

Raf's line of vision, limited by the door, framed a portion of scaled back, as it looked, immediately below him. His hand went to the blast bombs as he descended the runway, and his boots hit the sand just as the drama below reached its climax.

The furred one lay prone in the sand, uncaring. Above that mistreated body, the human stood in the half-crouch of a fighting man, the puny spear pointed up bravely at a mark it could not hope to reach, the soft throat of one of the giant lizards. The reptile did not move to speedily destroy. Instead, hissing, it reared above the two as if studying them with a vicious intelligence. But there was no time to wonder how long it would delay striking.

Raf's strong teeth ripped loose the tag end of the blast bomb, and he lobbed it straight with a practiced arm so that the ball spiraled across the arena to come to rest between the massive hind legs of the lizard. He saw the man's eyes widen as they fastened on him. And then the human captive flung himself to the earth, half covering the body of the furred one. The reptile grabbed in the same instant, its grasping claws cutting only air, and before it could try a second time the bomb went off.

Literally torn apart by the explosion, the creature must have died at once. But the captive moved. He was on his feet again, pulling his companion up with him, before the startled spectators could guess what had happened. Then half carrying the other prisoner, he ran, not onward to the waiting Raf, but for the gate through which he had come into the arena. At the same time a message beat into the Terran's brain—

"This way!"

Avoiding bits of horrible refuse, Raf obeyed that order, catching up in a couple of strides with the other two and linking his arm through the dangling one of the furred creature to take some of the strain from the stranger.

"Have you any more of the power things?" the words came in the archaic speech of his own world.

"Two more bombs," he answered.

"We may have to blow the gate here," the other panted breathlessly.

Instead Raf drew his stun gun. The gate was already

opening, a wedge of painted warriors heading through, flame-throwers ready. He sprayed wide, and on the highest level. A spout of fire singed the cloth of his tunic across the top of his shoulder as one of the last aliens fired before his legs buckled and he went down. Then, opposition momentarily gone, the two with their semiconscious charge stumbled over the bodies of the guards and reached the corridor beyond.

⭑16⭑
SURPRISE ATTACK

SO MUCH had happened so quickly during the past hour that Dalgard had no chance to plan or even sort out impressions in his mind. He had no guess as to where this stranger, now taking some of the burden of the wounded merman from him, had sprung from. The other's clothing, the helmet covering his head were more akin to those worn by the aliens than they were to the dress of the colonist. Yet the man beneath those trappings was of the same breed as his own people. And he could not believe he was a Peaceman of Pax—all he had done here spoke against those legends of dark Terran days Dalgard had heard from childhood. But where had he come from? The only answer could be another outlaw colony ship.

"We are in the inner ways," Dalgard tried to reach the mind of the merman as they pounded on into the corridors which led from the arena. "Do you know these—" He had a faint hope that the sea man because of his longer captivity might have a route of escape to suggest.

"—down to the lower levels—" the thought came

slowly, forced out by a weakening will. "Lower—levels— roads to the sea—"

That was what Dalgard had been hoping for, some passage which would run seaward and so to safety, such as he had found with Sssuri in that other city.

"What are we hunting?" the stranger broke in, and Dalgard realized that perhaps the other did not follow the mind talk. His words had an odd inflection, a clipped accent which was new.

"A lower way," he returned in the speech of his own people.

"To the right." The merman, struggling against his own weakness, had raised his head and was looking about as one who searches for a familiar landmark.

There was a branching way to the right, and Dalgard swung into it, bringing the other two after him. This was a narrow passage, and twice they brushed by sealed doors. It brought them up against a blank wall. The stranger wheeled, his odd weapon ready, for they could hear the shouts of pursuers behind them. But the merman pulled free of Dalgard and went down on the floor to dig with his taloned fingers at some depressions there.

"Open here," the thought came clearly, "then down!"

Dalgard went down on one knee, able now to see the outline of a trap door. It must be pried up. His sword-knife was gone, the spear they had given him for the arena he had dropped when he dragged the merman out of danger. He looked to the stranger. About the other's narrow hips was slung a belt from which hung pouches and tools the primitive colonist could not evaluate. But there was also a bush knife, and he reached for it.

"The knife—"

The stranger glanced down at the blade he wore in surprise, as if he had forgotten it. Then with one swift movement he drew it from its sheath and flipped it to Dalgard.

On the track behind the clamor was growing, and the colony scout worked with concentration at his task of fitting the blade into the crack and freeing the door. As soon as there was space enough, the merman's claws recklessly slid under, and he added what strength he could to Dalgard's. The door arose and fell back onto the pavement with a clang, exposing a dark pit.

"Got 'em!" the words burst from the stranger. He had pressed the firing button of his weapon. Where the passage in which they stood met the main corridor, there was an agitated shouting and then sudden silence.

"Down—" The merman had crawled to the edge of the opening. From it rose a dank, fetid smell. Now that the noise in the corridor was stilled Dalgard could hear something: the sound of water.

"How do we get down?" he questioned the merman.

"It is far, there are no climbing holds—"

Dalgard straightened. Well, he supposed, even a leap into that was better than to be taken a second time by Those Others. But was he ready for such a desperate solution?

"A long way down?" The stranger leaned over to peer into the well.

"He says so," Dalgard nodded at the merman. "And there are no climbing holds."

The stranger plucked at the front of his tunic with one

hand, still holding his weapon with the other. From an opening he drew a line, and Dalgard grabbed it eagerly, testing the first foot with a sharp jerk. He had never seen such stuff, so light of weight and yet so tough. His delight reached the merman, who sat up to gaze owlishly at the coils the stranger pulled from concealment.

They used the door of the well for the lowering beam, hitching the cord about it. Then the merman noosed one end about him, and Dalgard, the door taking some of the strain, lowered him. The end of the cord was perilously close to the scout's fingers when there was a signaling pull from below, and he was free to reel in the loose line. He turned to the stranger.

"You go. I'll watch them." The other waved his weapon to the corridor.

There was some sense to that, Dalgard had to agree. He made fast the end of the cord and went in his turn into the dark, burning the palm of one hand before he was able to slacken the speed of his descent. Then he landed thigh-deep in water, from which arose an unpleasant smell.

"All right—Come—" he put full force into the thought he beamed at the stranger above. When the other did not obey, Dalgard began to wonder if he should climb to his aid. Had the aliens broken through and overwhelmed the other? Or what had happened? The rope whisked up out of his hands. And a moment later a voice rang eerily overhead.

"Clear below! Coming down!"

Dalgard scrambled out of the space under the opening, heading on into the murk where the merman waited.

There was a splash as the stranger hit the stream, and the rope lashed down behind him at their united jerk.

"Where do we go from here?" The voice carried through the dark.

Scaled fingers hooked about Dalgard's right hand and tugged him on. He reached back in turn and locked grip with the stranger. So united the three splashed on through the rancid liquid. In time they came out of the first tunnel into a wider section, but here the odor was worse, catching in their throats, making them sway dizzily. There seemed to be no end to these ways, which Raf guessed were the drains of the ancient city.

Only the merman appeared to have a definite idea of where they were going, though he halted once or twice when they came to a side passage as if thinking out their course. Since the man from the arena accepted the furred one's guidance, Raf depended upon it too. Though he wondered if they would ever find their way out into the open once more.

He was startled by sudden pain as the hand leading him tightened its grip to bone-bruising force. They had stopped, and the liquid washed about them until Raf wondered if he would ever feel clean again. When they started on, they moved much more swiftly. His companions were in a hurry, but Raf was unprepared for the sight which broke as they came out in a high-roofed cavern.

There was an odd, cold light there—but that light was not all he saw. Drawn up on a ledge rising out of the contaminated stream were rows of the furred people, all sitting in silence, bone spears resting across their knees, long knives at their belts. They watched with round, unblinking eyes the three who had just come out of the side passage. The rescued merman loosened his grip on Dalgard's hand and waded forward to confront that quiet, waiting assembly. Neither he nor his fellows made any sound, and Raf guessed that they had some other form of communication, perhaps the same telepathic ability to broadcast messages which this amazing man beside him displayed.

"They are of his tribe," the other explained, sensing that Raf could not understand. "They came here to try to save him, for he is one of their Speakers-for-Many."

"Who are they? Who are you?" Raf asked the two questions which had been with him ever since the wild adventure had begun.

"They are the People-of-the-Sea, our friends, our knife brothers. And I am of Homeport. My people came from the stars in a ship, but not a ship of this world. We have been here for many years."

The mermen were moving now. Several had waded forward to greet their chief, aiding him ashore. But when Raf moved toward the ledge, Dalgard put out a restraining hand.

"Until we are summoned—no. They have their customs. And this is a party-for-war. This tribe knows not my people, save by rumor. We wait."

Raf looked over the ranks of the sea folk. The light came from globes borne by every twentieth warrior, a globe in which something that gave off phosphorescent gleams swam around and around. The spears which each merman carried were slender and wickedly barbed, the knives almost sword length. The pilot remembered the flame-throwers of the aliens and could not see any victory for the merman party.

"No, knife blade against the fire—that is not equal."

Raf started, amazed and then irritated that the other had read his thoughts so easily.

"But what else can be done? Some stand must be taken, even if a whole tribe goes down to the Great Dark because they do it."

"What do you mean?" Raf demanded.

"Is it not the truth that Those Others went across the sea to plunder their forgotten storehouse of knowledge?" countered the other. He spoke slowly as if he found difficulty in clothing thoughts with words. "Sssuri said that was why they came."

Raf, remembering what he had seen—the stripping of shelves and tables of the devices that were stored on them—could only nod.

"Then it is also true that soon they will have worse than fire with which to hunt us down. And they shall turn against your colony as they will against Homeport. For the merman, and their own records, have taught us that it is their nature to rule, that they can live in peace only when all living things on this world are their slaves."

"My colony?" Raf was momentarily diverted. "I'm one of a spacer's crew, not the member of any colony!"

Dalgard stared at the stranger. His guess had been right. A new ship, another ship which had recently crossed deep space to find them had flown the dark wastes even as the First Elders had done! It must be that more outlaws had come to find a new home! This was wonderful news, news he must take to Homeport. Only, it was news which must wait. For the sea people had come to a decision of their own.

"What are they going to do now?" Raf asked.

The mermen were not retreating, instead they were slipping from the ledge in regular order, forming somewhat crooked ranks in the water.

Dalgard did not reply at once, making mind touch not only to ask but to impress his kinship on the sea people. They were united in a single-minded purpose, with failure before them—unless—He turned to the stranger.

"They go to war upon Those Others. He who guided us here knows also that the new knowledge they have brought into the city is danger. If an end is not put to it before they can use it, then"—he shrugged—"the mermen must retreat into the depths. And we, who can not follow them—"He made a quick, thrusting gesture as if using a knife on his own throat. "For a time Those Others have been growing fewer in number and weaker. Their children are not many and sometimes there are years when none are born at all. And they have forgotten so much. But now, perhaps they can increase once more, not only in wisdom and strength of arms, but in numbers. The mermen have kept a watch on them, content to let matters rest, sure that time would defeat them. But now, time no longer fights on our side."

Raf watched the furred people with their short spears, their knives. He recalled that rocky island where the aliens had unleashed the fire. The expeditionary force would not have a chance against that.

"But your weapons would." The words addressed to him were clear, though they had not been spoken aloud.

Raf's hand went to the pocket where two more of the blast bombs rested. "And this is your battle as much as ours!"

But it wasn't his fight! Dalgard had gone too far with that suggestion. Raf had no ties on this world, the RS 10 was waiting to take him away. It was strictly against all orders, all his training, for him to become involved in alien warfare. The pilot's hand went back to his belt. He was not going to allow himself to be pushed into anything foolish, whether this "colonist" could read his mind or not.

The first ranks of the mermen had already waded past them, heading into the way down which the escaping prisoners had come. To Raf's eyes none of them paid any attention to the two humans as they went, though they were probably in mental touch with his companion.

"You are already termed one of us in their eyes," Dalgard was careful to use oral speech this time. "When you came to our rescue in the arena they believed that you were of our kind. Do you think you can return to walk safely through the city? So"—he drew a hissing breath of surprise when the thought which leaped into Raf's mind was plain to Dalgard also—"you have—there are more of you there! But already Those Others may be moving against them because of what you have done!"

Raf who had been about the join the mermen stopped short. That aspect had not struck him before. What had happened to Soriki and the flitter, to the captain and Lablet, who had been in the heart of the enemy territory when he had challenged, the aliens? It would be only logical that the painted people would consider them all dangerous now. He must get out of here, back to the flitter, try to help where unwittingly he had harmed—

Dalgard caught up with him. He had been able to read a little of what had passed through the other's mind. Though it was difficult to sort order out of the tangled thoughts. The longer he was with the stranger, the more aware he became of the differences between them. Outwardly they might appear of the same species, but inwardly—Dalgard frowned—there was something that he must consider later, when they had a thinking space. But now he could understand the other's agitation. It was very true that Those Others might turn on the stranger's fellows in retaliation, for his deeds.

Together they joined the mermen. There was no talk, nothing to break the splashing sound of bodies moving against the current. As they pressed on, Raf was sure that this was not the same way they had come. And once more Dalgard answered his unspoken question.

"We seek another door into the city, one long known to these tribesmen."

Raf would gladly have run, but he could not move faster than his guides, and while their pace seemed deliberate, they did not pause to rest. The whole city, he decided, must be honeycombed with these drains. After traversing a fourth tunnel, they climbed out of the flood onto a dry passage, which wormed along, almost turning on itself at times.

Side passages ran out from this corridor like rootlets from a parent root, and small parties of mermen broke from the regiment to follow certain ones, leaving without orders or farewells. At the fifth of these Dalgard touched Raf's arm and drew him aside.

"This is our way." Tensely the scout waited. If the

stranger refused, then the one plan the scout had formed during the past half-hour would fail. He still held to the hope that Raf, with what Raf carried, could succeed in the only project which would mean, perhaps not his safety nor the safety of the tribe he now marched among, but the eventual safety of Astra itself, the safety of all the harmless people of the sea, the little creatures of the grass and the sky, of his own kind at Homeport. He would have to force Raf into action if need be. He did not use the mind touch; he knew now the unspoken resentment which followed that. If it became necessary—Dalgard's hands balled into fists—he would strike down the stranger—take from him—Swiftly he turned his thoughts from that. It might be easy, now that he had established mental contact with this off-worlder, for the other to pick up a thought as vivid as that.

But luckily Raf obediently turned into the side passage with the six mermen who were to attack at this particular point. The way grew narrower until they crept on hands and knees between rough walls which were not of the same construction as the larger tunnels. The smaller mermen had no difficulty in getting through, but twice Raf's equipment belt caught on projections and he had to fight his way free.

They crawled one by one into a ventilation shaft much like the one he had climbed at the Center. Dalgard's whisper reached him.

"We are now in the building which houses their sky ship."

"I know that one," Raf returned almost eagerly, glad at last to be back so close to familiar territory. He climbed up the hand—and footholds the sea-monster lamp disclosed, wishing the mermen ahead would speed up.

The grille at the head of the shaft had been removed, and the invaders arose one by one into a dim and dusty place of motionless machinery, which, by all tangible evidence, had not been entered for some time. But the cautious manner in which the sea people strung out to approach the far door argued that the same might not be true beyond.

For the first time Raf noticed that his human companion now held one of the knives of the merpeople, and he drew his stun gun. But he could not forget the flame-throwers which might at that very moment be trained upon the other side of that door by the aliens. They might be walking into a trap.

He half expected one of those disconcerting thought answers from Dalgard. But the scout was playing safe— nothing must upset the stranger. Confronted by what had to be done, he might be influenced into acting for them. So Dalgard strode softly ahead, apparently not interested in Raf.

One of the mermen worked at the door, using the point of his spear as a lever. Here again was a vista of machinery. But these machines were alive; a faint hum came from their casings. The mermen scattered, taking cover, a move copied by the two humans.

The pilot remained in hiding, but he saw one of the furred people running on as light-footedly as a shadow. Then his arm drew back, and he cast his spear. Raf fancied he could hear a faint whistle as the weapon cut the air. There was a cry, and the merman ran on, vanishing into the shadows, to return a second to two later wiping stains from his weapon. Out of their places of concealment, his fellows gathered about him. And the humans followed.

Now they were fronted by a ramp leading up, and the mermen took it quickly, their bare, scaled feet setting up a whispering echo which was drowned by the clop of Raf's boots. Once more the party was alert, ready for trouble, and taking his cue from them, he kept his stun gun in his hand.

But the maneuver at the head of the ramp surprised him. For, though he had heard no signal, all the party but one plastered their bodies back against the wall, Dalgard pulling Raf into position beside him, the scout's muscular bare arm pinning the pilot into a narrow space. One merman stood at the crack of the door at the top of the ramp. He pushed the barrier open and crept in.

Meanwhile those who waited poised their spears, all aimed at that door. Raf fingered the button on his gun to "spray" as he had when he had faced the attack of the scavengers in the arena tunnels. There was a cry, a shout with a summons in it. And the venturesome merman thudded back through the door. But he was not alone. Two of the black guardsmen, their flamers spitting fiery death, ran behind him, and the curling lash of one of those flames almost wreathed the runner before he swung aside. Raf fired without consciously aiming. Both of the sentries fell forward, to slide limply down the ramp.

Then Dalgard pulled him on. "The way is open," he said. "This is it!" There was an excited exultation in his voice.

— 17 —
DESTRUCTION UNLEASHED

THE SPACE they now entered must be the core of the building, Raf thought a little dazedly. For there, towering over them was the round bulb of the globe. And about its open hatch were piles of the material which he had last seen in the warehouse on the other continent. The unloading of the alien ship had been hastily interrupted.

Since neither the mermen nor Dalgard took cover, Raf judged that they did not fear attack now. But when he turned his attention away from the ship, he found not only the colony scout but most of the sea people gathered about him as if waiting for some action on his part.

"What is it?" He could feel it, that strong pressure, that band united in willing him into some move. His stubborn streak of independence made his reaction contrary. He was not going to be pushed into anything.

"In this hour," Dalgard spoke aloud, avoiding the mind touch which might stiffen Raf's rebellion. He wished that some older, wiser Elder from Homeport were there. So little time—Yet this stranger with practically no effort might accomplish all they had come to do, if he could only be persuaded into action. "In this hour, here is the heart of what civilization remains to Those Others. Destroy it, and it will not matter whether they kill us. For in the days to come they will have nothing left."

Raf understood. This was why he had been brought here. They wanted him to use the blast bombs. And one part of him was calculating the best places to set his two remaining bombs for the widest possible destruction. That part of him could accept the logic of Dalgard's reasoning. He doubted if the aliens could repair the globe if it were damaged, and he was sure that much which they had brought back from the eastern continent was irreplaceable. The bombs had not been intended for such a use. They were defensive, anti-personnel weapons to be employed as he had done against the lizard in the arena. But placed properly—Without thinking his hands went to the sealed pocket in the breast of his tunic.

Dalgard saw that gesture and inside him some taut cord began to unwind. Then the stranger's hands dropped, and he swung around to face the colony scout squarely, a scowl twisting his black brows almost together.

"This isn't my fight," he stated flatly. "I've got to get back to the flitter, to my spacer—"

What was the matter? Dalgard tried to understand. If the aliens won now, this stranger was in as great a danger as were the rest of them. Did he believe that Those Others would allow any colony to be established on a world they ruled?

"There will be no future for you here," he spoke slowly, trying with all his power to get through to the other, "They will not allow you to found another Homeport. You will have no colony—"

"Will you get it into your thick head," burst out the pilot, "that I'm not here to start a colony! We can take off from this blasted planet whenever we want to. We didn't come here to stay!"

Beneath the suntan, Dalgard's face whitened. The other had come from no outlaw ship, seeking a refuge across space, as his own people had fled to a new life from tyranny. His first fears had been correct! This was a representative of Pax, doubtless sent to hunt down the descendants of those who had escaped its throttling dictatorship. The slender strangely garbed Terran might be of the same blood as his own, but he was as great an enemy as Those Others!

"Pax!" He did not know that he had said that word aloud.

The other laughed. "You are living back in history. Pax has been dead and gone almost two centuries. I'm of the Federation of Free Men—"

"Will the stranger use his fire now?" The question formed in Dalgard's mind. The mermen were growing impatient, as well they might. This was no time for talk, but for action. Could Raf be persuaded to aid them? A Federation of Free Men—Free Men! That was what they were fighting for here and now.

"You are free," he said. "The sea people won their freedom when Those Others fought among themselves. My people came across the star void in search of freedom, paying in blood to win it. But these, these are not the weapons of the free." He pointed to the supplies about the globe, to the globe itself.

The mermen were waiting no longer. With the butts of their spears they smashed anything breakable. But the damage one could do by hand in the short space of time granted them—Raf was surprised that a guard was not already down upon them—was sharply limited. The piled-up secrets of an old race, a race which had once ruled a planet. He thought fleeingly of Lablet's preoccupation with this spoil, of Hobart's hope of gaining knowledge they could take back with them. But would the aliens keep their part of the bargain? He no longer believed that.

Why not give these barbarians a chance, and the colonists. Sure, he was breaking the stiffest rule of the Service. But, perhaps by now the flitter was gone, he might never reach the RS 10. It was not his war, right enough. But he'd give the weaker side a fighting chance.

Dalgard followed him into the globe ship, climbing the ladders to the engine level, watching with curious eyes a Raf inspected the driving power of the ship and made the best disposition possible of one of the bombs.

Then they were on the ladder once more as the ship shook under them, plates buckling as a great wound tore three decks apart. Raf laughed recklessly. Now that he was committed to this course, he had a small-boy delight in the destruction.

"They won't raise her again in a hurry," he confided to Dalgard. But the other did not share his triumph.

"They come—we must move fast." the scout urged.

When they jumped from the hatch, they discovered that the mermen had been busy in their turn. As many of the supplies as they could move had been pushed and piled into one great mass. Broken crystal littered the floor in shards and puddles of strange chemicals mingled smells to become a throat-rasping fog. Raf eyed those doubtfully. Some of those fumes might combine in the blast—

Once again Dalgard read his mind and waved the mermen back, sending them through the door to the ramp and the lower engine room. Raf stood in the doorway, the bomb in his hand, knowing that it was time for him to make the most accurate cast of his life.

The sphere left his fingers, was a gleam in the murky air. It struck the pile of material. Then the whole world was hidden by a blinding glare.

It was dark—black dark. And he was swinging back and forth through this total darkness. He was a ball, a blast bomb being tossed from hand to hand through the dark by painted warriors who laughed shrilly at his pain, tossed through the dark. Fear such as he had never known, even under the last acceleration pressure of the take-off from Terra, beat through Raf's veins away from his laboring heart. He was helpless in the dark

"Not alone—" the words came out of somewhere, he didn't know whether he heard them, or, in some queer way, felt them. "You are safe—not alone."

That brought a measure of comfort. But he was still in the dark, and he was moving—he could not will his hands to move—yet he was moving. He was being carried!

The flitter—he was back on the flitter! They were airborne. But who was piloting?

"Captain! Soriki!" he appealed for reassurance. And then was aware that there was no familiar motor hum, none of that pressure of rushing air to which he had been so long accustomed that he missed it only now.

"You are safe—" Again that would-be comfort. But Raf tried to move his arms, twist his body, be sure that he rested in the flitter. Then another thought, only vaguely alarming at first, but which grew swiftly to panic proportions—He was in the alien globe—He was a prisoner!

"You are safe!" the words beat in his mind.

"But where—where?" he felt as if he were screaming that at the full power of his lungs. He must get out of this dark envelope, be free. Free! Free Men—He was Raf Kurbi of the Federation of Free Men, member of the crew of the Spacer RS 10. But there had been something else about free men—

Painfully he pulled fragments of pictures out of the past, assembled a jigsaw of wild action. And all of it ended in a blinding flash, blinding!

Raf cowered mentally if not physically, as his mind seized upon that last word. The blinding flash, then this depth of darkness. Had he been—?

"You are safe."

Maybe he was safe, he thought, with an anger born of honest fear, but was he—blind? And where was he? What had happened to him since that moment when the blast bomb had exploded?

"I am blind," he spat out, wanting to be told that his fears were only fears and not the truth.

"Your eyes are covered," the answer came quickly enough, and for a short space he was comforted until he realized that the reply was not a flat denial of his statement.

"Soriki?" he tried again. "Captain? Lablet?"

"Your companions"—there was a moment of hesitation,

and then came what he was sure was the truth—"have escaped. Their ship took to the air when the Center was invaded."

So, he wasn't on the flitter. That was Raf's first reaction. Then, he must still be with the mermen, with the young stranger who claimed to be one of a lost Terran colony. But they couldn't leave him behind! Raf struggled against the power which held him motionless.

"Be quiet!" That was not soothing; it had the snap of a command, so sharp and with such authority in it that he obeyed. "You have been hurt; the gel must do its work. Sleep now. It is good to sleep—"

Dalgard walked by the hammock, using all the quieting power he possessed to ease the stranger, who now bore little resemblance to the lithe, swiftly moving, other-worldly figure of the day before. Stripped of his burned rags of clothing, coated with the healing stuff of the merpeople—that thick jelly substance which was their bulwark against illness and hurt—lashed into a hammock of sea fibers, he had the outward appearance of a thick bundle of supplies. The scout had seen miracles of healing performed by the gel, he could only hope for one now. "Sleep—" he made the soothing suggestion over and over and felt the other begin to relax, to sink into the semicoma in which he must rest for at least another day.

It was true that they had watched the strange flying machine take off from the roof top. And none of the mermen who had survived the battle which had raged through the city had seen any of the off-worlder's kind among the living or the dead of the alien forces. Perhaps, thinking Raf dead, they had returned to their space ship.

Now there were other, more immediate, problems to be met. They had done everything that they could to insure the well-being of the stranger, without whom they could not have delivered that one necessary blow which meant a new future for Astra.

The aliens were not all dead. Some had gone down under the spears of the mermen, but more of the sea people had died by the superior weapons of their foes. To the aliens, until they discovered what had happened to the globe and its cargo, it would seem an overwhelming triumph, for less than a quarter of the invading force fought its way back to safety in the underground ways. Yes, it would appear to be a victory for Those Others. But—now time was on the other side of the scales.

Dalgard doubted if the globe would ever fly again. And the loss of the storehouse plunder could never be repaired. By its destruction they had insured the future for their people, the mermen, the slowly growing settlement at Homeport.

They were well out of the city, in the open country, traveling along a rocky gorge, through which a river provided a highway to the sea. Dalgard had no idea as yet how he could win back across the waste of water to his own people. While the mermen with whom he had stormed the city were friendly, they were not of the tribes he knew, and their own connection with the eastern continent was through messages passed between islands and the depths.

Then there was the stranger—Dalgard knew that the ship which had brought him to this planet was somewhere in the north. Perhaps when he recovered, they could travel in that direction. But for the moment it was good just to be free, to feel the soft winds of summer lick his skin, to walk slowly under the sun, carrying the little bundle of things which belonged to the stranger, with a knife once more at his belt and friends about him.

But within the quarter-hour their peace was broken. Dalgard heard it first, his landsman's ears serving him where the complicated sense which gave the sea people warning did not operate. That shrill keening—he knew it of old. And at his warning the majority of the mermen plunged into the stream, becoming drifting shadows below the surface of the water. Only the four who were carrying the hammock stood their ground. But the scout, having told them to deposit their burden under the shelter of an overhanging ledge of rock, waved them to join their fellows. Until that menace in the sky was beaten, they dare not travel overland.

Was it still after him alone, hunting him by some mysterious built in sense as it had overseas? He could see it now, moving in circles back and forth across the gorge, probably ready to dive on any prey venturing into the open.

Had it not been for the stranger, Dalgard could have taken to the water almost as quickly and easily as his companions. But they could not float the pilot down the stream, thus dissolving the thick coating of gel which was healing his terrible flash burns. And Those Others, were they following the trail of their mechanical hound as they had before?

Dalgard sent out questing tendrils of thought. Nowhere did he encounter the flashes which announced the proximity of Those Others. No, it would appear that they had unleashed the hound to do what damage it could, perhaps to serve them as a marker for a future counterattack. At present it was alone. And he relayed that information to the mermen.

If they could knock out the hound—his hand went to the tender scrape on his own scalp where that box had left its glancing mark—if they could knock out the hound— But how? As accurate marksmen as the mermen were with their spears, he was not sure they could bring down the box. Its sudden darts and dips were too erratic. Then what? Because as long as it bobbed there, he and the stranger were imprisoned in this pocket of the gorge wall.

Dalgard sat down, the bundle of the stranger's belongings beside him. Then, he carefully unfastened the scorched cloth which formed that bag and examined its contents. There was the belt with its pouches, sheaths, and tool case. And the weapon which the stranger had used to such good effect during their escape from the arena. Dalgard took up the gun. It was light in weight, and it fitted into his hand almost as if it had been molded to his measure.

He aimed at the hovering box, pressed the button as he had seen the other do, with no results. The stun ray, which had acted upon living creatures, could not govern the delicate mechanism in the hound's interior. Dalgard laid it aside. There were no more of the bombs, nor would they have been effective against such a target. As far as he could see, there was nothing among Raf's possessions which could help them now.

One of the black shadows in the water moved to shore. The box swooped, death striking at the merman who ran to shelter. A second followed him, eluding the attack of the hound by a matter of inches. Now the box buzzed angrily.

Dalgard catching their thoughts, hurried to aid them. They undid the knots of the hammock about the helpless stranger, leaving about him only the necessary bandage ties. Now they had a crude net, woven, as Dalgard knew, of undersea fibers strong enough to hold captive plunging monsters a dozen times the size of the box. If they could net it!

He had seen the exploits of the mermen hunters, knew their skill with net and spear. But to scoop a flying thing out of the air was a new problem.

"Not so!" the thought cut across his. "They have used such as this to hunt us before, long ago. We had believed they were all lost. It must be caught and broken, or it will hunt and kill and hunt again, for it does not tire nor can it be beaten from any trail it is set upon. Now—"

"I will do that, for you have the knowledge—" the scout cut in quickly. After his other meeting with the hound he had no liking for the task he had taken on, but there must be bait to draw the box within striking distance.

"Stand upright and move toward those rocks." The mermen changed position, the net, now with stones in certain loops to weigh it, caught in their three-fingered hands.

Dalgard moved, fighting against hunching his shoulders, against hurrying the pace. He saw the shadow of the flitting death, and flung himself down beside the boulder the mermen had pointed out. Then he rolled over, half surprised not to be struck.

The hound was still in the air but over it now was draped the net, the rocks in its fringes weighing it down in spite of its jerky attempts to rise. In its struggles to be free, it might almost have led the watcher to believe that it had intelligence of a sort. Now the mermen were coming out of the stream, picking up rocks as they advanced. And a hail of stones flew through the air, while others of the sea people sprang to catch the dangling ends of the net and drag the captive to earth.

In the end they smashed it completely, burying the remains under a pile of rocks. Then, retrieving their net, they once more fastened Raf into it and turned downstream, as intent as ever upon reaching the sea. Dalgard wondered whether Those Others would ever discover what had become of their hound. Or had it in some way communicated with its masters, so that now they were aware that it had been destroyed. But he was sure they had nothing more to fear, that the way to the sea was open.

In midmorning of the second day they came out upon shelving sand and saw before them the waves which promised safety and escape to the mermen. Dalgard sat down in there blue-gray sand beside Raf. The sea people had assured him that the stranger was making a good recovery, that within a matter of hours he could be freed from his cocoon of healing.

Dalgard squinted at the sun sparkling on the waves, Where now? To the north where the space ship waited? If what he read in Raf's mind was true the other wanted to leave Astra, to voyage back to that other world which was only a legend to Dalgard, and a black, unhappy legend at that. If the Elders were here, had a chance to contact these men from Terra—Dalgard's eyes narrowed, would they choose to? Another chain of thought had been slowly developing in his mind during these past hours when he had been so closely companioned with the stranger. And almost he had come to a decision which would have seemed very odd even days before.

No, there was no way of suddenly bringing the Elders here, of transferring his burden of decision to them. Dalgard cupped his chin in his hand and tried to imagine what it would be like to shut oneself up in a small metal-walled spacer and set out blindly to leave one world for another. His ancestors had done that, and they had traveled in cold sleep, ignorant of whether they would ever reach their goal. They had been very brave, or very desperate men.

But—Dalgard measured sand, sun, and sky, watching the mermen sporting in the waves—but for him Astra was enough. He wanted nothing but this land, this world. There was nothing which drew him back. He would try to locate the spacer for the sake of the stranger; Astra owed Raf all they could manage to give him. But the ship was as alien to Homeport as it now existed as the city's globe might have been.

—18—
NOT YET—

RAF LAY on his back, cushioned in the sand, his face turned up to the sky. Moisture smarted in his eyes, trickled down his cheeks as he tried to will himself to see! The yellow haze which had been his day had faded into grayness and now to the dark he feared so much that he dared not even speak of it. Somewhere over him the stars were icy points of light—but he could not see them. They were very far away, but no farther than he was from safety, from comfort (now the spacer seemed a haven of ease), from the expert treatment which might save, save his sight!

He supposed he should be thankful to that other one who was a slow voice speaking out of the mist, a thought now and then when his inner panic brought him almost to the breaking point. In some manner he had been carried out of the reach of the aliens, treated for his searing wounds, and now he was led along, fed, tended—Why didn't they go away and leave him alone! He had no chance of reaching the spacer—

It was so easy to remember those mountains, the

heights over which he had lifted the flitter. There wasn't one chance in a million of his winning over those and across the miles of empty plains beyond to where the RS 10 stood waiting, ready to rise again. The crew must believe him dead. His fists clenched upon sand, and it gritted between his fingers, sifted away. Why wasn't he dead! Why had that barbarian dragged him here, continued to coax him, put food into his hands, those hands which were only vague shapes when he held them just before his straining, aching eyes.

"It is not as bad as you think," the words came again out of the fog, spoken with a gentleness which rasped Raf's nerves. "Healing is not done in a second, or even a day. You cannot force the return of strength—"

A hand, warm, vibrant with life, pressed on his forehead—a human, flesh-covered hand, not one of the cool, scaled paws of the furred people. Though those hands, too, had been laid upon him enough during the past few days, steadying him, leading him, guiding him to food and water. Now, under that firm, knowing touch he felt some of the ever-present fear subside, felt a relaxation.

"My ship—They will take off without me!" He could not help but voice that plaint, as he had so many times before during that foggy, nightmare journey.

"They have not done so yet."

He struggled up, flung off that calming hand, turned angrily toward where he thought the other was. "How can you be sure?"

"Word has come. The ship is still there, though the small flyer has returned to it."

This assurance was something new. Raf's suspicions

could not stand up against the note of certainty in the other's voice. He got awkwardly to his feet. If the ship was still here, then they must still think him alive—They might come back! He had a chance—a real chance!

"Then they are waiting for me—They'll come!"

He could not see the soberness with which Dalgard listened to that. The star ship had not lifted, that message had found its way south, passed along by hopper and merman. But the scout doubted if the explorers were waiting for the return of Raf. He believed that they would not have left the city had they not thought the pilot already dead.

As to going north now—His picture of the land ahead had been built up from reports gained from the sea people. It could be done, but with Raf to be nursed and guided, lacking even the outrigger Dalgard had used in home waters, it would take days—weeks, probably—to cover the territory which lay between them and the plains where the star ship had planeted.

But he owed Raf a great deal, and it was summer, the season of warm calms. So far he had not been able to work out any plan for a return to his own land. It might be that they were both doomed to exile. But it was not necessary to face that drear future yet, not until they had expended every possible effort. So now he said willingly enough, "We are going north."

Raf sat down again in the sand. He wanted to run, to push on until his feet were too tired to carry him any farther. But now he fought that impulse, lay down once more. Though he doubted if he could sleep.

Dalgard watched the stars, sketched out a map of

action for the morning. They must follow the shore line where they could keep in touch with the mermen, though along this coast the sea people did not come to land with the freedom their fellows showed on the eastern continent—they had lived too long in fear of Those Others.

But since the war party had reached the coast, there had been no sign of any retaliation, and as several days passed, Dalgard had begun to believe that they had little to fear. Perhaps the blow they had struck at the heart of the citadel had been more drastic than they had hoped. He had listened since that hour in the gorge for the shrilling of one of the air hounds. And when it did not come the thought that maybe it was the last of its kind had been heartening.

At last the scout lay down beside the off-world man, listening to the soft hiss of waves on sand, the distant chittering of night insects. And his last waking thought was a wish for his bow.

There was another day of patient plodding; two, three. Raf, led by the hand, helped over rocks and obstacles which were only dark blurs to his watering eyes, raged inwardly and sometimes outwardly, against the slowness of their advance, his own helplessness. His fear grew until he refused to credit the fact that the blurs were sharpening in outline, that he could now count five fingers on the hand he sometimes waved despairingly before his face.

When he spoke of the future, he never said "if we reach the ship" but always "when," refusing to admit that perhaps they would not be in time. And Dalgard by his anxiety, tried to get more news from the north.

"When we get there, will you come back to earth with us?" the pilot asked suddenly on the fifth day.

It was a question Dalgard had once asked himself. But now he knew the answer; there was only one he dared to give.

"We are not ready—"

"I don't understand what you mean." Raf was almost querulous. "It is your home world. Pax is gone; the Federation would welcome you eagerly. Just think what it would mean—a Terran colony among the stars!"

"A Terran colony." Dalgard put out a hand, steadied Raf over a stretch of rough shingle. "Yes, once we were a Terran colony. But—can you now truthfully swear that I am a Terran like yourself?"

Raf faced the misty figure, trying to force his memory to put features there, to sharpen outlines. The scout was of middle height, a little shorter in stature than the crewmen with whom the pilot had lived so long. His hair was fair, as was his skin under its tan. He was unusually light on his feet and possessed a wiry strength Raf could testify to. But there was that disconcerting habit of mind reading and other elusive differences.

Dalgard smiled, though the other could not see that.

"You see," deliberately he used the mind touch as if to accent those differences the more, "once our roots were the same, but now from these roots different plants have grown. And we must be left to ourselves a space before we mingle once more. My father's father's father's father was a Terran, but I am—what? We have something that you have not, just as you have developed during centuries of separation qualities of mind and body we do not know.

You live with machines. And, since we could not keep machines in this world, having no power to repair or rebuild, we have been forced to turn in other directions. To go back to the old ways now would be throwing away clues to mysteries we have not yet fully explored, turning aside from discoveries ready to be made. To you I am a barbarian, hardly higher in the scale of civilization than the mermen—"

Raf flushed, would have given a quick and polite denial, had he not known that his thoughts had been read. Dalgard laughed. His amusement was not directed against the pilot, rather it invited him to share the joke. And reluctantly, Raf's peeling lips relaxed in a smile.

"But," he offered one argument the other had not cited, "what if you do go down this other path of yours so far that we no longer have any common meeting ground?" He had forgotten his own problem in the other's.

"I do not believe that will ever happen. Perhaps our bodies may change; climate, food, ways of life can all influence the body. Our minds may change; already my people with each new generation are better equipped to use the mind touch, can communicate more clearly with the animals and the mermen. But those who were in the beginning born of Terra shall always have a common heritage. There are and will be other lost colonies among the stars. We could not have been the only outlaws who broke forth during the rule of Pax, and before the blight of that dictatorship, there were at least two expeditions that went forth on Galactic explorations.

"A thousand years from now stranger will meet with stranger, but when they make the sign of peace and sit down with one another, they shall find that words come more easily, though one may seem outwardly monstrous to the other. Only, now we must go our own way. We are youths setting forth on our journey of testing, while the Elders wish us well but stand aside."

"You don't want what we have to offer?" This was a new idea to Raf.

"Did you truly want what the city people had to offer?"

That caught the pilot up. He could remember with unusual distinctness how he had disliked, somehow feared the things they had brought from the city storehouse, how he had privately hoped that Hobart and Lablet would be content to let well enough alone and not bring that knowledge of an alien race back with them. If he had not secretly known that aversion, he would not have been able to destroy the globe and the treasures piled about it.

"But"—his protest was hot, angry—"we are not them! We can do much for you."

"Can you?" The calm question sank into his mind as might a stone into a troubled pool, and the ripples of its passing changed an idea or two. "I wish that you might see Homeport. Perhaps then it would be easier for you to understand. No, your knowledge is not corrupt, it would not carry with it the same seeds of disaster as that of Those Others. But it would be too easy for us to accept, to walk a softer road, to forget what we have so far won. Just give us time—"

Raf cupped his palms over his watering eyes. He wanted badly to see clearly the other's face, to be able to read his expression. Yet it seemed that somehow he was able to see that sober face, as sincere as the words in his mind.

"You will come again," Dalgard said with certainty. "And we shall be waiting because you, Raf Kurbi, made it possible." There was something so solemn about that that Raf looked up in surprise.

"When you destroyed the core of Those Other's holding, you gave us our chance. For had you not done that we, the mermen, the other harmless, happy creatures of this world, would have been wiped out. There would be no new beginning here, only a dark and horrible end."

Raf blinked; to his surprise that other figure standing in the direct sunlight did not waver, and beyond the proudly held head was a stretch of turquoise sky. He could see the color!

"Yes, you shall see with your eyes—and with your mind," now Dalgard spoke aloud. "And if the Spirit which rules all space is kind, you shall return to your own people. For you have served His cause well."

Then, as if he were embarrassed by his own solemnity, Dalgard ended with a most prosaic inquiry: "Would you like shellfish for eating?"

Moments later, wading out into the water-swirled sand, his boots kicked off, his toes feeling for the elusive shelled creatures no one could see, Raf felt happier, freer than he could ever remember having been before. It was going to be all right. He could see! He would find the ship! He laughed aloud at nothing and heard an answering chuckle and then a whoop of triumph from the scout stooping to claw one of their prey out of hiding.

It was after they had eaten that Dalgard asked another question, one which did not seem important to Raf. "You have a close friend among the crew of your ship?"

Raf hesitated. Now that he was obliged to consider the point, did he have any friends—let alone a close one—among the crew of the RS 10? Certainly he did not claim Wonstead who had shared his quarters—he honestly did not care if he never saw him again. The officers, the experts such as Lablet—quickly face and character of each swept through his mind and was as swiftly discarded. There was Soriki—He could not claim the com-tech as any special friend, but at least during their period together among the aliens he had come to know him better.

Now, as if Dalgard had read his mind—and he probably had, thought Raf with a flash of the old resentment—he had another question.

"And what was he—is he like?"

Though the pilot could see little reason for this he answered as best he could, trying to build first a physical picture of the com-tech and then doing a little guessing as to what lay under the other's space-burned skin.

Dalgard lay on his back, gazing up into the blue-green sky. Yet Raf knew that he was intent on every word. A merman padded up, settled down cross-legged beside the scout, as if he too were enthralled by the pilot's halting description of a man he might never see again. Then a second of the sea people came and a third, until Raf felt that some sort of a noiseless council was in progress. His words trailed away, and then Dalgard offered an explanation.

"It will take us many, many days to reach the place where your ship is. And before we are able to complete that journey your friends may be gone. So we shall try something else—with your aid."

Raf fingered the little bundle of his possessions. Even his helmet with its com phone was missing.

"No," again Dalgard read his mind. "Your machines are of no use to you now. We shall try our way."

"How?" Wild thoughts of a big signal fire—But how could that be sighted across a mountain range. Of some sort of an improvised com unit—

"I said our way." There was a smile on Dalgard's face, visible to Raf's slowly clearing vision. "We shall provide another kind of machine, and these"—he waved at the mermen—"will give us the power, or so we hope. Lie here," he gestured to the sand beside him, "and think only of your friend in the ship, in his natural surroundings. Try to hold that picture constant in your mind, letting no other thought trouble it."

"Do you mean—send a message to him mentally!" Raf's reply was half protest.

"Did I not reach you when we were in the city—even before I knew of you as an individual?" the scout reminded him. "And such messages are doubly possible when they are sent from friend to friend."

"But we were close then."

"That is why—" again Dalgard indicated the mermen. "For them this is the natural means of communication. They will pick up your reaching thought, amplify it with their power, beam it north. Since your friend deals with matters of communication, let us hope that he will be sensitive to this method."

Raf was only half convinced that it might work. But he remembered how Dalgard had established contact with him, before, as the scout had pointed out, they had met t was that voiceless cry for aid which had pulled him into his adventure in the first place. It was only fitting that omething of the same process give him help in return.

Obediently he stretched out on the sand and closed his im eyes, trying to picture Soriki in the small cabin which eld the com, slouched in his bucket seat, his deceptive osture that of a lax idler, as he had seen him so many mes. Soriki—his broad face with its flat cheekbones, its vide cheerful mouth, its heavy-lidded eyes. And having xed Soriki's face, he tried to believe that he was now onfronting the com-tech, speaking directly to him.

"Come—come and get me—south—seashore—Soriki ome and get me!" The words formed a kind of chant, a hant aimed at that familiar face in its familiar surround-igs. "South—come and get me—" Raf struggled to think nly of that, to allow nothing to break through that chant r disturb his picture of the scene he had called from iemory.

How long that attempt at communication lasted the ilot could not tell, for somehow he slipped from the deep oncentration into sleep, dreamless and untroubled, from hich he awoke with the befogged feeling that something nportant had happened. But had he gotten through?

The ring of mermen was gone, and it was dawn, gray, iill with the forewarnings of rain in the air. He was eassured because he was certain that in spite of the oom his sight was a fraction clearer than it had been the ay before. But had they gotten through? As he arose, rushing the sand from him, he saw the scout splashing it of the sea, a fish impaled on his spear.

"Did we get through?" Raf blurted out.

"Since your friend cannot reply with the mind touch we do not know. But later we shall try again." To Raf peering gaze Dalgard's face had a drawn, gaunt look as i he had been at hard labor during the hours just past. H walked up the beach slowly, without the springing ste Raf had come to associate with him. As he settled down t gut the fish with one of the bone knives, the scout repeated "We can try again—"

Half an hour later, as the rain swept in from the sea Raf knew that they would not have to try. His head wer up, his face eager. He had known that sound too long an too well ever to mistake it—the drone of a flitter moto cutting through the swish of the falling water. Some tric of the cliffs behind them must be magnifying and project ing the sound, for he could not sight the machine. But was coming. He whirled to Dalgard, only to see that th other was on his feet and had taken up his spear.

"It is the flitter! Soriki heard—they're coming!" Ra hastened to assure him.

For the last time he saw Dalgard's slow, warm smile clearer than he had ever seen it before. Then the scou turned and trotted away, toward a fringing rock wal Before he dropped out of sight behind that barrier h raised the spear in salute.

"Swift and fortunate voyaging!" He gave the farewe of Homeport.

Then Raf understood. The colonist meant just what h had said: he wanted no contact with the space ship. To Ra he had owed a debt and now that was paid. But the tim was not yet when the men of Astra and the men of Terra should meet. A hundred years from now perhaps—or a thousand—but not yet. And remembering what had summoned the flitter winging toward him, Raf drew a deep breath. What would the men of Astra accomplish in a hundred years? What could those of Terra do to match them in knowledge? It was a challenge, and he alone knew just how much of a challenge. Homeport must remain his own secret. He had been guided to this place, saved by the mermen alone. Dalgard and his people must not exist as far as the crew of the RS 10 were concerned.

For the last time he experienced the intimacy of the mind touch. "That is it—brother!" Then the sensation was gone as the black blot of the flitter buzzed out of the clouds.

From behind the rocks Dalgard watched the pilot enter the strange machine. For a single moment he had an impulse to shout, to run forward, to surrender to his desire to see the others, the ship which had brought them through space and would, they confidently believed, take them back to the Terra he knew only as a legend of the past. But he mastered that desire. He had been right. The road had already forked and there was no going back. He must carry this secret all the rest of his life—he must be strong-willed enough so that Homeport would never know. Time—give them time to be what they could be. Then in a hundred years—or a thousand—But not yet!

Epic Urban Adventure by a New Star of Fantasy

DRAW ONE IN THE DARK

by Sarah A. Hoyt

Every one of us has a beast inside. But for Kyrie Smith, the beast is no metaphor. Thrust into an ever-changing world of shifters, where shape-shifting dragons, giant cats and other beasts wage a secret war behind humanity's back, Kyrie tries to control her inner animal and remain human as best she can....

"Analytically, it's a tour de force: logical, built from assumptions, with no contradictions, which is astonishing given the subject matter. It's also gripping enough that I finished it in one day."

—Jerry Pournelle

1-4165-2092-9 • $25.00